JEAN-YVES FORTUNY

Elsewhere

Certain realities escape us

Éditions

Acknowledgement

To Sylvie, my co-worker who kindly offered her help with typing this story. Indeed, the progress I would have made in this area would have been like a race of overtrained snails. Today, I'm typing directly on the keyboard. Still, I miss my pen. It's like that, I love writing! I like my cross outs and my corrections on the margin.

To all our learned researchers who inspired me a lot; our conclusions are not always the same, for I romance a few. I voluntarily do not quote them.

To those rare 'magical' days that change certain things in the perception of our surroundings and our priorities and which, therefore, are to be marked in red on the calendar of our lives.

To the magazines 'Sciences et vies'[1] and 'Le monde inconnu'[2] who have given me some ideas for this story.

To the authors who write, like me, in this register, at least for the moment, that I read with interest if only to make sure we don't say the same things.

---

[1] 'Science and lives'

[2] 'The unknown world'

PROLOGUE.

Sunday, the 14th of August, 2017, 1 pm. Jocelyn and his wife Emma are in a beautiful restaurant in southwestern France, 'The beautiful candle', whose terrace offers a splendid and unique view of the Pyrenees. The ambience is exclusive, but remains simple. Jocelyn, nicknamed 'Joss' literally devours what's on his plate. Emma observes him with an amused and loving eye, continuing to discover him with delight, despite their ten years of living together.

"These prawns are excellent!"

"Seeing you, it would be hard to contradict you!"

"You had something important to tell me, I think… I'm listening…"

"I was planning to tell you at dessert, but if you insist, I'll tell you now."

"I'm not forcing you, however you feel…"

She let one or two seconds pass, then continued.

"It's a boy!"

Happy with what he had just heard, Jocelyn stopped eating and stared at her.

"What did you say?"

"It's a little boy!" she said, adding a broad smile.

"When did you find out?"

"Thursday morning, and I wanted to surprise you on your

return. I succeeded, didn't I? "

"You dared hide this from me!", he went on jokingly.

"Yes, I did, darling."

She got up, and put her napkin on the table.

"Where are you going, did I say something wrong?"

"No, love, I'm going to the bathroom and coming back."

Joss was both stunned and happy; he began to imagine the young father that he never thought of becoming one day.

For some time, many things had changed in his life. He knew deep down in his soul that his life was about to tip over. Something changed inside of him. It's true that if he could open the drawers of his mind, he would find one that contained a story erased from his conscience. A story he could probably have lived in other circumstances, or in another life like this one, for example...

VARIOUS FACTS…

— "Time destroys what is not real."
Jean Grenier.

On that beautiful morning of May 8th, 2016, promising a warm and sunny day, Lucien and Michel, constables in the Chartres region, patrol the straight roads of the area. It's a quarter past seven in the morning, and they'll be going back to base to leave the round to their rested colleagues, ready for another day. The night had been calm. Some speeding penalties and a license withdrawal due to alcohol. No more than a few kilometers separate them from their unit. Lucien is relatively eager to arrive; he's tired and in a hurry to find his bed.

"Try not to fall asleep at the lights", jokes Michel.

"What is that?", Lucien said, whose attention seemed drawn to a black and motionless dot in the distance.

"It's a three-color flag we salute every morning!"

"Be serious for a second; look there."

"I saw… Surely a flat tire. He could have pulled on the side instead of staying in the street. Moreover, the door is open and anyone could knock it over!"

"Accelerate and go without the siren, just in case…"

"Something doesn't add up; I don't see anyone in the car, nor around."

"It's true, and the hood isn't even open."

Arrived on place, they discover a black Chrysler, with all the lights on, the engine still running, the door open, the documents, the wallet, and all the things there, the driver absent. While Michel looks through the contents of the bag left on the passenger seat, Lucien examines the surroundings, thinking to maybe discover a man urinating, but in vain.

"*Strange*", he thinks, "*you don't leave your car in the middle of the road with all your papers inside...*"

"Did you see anyone?", asked Michel, getting his head out of the car.

"No, no one."

"The car starts and the tank is three-quarters full; why leave it here abandoned?"

"Did you see that?"

"What?"

In front of the car, something that looked like a jacket, or rather a half of jacket...

"Well, there you go", Michel resumes, approaching the piece of cloth.

"Strange... It looks like he wanted to cut it in two in the back. But why?"

"Yes, why", Lucien went on, perplexed. "Maybe he was kidnaped."

"I don't know, but if that's the case, I don't see why he would have cut his jacket in half."

"I have a feeling that this end of night will last much longer than expected."

"And it had to fall on us. What do we do?"

Michel couldn't take his eyes off the piece of fabric and looked pale.

"Michel?"

Seeing him like that, Lucien he calmly shook his shoulder as if to wake him up.

"Hey, Mich, you ok? I feel like we're on the verge of something huge…"

"It's just an abandoned car after all", Lucien resumed; "it's not the first and it won't be the last!"

"I know, Lucien, but trust my experience. Let's take some photos and do the necessary to have it towed."

While Lucien executed his orders, Michel seemed to have invented a new form of meditation, his eyes raised to the sky. Lucien could see that something worried his colleague and friend; but this is how he dealt with problems he encountered. He preferred to keep silent a secret that only his wife knew. It was enough for him to 'disconnect' from reality for a few minutes to allow a series of flashes and feelings to happen. Such had been the verdict of his attending physician, assisted by a specialist when Michel was a child. He had undergone a series of tests that had proved revealing. His parents then decided to let him handle this gift while keeping a lookout; and as the years went by, he had made an ally out of it.

Lucien was on the phone, transmitting the facts of which they had been witnesses of and at the same time, collecting significant information.

"An abandoned car in the middle of the road? Imagine that a unit discovered a car in the South. But it was cut in two and the back was against a plane tree."

"Quite, the front shouldn't be pretty a pretty sight!"

"Surely!"

"What do you mean surely, they must have seen it?"

"Well, no! They only found the back of the vehicle embedded in a plane tree…"

"It must have made some serious swerves… and the driver?"

"No, you didn't understand; it's not the boot that is planted in the tree, but the 'middle of the back' of it."

"Just a second; you mean that the front of the car disappeared with the driver?"

"Yes, just the back is cut as clean as that jacket."

In that moment, Lucien looked at the flap of fabric hanging from Mich's hand.

"It's properly cut, you say?"

"Yes, well, there is a little broken glass around the body of the car and the ends are slightly veiled inwards, and all over the cut-out part as if it had passed in a giant guillotine, but with a circular blade that would have closed on itself in the center of the car."

"Something compressed this car by cutting it… Did I understand correctly?"

"They sent a photo by e-mail, because I was also having a hard time believing it; you'll be able to see it in a bit, it'll be better than anything I could give you as explanation. Anyway, I see a common point with these two cars. Besides the fact that one is in one piece and the other isn't, the driver disappeared in both cases."

"Yes, that is certainly what we'll remember about these two cases… what do you think, Mich?"

"It's puzzling…"

"Oh!"

"What?"

"I just received another e-mail. Apparently, there is someone in the Alps, completely crazy, walking around with half of a vest."

"They wouldn't have seen half a car, by chance, would they?"

"No, I would have told you. I might have an idea about what's going on, but it doesn't fit both cases. For yours, it could be a settlement of accounts. They would have taken him to get a word with him."

"And they would have released him in the Alps after driving all night, is that it?"

-"Well, to scare him…?"

"No, it doesn't make sense. Thanks a lot for the info, I'm going to talk to Mich."

"Experience is irreplaceable, isn't it?"

"Yeah, as you say… Talk to you later."

"OK, I'll send in the guys. Later."

He hung up, heading for 'Mich', relieving himself of some thoughts…

"Idiot! I kidnap someone and invite him to travel all night to scare him; now that's logic! He must have invited him for coffee before releasing him in the Alps…" Lucien thought, amused.

"So, what did they tell you all this time?"

"He'll send us a team and ask for an inquiry."

"Another car was discovered in similar circumstances; but this one was split in two. They only found the back of the car."

"I presume the work is flawless…"

"Yes, and that's not all; our driver is safe and sound, on the verge of a nervous breakdown and in the Alps!"

"In the Alps! Curious… How did he get there in such a short period of time? What do our buddies say?"

"They will open an investigation on their side as well."

"We'll do it together, the two are tied; I can bet on it."

"So, you have an idea… Out with it."

"No, Lucien; I'll do it later."

"Why, I remind you that we work together!"

"Don't insist", Michel said gently; "this won't be on the report."

"Ok; I'll leave it be."

"Don't take it the wrong way, but I'm not sure of anything and you would take me for a crazy person anyway."

"Yes, Lucien; you'll be the first one to know."

"Let me think it over for a while."

"As you wish… But, I would have told you!"

"Lucien…"

"OK, whenever you'll feel like it."

This was taking Michel back over thirty-five years. He was eight years old, he was out for a walk with his friend, Mathias at the edge of a forest not far from their house. That day, Mathias had become the focus of all the talks in the village and even beyond. The investigators had had a hard time believing little Michel who was claiming his friend had disappeared before his eyes just after a race. He would never be found and little Michel will follow his destiny with this feeling of helplessness. It was decided; later, he would be a part of law enforcement, and who knows, maybe someday he would be able to investigate this disappearance…

SUCCESSFUL INVESTIGATIONS.

*— "I could never pretend to be
perfect, for if this were the case,
no one would understand me."
MM.*

Beaulieu University, PARIS

"Garvey, please give me my spiral notebook, please."

"Yes professor, I'll bring it to you right away."

Finishing a calculation, the 'teaching assistant' made him wait two minutes before executing.

"Garvey, I need it now; when you'll be in a position of responsibility, you'll be able to make people wait, but for now, you are 'my student', and until you finish your studies and become a licensed scientist yourself, when I ask you something, I want to be served on the spot! If this bothers you, there are many other volunteers to work with me on this project."

"Pardon me, professor, but I couldn't leave this calculation hanging, I would have had to start again had I lost the thread."

The professor continued to go on 'for form', but he greatly appreciated his young scientific apprentice; he had chosen him for his seriousness, his knowledge, his insight and his simplicity. For his part, Garvey loved working with professor Thibault, but knowing exactly what he wanted to do, it wouldn't have bothered him to tell his 'science master' to take a hike when he asked for too much.

For sure, their relationship was tense at times, but to tell the truth, the young man of twenty-one had the potential to become as good as the teacher in his work, and perhaps become the same annoying kind of person.

Busy with their tasks, an hour and a half had passed and it was now seven thirty.

Still engrossed in his calculations, Garvey felt he had succeeded.

"Professor", he shouted, "I think I have it!"

"Well, do show it to me, my young friend."

The teaching student proudly brought his results, and the teacher scrutinized them carefully.

"Hm… You made a mistake here, see, yet it is the basis of any good physicist who respects himself, you didn't take into account relativity!"

"Of course not, professor, but you have to admit that for our project, this formula could be it!"

"It's true that it takes out a lot of problems, however, it seems to me unrealistic and too risky if we tried anything."

"But, why professor; what do you find faulty with my calculations besides relativity?"

"What you don't want to understand is right under your nose, young man. No relativity, no safety, it's as simple as that! Do you think I didn't take this possibility into account? Are you forgetting who you're working with?"

"But, professor…"

"Enough; with your formula, we risk triggering a chain reaction and you know it very well! So go back on your calculations, but take into account this damn relativity, and I don't want to talk about any further."

Forced and resigned, Garvey returned to those calculations, patiently waiting for the day to end to put his discovery into practice.

At ten thirty, the professor noticed the time and decided to stop for the day.

"It's getting late, Garvey, call it a day and I'll see you here tomorrow after your classes."

"Alright professor, I was done, anyway…"

The professor put on his old leather jacket, and got ready to get out of the 'workroom'.

"Don't be too late Garvey, I'm going to need you tomorrow."

"Don't worry professor, I'll finish this fraction and I'll go home."

"And forget that formula… I'm counting on you."

"Understood, professor."

Knowing his 'stubborn as a mule' student, the old man left the room, letting the door close behind him. He took the corridor that lead to the exit of the University, opened the large front door leading to the parking lot of the building where only mopeds and bicycles were parked, and let it close in front of him, making it believe he had went out. But he decided to go back in the hall.

For his part, the young man stood waiting patiently for the sound of the engine of the teacher's moped, for it to start.

"I could have bet on it, he thought, he's watching me…"

So he gathered his things, put on his jacket, and went out himself, acting as if he hadn't noticed anything. He went out the front door, got on his bike, and headed for his building, three blocks away.

Surprised, the professor hesitated for a moment, thinking his student might be playing a trick on him. He waited another twenty minutes, then headed for his moped to go home.

"If it were me, I would have gone back", he thought.

But Garvey hadn't said his last word, and had also hid not far away, watching the incompressible bright red helmet of his physics' professor.

"There you go", he told himself as he watched the two wheels move away.

He let a few minutes go by, straddled his bike again, and returned to the University. He took care to go to the night guard first to talk to him for a few moments, explaining, among other things, the reason of his return, which was to finish a work that he couldn't possibly postpone.

"Good luck Garvey", replied the fifty-year-old Auguste, who was accustomed to seeing him finish work late.

"Thanks", said Garvey, walking straight ahead, determined to achieve what he had in mind.

He parked his bike in one of the five staircases that lead to the basement of the building and again crossed the entrance by walking enthusiastically to the physics room. Upon his arrival, he threw his jacket on one of the desks, went to take the control box he had secretly developed, and inserted the data that resulted from its non-relativized formula. He did the same on the computer to which the box was remotely connected to. After some manipulation on the keyboard, he proceeded to a first test that was inconclusive. He then plunged back into his calculations to detect the fault.

It had been more than an hour and a half since he had resumed his work. Auguste decided to make a round at 10 pm, as he often did during the nights when he was on guard. On the way, he noticed the still lit light in the room where Garvey was and went to visit him. As he entered, the young physicist was about to finish his calculations and put them into effect. Surprised by this intrusion, he turned abruptly, praying that it wasn't the professor.

"Auguste, you really scared me out of my wits!"

"Until what time do you plan on staying?"

"Would it be a problem, Auguste?"

"Not a one, but it's my job to know who's still here and who left."

A bit chubby, but sturdy and beefy, Auguste wasn't the type that invited you to tell stories to.

"I'm going to stay for another hour or so, and then I'll go to bed", Garvey said, somewhat uncomfortably aware of disobeying the teacher's instructions.

"You scientists, have no sleeping hours."

"It's a passion Auguste, when we love it, we don't really matter!"

"Well, I'll leave you to your equations, I'll continue my round. If you need anything, don't hesitate, to dial '213'."

"Got it, thanks Auguste."

"It's nothing, little one, good luck."

"I hope he doesn't come back" Garvey prayed.

Auguste had noticed that 'the little one' was embarrassed, but didn't worry too much about it, as he knew very well that he impressed many people by his presence, by his molosse stature, and his serious Savoyard voice.

Garvey had finished, and was ready to retry his experience. He entered the new data into the computer, as well as into the case. Some settings were still missing. But against all odds, the fourth attempt was crowned with success. It worked!

So, he pressed one of the buttons on the box that was no bigger than a TV remote, and activated the process.

"It's now or never", he thought.

Like daylight becoming night when the switch was operated, he disappeared just as quickly, without leaving any other trace than his jacket on the desk.

Making a round every two hours, Auguste was preparing to do the next one. He left his station at 10:50 and began his 'walk'. At the floor of the science room, he was surprised to see the light still lit, and thought naively that the boy had collapsed of tiredness on his desk. He pushed open to room door again and found it empty, but noticed that the young man's jacket was still there. *"He must have gone to the bathroom."*

He stealthily looked at his work while waiting for his return, if only to suggest that he go home, given the late hour. Five minutes passed.

"He must be doing the number two", he continued thinking.

Another ten minutes passed. He went out of the room, and went straight to the bathroom to clarify the situation. When he got nearby, he realized there was no light there.

"Strange", he thought *"Crappy nights for a scientist!"*

"Garvey!", he yelled.

No one answered him. He finally concluded that the young student had probably gone home, forgetting his jacket and the light on.

"One day, this young man is going to forget his head", he said to himself, turning off the light and closing the door. The computer was still running, but had gone to sleep mode, displaying a completely black screen.

He continued his round, got back to his station and made his report as he did every time he returned. In the same way

14

he had written in the space for the 10 o'clock round, *"Garvey Dubois in the science room"*, he wrote this time, in the space for the midnight box *"Garvey went home"*.

He continued his rounds until six o'clock in the morning, when he was relieved, and had no other facts to report.

Seven o'clock in the morning in that beautiful world, Christian, a former 'commando' of the retired national navy, took Auguste's place, and began to see the first teachers arrive to prepare their classes. Professor Thibault was one of them. In passing, all didn't fail to greet 'The Guardian of Culture', as they called him. Christian, only forty-two years old, unlike Auguste, who was fifty-five, but he was of the same size as his colleague, and inspired respect, as well as a little fear.

It was only when everyone went to the halls he left his station to inspect the car park and the garden, in case he found 'young on's' smoking weed, or moped thieves, or young thugs not part of the establishment, going there to wreak havoc. During his round, he noticed a bike in a stairwell. The latter wasn't attached with a lock, and seemed to have been hidden there.

"But, I recognize this bike, it's Garvey's bike."

The two of them had forged a bond of good fellowship, for besides the character that he exteriorized from time to time, Garvey was insecure and always discussed a little bit of everything with Christian, when he arrived in the morning. As for the 'day guard', he appreciated those brief discussions with the young boy, who, unlike almost everyone in the University, didn't judge him on his appearance of 'big muscles without brains'. Christian had noticed his absence, and thought he must be sick from the flu epidemic that was going round at the time. But seeing his bike sitting on the stairs and not having had his visit that morning bothered him. So he decided to share it with the dean, who was also absent.

At the same time, professor Thibault, who was drinking a last coffee with other teachers present in the room where they gathered, to discuss the students, the job, and a little of their lives, took his things, and went to his hall to prepare for his course. When he saw Garvey's jacket upon entering, he understood immediately that something was wrong, as the young man wasn't the type to leave his belongings laying around. He rushed to the computer and presses a key to revive the screen. The calculations and data that Garvey had entered into the computer before disappearing appeared.

"Garvey, what have you done?", he said aloud, taking his head in both hands. "I warned you, didn't I, about the risks of ignoring relativity, you have no idea of what you have probably done." He sat on one of the chairs and began thinking about a possible solution.

"I have to bring him back at all costs, I am the only one responsible; I should have locked the computer", he told himself.

Still engrossed in his thoughts, he suddenly thought of a solution. He locked the door so as not to be disturbed, deliberately ignoring the class he had to give to the students and settled himself in front of the computer.

"Ok, calculating the rotation of the Earth since he entered this formula, I should find the passage... The radius of the Earth... Latitude point... The time... And finally; Speed... 307 m/s!"

It only took him about ten minutes to find what he was looking for.

"It's not true, it had to be up there!"

Having found the door closed, the students who gradually came, waited patiently for him to arrive. Getting up quickly from the chair, the professor put on his jacket and stormed out

16

of the room, heading to the upper floors. The students looked at each other without understanding anything.

"Professor", one of them said.

He paid him no attention, and continued his run to the roof of the building.

Christian was still looking for answers by bustling on the phone when suddenly, one of the science students came to find him.

"Christian, come quickly, I think professor Thibault wants to kill himself!", he announced, panicked.

"He want to kill himself?"

He immediately got up from his seat and followed the student who told him where he had seen the professor go. Arrived on the floor, 'Rambo' took the lead.

"Stay here, I'll go up. He took the stairs leading to the roof, is that right?"

"Yes Christian, when he got out of the room, I followed him, and when I saw that he was taking this staircase, I thought I would better come get you."

"And you thought very well. Now, one of you go down to the parking lot to watch for him, if you see him."

"Yes Christian, I'll go", one of the students said.

They almost all went down, eventually, while the guard arrived on the roof. The professor was standing in the middle of the roof, looking like someone waiting for a bus.

"Professor", Christian shouted, "come with me, we'll talk, there are people who count on your here, and a family who loves you!"

This was the only thing missing", the professor thought, *"he thinks I want to kill myself*".

"It's an experiment", he answered, "and nothing more, don't

get any closer."

"Then do it downstairs so everyone can enjoy it!"

"You don't understand; this is where I have to be. Besides, I must leave you, duty calls!"

"No", Christian shouted, "don't do it!"

He saw the teacher walk towards the edge, then disappear just as quickly as Garvey had, before his amazed eyes. He was having a hard time believing what he had seen.

Like a hermit who found civilization again, he went down, and went to take refuge in his station, without saying anything to the students, as well as to all the people who, alerted by the ruckus had come down to see what was happening

"So?", one of the students asked, looking at Christian.

But he didn't answer, he was withdrawn into himself. At that precise moment, he couldn't see, nor hear anything, and he was sure that the same phenomenon was happening, a little, all over the world, at the same time.

PHENOMENA.

*Calculator: Computer
— *"Because the paths of day
rub shoulders with those of the night."*
Homer.

Berlin, in Germany, on the same day, at 8:15 in the morning, a little less than half an hour after the professor's 'stunt' on the roof.

'The Wall of Shame', the place that Enke and Klaus were crossing, still had some vestiges of the 'dark years', a passage had been converted into a pedestrian zone to cross on foot or by bike, unlike some other places where the wall was only cutting a street, a boulevard or a square in two.

Enke was accompanying her son to school, found on the west side of the city. Suddenly, an unexpected phenomenon took place.

Five minutes later, an old man sitting on a bench not far from there, will claim to have seen them enter the tarred road and simply disappear from sight.

* * *

New York in the United States of America, 4 am for them, and precisely 9 o'clock for us, in Europe.

Four construction workers working at 'Ground Zero' also disappeared under the bewildered eyes of their colleagues, as they were heading towards the exit of the yard, because for once, they had finished earlier. Among those who witnessed it, some will say that they should have never drunk so much alcohol the day before, others will say that God got angry and He called them back to Him without any other form of judgment, and others, a little more logical, will simply state what they had seen... They were walking towards the big climb that led to Wall Street and suddenly, nothing, they had volatilized!

* * *

Pekin in China, around 9 pm local time.

Ching-Changsung Boudsang was going home from the factory where he worked at. Traveling on an old bike, he made more than twenty kilometers return every day of the week, except Sunday. He will also experience the same setbacks as the others who went missing that day. There won't be any witness for Ching-Changsung. All we know, is that he left the factory at the usual time on his bike. It's only the next morning that someone working in the urban watch service will notice something unexplainable about one of the recordings made the day before. It will be revealed that a man cycling on the big boulevard parallel to the expressway that goes to the center of the city, disappeared from the screen from one second to the next. Only after some research will they get some clues. It wasn't a ghost, but Ching-Changsung Boudsang, a worker living, working in the outskirts of the city, in the big Siunsyao factory.

* * *

Italy, 9:47 am.

Hubert, accompanied by his wife, Tiffany and their son, Félix went on vacation to 'Lake St. Cross' for a week. That morning, they were in a small boat they had rented for the day. After sailing for an hour and a half, they made a stop on one of the many lakeshores they had been selected as their little paradise of the day.

While Tiffany installed 'a camp' with the help of her husband, Félix, who from the height of his nine years of age had never sailed, asked his father to accompany him for another 'float' ride.

"Don't worry, I'll take care of the rest", Tiffany said, "go, I'll finish and I'll take advantage of the sun, reading a book while you guys sail."

Father and son went on the water again, letting themselves be carried away by the waves, while rowing from time to time, so as not to get too far away.

Turning the pages of her thriller one after the other, Tiffany looked at her husband and son about every two pages, making a small wave of her hand.

It was about twenty pages since they had left; Tiffany took a break, and prepared a small snack in the form of coffee in a thermos with some croissants.

In doing so, she looked at them and shook her hand in front of her mouth.

"Come eat!"

The two navigators understood the message and initiated the return. With a teasing spirit, she bent and took a croissant, crunching it in.

"Look, I'm enjoying myself!"

She bent for a second time for a cup of good coffee. But when she got up again and looked in their direction, Hubert, Félix and the boat were no longer there. In their place was what seems to be the front half of a car that emerged from the water, with a man inside, who tried to get himself out.

"What's the meaning of this?", she thought, *"Where are they... But that's a car!"*

Focusing on the urgency of the situation, she screamed with all her strength so that someone might notice what was happening. Immediately alerted by Tiffany's screams tearing the tranquility of the lake and by the obvious panic of some people running to the rescuers' station, they embarked in less than a minute and headed straight for the car that only had a few moments left before sinking into the water.

"Where does this car come from?", the rescuers asked themselves.

Quickly arriving at the place, they stopped at a few meters' distance from the roof of the car, while two of them dove to get the man out before he was fully engulfed by water.

The situation itself was already surreal, but one of the men noticed another strange and disturbing phenomenon. The lake seems to 'run away' in this point, not from the bottom as if a plug had been removed, but at the precise location of the car. The rescuer didn't move, he stared at that precise place, trying to understand. His colleagues are actively working on the preparation of materials to save the man, but they couldn't help but observe the unusual movement of water.

This lasted for a few moments more, then completely stopped.

No movements, nothing, only the lake's normal current. The three men were looking at each other without saying anything. Although intrigued, they continued to fulfill their mission of urgency, and delicately extracted the man who was really wondering what was happening to him.

The operation finished, the man was out of danger. They hoisted him on board and heard Tiffany as she continued to scream, making signs that they couldn't interpret. In that moment, the car was completely swallowed by the lake. So they made haste in the direction of the young woman, and found someone completely panicked, on the verge of a nervous breakdown.

"There is a float that sank with two people on board", she hastened to say, "you have to go right now!"

"OKAY Signora, parla piano!", one of the rescuers said.

"Un uomo et un bambino in acqua", she said.

Despite her very rough Italian, rescuers fully understood that a man and a child were in the water. Following the indications of the unfortunate young woman, they went again to the place where the car had sunk. They were really surprised by her indications, but as long as there were lives to be saved… Arrived again at the place, divers went back to the water, equipped this time with a powerful waterproof lamp to ward off the darkness of the depths and oxygen tanks to go down the sixty meters that were in that spot of the lake. When they arrived at the bottom, all they could see was a half car, resting on its two front wheels. They scanned the underside of the vehicle, but it seemed unlikely that anything was stuck under the inclined frame. They searched the surrounding area until exhausting their supply air, but to no avail. Resurfacing about half an hour later, they gave Tiffany some bad news. There was no boat, neither man, nor child below.

No need to say what the young woman felt in that moment, but Hubert and Félix were added to the black list of the nine people missing at the beginning of that day. So that's now eleven people who had vanished.

It was only the beginning. While some people continued to disappear, others appeared...

But contrary to the disappearances, the phenomenon began at the end of the afternoon, at exactly eleven o'clock in Bollène, not far from Orange...

SUCH JEANNE.

Float: Boat
— *"It is always that which illuminates
that is measured in the shadows."*
Edgar Morin

Béatrice was on a bike ride with her young sister, Annie. They chose a small departmental road with little traffic. "We shouldn't be long in going back", Annie said; "mom will worry if we get back too late."

"You're right, little sister, but don't worry, we're only seven kilometers from the house."

The two sisters were riding quietly, with Annie at the head of the pack, so that Béatrice could keep an eye on her, given her young age and her ardor. As she began to be outdistanced by her sister, Béatrice called her to order.

"Don't distance yourself, Annie; if mom and dad see you coming alone, I'm going to get bawled at."

She didn't have time to say more, as a strange-looking man suddenly appeared a few meters away, right in front of her. Having taken up speed to catch up with her sister and surprised by this apparition, she didn't have the reflex to 'overtake' him and ended her race in the forest that bordered the road. Spread down completely on the ground, next to her bike, she began to wonder if she had had a hallucination. She got up, looked at the state of her legs and arms, skinned in the fall. Annie had apparently not noticed anything, and was now out of sight.

"What was that", she thought, "I dreamed it!"

Arriving on the road, pushing her bike, she saw again the man from nowhere. His clothes looked like an off-white uniform; his body seemed frail, and most unsettling was his slightly larger head than normal; but he didn't seem vindictive, and looked just as surprised as the young woman. She decided to move slowly towards him, but with caution. She stopped three meters in front of him, unable to look at anything else but his big head. She thought of Annie, but perhaps it was better she returned home alone, in case the man had bad intentions. For sure, his face wasn't really 'normal', considering its deformity; she thought he probably had an illness. But that wasn't the question, how had he arrived there, on that small country road?

"Where do you come from?", she said, cautiously getting close to him.

But the man, against all expectations, seemed frightened, at least as much as she had been, seeing him.

"You have nothing to fear", she said, trying to get close again.

But he stepped back. Suddenly, she heard someone talk to her... in her head.

"What's happening?", she said, putting her hands on her head, thus letting her bike fall to the ground.

"Where are we?", the voice was saying, "and what is this ridiculous device on which you move?"

"How do you do that, it's telepathy, isn't it?"

"Yes, that's what we used to call it, but nowadays, it's our way of communicating, we don't talk anymore. Seeing you as you are, and to hear you express yourself as you do worries me."

"What are you trying to tell me... you're not from these parts?"

Béatrice was beginning to wonder about the mental health of this mysterious stranger.

"You're probably not going to understand what I'm going to tell you, but there is someone who has found a way to walk in the 'corridors', but without the coordinates, I'm stuck here!"

"Don't get me wrong, Mister, but I think I'm going to go home, I wish you good luck!"

With a simple look, the man blocked the brakes of the bike and made Béatrice stop completely, just as she was wondering what to do. She got on the front handles on the frame of her bike, turned towards him and looked at him one last time, before deciding what to do for a few seconds.

"Help me", the voice continued.

"After all, he doesn't seem evil, even if he tells funny stories", she told herself.

"Do you happen to also talk?"

"I just did!"

"I meant out loud", she said, stirring her lips as if she were speaking to a deaf person.

"We have not used our vocal cords for a long time."

"Either he's a real wacko, or I'm living the craziest adventure of my life."

"OK, I'm going to help you, but we'll have to be discreet. I'm sorry, you'll have to sleep in the garden shed tonight, will that suit you?"

"I'll follow you", he said getting close to her, without moving a single leg and at ten centimeters from the ground.

Béatrice couldn't believe her eyes.

"How... But how? Let me guess, it's your way of moving?"

"Only for short distances…"

"Before helping you, you'll first have to satisfy my curiosity on some points, when we'll see each other again tomorrow. For now, follow me from a distance without getting yourself noticed, for I have to catch up with my younger sister, well, what I meant to say was 'Miss intermittently little pest'. "

The man took Béatrice's hand, as well as her bike, and made her advance with such speed that in a few seconds, she found herself right behind Annie, who was starting to show signs of exhaustion.

Béatrice was scared of what was happening to her. She waved the man to hide in the woods along the road in order to put their plan into action, then she caught up with her younger sister to ride next to her this time.

"So, you thought to plant me one?"

Surprised, the girl screamed.

"I didn't hear you, you scared me out of my wits!"

"That's wasn't my intention, little sister; let's get back, our parents are going to worry otherwise."

Annie noticed the scratches on her sister's legs and arms.

"What happened to you; did you fall?"

"No, little sister, I went with such a speed to catch up to you, that the wind blew hard my skin!"

"It even left you foliage in your hair…"

Having not paid attention to that, Béatrice passed her hand in her hair several times to remove it.

"As a conclusion, sister dear, speed isn't good!"

"Speak for yourself, me, the wind didn't do anything to me, and I stayed on my wheels… ME!"

"Wait until I introduce you to Big Magic Head, and we'll see how you'll react", Béatrice thought.

"She fell, she fell", Annie laughed!

"Yes, and thank you very much for turning around and worrying about me!"

"Don't mention it, big sister!"

Arrived home, Annie went to the wooden cabana to store her bike.

"Leave it here, if you want, I'll take care of it…"

"Thanks, Béa", 'Miss intermittently little pest answered, on her way to the house.

Béatrice looked around her, taking both bikes into the garage.

"What is he doing?", she thought, *"This is the moment, get yourself here!"*

She opened the door to put the first bike in and found, to her great amazement, the man, who had been waiting there for a long time?

"Is this moment alright for you?"

"What! You can also hear what I'm thinking?"

"Yes, young lady, and I'm not good at being locked up!"

"OK, I'm sorry, but we don't often see people who walk without walking, who talk with their heads, and who appear out of nowhere in front of us, around here!"

"Do you want me to bring you something to eat?"

"If you have 'Miosistak', I won't say no!"

"Listen, I'll ask you tomorrow what that means, you'll have to do with what I bring you when I come back, in a sec. While waiting, you can rest here", she said, pulling out a tatami.

"Thanks, Béa."

"Trice, please, we barely know each other. Will this do?"

"Yes, it's perfect, thanks…"

"Primitive, but with a good character", he thought.

"I have to go now, they're going to wonder what I'm doing,

see you soon... Actually, what's your name?"

He got out with The Small Voice a mixture of inspired and expired letters of which Béatrice didn't understand a thing.

"OK, we'll come back to this later!"

She went home, to join her family. On the way, she asked herself... How did he know about the shed, maybe he saw it in my thoughts... I'll have to be careful what I'll be thinking of when I'm with him...

Suddenly, the small voice made itself heard again.

"There's no need to bring me food, Béatrice, I'm not hungry, I'll just rest till tomorrow. Thank you for your warm welcome."

"You're welcome", she thought, "can you still hear me?"

"Of course, Béatrice..."

At the table with her parents and Annie, she couldn't contain a grin. Intrigued by this reaction, her parents questioned her with a look.

"It's nothing", she reassured them, "I thought of something funny..."

"Let's all laugh together", Roger, her father, said.

"Yes, tell us", Annie said.

Quick-witted, she told a joke she had recently heard during a break with her colleagues, the contents evoking a funny family meal.

While everyone was laughing at her good joke, she was still thinking about her new friend... "I met 'E.T.'", she told herself.

"Does it hurt?", her mother asked, seeing her clean her wounds.

"No, Mum, it's really nothing", she reassured her, "it wasn't a great fall!"

After the meal she pretended a 'digestive walk', as she often did, to visit 'E.T.'. In that moment, she had no doubt that the next two days were going to be intense and informative at different levels…

* * *

That apparition, though surprising wasn't spectacular, compared to others. Like that from Thouard, a small village, not far from Digne-les-Bains, in the Alpes of Hautes Provence.

Today, Pascal, an electrician working at the E.R.D.F., was sent to a special intervention on an electrical pylon to perform a repair, so that the neighborhood he covered could have power that evening. As well as his colleague Henri who accompanied him, he had agreed to work overtime to his normal workday. After all, they owe us more than the light…!

Arrived in place, the two men equipped themselves and prepared their tools on the platform of their van that would allow them to perform their task without having to be attached to the pylon. Pascal went first and waited for Henri, who was fighting with his suit.

"So, are you coming, are we doing it?"

"I've got it, I'm coming…"

Henri joined his colleague on the platform, and they started going up towards the top of the pylon. Manipulating the joystick of the box which controlled the rise and descent, Pascal stopped at a box fixed under the cables. Henri unscrewed the four bolts that held the case cover while Pascal prepared a device to perform some tests, and see where the failure was coming from. What will follow will traumatize them somewhat.

Suddenly, at a height of two meters above them, Henry

pointed out to Pascal something strange in the sky.

"Look", he said, patting him on the elbow.

"Yes, what is it; did you see a UFO?"

"No, look at the sky", Henri said again.

At that hour, the night was beginning to softly descend. Indeed, something unusual was just above them. Pascal consulted his watch which indicated 7:20. Both looked towards that anomaly, and were blown away by what they saw.

As the sky darkened more and more, a significant portion, delineated like an ink spot still remained sunny in the middle of the afternoon.

"Strange", Pascal said, "I have never seen such a phenomenon. I'll take a picture with my phone."

He got the phone out, framed the space and took a small series of photos. Suddenly, a huge bird, like an eagle or a condor, suddenly appeared in his viewfinder, coming straight from that part of the sunny sky. Surprised and frightened, both men had the reflex to squat on their small iron platform to protect themselves from the animal. The bird didn't attack them and continued its flight, probably shocked itself by the 'so fast a change of sky'. Instantly, Pascal dropped his phone, as both him and Henri were paralyzed with fear, and dared not get up. Eyes focused on the bird that they ended up losing sight of, then on 'the small encrusted sky', still clear, the two electricians were trying to recover from their emotions. They looked at each other as if to reassure themselves, but also with questions in their eyes.

"What was that… and where did it come from?", Henri said.

"In any case, it wasn't a canary!"

But the surprises hadn't finished, because what they were going to observe next was going to make them drop everything and go back into fourth gear, wondering if they weren't hallucinating.

In less time than it took to say it, the spot disappeared before their amazed eyes, as if a giant hand had closed a zipper. In the panic, Pascal thought of the pictures he had taken. But after a fall of more than ten meters, the phone was shattered, and it will be impossible for him to prove what they had seen. So, he wondered what attitude to take. Should they explain that the sky released a living Boeing, just to close up after, taking the risk of being prescribed a stay in a psychiatric hospital, or should they lie?

They would never forget what they saw that day. They will ultimately decide to keep it silent and leave the work that was ordered on the account of an emergency. They would later understand, watching the news on TV, that they had witnessed an unusual phenomenon.

INTERFERING ELEMENTS.

— *"In the thick night that*
surrounds us, is there a glow that we could
push back?"
Benjamin Constant.

We are still Monday, May 8th; Jocelyn is a truck driver and is driving towards Italy. This tall fellow, of one meter ninety-three had been traveling the roads of France and Europe for twenty years. He has what is called 'experience' and knows his job very well. That wasn't actually his vocation. Physical stuntman and amateur mechanic, he had stopped his career to slip behind the wheel of a truck during his military service at the age of twenty-five. But that was just an excuse. The real reason he had stopped his acrobatics at the time was the accident of one of his friends. Her name was Corinne. She had broken the seventh cervical vertebra after falling two and a half meters and had remained paralyzed. He had done everything he could to help her, but their relationship had been cut short the day when she could no longer endure her condition and she had killed herself by swallowing a whole bottle of pills. Afterwards, having gone through a long period of sorrow, he gave up everything overnight and had gone to the army to do his service, which he had always rejected. At times, he remembered, and thought about that moment during his long hours of driving. It was one of the biggest advantages that job had. You really had time to ponder and think about a lot of things. If you're going through a bad time, it's a nightmare, but if it's the other way around, it's excellent... It becomes a real pleasure, whatever the context.

That day was the beginning of a week like all the others. It was close to 7 am.

Like in all other days, he was looking for a radio station transmitting the information of the day, then the information on the conditions of the road, when he got close to the highway. Leaving at 5:15, he planned a twenty-minute stop at the 'Béziers-Montblanc' area to have a coffee and complete the difficult task of becoming fully awake. He knew the place very well, for there was where he stopped every week. It was with a smile and a handshake that he was welcomed.

"Hi, Joss!"

"Hi, Michel, you doing ok?"

"Yes, I'm great, and you, did you have a good weekend?"

"Excellent!"

"Are you having a coffee, as usual?"

"Yes, please."

"So, what's new besides this?"

Alone in the shop, the two men quickly talked about the world, then he went back to his truck. He looked at his delivery notes, took a look at the clock and then took the road towards Vitrolles where he had to deliver to his first client.

At the moment when he started the truck, he had the feeling that a car or 'something else' passed a few meters in front of his truck, but without seeing anything concrete. It was the second time that day he had felt it, but he thought he was imagining it. Still, everything was there... the noise, the speed... He started off cautiously and noticed other people were behaving strangely, stopping to look right and left. Some seemed to want to avoid people that weren't there. Others turned abruptly, probably thinking they heard a noise right behind them or a voice...

Jocelyn started to ask himself questions.

"What's happening around here? What got into all these people?" Was it a collective hallucination or were supernatural phenomena occurring? It was better to leave that place as soon as possible and see if such behavior would be met further on.

One might have thought they were in the middle of a farce organized by the gas distributor throughout the area to promote the brand. At the same time worried, surprised and amused by what he had seen, he continued to change gears and went back to make his first delivery. As the miles went by, he set this episode aside and began to think of where he would make his daily break in the evening. "It will be at the Vintimille or Cériale", he told himself. It had been about half an hour since he had left, when his attention turned to a car far ahead of him. It seemed to have vanished from one second to another. Accustomed to look far ahead, he had focused his attention on that group, and that car seemed to have disappeared before his eyes. After having put it out of his mind, he immediately made the connection with the events of which he had been the privileged witness of.

"But, what's happening today!", he thought.

His gaze was fixed on that group of cars, 500 meters from him, when a second car disappeared in the same way as the first one had.

"That's it, I'm now paying the excesses of my youth, I'm growing

36

old!"

Now it was impossible to turn away from that scene; the cars that drove alongside stopped at once. The drivers were probably as dazed as he was.

"But, what's all this mess?"

Arrived at the cars, he slowed down, like many other drivers who probably had seen the strange phenomenon. Some had gotten out of their cars, completely baffled. Others were nailed to their seats, paralyzed by fear.

Suddenly, Jocelyn became very worried… His wife, Emma. Those that had stopped were signaling him to do the same. But after a moment's hesitation, he continued on his way at thirty kilometers an hour, telling himself that the cars had disappeared from the left lane and that logically, he wasn't risking anything going on the right lane, for some of them had continued on that side, not seeming to be aware of anything. He was moving cautiously. On the way, he took his phone out to call Emma.

"And if this phenomenon wasn't local."

Two kilometers further on, he didn't seem to have disappeared and decided to resume his cruising speed. Emma answered on the second ring.

"Hello, kitten?"

"Jossy", she said, with a sleepy voice, "do you know what time it is?"

"Yes, I know, but I wanted to make sure everything was OK…"

"And why wouldn't it be?"

"It would take too long to explain, I would rather tell you tonight when I'm done with everything."

Reassured by what he heard, he didn't want to worry her.

"The radio announced some bad weather in the area and I was wondering…"

Emma looked towards the window, intrigued by the strange call.

"Some bad weather and this is why you called? Are you sure everything's OK, Jossy?"

"I'm sorry, kitten, go back to sleep, we'll talk again tonight."

"Yeah… Now it's me who's worried!"

"No, don't be, everything's OK. Go back to bed, we'll talk tonight. Have a great day, darling…"

"Be careful, Joss…"

"Sure I will; I'll hang up; I have the phone to my ear…"

He had made about fifteen kilometers, when he suddenly heard a loud thump sound coming from the inside of his trailer, which he felt the vibrations and shakings of all the way to his cabin. He immediately thought of the big two-and-a-half-ton reel of paper that was standing on a pallet in the middle for the balance of the load.

"This isn't real", he said, slowing down and turning on his hazard lights. **"I don't need this, not now…"** He also considered the possibility that it could roll back and forth, and violently fall from behind. He prepared his attitude accordingly, hoping not to cause a disaster. The truck stopped a little more than a minute later on the emergency lane. He got out and quickly went to the back of the vehicle. He carefully opened a first door, preparing to 'jump' to the side in case the coil was patiently waiting to fall from behind the doors. Nothing, no coil; oh! He opened the door and found the coil still in place and proudly standing on its pallet.

"What was it then?" He asked himself, thinking about other possibilities. He began to go around, inspecting every corner, but saw nothing abnormal. He climbed into the trailer to check the stowage, which was irreproachable.

"I'm not crazy, I heard that damn coil fall.   And about the vibrations? And that devilish fuss?"

He climbed down again, closed the door and returned to his cabin with his mind boiling. *"What was it, damn it!"*

He restarted and went on the road smoothly.

"Maybe it was just a warning... Who knows! "

Jocelyn continued to chase the kilometers. He looked at the landscape around him, the trucks that crossed and the ones that went ahead of him. One of the cars that quickly arrived in his rearview mirror made him headlight signs, honked when it reached the cabin of his truck, then slowed down a little, just in time for the driver to lower his window, take out his arm and give him the splendid finger of honor… Finally, he got his arm back in and accelerated again.

"He didn't look happy", thought Jocelyn, searching vainly for a reason for that conquistador like behavior. *"I know, it's windy, and the trailer is swaing a little... If it's that, I can understand",* he thought, addressing the car, which was nothing more but a black dot on the horizon now, *"and I'm sorry..."*

To kill the long hours of driving, he would often 'have fun' raving about anything. Those who passed him or crossed him could see him talking by himself, or do what he called 'seated dances', or mimicking a groan by accentuating it in a funny way, preferably. Then he put a CD on – 'Always Blues', appreciated the landscape at the same time as the road, thinking of his beloved, longing to talk to her every night, on the phone. Above all, he wanted to change his state of mind, hoping that he would no longer have to deal with those phenomena which, even if he didn't admit it, made him anxious. He arrived at his first client in Vitrolles. It had been a good hour and a half since he had been driving, without seeing anything abnormal. The delivery was just as relaxing. He then went to Berre-l'Étang where he put gas in the tank and took a break at the roadside restaurant next door. He went there every week and had his habits. When the tank was full, he parked in the adjoining car park, stopped the engine, wrote his weekly report on the number of liters put in the tank, then got down. When he stepped on the ground, he heard.

"Sorry, Sir!"

"Yes, please!" he automatically answered, with a smile.

He was suddenly terrified, realizing he was alone in the parking lot. He looked to his right, to his left, all around him and saw nothing but a truck in the background whose driver was sitting in front of his steering wheel.

"But it's not true, my mind is having a melt down! What was that, again... A ghost!"

No doubt, inexplicable events were happening and they seemed to emerge from everywhere and from nowhere at once. The poor man didn't know what to believe anymore. Between the strange behavior of the people in the area where he had stopped in the morning, the disappearances on the highway and this voice out of no one knows where that he had just heard, it wasn't easy to form a clear opinion.

"Ok, so I lived this too. A small coffee and I'll be on my way."

It wasn't in style to let oneself be annihilated. He made as if nothing had happened and headed for the bar-restaurant.

"Hi, Daniel!", he said merrily, going in.

"Hi, Big Guy; what do you want, a hazelnut one?"

'Big Guy' was a nickname a lot of people gave him.

"Yes, please..."

Daniel saw that something was wrong, he wasn't as expressive as usual.

"Everything ok?"

He looked at him, trying to reassure him, but his pupils were saying "NO".

Daniel didn't say anything more, but kept an eye on him from time to time. Jocelyn was worried about Emma and for him, as well.

Comfortably seated on one of the high chairs in front of the bar, the elbow resting on the zinc and the cup of coffee in his left hand, he was looking outward, with the strong feeling of being the only one to have seen those phenomena and yet not. He was quietly enjoying his coffee without putting the cup down between sips. Some minutes passed, throwing from time to time a furtive look towards Daniel, always ready to listen if needed, and outside looking at the incessant coming and going of the sparse traffic at that hour of the morning, until the moment, that short second when his attention was drawn to a shadow passing in front of the restaurant, a strange and stealthy shadow, for it disappeared as quickly as it had appeared. Jocelyn kept looking at that place, and suddenly saw a huge head, seeming to belong to someone forced to bend down by putting a hand on the roof, to look inside.

Jocelyn uttered a cry of surprise, similar to the 'how', a little sharper, said to the horse as a command to stop. Busy, Daniel hadn't seen anything and turned at once.

"What happened, Big Guy?"

Knowing him, Jocelyn preferred to simulate a catch-up in extremis of his cup, unexpectedly thrown over.

"Nothing, Daniel, I was clumsy and I thought I would spill the cup on me.

"Oh, OK, I thought you had seen a ghost…"

Jocelyn looked at him without saying a word and decided to

walk to the entrance with his cup in his hand. Daniel wasn't the type to insist too much; but Jocelyn was one of his most valued customers and he began to discreetly observe him between two storage boxes. Jocelyn was seriously starting to ask himself existential questions. Standing in front of the front door, his cup in his left and the right hand in the pocket of his pants, he drank the penultimate sip and saw an apparition again. He saw in front of the building a man so big that ten thousand kicks in the back would not have been enough to generate such a size. That giant had to measure at least three and a half meters, maybe even four. He was dressed like a pharaoh and the landscape behind him was nothing like the parking lot. It was as if a movie was projected there, right under his astonished eyes. After leaving his cup, he pushed the door so he could see the scene closer, which disappeared less than three seconds after it had appeared.

"Hey!", he screamed.

Daniel looked at him curiously, wondering if poor Joss was going crazy right under his eyes. He decided to join him outside, wanting to get what was happening out of him.

"What's the matter, Big Guy? Something's wrong, tell me what."

Jocelyn didn't answer promptly, so he repeated.

"Hey", Daniel insisted, "can you hear me?"

This time, he was heard. Joss looked at him as if he had just buried a loved one by simply replying:

"I would rather you keep a good opinion about me, Daniel. Thank you for coming out and I'm sorry about the cup. I'm leaving", he concluded, walking towards his truck.

Daniel scratched his chin, making the few questions coming to his mind wait.

As for Jocelyn, there was no rest. Where did all these phenomena come from? Would they last? And if this was the case, were they going to spread like wildfire...?

Ten minutes passed. Jocelyn picked up his truck keys, his wallet, and then went back to work saying in an almost inaudible voice,

"Ciao, Daniel, I'll probably see you on Thursday."

He didn't stop there systematically every weekend. Everything depended on his work.

"Bye, big guy, have a safe drive!"

Leaving the establishment, he looked straight ahead, went back to his work truck, then made his way to Nice where his second client was waiting for his goods. At 2:30 pm, he arrived at the first toll before going on to the French Riviera.

"Until now, things are ok", he thought.

The road had been the same as usual. He had literally scanned the area every kilometer he had traveled since leaving. Nothing to complain about. No disappearance, appearance or weird behavior. A toll was announced at two thousand meters. This symbolized the entrance to the French Riviera. Sustained traffic caused some slowdowns five hundred meters ahead. Seeing this, he raised his foot, quietly let the truck 'die' to the queue he had chosen and took no less than ten minutes to get to the barrier. Equipped with 'Télépass', he didn't need to lower his window. His turn finally arrived.

"Well, *'The angels of the road'*," he said to himself, seeing policemen on the right. "Seeing how this damn day started, I might get the whole service!" He watched them work... They seemed to be asking for 'the total' or about forty-five minutes of control between the twenty-eight days of records and the papers.

"I focus on the barrier, I ignore them..."

They seemed to be spying on any suspicious behavior of every driver. Jocelyn knew that despite this new era of systematic verbalization, the best behavior was one that reflected what we had done when we had nothing to reproach ourselves with. He acted as if they didn't exist and went through the barrier that had just risen on the order of the 'Télépass'. He drove for about ten meters and stopped. At that moment, he thought he saw another truck pass by on his right, at a brisk pace.

"It can't be true, it's starting again!"

A car passing on the lane next to his had the same reaction. The driver was just as helpless. Realizing that the policemen only had eyes for them, Jocelyn pretended to have a problem on his dashboard by tapping lightly on it, then started again softly, praying to all the saints that he wouldn't be arrested, as he wouldn't have time to deliver in the early afternoon to his other client. It wasn't imperative, but he just wanted to avoid the busy rush hour, if only to be able to park easily once he arrived there. He had the impression that a hundred policemen eyes were encircling his cabin while advancing with him; a hundred meters, two hundred meters, he passed them, three hundred meters, he had virtually won, like the motorist who doesn't escape.

"Wow, safe!"

He changed gears one by one and then began to think about the phenomena.

"Maybe ghost trucks exist, but why is it all happening today?", he asked himself.

"It's the national celebration of the ghosts... Maybe by seeing us they got scared!"

Something bright suddenly caught his eye in the sky. It stayed for a few moments and then disappeared as quickly as the light. Having his eyes on the road and on the sky, he didn't understand what that was and continued his way.

"A shooting star in broad daylight, an asteroid passing close enough to the earth so it's well visible, a UFO....! Whatever it is, nothing will surprise me today... Let's drive without asking questions", he thought.

The radio was reporting often more and more phenomena of disappearances and appearances. The anxiety of general opinion grew as time passed. The events became the main subject of the FM bandwidth.

He had to drive about one hour and fifteen minutes to get to his second destination. He thought of Emma; everything he heard didn't reassure him.

"If something happened, she would call me... but, if she disappeared?"

He decided to call her on the pretext of having forgotten something. He put his headset back on and pressed twice on the side of the headset to automatically redial the number.

"Come on, answer…"

At the fifteenth ring, someone picked up.

"Hello, darling", he was relieved, "could you look…"

"Hello, you have reached the voicemail of…"

"Oh, no!"

"Talk after the Beep…"

He clumsily tried to hide his concern, but the tone of his voice betrayed him.

"Yes, my angel, it's me, it's nothing important, I'll call again in five minutes."

He called three times in fifteen minutes without leaving a message.

"Answer… Answer!"

At that point, if concern could be measured, he was at ninety-nine percent. He put his hand on the phone to try a fifth time, but it rang just before. Being in a state close to a nerve crisis, he picked up without a headset.

"Hello!"

Emma had to move the handset away from her ear for a moment…

"Yes, my love, what is it? You called five times in less than half an hour!"

"Yes sorry, but I absolutely wanted to know where my brown belt was; impossible to remember where I put it!"

"And it's for a belt that you get yourself in a similar condition!"

"Don't be upset, honey; my nerves are a little stretched today…"

"No kidding; do I have to worry or do I leave it like this?"

"No, don't worry", he retorted, most calmly, "call me when you find it…"

"I'll go look for it right now, so we can both be at ease."

He knew she wouldn't find it; it was just to hear from her in the next hour or hour and a half without needing to call back, without alarming her.

"No, no need, take your time…"

"You're strange this morning, Jossy… OK, I'll call you back."

"Thanks, honey, talk to you soon."

"Later, Joss…"

Emma started worrying.

"What's happening to him today? Jossy, if I didn't know you, I would say there's something wrong with your head", she thought, hanging up.

She knew nothing of what was happening. She listened to

the news of the day in the evening at the 8 o'clock newscast. However, phenomena were regrettably happening in that region as well. But although special flashes were broadcast on television and radio, the panic wasn't general. Information seemed to go unnoticed. And anyway, between the two lovebirds, it was agreed that 'as long as the phone doesn't ring, everything is fine'; it wasn't much consolation. He had to hold himself in check not to call her more and start wondering if he should continue, or call his boss, Gérard, to explain the situation to him if he didn't already know it, and force him to make him turn around so he could be with his beloved. It was certain, however, that if Gérard had heard of anything, he would have telephoned to inform him.

It was now 1 pm and he was only ten minutes away from his second delivery point.

"Let's deliver this, we'll see what happens after!", he thought.

When he arrived there, he realized that access was impossible with his big truck. He decided to park a little further and wait for 1:30 to call his client to explain the situation. He didn't have long to wait. In the time it took him to park his truck and stop the engine, he heard drumming at the door. Quite polite, he lowered the window and displayed a 'commercial' smile.

"Yes, hello sir…"

"You're bothering here and you have nothing to do in this neighborhood with such a big truck!"

Jocelyn immediately understood that he had to do with the 'annoying person of the day'. The man was old enough to be retired and seemed to have nothing else to do. Polite, Jocelyn kept calm and replied kindly.

"I don't have a choice, Sir; I have to deliver two streets over, but there isn't enough room to park in front and you'll easily understand that with my truck, I have no desire to cross your beautiful city, then come back when traffic jams are."

"But that's your problem!"

"I fully agree, sir, and I found the solution!"

"I'm going to call…"

"Excuse me again; if you're having a hard time taking your car out, just tell me and I'll move a few meters away."

"I'm telling you that…"

"Look at my delivery ticket; you can see that I can't move from here. Besides, it would be really ridiculous to do it…"

"Ok, fine, I'm going to call…"

Jocelyn got out of his cabin and again cut the man in mid stride.

"Don't bother, I'm going to do it for you!"

The man was starting to be worry, but Jocelyn had decided to not let himself go.

"Hello… Good day; did I call the police station?"

"Yes, Sir…"

"OK, here's the problem; I'm Road-Driver, I have a delivery on Venus Street in the early afternoon, and being in a semi-trailer, I can't park there, waiting for an hour and a half. So I went to park two streets away where there is a small parking lot, so as not to impede traffic. Upon arrival, I got out to make sure it's OK, and I am even able to send you a picture by phone to prove it to you. I know, you're probably wondering why I'm calling you to tell you that. It's simple; there's a gentleman here…"

"Your name, please?"

The man was embarrassed and he began to regret his gesture, trying not to show it.

"That's enough, I'm leaving; please, excuse me…"

"He's excusing himself", Jocelyn thought… *"I'll give you a little*

lesson that you will remember for a long time and in the future, YOU WILL LEAVE US ALONE!"

"I'm sorry, officer, but I think he changed his mind, I won't bother you further! You want me to pass him to you... OK, very well... Here you are, Sir, they want to talk to you, come on, go all out!"

"But I..."

"Here you go!"

By chance, it was an 'old' cop who had taken the call, not far from retirement. He was old school...

"He... Hello..."

"Hello! This is the national police; you wanted to call us to report a heavy vehicle that is badly parked and obstructing traffic, is that right?"

"Uhm... Yes, officer, Sir, but I..."

"Alright, we thank you very much for your civic gesture; we'll come immediately to draw up a report to this unseemly driver. Of course, it goes without saying that we won't be bothered for nothing, as we have the opportunity to check if it has moved during this last half hour. Give us your name and address, please; we'll summon you, because you don't seem like the person we arrested and imprisoned last week. He made us go there for nothing, the animal! Alright, I'm listening, you're Mister... OK, and you live... Perfect, we're on our way; will you pass me the indelicate driver of the truck, please..."

The man was in a state similar to that of advanced decomposition. On his part, Jocelyn was secretly laughing.

"He... Here, they want to talk to you..."

"Ouch... They're going to come see how badly I'm parked, is that right?"

"You can make fun if you want, but you have nothing to do

here", the old grumbler insisted, "it's forbidden for trucks here!"

"You have the soul of a model citizen Sir, you are the protector of this city... I only have one word for you: 'Bravo...'!" and go show your wrinkled, crumpled face elsewhere while waiting for them to arrive.

He pulled his hand away from the speaker and resumed the conversation with the policeman.

"Hello..."

"Are you staying for long in the parking lot?"

"Between us, fortunately, no!"

The policeman laughed heartily and continued...

"We don't intend to move from headquarters for this, but I think there's someone who isn't so calm, is the?"

"That's the least we can say Mr. Officer!"

"Go make your delivery and leave quickly before someone reminds us of you, we're a little overwhelmed today with these appearances and disappearances."

In that moment, he thought of Emma.

"Damn it, she hasn't called me back!"

"Yes, I understand, Mr. Officer, good luck!"

"Safe roads and good luck to you too with your big truck in our small streets."

"Thank you, Mr. Officer, goodbye!"

"Goodbye, Sir!"

Worried, he took his phone again to call Emma.

"No", he told himself, *"it's going to be too much... She's going to lose it if I call her now. And if I told her the honest truth... No, then she'll worry about me."*

Trusting destiny, he resigned himself.

"Oh, it's 1:30, I'm leaving!"

As he put his phone down to start the engine and leave the

parking lot of discord, the 'grumpy old man' came after him again. Jocelyn saw him approaching in his rearview mirror. Although patient, he was like everyone else; if one insists too much, he answers… He always did what he wanted and it was not this two-legged antiquity whose behavior was influenced by the opposite definition of the expression 'good manners', which would ruin the day. In cases as these, he had his own methods… For him, his tranquility was paramount and he didn't hesitate to appear the opposite of what he was to get the desired reaction when he was working, for example, or to get rid of an unwanted person, as was the case now. It was a 'game' he always won.

"Him again; quick, I'll start the engine and leave!"

Seeing this, the man picked up his pace.

"So, what did they say?", he shouted, trotting.

Well educated, Jocelyn lowered his window and looked at him a little amused.

"Don't worry, grandpa, they'll be here in five minutes. You have to wait for them and join me with them at my place of delivery. See you soon!"

Then, he left towards his client.

"He might be capable of coming on foot, this freak, when he won't see me arrive; if he could disappear!"

The rest of the afternoon was laborious. He had to wait for more than an hour to make his delivery, which lasted for two hours and a half; the place offered no convenience, starting with its narrowness. Result… He left the flamboyant Riviera town at 5:40 pm; the time of the first traffic jams in formation.

"Damn it, this can't be happening! How much time will it take me to cross the border?", he told himself, disgusted by his day.

Stuck in the traffic that was becoming denser by the minute, the ringing of his phone sounded.

"*Emma*", he thought…

"Yes, my love…"

"It's Gérard and please remove this transfer number on your phone."

Embarrassed, Jocelyn tried a vain easy-going explanation.

"Sorry, Gérard, I wasn't looking for an increase, but your phone picks up a little less than mine in places, so…"

"It works very well with me and it's the same as yours!"

"In Mazamet maybe, but not in the tunnels in Italy, unlike mine."

"You're the only one with whom it doesn't work, the others don't have this problem."

"*That's it, international airwaves have conspired against my phone*", he thought, smiling.

"Then, there's gotta be a problem", he thought again.

"You'll bring it to me when you get back on Friday, we'll take a look together."

"Ok, Gérard…"

"I called to know where you were."

He explained the road to him, finishing on these beautiful words…

"Sorry again for earlier, you should have seen my face when I head your voice!"

"It doesn't matter, but remove my number from this phone."

Gérard was someone you could count on. He was 'Grumpy' sometimes, but had a strong character and spoke with a little difficulty, swallowing most of the words. Those who knew him for a long time called him 'the bear'. But he was a gentle bear; straight, righteous and hardworking. Jocelyn had never complained and got on very well with him, even if on a day of anger he had asked for his balance of all accounts. It had happened only once in a little over twelve years of collaboration. The attitude to take was simple... Be honest and forthright; it wasn't difficult for Jocelyn, even if he told him little lies from time to time that made life easier.

FROM DISCOVERY TO DISCOVERY.

— *"Of all the prodigalities, the most
blameworthy is that of time."*
Marie Leszczynska.

W hen he made the crossing of the cursed sector, he took the road back to Italy, more precisely towards Venice, to deliver to his last client. The highway he usually used to get there was lined with tunnels and high viaducts for nearly two hundred kilometers. Some tunnels were up to two kilometers long and if one had been driving for more than eight hours, not counting the unloading operations and that he had approximately two hours left to drive, the end of the day was sometimes very long; it was in those moments of tiredness that 'small moments of sleep' occurred on average once an hour, which didn't mean losing control of the vehicle, but resulted in the form of memory lapses. It was then impossible to remember where you went, even if you know the road well. Thus, Jocelyn was traveling at ninety kilometers an hour, since that was the maximum speed allowed for a truck. He saw the long white lines that marked the tracks pass by, listening to the rebroadcast of a show, in which listeners expressed themselves on different topics on a station he particularly liked. They varied, but all had a near or far relationship with paranormal and supernatural phenomena.

On that day, it was a special live broadcast. That day's theme, testimonies of people who had seen a loved one disappear or a stranger appear in their living room, but not only. A man was talking about the ghost of his son with whom he had regular communication with. Another told about his dreams of dying people, happening in the night before the official announcement of their death. He explained that he saw them happy and fulfilled, as if they were coming to say 'Goodbye'.

A lady was saying she was in direct contact with her late husband in the form of trances and would start writing on a sheet of paper whatever he dictated.

Jocelyn was fond of those extraordinary stories. But tonight, it was him who would, unintentionally, enter the supernatural.

It began with a distant explosion to which he paid no attention to. Out of a long tunnel, he began feeling a certain monotony, he was tired; he started on an equally long viaduct. Below, thousands of small lights that formed villages more or less distant from each other could be seen. Suddenly, the radio began to crackle. He took his eyes off the road for a moment to search for a new station. In that moment, he had the impression that the landscape was passing at the speed of sound, as if he were driving at 1300 kilometers an hour. He immediately put his eyes on the road again and realized that it wasn't a simple impression, it was reality. He was rolling like a pinball pulled by the striker. He pulled himself together and literally stood on the brakes. But nothing happened. All this only lasted for a short moment, but it was enough to get his adrenaline level in the red.

"What is this?", he thought.

He was scared and had the very bad feeling of not controlling anything anymore. The whole thing was accompanied by a serious and continuous humming; it was a mixture of different noises like car engines in circulation, honking, voices, a powerful torrent of water, as well as a multitude of other noises constituting our environment on Earth, all this focused on two small seconds and in a rotational movement, at least disturbing. Everything was vibrating from the chassis to the roof. The direction seemed to be held straight by two invisible arms; impossible to move anything. Still trying to stop, he literally crushed the brake pedal, praying to all the saints to 'stay on track'. He had the impression of crossing the drum of a giant washing machine.

"Damn it; it's not true!", he screamed, *"It's a nightmare!"*

"The world went crazy!" he continued his thinking.

Suddenly, the vibrations and the noise diminished and moved away behind him, leaving room for total silence. He was in shock; his entire body was trembling, thus making the pounding of his heart felt. As long and painful this unusual situation had been for him, it only lasted a lapse of time. Two seconds later, the landscape around him had nothing in common with the one he had just been in before. As if the framework in which he was had changed. He recognized nothing. He had just passed from one second to the other from the highway to a national road.

"What toll did I cross?" Jocelyn thought, not understanding what had happened to him.

"I want to believe in my small phases of sleep, but right now, it's just not possible! There's no toll around here... And, anyway, I could never have passed by it had I been sleeping... Where are the tunnels and the bridges? Where's the highway? My God, where am I? And

why do I feel like scratching myself so badly, damn it?"

To top it off, his watch still showed 8:30 pm and continued to work. But in that precise moment, he was lost, because right then, the sun was shining brightly. There were only mountains around him; no houses, no cars... Nothing else except him. He decided to stop in the middle of the road, killed the engine, got out of the cabin and pinched his skin to make sure that this whole charade wasn't a bad dream. Checking made, he sat down on the asphalt and pondered. The tingling sensations he had felt were slowly fading away.

"If there's a road, there are cars." He couldn't believe what was happening to him.

"But what am I saying... I was probably dead tired and I went out somewhere without realizing it... But still, even so, that should have been a conscious decision! Yes, but then why did I have the feeling that the landscape was a hundred times faster than the truck? I didn't dream that, it was too intense! In any case, obviously, the night has passed and I'm on this national in the middle of nowhere. Moreover, given the traffic and the width of the road, it seems to me to be a county road."

Anyway, that didn't change anything; there was a black hole in his schedule and it wasn't sitting on that road that he would find an answer. He tried to make a phone call, but there was no network. What to do? He decided to resume the road, till he found something that would indicate where he was. As he climbed back into his truck, he saw a car coming in the opposite direction, driving at a slow pace, without stopping.

"Nothing much changes, one could die alone out here!", he thought.

He sat on his seat, started the ignition, peeked in his rearview mirror and saw the driver backing up.

"What is he playing at", thought Jocelyn, suddenly hesitant to

leave.

In the situation he was in, he decided to wait. The car didn't look like anything he knew. He, who was unbeatable with brands, types and different models of everything that existed on the subject, was unable to recognize it. Arrived near him, he saw an old man of at least eighty-five years get out of his car. Jocelyn did the same; he was intrigued by this little old man who seemed quite alert for his age.

"Hello, 'young one'", he said through his thick white mustache and his Savoyard accent.

Jocelyn was amused by his strong accent and manner of speaking. But something wasn't adding up, he was supposed to be in Italy, and not in France; nonetheless, he returned the politeness and started the conversation.

"Hello, Sir."

"You're having problems with your damn motor!", the old man continued.

"No, Sir, but maybe you'll be able to help me."

"Gladly, my boy! So, what can I do for you?", said the old man, rolling the 'R's'.

"For starters, tell me where we are", Jocelyn said, a little embarrassed to ask such a question.

"How so… This cart driver doesn't know where he is?"

"This what?"

"But who is this old fool?", Jocelyn thought. *"He pretends to speak my language to please me, or he doesn't care about that at all, with his plutonic accent. And if, to top it off, he uses words from another age, we aren't going to get along!"*

Exasperated, the old man continued…

"The damn cart driver; is he deaf or drugged?"

Understanding only one tenth of what the old man was saying, and having in all and for all just 'Grandpa' as the only source of information to understand what was happening to him, he chose to act as if he understood and replied tit for tat.

"Well, no, he doesn't know where he is and he isn't drugged either!"

"Say… Are you mocking me, you cart driver?"

"Sir", Jocelyn said, very seriously, "I do not mock you, I wouldn't allow myself; but please… Where are we?"

"In the Vosges my boy", the old man proudly replied. "God Almighty… This is the first time I see a cart driver who doesn't know where he is!"

"You said in the Vosges!"

"Yes, my 'young one', in the Vosges! Do I have to write it for you? You're not normal, are you! Furthermore, from where do you have such a art?"

"Are you talking about the truck?", Jocelyn was surprised.

"How did you call it? What is a 'truck'?"

"Fell again on a fan from another planet, I did!", thought the old man.

Jocelyn kind of thought the same…

"Not only is he deaf, but he completely takes Granpa Mousot! Only one solution; say 'Yes' to everything he says. Maybe I'll finally open my eyes and wake up in my bed at home!"

"Never mind", Jocelyn said, resigned; "what does my truck have that is so extraordinary?"

"I have never seen one like it before", said the old man, seeming quite amazed to see such a truck! "Come with me, I'll show you a place where you'll feel more comfortable."

Jocelyn understood he had to get into the car on the passenger side and started to open the door.

"But what are you doing?", said the old man in an angry tone.

"Climb into your 'UFO' and follow me, damn it!"

"Yes, sorry", said Jocelyn timidly, "I didn't understand!"

"Luckily he is a cart driver, that one!", grandpa thought, *"I wouldn't do this for just anyone!"*

Jocelyn's phone suddenly rang. He took it out of his pocket, looked at the displayed number...

"Finally, I was beginning to wonder if I wasn't dreaming while awake", he thought, then answered.

"Hello..."

All he heard was a mixture of frying and a very distant female voice seeming to come and go, as if the person had put the phone on a table, talking while on a rocking chair.

"Hello..." he repeated, in vain.

Intrigued, he decided to hang up. Meanwhile, grandpa was growing impatient.

"So, are you coming?"

"Yes, I'm coming..."

Jocelyn was disappointed and was feeling lonelier by the second. The old man stopped, stepped back a bit and invited him to follow him with an arm sign. He drove about a dozen kilometers, to a large parking lot, where there were already other trucks, which had spent the evening and the night there. There were about fifty trucks lined up. Some drivers were having breakfast before starting their day's work; others were barely getting up and crossing the parking lot towards the restaurant. The two vehicles stopped. The old man got out of his car and went to talk to one of them. Jocelyn looked around him, desperately searching for a landmark, something he could hang on to. All the trucks he was seeing didn't look like anything he'd seen in his twenty-five years on the job. Their shape was totally unknown to him. They looked like Japanese trucks, somewhat Americanized, with their beauty and their presence. Even more strange; they all had the same line and all seemed to come out of the same factory. Their only difference was in the color and logos of different companies. The drivers who had seen Jocelyn arrive at the wheel of his 'Scania' looked at him strangely, and yet, it wasn't malicious. One of them came close, while the old man left in his car, greeting him with a wave of his hand. Jocelyn returned the courtesy and greeted the driver who arrived in front of him.

"Hi, there, buddy" the man told him politely, "My name is Jordan; would you like to have coffee with us?"

"Hello Jordan", said, Jocelyn completely baffled, "one never says 'no' to coffee."

"Then come with me, I'll introduce you to the others", he continued, and seemed pleased to make a new acquaintance.

The two men joined the others who were waiting to see the driver of the strange truck before returning on the road. Jocelyn was still wondering what was happening to him. While walking, Jordan questioned him.

"Who sold you such a cart?"

"Better and better; a cart... There's room for some courses here!"

"Why, are you going to tell me you never saw one like it before?"

Jordan looked at him with such an expression, that he immediately understood that the answer was "No".

"Your face seems familiar", Jordan continued; "you wouldn't have gone to the videophone by any chance?"

"By what?"

"What's wrong with all the people here; they have been drugged since birth!"

He guessed, however, the meaning.

"By the videophone!"

"Yes, I think I have seen you there not so long ago, but I don't remember in what context." Jocelyn didn't know if he should be happy that someone recognized him or whether he should continue to worry about the situation he was in. They arrived among the group that was watching Jocelyn as if his skin color had turned to something akin to 'green meadow'. Everyone, without exception came to introduce themselves. A warm atmosphere reigned, all seemed to be relaxed, not an ounce of stress in their looks. Bruno was one of them, and when he saw Jocelyn, his heartfelt cry didn't leave room for a 'hello'…

"Look, guys", Bruno said enthusiastically; "it's Jocelyn Martin, a sacred monster!"

"He seems familiar to me too", Jordan continued, "but I can't remember where!"

"What about you, guys?" Bruno spoke again, "You don't recognize him?"

Some were with the same hypothesis as Jordan, but didn't understand Bruno's craze.

"Oh, come on guys" Bruno insisted, "Jocelyn Beaumont the famous stuntman who has set several world records! Besides, if he's here with us to drive his spacecraft, it's surely to promote his next show!"

"You planned something with the carts this time?", Bruno chanted, no longer able to contain his curiosity.

Jocelyn was clueless. In one go, he was promoted to the rank of star and moreover in the field of stunts, something he hadn't practiced for many years. Was it a general hallucination, a bad joke or was he just becoming crazy? Why this relentlessness on Bruno's part to recognize him as a stuntman, when he had been driving for twenty years? Should he realize that something in this world was playing a bad trick on him? Sure, it was the life he once wanted to have, but if this was a joke, it was a really bad one. He decided to let it go on, to better see what was coming to him. Like this, he could have a fairer opinion. Without answering in the affirmative, he made the decision not to contradict Bruno.

"This guy is the first man to have rolled upside down!", assured Bruno. "He's the one who made 'the jump of the angel' with a car between the two banks of the Hampton dam in the United States! I tell you guys, it's "The" driver we have with us this morning."

As Bruno listened to Jocelyn's acrobatic exploits, the others slowly began to remember all they had seen and heard about this world-famous fearless stuntman. But it's true we speak much less of stuntmen than we do about the stars of song or cinema. This explained the delayed reaction of his 'road friends'. Still, they began to evoke TV shows of which he had been the star of. And soon, it was the whole group or almost who agreed with Bruno's comments about Jocelyn's notoriety. He suffered a veritable avalanche of questions, just like a star interviewed by a journalist. He didn't know where to turn anymore. All that was nice, but he was in the presence of people who took him for someone else, or more precisely for what he could have been in other circumstances. He absolutely had to know where he was. Driver, stuntman, what magic was he facing?

He was more than five hundred miles from where he had been the moment before, and besides, stuntman was a life he had left far behind. He knew well what he had done in the last twenty years; he had driven and apart from a few skirmishes, he hadn't done any acrobatics. So why were they all trying to remind him of memories that were not his own?

After a while, he felt the need to concentrate to see a little more clearly into this charade. It suddenly occurred to him to borrow the phone from one of them, claiming a battery problem with his. It was Philippe who gave him his. This little man of one meter sixty-five looked nice and without manners. He was a little bumpy and when it was pointed out to him, he simply replied that it was nothing but a little 'cumulated pleasure'. He took Jocelyn to his truck because his phone was fixed on the dashboard.

"Here you go"... Philippe said, "you can go up in the cabin and take your time."

He complied, settled down, picked up the phone and dialed Gérard's number without knowing exactly what he would tell him to explain the situation.

"Hello", a soft, feminine voice answered!

"Hello", said Jocelyn, who had just understood his mistake, "I dialed the wrong number, I'm sorry..." "Could I look for a number?", he said, looking at Philippe, who nodded his approval.

"Hello, good day Madam; I would like the number for Mister Gérard Galland, please... I'm listening... 07. 32. 18. 54. 91. 01. 27!"

"Thanks for the additional numbers, I'll play my luck... 14 numbers; only this much!", he thought.

Still, he dialed the number.

"Ah, finally; I managed to get through to you", Jocelyn said, enthusiastic. "You'll never guess what happened to me!"

Gérard had the same voice, but spoke much more clearly than usual. He did not seem to muter anymore.

"Who are you?", Gérard continued, surprised.

For the moment, Jocelyn couldn't believe his ears.

"If this is a joke, I'm really not appreciating it", he replied curtly.

"Obviously, you've got the wrong number, Sir", said Gérard, who was not angry, however.

It was quite the opposite reaction the Gérard he knew would have had. He could see that it was not a joke. He understood less and less of what was happening to him. So he didn't insist anymore.

"I'm sorry to have bothered you, Sir", he said before hanging up.

He decided to dial Emma's number. But this time, with her voice that remained the same, she let him know about the unthinkable. When she picked up, she had an icy reaction.

"Hello…" she answered curtly, "how come you're calling, have you already forgotten we're divorced!"

He would have preferred to be clubbed on the head instead of hearing that. He was silent for a moment.

"So you, too!", he went on, confused.

"Me too, what?"

"Nothing, never mind!"

Jocelyn was starting to be really scared about the situation.

"Everything OK, Joss? I know you and I know when something's wrong. If you need help, tell me."

Emma was always so nice. He decided to take that helping hand, thinking to explain what was happening later.

"OK, Emma, I accept your help… Truth be told, I'm a little lost at the moment."

Emma knew this type of reaction wasn't like him. Until that moment, he had always refused help, no matter the circumstances.

"For him to be like this, something serious must be happening to him…"

"Are you already in Paris or are you still on the road?", she asked, ready to help her ex-husband.

"I don't even know where I am, all I can say, is that I'm in the Vosges! Reassure me on one point... Do you live in Mazamet?"

"Well, now, I really know you have a problem! Must I remind you that I live in our old house with the children?"

"The children? Our children?"

"What's wrong with you, are you doing it on purpose? I'm starting to wonder if you haven't gone crazy!"

"If it's any reassurance, I'm wondering the same thing..." He said in a fragile voice.

This situation was bothering Emma a little, as they had divorced only because of his too demanding job, but they still loved each other, and all of this was definitely going to cause one of those unmanageable situations that comes about in these cases.

"Tell me what I can do, do you want me to come get you from somewhere", Emma proposed who, despite everything, was happy to see him again.

"No, that would be too far, but first of all I'll ask you for a little favor... Look on the directory and tell me if 'Gérard Galans' transport exists", asked Jocelyn wanting to be sure not to make a mistake.

"The what; why are you talking about transistors?"

Jocelyn didn't know how to go around this anymore.

"This can't be", he thought, *"they managed to create the contagious lobotomy virus!"*

But he didn't give up and continued ...

"I'm talking about a company, of a professional activity that a person creates to earn a living, maybe allowing others to work for him; and this one is about trucks, I'm sorry, about 'carts', who take goods from one place to another!"

"You're a driver now?"

Jocelyn immediately made the connection.

"Yes, that's exactly it, I wanted to see if you knew!"

"What is happening to him?", Emma thought, *"he got knocked over the head! Poor Joss; I told you time and again not to continue that crazy job of yours! I have to be understanding with him and not jostle him".*

"'Gérard Galans' transport in Mazamet, is that it?"

"Yes, that's it…"

Emma searched and answered quickly.

"No… No transporter with that name, just an accountant!"

Knowing he had someone to count on, he decided to take the bull by the horns.

"This is what I'm gonna do: I'm going to go directly to Mazamet, and I'll be there around 7."

"At 7?", Emma was surprised.

"What do you mean, I'm with my cart."

"Since when do you go around in a cart?"

"Don't ask any questions", Jocelyn said, decided to do what was in his power to get out of that bad dream, "I'll tell you when I get there."

"Alright", Emma answered, "I'll be there when you arrive; see you tonight."

"See you tonight, Emma, and thank you…"

While hanging up, she had a small smile of satisfaction; what was at the forefront of her mind was that he had called her and no one else. He got down from Philippe's truck, thanked him again and went towards the other drivers to say goodbye, thank them for their welcome, to then resume the road towards his point of departure.

"So, tell me, my friend", Jordan said, "You still haven't told me from where you bought this weird cart from!"

Jocelyn looked him straight in the eyes, sure of himself.

"Maybe I'll be able to tell you one day, who knows; but for the moment, it's a long story, whose ending I do not yet know. Call me one of these days, after my stunt in Paris, if I don't answer, there will always be someone to take a message, don't worry, I'll tell about you too, Bruno!"

He hadn't asked for anything, but he was delighted. He suddenly had a thought for his double …

"Poor Joss; they're going to call him and they won't understand anything!"

"Here", Jocelyn continued, "this is my phone number…"

"You have a strange number", Bruno said, "it starts with '05'."

"Damn it!", Jocelyn thought again, *"I had forgotten that detail!"*

"I never did have a mind for numbers; look for it, you'll find it easily. I have to go now; safe roads!"

"OK", Bruno said happily; "You too!"

"No problem!", Jocelyn proudly concluded, "Thank you, guys!"

He climbed in his truck, started the engine and left slowly, greeting them one last time. For the time being, the most important thing was to understand what was happening, no matter what discoveries he might make. Obviously, he was not taken for himself, but for someone who had the same traits as him, and who had the life he would have had if he had made other decisions. It couldn't be a general hallucination, for, if that were the case, why would he be the only one to stand out? Maybe all of this was a bad dream; he was hoping to wake up in a parking lot along his initial route sitting on the seat, with his head on the wheel, having been too tired to lie on his bunk. But everything was so real… That being said, he wasn't one to be taken under by events; *"time will tell"*, he thought.

As he drove towards his starting point, he noticed that apart from trucks and cars, everything was the same as he knew it, except for the road signs, which were dark red and the somewhat surreal behavior of the people he saw on the road and at the rest stops where he stopped occasionally to stretch his legs. They seemed calmer, more courteous, friendlier and less stressed. No one in a hurry to arrive to their destination. Mutual respect prevailed even between truckers and motorists! During a break he took at a highway area, people who came out of the shop, stopped, to let in Jocelyn, who arrived at that time. He could hardly believe it.

"Who could imagine such a thing in the world I know! I must be in the magic world of Tinkerbell!", he thought, smiling. And it is with this thought that he had a revelation. Nobody understands me when I speak and it's the same for me. I went from night to morning with my eyes wide open in just a few seconds, and I only saw that surge in the tunnel. Something unusual must have happened in there. There have been too many quirks since this morning. This car who comes out of nowhere, these strange trucks, not to mention the passage from Italy to the Vosges... Jocelyn hardly dared to believe the idea that was behinning to form in his thoughts.

"What if I passed to another dimension, a world parallel to ours... No... It's not possible, could this be really happening to me? Another world... Another world... My good old Joss, you're cracked enough to be locked up! Had I been sleeping, I would have noticed! No, that's where I stop..."

Looking at the sky, he ended up considering the impossible.

"After all, it may not exist only in science fiction movies... Maybe I really am elsewhere."

He suddenly realized it wasn't the first time he was asking

himself that question. He remembered that huge reel of paper he had carried the week before. Had he dreamed what he had heard and felt the vibrations of up to the wheel? Joker or thoughtful spirit? Reality or furtive crossing of another dimension?

The only certainty, the reel couldn't have gotten straight by itself. It seemed unrealistic... And if all these questions that arise in similar cases were founded? So maybe this time he had not just quickly crossed through a parallel dimension.

"Why is there a different today? Why am I, then, in a different place? I should have still been on the highway; elsewhere, but on the highway, not here, in full countryside. It doesn't make sense. I can't believe I'm thinking about this!"

But, then... Maybe the reel had actually fallen into another dimension I went through and I only heard the noise... Yes, but that doesn't explain the vibrations and the jolts...

As he intensely thought about his sad fate, a voice was heard.

"They're offset!"

"That's surely it", Jocelyn answered, "you're right..."

Suddenly realizing he was alone, he looked around him, frightened.

"Who, who said that?"

This same voice suddenly began to laugh, then resumed:

"It's nothing Joss capich, don't be afraid!"

"Joss Capich?"

"Show yourself! Who are you, a ghost, a spirit? And, here, I bet you're having a good laugh?"

He suddenly saw a man, all dressed in white about 200 meters from him on the small country road. He held his breath for a moment and started slowly walking towards him. The man was really laughing on Jocelyn's account.

"You will never change, Mr. Chaos!"

"'Mr. Chaos now; better and better! I forbid you to skin my name. My name is 'Beaumont', damn it!"

He stopped short, looking, with his eyes, which were asking three questions a second, to the man who seemed not to be getting closer despite the distance he had walked to join him.

"I hadn't fallen far!"

"And he's also mocking me!"

"Continue your road, Joss, your life has already changed. You'll never be the same again!"

He took a step towards Jocelyn, then disappeared altogether. Joss couldn't believe his eyes.

"I didn't dream it! No, I'm not crazy... My life simply changed! He seems to know me... Strange..."

He went back to the truck. Since then, he looked at everything around him with new eyes, like a researcher doing a scientific experiment. He couldn't believe it. I'm in another world! He didn't know if he should rejoice at this discovery or worry about never being able to return to his own. In that moment, a ton of questions crossed his mind.

"Who's the president of the Republic? Are celebrities the same ones? Right, maybe not, since I'm one of them! And inventors... Maybe there are things here completely unknown to us. What a strange feeling to be in a world we don't belong to."

Suddenly, while enjoying quietly a moment of relaxation, sitting on a bench outside the shop, a group of excited young people came to ask him for an autograph.

"Hello, Jocelyn, we immediately recognized you! We're fans of your acrobatics and what you do with the wheel of a car and now, we're going to Paris to see you beat the world record. Here is a poster of you next to the 'rocket car', please sign it for us?"

"But, of course", he answered, amused by the situation, "do you have a marker?"

They had planned everything; one of them handed it to him. Not knowing how his double signed, he opted for the simplest, by signing his name and surname.

"Thank you, Jocelyn", one of them said "and good luck on Sunday!"

It was surreal. He would never have thought of signing an autograph with his effigy for stunts he had never made. In any case, not for those of the last twenty years. But what did his wife have to do with all of this? It couldn't be Emma, since they were divorced. The only plausible explanation was that his double had married another, who was also interested in this demanding job.

"Maybe Corinne", he thought with certain emotion.

"But maybe here..."

Despite what he felt about returning to his world, this story began to grow on him. It was certainly not reasonable, but it was stronger than him. What more would he discover?

He decided to take the wheel to go to Mazamet at once, where he would find Emma's double. He knew that from where he left off, it would take a little less than four and a half hours to arrive safely. Circumstances may have been exceptional, but he preferred to respect the legislation in his world, which imposed a stop of at least forty-five minutes after four hours and a half of driving. After all, maybe the rules were the same in this world. And during this long 'Rolling', since that is the name it carried in the jargon road, he had time to think over and over. What would his reaction be when he saw the children his double had had with this world's Emma?

"They're surely going to call me 'dad'," he thought, a little worried.

"What will I answer? They're now my children, but his."

"How am I going to explain all this? Hi, it's me, Jocelyn, the driver and I come from a parallel world!"

No, he couldn't say that…

"Hello, Emma, listen to me well, don't interrupt me and try to keep an open mind; look, I'm Jocelyn, but I'm not the Jocelyn you know and with whom you had children with... In short, I'm from another dimension!"

"No; this won't do either. Then, how to go about it? Is there an interdimensional traveler manual in bookstores?"

He, who generally, allowed things to come and waited to see how it would unfold in order to react, was confronted with a cruel dilemma. If he told her the truth, he would probably scare her and wouldn't get anywhere good. But, on the other hand, if he lied, she would inevitably end up realizing it and risk blaming him, thinking she had been misled; furthermore, this would hurt the other Jocelyn. He felt trapped. It was an impasse that he was going to have to get out of by doing something he hated: lie to the woman he loved, even if it was only her double.

The trip was long and distressing. It was almost 6:30; he was only fifteen kilometers from Mazamet. His heart beat like crazy. He was both happy and worried about seeing Emma again. Upon his arrival, he had a first surprise. The house Emma lived in was in the same place as the one he shared with his double, but three times bigger.

"I would have had the means, had I continued with the stunts", he thought.

It was a real palace disguised as a luxury villa. Two floors above the ground floor were overlooking a huge garden in which a large Olympic pool had been built, equipped with a diving board.

"I always knew I had good taste", he told himself, thinking about his double. They weren't that different, after all!

When she saw him coming, Emma was happy, almost shining with it, but she tried not to let it show due to the situation, even though she had the feeling that he had spoken to her as if they were still together… On his side, he had conditioned himself not to make the mistake of kissing her as he would have done with the other Emma. Moreover, that could have serious consequences with his double, since he had remarried. Arriving, he parked in a parking lot not far from the house and made the hundred and fifty meters separating him on foot.

"What a strange cart", she thought. Leaning on the railing of the long balcony at the front of the house, she watched him walk in her direction with the same loving eyes as when they lived together. It was nice to see him again. He was the same, a simple walk, but decided; she who didn't measure more over one meter sixty-five, with long curly brown hair, immediately fell in love with this tall blond guy of a meter ninety-five, the Hispano-Swedish type. Looking at him, he was now forty-five years old, still a slender and handsome man. How could she have let him go? Certainly, he came by as often as his job allowed him, to see the children, but it was different. Perhaps she should have been more understanding of his perilous passion, although it wasn't his style to take unnecessary risks. On the advice of some of his relatives, he had decided to do an analysis on himself, and it came out that he wasn't doing this job to play with death, but simply because he loved what he did. He just wanted to present extraordinary shows. And for the preparation of each stunt, everything was studied by computer, or rather by calculator; the distances, the speed, and even the wind, he left nothing to chance!

Seeing him coming to the door, Emma went down to greet him and stopped herself from jumping around his neck, as she did every time she saw him. Both kissed each other like two longtime friends.

"Hello Emma", Jocelyn said cautiously.

"Hi, Joss", she replied, a little surprised by this unusual situation. "Go up, you know the way…"

"Yes, I know it", he said, striving to act as if that were the case.

Emma was heading straight for the stairs to the other wing of the house, which was once the place where he worked in the development of those various acrobatics with his team, in the form of a multitude of very specific plans. Occasional musician, he even happened to make little 'personal oxen' as he called it, playing alone on his drums over music he liked like rock and roll, blues or jazz.

Both 'Joss' were able to play many songs to perfection. It was their hobby.

"Do you feel like hitting your drums?", asked Emma, intrigued by the direction he was taking; "you got them when you left, you know…"

"Drums", he thought; *"then, he also…"*

He immediately understood that he was taking the wrong staircase; he walked towards the other one, giving Emma a rough explanation.

"No, you're right, let's go to the living room instead!"

In that moment, Emma looked at him strangely and decided not to say anything.

"Yes, I think it would do better for a talk…"

When he set foot on the last step of the stairs, he discovered a piece worthy of the greatest luxury hotels. He wanted to stop for a moment to contemplate, but he was supposed to have lived there, and therefore should not reveal his amazement. The furniture was all made of solid wood; a magnificent chandelier that seemed to be made of diamonds was suspended above a marble table, with a large smoked glass in the center, attached to the same level as the plate. He was charmed. If he had the financial means of his double, he would probably have chosen something similar.

Emma realized he wasn't himself by his attitude, but decided to keep silent for the moment.

"Do you want me to extend an invitation for you to sit on a chair, or could you do without?", she joked.

He was frozen in front of the family photo that showed Emma, his double and... their two children.

"They look so much like me."

"No, dar... Emma, you don't need to extend it", he said.

She had noticed the beginning of the word "darling" in his sentence, and began to think, in spite of herself of another future than the one she had imagined till then.

"Still, he seems happy in his marriage", she thought.

He pulled one of the chairs from under the table and sat down.

"Do you want anything to drink; coffee, tea?", she offered him, almost lovingly.

"Would you happen to have whiskey?", Jocelyn said, needing something strong.

"Peated, as you like it?"

"But... It can't be, he's my true copy, this guy!"

"Yes, thanks!" he replied, still wondering how he was going to explain all of this to him.

Emma prepared a cup of tea for herself, and came to join him, taking a seat in front of him.

"So, tell me", she said with an air that wanted to be detached.

He looked at her, stared at her as if he were discovering her; she was the same, with wrinkles and lines and all, but it was very difficult for him not to look at her with loving eyes.

"If only you knew", he thought.

The Emma he knew was very open-minded; so there was no reason for him to be different with the one sitting in front of him. He decided to tread carefully.

"If you had to describe me in writing or verbally, what would you say?", he said, satisfied with his introduction.

"I would say that you are a sensible person, down to earth, who knows what he wants, with a character that's not always easy to take, but not mean, at the same time", Emma answered, a little surprised by the question. "Why do you ask?"

"Well, what I'm about to tell you is so crazy, that you'll be entitled to ask if a screw isn't loose in my head! Before starting, did you ever think I could have a crazy side or not?"

"Now I'm wondering what you're going to tell me that would make me believe that", said Emma, who was now really worried; "tell me what's wrong and stop turning in a circle!"

"OK… I'm Jocelyn, but not the one you knew!", he continued like a salesman looking to sell the Eiffel Tower for the second time to the same person.

"That's actually good news", Emma said.

Jocelyn was speechless for a moment, and realized she had misunderstood what he had told her.

"I don't think you understood, Emma; I'm not talking to you about any awareness that made me another man, but that I'm simply not the 'Joss' who is currently in Paris, preparing for his stunt!"

Emma was still far away from reality.

"If you have problems with drugs, I can help you, you know", she continued "and I promise it will stay between us!"

He didn't know what to say anymore so she would understand, and at the same time, he understood her reaction.

"Emma", he said, looking at her in the whites of her eyes and taking her left hand in his, "listen to me carefully, I don't take any drugs, I haven't been a stuntman for twenty years, I'm a truck driver..."

"Just a second; you want to say cart driver?"

"Cart driver, that's also funny."

"Yes, that's it, and the tru... cart that you see there in the parking and that everyone has looked at strangely since I came here, is my means of work. The 'Joss' you knew is actually in Paris and me, I'm his double!"

Frightened, Emma, suddenly let go of his hand and got up from her chair.

"Now, you did it!", she said, "I honestly think you're crazy!"

"Look at me, Emma", he continued, "where I come from, we're still married and I love you more than life itself, but you have to believe me... Trust me, and please... Help me!"

He couldn't go back now; now he had to find the words to reassure her, convince her of the truth of his words, and he couldn't help but think that if a door had opened when he had entered this world, it could just as quickly close if that wasn't already the case. He thought he had to act quickly.

"Emma, take me for a fool if that works for you", Jocelyn insisted, "but I really need help."

By saying that, Emma could well see he was truly scared as well; she still loved him and didn't have the heart to leave him to his sad fate.

"Very well", she answered, trying to remain objective; "admitting I believe you, what do you want me to do?"

"If you know where to find me in Paris, I mean, my double, then take your phone and check my story, and after you talk to him, then maybe you'll believe me more easily; that would be a good starting point."

Emma had a phone number with which she could reach him anytime, for the children. She had trouble taking in the situation. She was about to call a man who was supposed to be in Paris, but who was under her eyes.

"*I must be completely crazy*", she thought.

She took her mobile phone, dialed the number listed under the name 'Joss without letting out of her eyes the one who was sitting in her living room. To her big surprise, no phone was ringing in the room, but that didn't mean much; he could have very well have left it in the cart. At the end of the fourth ring, she heard.

"Hi, it's Jocelyn, but I can't answer you right now, leave me a message after the beep and I'll call you as soon as possible."

"Hi, Joss, it's me", said Emma who was almost scared to see herself doing what she was doing, "call me back when you get this message and don't worry, it's nothing major."

Her voice was trembling and it could be heard. In that moment, Jocelyn's eyes grew round, as for him, the situation was major, it was catastrophic! What would he do in this world if he couldn't go back to his dimension? It was out of the question he lost his life, even if there was another Emma here who was practically identical to the one he loved. And it was unthinkable for him to live in the shadow of his double who had become famous in this world, to his fans, in any case, with mechanical acrobatics.

"How do you see this continuing?", Emma asked, a little lost.

"Do you know someone around you who is interested in this

kind of phenomenon? A researcher or a professor, for example?" he ventured.

"No", she answered, "but there may be someone who could inform me. I'll give him a call."

"Thanks, Emma."

"Now that I decided to help you, you risk thanking me often if you go on like this."

Jocelyn had a grateful smile, while Emma was dialing the number.

"Hello, Mira?"

Surprised, Jocelyn's eyes grew round.

"Hi... Would you happen to know someone working for NASA?", she joked.

"Well, they have a NASA here", Jocelyn thought!

"Yeah, I'm OK, thanks... No, I was joking, but it's very important... I can't tell you anything, let's say I'm preparing a surprise and I don't want to talk about it yet... No, don't worry, I'm not in trouble... OK, then listen, I wasn't serious with NASA, but I'm looking for a..."

She stopped and continued.

"Yes, Mira, I'm still here... No, it's fine, I got my answer... Yeeeees, I'll say it again, everything is fine... I'm sure, I have to hang up, I'll call again... No, I don't want you to come over! I'm sorry to be carried away, I'm hanging up, later!"

Jocelyn was looking at her with a questioning look.

"So, what did you think of?"

"I didn't recall right away, but there's a certain professor 'Thibault' in our friendly circle and we could have our solution with him. Just the time to look for his number and... by the way, now that I think about it, why did you look surprised when I spoke to Mira, the Emma in your world doesn't have a sister with that name?"

"Yes, but it isn't what could be called a good sisterly relation, contrary to what I have just seen."

"They don't get along?"

"You could say that again… You smile when you see each other and you tear yourself to pieces afterwards… Especially since her husband's death…"

"Her husband's death, you're talking about Max?"

"Yes, that's right, so he's called Max here too, and apparently, he's still alive!"

Emma finally found the number and put the notebook on the table, leaving it open to the page she had found, to continue the conversation.

"Yes, but what did he die of?"

"A bullet to his head!"

"You mean a missed bullet?"

"No, he put it there himself…"

"Why did he do such a thing?"

"He was pushed to the brink of his nerves. It was a complicated story."

"Tell me!"

"No. There's nothing interesting in this story. I wouldn't want to rush you, but if you phoned this famous person who could help me…"

"Yes, you're right, I'll phone him right away."

"What's his name?"

"'Professor Allan Thibault, do you know him?"

"No, it doesn't ring a bell… do I know him here?"

"Yes, you know him very well."

"And what does he do in life, this gentleman?"

"Well, like I told you, he's a professor and he works at a

university in Paris; and we made his acquaintance when he was staying here with his wife, visiting his children..."

Emma recovered:

"That your double and I have known for about the last ten years, they came to greet me, as Joss had worked with him on the set of a sci-fi visionary; he did the stunts, while Allan was there only as a consultant for his knowledge and his research on the universe. Maybe he could help you see a little more clearly into what's happening to you."

"Then, you believe me now", he said enthusiastically.

"I told you. Such a story isn't easy to believe, but if I told you I believe you, you can count it's true. The Emma in your world doesn't have this virtue?"

"Of course she does, and it's not the only one she has..."

Despite the situation, she was starting to feel comfortable with this man she knew without ever having seen, but he seemed to really like the other Emma and that comforted her somewhat.

"Thanks for the compliment... Apparently, we're not so different..."

"No, and I'm beginning to wonder if I'm not dreaming all this!"

At that moment Emma's phone rang; she took it and picked up without looking at the number on the screen.

"Hello?", she said in a calm voice.

"It's me!", the voice in the headset said, "You called me just now, is there a problem?"

"Joss... No, none... I'm going to ask you a question which will seem a little strange."

"I'm listening..."

"Have you ever had a twin brother?"

Jocelyn frowned; but he might have done the same if the

82

situation was reversed. He understood at that moment that she was talking to his double; he was all ears.

"Why such a question?", he asked, surprised; "Have you seen someone resembling me?"

Emma wasn't planning on talking about the presence of the other Jocelyn and so, she justified herself:

"I went to town today and I thought I saw you; I knew it couldn't be you, but from afar, he looked so much like you!"

"And you called to ask me this?"

"No, I called so you wouldn't forget Lionel's birthday", she said, falling back on her words.

"Don't worry, Emma, I already thought about it... You know very well I never forget my brother! But thanks for having reminded me."

"You're welcome, Joss... OK, I'll leave you to your work... Later!"

"Later, Emma and you didn't tell me, but I'll be careful! I'm hanging up... Kiss Quentin and Gaël for me... And for your information, I don't have a twin brother... 'Ciao Bella'."

"I'll keep in mind... Bye", she concluded.

Impatient, Jocelyn wanted to know everything.

"So?", he said cheerfully!

"So, what?", Emma teased.

"It was him, wasn't it?"

"Yes, it was you!"

Emma was starting to be amused by this unusual situation.

"Reassure me on one point", Jocelyn continued; "he doesn't have a twin brother apart from Lionel?"

"No, no twin; you also have a brother named Lionel in your world?"

"Yes; he works in computer science, in Paris, precisely."

"Decidedly, this doesn't sum up", Emma thought.

"What do you mean by that?", she asked.

"It's not going to be easy!", Jocelyn thought.

"Well, to keep it simple, he types on a keyboard where there are many keys marked with letters of the alphabet; and in front of him, there is a small bright screen on which he can see the result of his work."

"If I understood correctly, he works with a calculator!"

"A calculator... Funny that."

"Yes, that's exactly it", he continued; "Why, what does 'his Lionel' do?"

"He manages the bakery at the corner of the street with his wife, Grégorine."

Jocelyn couldn't hold back an ironic smile.

"This is all crazy", he said.

He was also beginning to get a sense of the dimension he was in.

"And you, I presume you're not a seamstress?"

"Absolutely not; but I still know how to get by. I wouldn't be scared to start making a sweater or a suit."

"Still! It's pretty good for someone who claims not to be a sartor, don't you think?"

Emma sighed, then continued.

"I just wanted to say I don't do it often, but I don't have any problems with it. Maybe we have it in our blood, who knows?"

"Who knows, as you say; it's true she always had it in for foreign languages. Maybe we have a different destiny in each dimension; different life lessons, challenges... I confess I still have a hard time believing what I just said and parallel to that, I'm convinced, like I have always known it..." He pulled himself together, "Talk to me a little about your work."

84

"My job, I do it at home on my calculator."

"And what do you do exactly?"

"Commercial translations… English, Chinese, German and Russian translated into French and vice versa."

"Well, I'll be…, just that; you didn't mess around. You really chose Russian and Chinese! Since my arrival, I find all the people I know, but you've all taken at one time or another, different ways… All this must mean something, but what…? On the contrary, I don't know professor Thibault; although I seem to have heard this name somewhere. By the way, could you call him and ask if I could go see him in Paris?"

Emma took her phone and complied. Thinking he would probably be at the University, she started from there. But she had a negative response. The teacher was away from work and he wasn't at home either. So she phoned Benjamin, one of the professor's children, who, she knew, was home at that hour of the day.

"Hello… Benjamin?"

"Hello, Emma", he replied in a tense voice.

"What's happening, you seem worried?"

"You wouldn't have talked to my dad on the phone lately, by any chance?"

"No, why?"

"My mother hasn't had any news for two days; no phone call, no word, no message, nothing since he left for University the day before yesterday and it's not his style to do this. When we called, they simply told us he wasn't there. But I have a feeling they haven't told us everything…"

"Jocelyn is in town", Emma said, "and, furthermore, I think the place he's at in Paris isn't very far from the University; I'll call him and ask if he can go inquire."

"That's nice of you, Emma; I didn't remember he was in Paris. Keep me informed, would you?"

"Of course, Benjamin", Emma assured him, "I'll call you as soon as I have something. Talk you later and try not to worry too much; it's probably not serious."

Emma was reassuring, but thought no less.

"What's happening?", Jocelyn asked, seeing her worried.

"The professor..."

"Well?"

"He disappeared two days ago, without a trace!"

Emma hadn't thought about the professor's activity, but Jocelyn immediately made the connection.

"Maybe he did some tests in his research..."

In that moment, he didn't know if he should rejoice or be afraid.

"Emma", he said like a captain giving an order to a sailor, "call 'Joss' and tell him to check with one of his colleagues; I'm sure there must be at least one who knows something... No, never mind; I'll go there myself."

"Why do you say that?", she asked, surprised.

"Think about it for a second", he said, sure of himself; "what was he working on?"

Emma immediately understood where he was going to this.

"Oh, my God!", she exclaimed with fright. "You think he could have..."

"I know nothing, Emma, and I know nothing of the exact nature of his research, but if his disappearance has any connection with my appearance here, then I have to go there and talk with his collaborators. The car parked downstairs is yours, isnt' it?"

"Yes, whose else would it be!"

"I don't know; there might be someone in your life, who might have gone somewhere on foot!"

"No, there's no one", she replied; "your double has completely taken over my being!"

"I see… Would you agree to lend it to me to go to Paris?"

"Of course, but I think it would be better to go together, since I know more people than you do here… Furthermore, you drove all day to get here; you must be tired and it's almost 8 o'clock; it's late!"

"And your work?"

"Don't worry about it, I'll be fine; I don't know how it is in your world, but here, we have portable calculators!"

"Oh, they're portable here as well?"

"Not real; you don't have this in your world?"

"I think I heard a story about it sometime", he continued, joking, "could we brew some coffee to take with?"

Emma giggled.

"I promise to try when we're in Paris!"

Without realizing it, he joked with her as he would have done with the Emma in his dimension; but he suddenly pulled himself together, striving to refrain from any familiarity with this Emma who, despite the disconcerting number of behavioral similarities, was still a woman he was seeing for the first time in his life.

In that precise moment, she was looking at him out of the corner of her eye and began to be seduced by this man who was the spitting image of the one whose life she no longer shared, despite some small insignificant differences.

For him, it was harder to resist temptation, since he was married to her in the other world; but for her, he represented the 'forbidden fruit', as she was divorced from the original, but they still loved each other. Only the life that Jocelyn led in this world had been right for their couple. So, how to resist this exact copy fallen from the sky and who in addition, still lived with her double!

It wasn't easy for either of them to face this extraordinary situation.

"I'll inform Benjamin of my trip to Paris and Lionel to go pick up the children at school and we can go", Emma said, somewhat troubled.

Jocelyn, however, felt the need to clarify their relationship.

"Very well", he continued, "I will ask you to allow me a shower before departure if you don't mind, and while I'm on this point…"

He paused for a moment.

"It's the other Emma I'm in love with, not you…"

She got close, kissed him on the cheek and nodded in the same direction of thought.

"And I'm in love with your double; even if there's nothing harder than being in the presence of the clone of the man with whom I have lived with, whom I divorced and with whom I would have less to blame than with the original…"

They exchanged an intense look and both curbed their impulses.

"Show me where the bathroom is, please", he asked.

From that moment on, it was a story without words until they left. Under the shower, he thought of all the eventualities about this so different and resembling Emma and the mysteriously disappeared professor.

"And if it was him the key to return? But for that, he should be here… His collaborators will surely be able to help me… It would be enough to succeed in convincing them I come from another dimension… Would they put me to a divine test? And this Emma

similar to the one I love, will I be able to resist her? If anything happened between us, somewhere, I would betray her... But, at the same time, it's her! How could I explain that if I had to do it?"

While he was taking his shower, Emma had prepared a little spare business bag and was waiting patiently on the living room sofa. Out of the bathroom, he looked at her there and thought of Emma, his Emma who was never ready on time; he concluded that there was at least this difference between them.

A climate of mutual embarrassment reigned in the room. They dared not look at each other in the eye and behaved like two guilty people, while there had been nothing more than a simple complicit look and an innocent kiss.

Emma got up, took her bag and went towards the car, taking care to leave the house key in the lock of the front door, so that Jocelyn could close it behind him. He arrived in turn and took a seat on the passenger side.

"Don't get upset, but I have to break the silence; we have to stop for a moment at my truck to take some extra stuff."

"I had already thought about it", Emma assured him; "and you're right, our reaction is ridiculous… We're behaving like two teenagers after an argument."

Jocelyn didn't answer to that.

"Let's go, Emma, we're wasting time."

"Alright, Sir!"

They stopped in front of the truck, Jocelyn took his bag and got in the car.

"While we're on this subject, when you pass the pharmacy at the corner of the boulevard and the national road, take the street on the left; we can then go around from behind to retrieve the main road", said Jocelyn, who wanted to make a comparison with what he knew in his world; "and drive slowly."

"Very well, my Lord and Master!"

"Why do you want to go this way?", she asked.

As she drove slowly down the street in question, Jocelyn looked at a building that in his world was only an old shed, and in this one, a shop.

He suddenly realized he might never see the building as he knew it and its boss again, with whom he got along so well.

And if he couldn't go back… Several moments of life, faces and good memories passed through his mind. He scrutinized every detail and made a complete survey by sweeping with his eyes the neighborhood he knew well and which was dotted with tiny differences regarding its size.

"You see that building on the right? This is where our store is."

It made him see the shed in the form of a ready-to-wear clothing store.

"Well, this is where I bought these pants from", Emma continued.

"The rest seems to be about the same as what I know", he continued, observing the place.

"It must be strange to be in a place where everything seems like what we have always known and diametrically opposed at the same time, in certain aspects", Emma hazarded… "Tell me about myself from your world, if you will… my character, my wishes, my work, tell me everything!"

He looked at her out of the corner of his eye, laughing.

"That's so much like her what you just did! But, to be honest, you have a lot of similarities in your behavior. Forged steel is like modeling clay compared to your character; I don't know you enough to talk about your wishes, but yours seem to vibrate as high as hers. As for her job, you know it, I'm sure that you, like her, are able to exchange them. To tell you the truth, I think I understood something important since my arrival... All I see here is identical to what I know or almost; only the decisions and directions of life that the characters have taken in this world are different."

"If you told me something about yourself... Why did you stop doing the stunts to travel the roads, for example; or do you also make music in your spare time?"

After a good relaxing shower, he let himself be led without doing anything other than listening to her speak, not to mention the day he had had, Jocelyn was a little tired, but thought it wrong not to reciprocate by falling asleep on the seat. So he undertook to tell a little to this Emma, so full of energy.

"Well, I did acrobatics up to twenty-six, when I had to go to do my military service and when I came back from the army with my per... my cart approval in my pocket, I decided to travel the roads."

"You would have me believe that it was the army alone that deterred you from doing stunts?", Emma interrupted, who saw well that something was missing from his story.

"Very well", Jocelyn said, sadly; "at that time, I was with someone named Corinne..."

Emma had a semblance of reaction, but immediately recovered.

Jocelyn noticed...

"He too?"

"Never mind, go on..."

He continued with some emotion.

"We used to work together; she did stunts as well. One day, she fell from the first floor during training and she didn't land well. She fell on her head, violently bent her spine and broke the seventh cervical spine. After that, everything changed. She became irascible, distressing to the highest point. It quickly became a hell to live in. Doctors were optimistic about her remission. But she preferred not to believe it; she got it through her head that she would never get up from her chair. I tried everything in terms of deterrence and motivation, but nothing. She finally let go completely and I saw her get a little unhappier every day. She had convinced herself that I would leave her sooner or later; she just didn't want to impose on me. Betwee,n us I would never have believed her capable of being overwhelmed by such a feeling, she, who loved life so much and who still had the energy of ten people, I realized that I didn't know her, or at least, I did very little."

Jocelyn didn't talk about it, but this story touched him in the depths of his being; he kept a short silence before continuing as lucidly as he could.

"Then I accepted the help that friends offered me. They managed to persuade her to go to practice, putting one foot in front of the other during workouts and I even thought that she liked it at first; we kept her standing and we helped her move slowly. I had the impression that she came back to life in those moments. Everyone ended up believing it... except her. One morning, I woke up like every other day, at six thirty. Not seeing her in the room, I went to the living room to see what she was doing. She was lying on the couch; I hadn't heard anything, for I sleep soundly. I thought it was better I let her sleep and I went to get a blanket so she wouldn't catch cold. I came back, I bent over to cover her and I kissed her on the forehead."

In that moment, a tear escaped him, but went on to tell the whole story.

"Her forehead was as cold as the leatherette sofa. There, I saw a tube protruding under her pillow; an empty tube of tablets. That's when I understood and I broke down in tears, holding her tight against me. Not very cheerful, is it?"

Emma was struggling to hide how she felt when she saw him in this state of anxiety.

Jocelyn continued.

"Afterwards, I didn't have the heart to continue with stunts, so I decided to do my military service that I had until then rejected."

He let a few moments pass, then resumed.

"Is there one here as well?"

"A what, a Corrine?"

Jocelyn nodded.

"Yes, there is one; she's the one who stole your double to my ex-couple."

"They're together?"

"For some years now."

"I'm sorry; I didn't want to make you feel uncomfortable."

"I know."

Jocelyn was dying to know the course of her fall in this world. Had it happened? If so, how had she avoided the accident? Questions jostled in his mind, but he didn't dare insist. Furthermore, Emma probably knew nothing.

"Your double told me about the fall that nearly cost her life."

"I'm not asking you, Emma."

"I would want to know if I were you, and believe me, it's in the past."

"As you wish."

"He told me about it one night when we were talking about our respective pasts."

"You had… Actually, I meant to say, he had noticed the bad

posture she had taken from the start and he had intervened before she touched the mat so that she landed without breaking her neck."

Jocelyn had always blamed himself for not doing that; that day he had held a reflex in check, as she had asked him all the time not to take care of her as if she were a kid… Obviously, his double had paid attention all that time. Had it been the right decision to take, in view of the consequences? There were so many details that came into play in his decision that it was better not to start regretting it.

"Thank you, Emma", Jocelyn concluded.

"That's OK… Why didn't you want to do your military service?", she asked, trying to relax the atmosphere.

"When I made that decision, I had far too many plans to lose a year holding a rifle", replied Jocelyn, who was recovering little by little from his emotions.

"However, when I went, I wanted to get employed; such an irony, right? But they refused my application because I was too old. So, I decided to find out about the jobs that were on offer when I left, and that's how I started to drive, while waiting to realize my goals."

"Too old to be military?", Emma was surprised.

"Too old for the specialization I wanted", he answered.

"What specialization?"

"I wanted to be a 'submariner'; because, were I to be employed, I preferred to do something that I would never be able to do in civilian life, unless to convert myself to an underwater explorer. But, the worst thing is they sent me a mail six months later telling me I was finally fit for the submarine, while I was already working for a shipper… Go figure!"

"You didn't accept?"

"No… It might seem funny, but I had met you!"

"I don't remember!", she joked.

"For sure", Jocelyn continued; "only the one I married could remember!"

"I imagine there are also a Quentin and a Gaël…"

"No; that's part of the differences… We can't have any."

"I'm sorry", she continued, trying to catch up with her indelicacy.

"Don't worry about it, it's not a problem. Had we had children, we would have had another life; that's all!"

"Wasn't it too hard to take in?"

"More for her than for me, for I have never lived to have an offspring, but to be happy with my life… with or without children; that being said, nothing is ever final."

"Why, are you going to adopt one?"

"No, I don't think so, for she's too old for that!"

"What! Me, too old!?"

"No, her…"

"What's wrong with her! If I see her one day, I'll tell her!"

Jocelyn couldn't restrain an eloquent smile …

"As I was saying, it's OK, because we talk from time to time about sponsoring a child."

"That means you'll pay his studies and that you'll make sure he doesn't miss anything, but it's not the same thing."

"Yes and no… We could end up loving him…"

Emma looked at him without saying anything, while Jocelyn continued.

"Whatever will be, for the moment we don't have one, and we take advantage of it to the maximum."

"I understand", Emma said with compassion.

"It's okay, we don't have all the weight of the world on our shoulders either even if, I confess, I think of it from time to time. Anyway, I have always believed in destiny, no matter what that would be."

"Yes, but... Life is also what we make of it..."

"There are unknown factors..."

"Maybe, but it is up to us to deal with what comes before us."

"Anyhow, I can tell you that these are two different lives and if this is what we must have, then so be it! But, today, all is well for us, if we don't take into account our worldly separation..."

"You have a little of the same philosophy as him", Emma continued, smiling. "I'm sure he would have had the same reaction as you, had he been in your place..."

"If I understood correctly, I'm a lot like Joss", he said jokingly.

"Even if I accepted the idea you come from elsewhere, this situation will seem strange to the end, no matter what you say!"

"Yes, I understand, it's not common, and I don't know how I would have reacted in the opposite case... I must admit that I feel a certain apprehension to meet myself!"

At that moment, he inclined his seat a few notches to rest; he was, literally, dead on his feet.

"Don't hold it against me, Emma, but I'm going to sleep a bit; I'm exhausted!"

"No problem, Joss, that's why I'm driving... Sleep well, 'till later."

"Thanks, Emma; drive safely."

Jocelyn didn't take more than two minutes to go to the arms of Morpheus. Emma looked at him furtively, wondering how all of this was going to end. She didn't want to admit it, but finding 'her Joss' through this one, didn't displease her at all; at the same time, she didn't want to ruin this budding friendship. She decided to focus on her road and turned the radio on to keep her company.

A few tunes of music and commercials later, she heard some information that made her stop on the spot to make a call.

"Hello, Benjamin, it's Emma… Phone your mother to tell her the good news!"

"You have news?", asked Benjamin, excitedly.

"Yes, from the radio. Your father was found hitchhiking on the road near Limoges. He's at the police station and we'll be there in two hours…"

"Hitchhiking in Limoges, my father!? Thanks, Emma I'll call right now."

"OK, I'll talk to you later…"

"But, what is he doing there?", she thought. She looked at Jocelyn again, thinking he was probably right in wanting to meet the professor. Perhaps he had had the same misadventure as himself, except that he would certainly have provoked it with one of his extraordinary experiments. She pulled herself together and she went on her way towards the Limoges police station.

Jocelyn was fast asleep and didn't realize anything. He was having a dream in which he was with his double's two children and he was having fun with them as if they were his own; the whole thing was reinforced by the conviction of being a good father, since he had often been told that he would have been an excellent one with his behavior and his upright mindedness.

When they arrived in Limoges, Emma woke him by touching his shoulder with a calm and thoughtful gesture. It was now 8:30.

"Joss… Joss… " Emma said, in a soft voice.

He painfully opened his eyes, wakened by the light of a street lamp that lined the road in that place.

"We arrived?", he asked in a thick voice.

"Yes, but we're not in Paris yet; we're at a police station in Limoges…"

"So, you're going to stop at police stations to say 'hi'?, Jocelyn joked, waking slowly.

Emma laughed.

"Yeah, something like that!"

"So, what are we doing here?"

"I'm just simply making the route for tomorrow, we'll spend the night here."

"If you're tired, I can take the wheel…"

"No, the professor I told you about earlier, is at this police station."

"You're talking about the same person who has the ability to get me out of here?"

"Yes, the professor with whom you're supposed to have worked with. We'll talk about it later, if you want; rather, help me find a 'roof for the night'."

"A roof for the night?"

"A 'Dwelling', if you prefer."

"It must be a hotel", he thought, amused.

"Look", Emma pointed out to the beautiful little rustic façade, cleverly highlighted by lights, "I think that's it!"

Arrived on the car park of the 'Roof', Emma parked the car; they took their things and headed for the entrance. Calculating and travelers at heart, their travel bag wasn't bulky. Arrived in the lobby, Jocelyn took the lead and spoke directly to the receptionist.

"Good evening sir, do you still have a 'roof' available?"

The man laughed out loud, just as Emma did.

"Yes, sir; when I saw you arrive, I sent the maid to mop the

98

tiles a bit!"

Jocelyn could see that he had goofed and decided to react as if he had told a good joke, while laughing in turn. He reformulated his request, this time being a little less precise, to be sure not to make a mistake.

"You never heard that one before, did you?", he continued in an amused tone. "OK, let's be serious now; do you have a place for us for the night?"

"So, we'll leave the tiles aside?", the receptionist continued to joke.

"Yes, since they need cleaning!"

"I'll remember that one, you made me laugh real good."

He quickly looked at the register. Jocelyn meanwhile, looked at the walls, the ceiling and the decoration. Apart from some insignificant differences, like the colors that didn't go together at all, or the hanging frames with unusual patterns, the hall really looked like a hotel lobby!

"Here you are, Ladies and Gentlemen, the 18 is free; it's between the ground floor and the first floor."

Jocelyn mechanically took the pen on the counter for the 'autograph' on the hotel file.

Emma was surprised to see him take the pen with his right hand.

"Well, he's a righty."

Leaving the receptionist to finish filling out a document, Jocelyn turned to Emma and noticed her pointed look on his hand.

"He's a lefty, isn't he?"

"Not you, apparently; how is that possible?"

"I was born a lefty, like him. But it was considered a flaw in the school I was in when I was a kid and they didn't let me.

Obviously, we didn't go to the same schools!"

He smiled, then waited for the receptionist's answer. A detail, however, crossed his mind. Not knowing if he had to pay in advance, he preferred to pass the baton to Emma, the only one holding the current currency. "We'll get up around eight o'clock tomorrow morning, must we pay you now?"

"No, tomorrow morning will be fine", said the man, confidently. "I can accompany you if you want, but it's real easy to find. When you reach the first, it will be the second door on your right."

"We'll find it", Emma said, "Thank you, Sir."

"In that case, I wish you a good nighty."

"A good nighty", Jocelyn thought; *"We are still in the time of the Revolution here!"*

"Here, darling, you take the bag!", Emma said, lovingly.

Surprised, Jocelyn's eyes grew round, then understood that she didn't want to give useless explanations.

"Of course, my angel", he replied, "take the lead, I'm right behind you."

Arrived at the first 'floor', Emma looked to the right then left to locate the location of the rooms.

"It's that way", she said, taking a left, "here it is."

As they entered the room, Jocelyn noticed a television.

"Allow me fifteen minutes of TV before sleeping, I want to watch your news."

"That I allow you what?"

"That thing; the box with images…"

"The videophone… You really want to look at it now?"

"It's only curiosity, I won't watch it for too long, I promise."

"I'll prepare to go to bed, I'm tired, and the only thing I want is to sleep."

"OK, 'My Angel'" he continued, pressing on the 'My'.

She gave him a quick look and headed for the bathroom to change.

During this time, Jocelyn sat down in front of the 'Videophone'. Apparently, it was the ending of a movie. The actors were almost unknown to him. Still, he recognized one.

"Not true, he's an actor here as well", he thought.

"But, he's old; he must be at least eighty-five years old!"

Suddenly, he realized he must still be alive, considering the way the movie was made.

"Louis de Funès is still alive, imagine that!"

Surprised by this discovery, he watched with interest the last five minutes of the film, hoping to catch the news. His wish became reality.

"Ladies and Gentlemen, good evening", the journalist began; "in this flash, no less than thirty strange appearances, including one fatal and twenty-two disappearances, just as inexplicable…"

What he heard then, left him speechless. But the surprises didn't end there…

The journalist enumerated the facts such:

"To begin this surreal flash, know that no rational explanation was found at the time I'm talking to you.

* Four Americans also appeared in the port of Marseille under the gaze of dozens of people. They are currently being questioned by policemen and declare that they understand nothing of what is happening to them."

He continued to enumerate several other suspicious apparitions and arrived at the tragedy.

* A Chinese man appeared right in front of a cart traveling at full speed on the highway to London, England. Violently hit by the engine, the man died on the spot. Now, look at these pictures; sensitive souls, please refrain…"

The film recorded by one of the cameras in the truck appeared on the screen, showing off a car in the distance and suddenly a man on a bicycle coming out of nowhere, being hit hard on the radiator grille of the engine.

At that moment, Jocelyn recoiled.

"Still in shock, the driver didn't return to the wheel", the journalist continued, "but the strangest thing is that everything indicates that he came directly from China with his bike. Indeed, no 'Frontier-Pass' nor any visa were found on the unfortunate man. Twenty-two disappearances; yes, there is a real mysterious wave surrounding these facts."

He enumerated, this time, the phenomena one after the other, also that of Professor Allan Thibault, who had disappeared under the eyes of the guard Christian, on the roof of the building.

"The professor would have been found in Limoges, from where our special envoy should give us more information shortly."

The journalist proceeded in the same way with the twenty-one other cases, treated two or three other subjects and finished with the weather.

"*So that's it*", thought Jocelyn, who didn't really know what to think of all this.

Firstly, this professor could surely help him, since he had just experienced the same thing, but he was still in his dimension. How was that possible?

By what miracle could he not be in another world, while Jocelyn was forced to face the perfect look-alike of the woman he loved; and he knew he would face himself in a short time, in all likelihood

Emma, who had finished changing, came out of the bathroom dressed in a nightgown such as the one worn by the Emma of his world.

"Is the news good?", she said as she replaced a lock of rebel hair over her head.

Eager to play 'Cards on the table', Jocelyn entered the heart of the matter.

"He also 'travelled', didn't he?"

Surprised, Emma had trouble answering.

"What… what are you talking about?"

"They talked about professor Thibault at the T… On the videophone and they described a very strange story…"

"It's what I wanted to talk to you about", she said, taken aback. "What did they say, exactly?"

"They simply said that he had suddenly vanished on the roof of the University where he teaches and that he was found here in Limoges."

"They didn't say anything else?"

"He isn't the only one to have vanished; they announced twenty-two in all!"

"Not possible!", said Emma, scared, sitting on the bed.

"But then, if they talked about disappearances, they probably had to evoke appearances like you."

"Yes, about thirty, but the number is incorrect, since I'm not part of it. So, how to know if there have been others?"

"But, what's happening right now?", Emma said, thoughtfully; "The world became crazy!"

"I don't know, but these phenomena have already cost the life of a man, who found himself aimlessly in front of a truck, I mean, a cart launched at full speed and seeing that, I felt happy to have landed on this small country road!"

"They showed it on the videophone?"

"Yes, it was awful; he didn't even have time to turn around, you can imagine..."

"Such horror!"

"Fortunately, the driver had placed a camera on his dashboard, otherwise I hardly dare to imagine the mess in which he would have found himself!"

"All the carts and cars are equipped, you know..."

"I see!"

"Yes, there has been too much abuse. You are equipped too, aren't you?"

"No, we don't have them, but we mustn't despair, given that we are in a time dedicated to road safety, I think we're right in presuming their time will come."

"You really have time to catch up!", Emma teased.

"Yes, I'm almost ashamed to tell you about my world."

"Don't worry about it, we also had our 'folk' era."

Seeing him worried, she approached him. They were half lying on the bed, each on his side, taking support on the left elbow for one and right for the other. She put her hand on Jocelyn's and looked him straight in the eye, trying in vain not to devour him.

"It's going to be OK; tomorrow, we'll go get the professor and he'll probably get you out of here."

For an answer, Jocelyn provided her with a smile that wanted to be approving. He couldn't help but see the differences. This other version of his beloved seemed much less exclusive; it was true that this one had had a much happier childhood and was therefore not in excessive demand of attention, contrary to her double. Sometimes, it was to such an extent that some situations had plenty of time to turn into a true marital cancer.

This exasperated him to the highest point, but he strove to be lovingly understanding. He even silenced his feelings until the final explosion. How could he be mad at her? Her brothers and sisters also suffered from the same syndrome almost to a T; she was really trying to get rid of this heavy and evil family burden.

What a pleasure to be there, in front of the woman he loved, without them; anyway, not with those hanging around. Maybe it would be better to take advantage, as this kind of opportunity would probably not be forthcoming anytime soon, and would certainly give him some breathing space, starting with his personality that he had lost somewhere in the early years of their relationship. He knew deep down that he should never have given up by accepting some unlikely situations, with catastrophic consequences. The fear that Emma felt in her being was always translated by 'Test Situations', to make sure that trichlorethylene really dissolves everything. So, what to think of this clone, that didn't even seem to need to assert or draw attention to herself. All these details made her much more pleasant, even if it was only a facet of the character that Jocelyn didn't know that well. But he had to admit that what he saw made them stand out from each other. He was just discovering an Emma devoid of anger, able to give a confidence and a love unrestrained by the fear of living, engendered by a heavy repetitive invading past, and present in all her acts and actions. Jocelyn knew perfectly well that 'his Emma' would never be able to give herself completely without having done a whole lot of tests beforehand, often clumsy, sometimes destructive. In addition to the long periods of reflection he was used to in his work, during which he was reviewing everything, he was thinking at that very moment of the various disputes they had had in the past on sensitive subjects, whose consequences were still felt in certain circumstances. For him, to love is above all, a question of well-being...

Seeing him so thoughtful, Emma hesitated a moment, then wanted to have a clear heart.

"Joss...?" she said in a soft voice.

"Yes, Emma; I'm sorry, my mind wanders... Where were we?"

"What happened?"

"Are you talking about us?"

"Who else would I be talking about!"

"I don't know you that well, but you resemble each other in your essence. I see very well that there's something wrong; for once, you can refrain from protecting me... Tell me, Joss."

"What's happening; what happened!?", Jocelyn told himself.

"What's the matter, is something wrong, Joss?"

"It's strange... I want to tell you about it, but the memories go in a swirl every time I want to pick one!"

"You have memory loss at your age?", Emma joked.

"That's doesn't make me laugh as much as you; I remember the feelings, but not the situations that caused them. It's still worrying! On the contrary, I can remember everything else..."

"Everything else?"

"Yes; the rest of my life... I may be starting to select my memories; the good ones to one side and the bad ones in the back! I don't remember Emma, I don't know anymore... All I know, is this profound sadness I feel right now; but from here to getting to the bottom of it..."

"I believe this disease has a name..."

"Yes, thanks, I know it; but I doubt it's that. I couldn't tell you why, but it's linked to all of this. I have a deep conviction..."

"All of this?"

"What's happening to me right now."

"How can you be so sure?"

"Because I'm not the type to run away from my problems!"

"That, I know!"

"He was the same?"

"From that point of view, yes; but hearing you, he doesn't go as far as you in regards to concessions…"

While Jocelyn's thinking machine was running at full speed, Emma took her mobile phone, sat next to him and took a picture of their two faces, aiming approximately. Taken by surprise, Jocelyn didn't put up any resistance.

"What are you doing?"

"As you can see, I'm taking a photo of us!"

"You want a souvenir?"

"A souvenir that won't get erased so easily…"

Emma was excited, hilarious. It was a simple moment to consume without moderation. A scene of crisp life. Precisely what he missed at the beginning of his relationship. But he couldn't remember. At the moment, he had the feeling of rewriting a page of his life. He watched her react and be.

"Joss!"

"If my thoughts are true, then what makes me doubt like this?"

"Joss!"

"What's confusing my mind, damn it? The changing of worlds? Maybe. An intervention in the past? No, not possible, I have no intention of doing that, anyway, I don't think so!"

"JOSS!"

"Yes, I'm sorry Emma, what do you intend to do with this photo?"

"Keep it and share it, if you want."

"You want to send it to me?"

"Yes", Emma continued, "I'm going to try to send it to you.

What's your number?" Jocelyn listed the eight digits and then pulled himself together.

"Never mind, it won't work."

"Why not?"

"Send it to me by Bluetooth, are you familiar with it?"

"No, we're completely stupid and ignorant!"

"Gently, I didn't want to make you angry!"

"I was kidding, Joss."

He tried to abound in the same direction, but his eyes betrayed him. The "videophone" news he had seen had made him more aware of the surrealism of what he was living.

"And it there isn't any solution to all this" he thought. *"If I can never go back?"*

Morally, he was at his lowest. There were lots of catastrophic questions and scenarios in his mind.

"I have to pull myself together" he told himself. *"She's helping me understand what has happened and I don't have the right to feel sorry for myself, I have to help her help me. Come on, old man, you have been through other situations"* he encouraged himself.

He looked at Emma again, approached his face to hers and tenderly applied a kiss on her forehead.

"I'm very grateful you're doing this for me, you give me, by your behavior and, especially, by your presence here with me, the hope that I could have lost had I been alone. Thank you, Emma."

They looked at each other intensely. In that moment, both wanted to go beyond the forbidden.

Suddenly, Jocelyn felt the vibrator of his phone in his pocket followed by the ringing 'Emma' that he had particularly created. Joss smiled.

"Saved by the bell, one could say! It's her…"

"Who, me?"

"No, Emma, her."

He didn't let the second ring end and picked up.

"Hello!"

All he heard was a heap of crackles, interference and a multitude of voices seeming to converse with each other. For the moment, he felt the need to move the phone away from his ear. Emma understood that there was a problem.

"I didn't want to tell you, but it seemed strange that you could get a call."

"It's true, but her name came up and it's her ringtone. Look", he resumed eagerly, "it's disappearing!"

"It's true, it disappears and it reappears. It's funny!"

"She must be watching us!"

"Who knows!"

"I don't think I could have done it."

"I don't follow! You're talking about our look before the phone rang?"

"Yes, I…"

Emma hastened to reassure him in her own way.

"It's true that it's a little special, as situations go. I resemble her and you resemble the Joss I married…"

For him, it was a little confusing in his mind, and yet he didn't want to let himself go with another who was, still, the same. What a strange feeling that of cheating on his wife with herself!

"We have to be reasonable", he continued, "you're not her."

Although she wouldn't have judged him, she appreciated his righteousness, just like his double, who also had this stability of mind, but who was sometimes questioned by the life he lead.

"We should get some sleep", Emma said with a touch of regret, "will you turn the videophone off?"

When he put his hand on the remote that had nothing different than the one he knew in his world, he saw an old man on the screen. The latter looked completely confused. He turned up the volume and realized that the old man was the subject of special news.

"You're not turning it off?" Emma exclaimed, still exhilarated.

"Wait a minute, I know this man."

"Holy cow!", said the old man, "I was driving towards 'my farm, and here I am found, here in Toulon!"

"But, it's daddy Mousot", Jocelyn said, "he's the one who helped me in the Vosges, apparently he went in there too! But he didn't change dimension, he's still in his, just like the professor."

"Am I the only one who's unlucky, or am I the chosen one of the universe!" he was exasperated.

Emma put a warm hand on Jocelyn's neck as if to draw him to her.

"Don't worry, Joss, we'll find a way".

Jocelyn was uncomfortable in this position of plaintiff, it seemed to him that the situation escaped him, no matter what he did.

"You can't begin to imagine how frustrating this is for me. Usually, it's me who reassures."

"Who, me?"

He smiled.

"Maybe we met to reverse roles!"

"Know it all!" he ventured.

He thought of the old farmer who hadn't hesitated to help him.

"He must be wondering what's going on, the poor old man! Tomorrow, I'll talk about it to the professor, if I manage to fit him into the conversation" he told himself.

"Joss, I'm exhausted and it's already 00:35. If we want to get up early tomorrow morning, we should rest."

"You're right, good night, Emma."

"Good night, Joss."

He turned off the 'videophone', as well as the light. Emma fell asleep in no time at all. Joss didn't manage to, he kept on visualizing that passage in which he had fallen into, the acceleration of particles that had generated this, the Emma who was lying next to him, the Chinese man who had been thrown violently in front of the truck. All this kept him awake until 4:30 in the morning.

Literally exhausted, he succeeded in finding sleep.

In the early morning, while Emma was 'snoring', Jocelyn, who was still sleeping soundly, didn't hear the alarm that she had set at seven o'clock. But that wasn't something new. For a long time he had harbored enmity with everything near or far to 'a morning disturbance' as he so often called it.

Emma woke up slowly and gently shook Jocelyn to 'revive' him.

"Joss!"

"Mm!"

"Joss, it's time, we have to get ready."

Being still half asleep, he had a reaction that, far from displeasing Emma, surprised her so much that she hesitated to continue. He had his lips forward, and was inviting her to do the same.

"I won't move 'till I have had my kiss", he said in a voice still heavy and asleep.

Emma didn't know if she should kiss him or not.

"I'm waiting!", he insisted.

She smiled, approached his face and kissed him on the mouth.

"You think I'll be convinced with that!"

She came closer again and kissed him greedily full mouth, without any restraints. Eyes still closed, he appreciated the act at its fair value. In his sleep, he thought he was home, in Mazamet. For him, it was the weekend and he was with Emma, his Emma.

"More", he said teasingly, half asleep.

Emma, who was taking more and more pleasure from it, didn't wait to be told twice. She kissed him again with passion, when suddenly, he opened his eyes, discovering the dwelling where they were and all the circumstances that went with it, like this Emma with whom he was behaving as if she were his wife. That really woke him up.

"I almost asked you to stay home with me", he said, a little embarrassed by what he had done, "but it was still nice! I imagine it was torture for you, could you forgive me one day?"

"I'm already starting to compose myself, minus your horse's breath! Let's leave it behind and let's get ready! It's 7:20 and we still have to have breakfast."

Stomachs full, they paid and then went to the car. *"Under way!"* Jocelyn thought.

Arrived in the parking lot in front of the police station, Emma made a final recommendation.

"There's something important I forgot to talk to you about. When we'll get there and we'll see the professor, you will have to act as if you know him, because you're supposed to have worked together."

"Yes, on the set of the sci-fi movie?", Jocelyn said.

"Exactly, and I even think you called him by his first name Allan, but I'm not sure. And it's not a movie, but a 'visionary'..."

"Don't worry, when I'll see him, I'll tell him: 'Hello, old chap, what's up!'"

"Old chap! And me, what am I then?"

"A young sapling!"

"Oh, come on, that's all you have?"

"You're even better than a sapling… You're a flower!"

Emma gave him an evocative look, then resumed.

"Be serious for two minutes and come with me."

Still tired, he got up painfully and they both went to look for the professor, who was in a delicate situation. They crossed the street between the car park and the police cars and arrived in the lobby. A police man sat behind a reception desk and was busy filling out documents.

"Let me talk and all will be well", Emma said in a decided tone.

"Hello, officer", said Jocelyn cavalierly, extending his hand forward, to Emma's surprise.

He didn't know he wasn't supposed to do that with an officer. In a certain world, and in a circumstance such as this, it would seem very equivocal, but in this one, it was the last kind of behavior to have. The officer naturally took it for a provocation, as well as three other colleagues present in the hall.

"Joss", Emma whispered, glaring at him.

She didn't even have time to finish her sentence that the officer at the counter grabbed Jocelyn's outstretched hand and twisted his arm, so that he had no choice but to turn on himself, with his back on the counter and the three other officers that had come in the meantime finished the job by grabbing him and putting him face down.

"Don't move!", one of the officers ordered roughly.

"Very well, Mr. Officer, I won't", Jocelyn answered, now well awake.

He suddenly heard a voice seeming to come from everywhere

and nowhere at the same time: *"You always have to get yourself noticed, one way or the other!"*

Joss looked up, looked right, left, behind.

"Who said that?"

Being only surrounded by officers, one of them replied dryly, stammering.

"You d… You d… You d…"

In that moment, Jocelyn wanted to laugh, but chose not to. *"What's he doing, is he accelerating, is he taking off!"*, he thought amused by the situation.

He heard the same voice laughing again and looked around the room.

"Who laughed?"

"You d… you d… you d… And stop right there!"

"He finally managed to line up two words in a row! Bravo, Mr. Officer!"

"I'm going to show y… show y… to show you who's who's who's laughing!"

"I won't say anything more, Mr. agen… officer", said Jocelyn, who was still looking from where the voice he had heard twice had come from.

Seeing his colleague stammering, one of his colleagues took over the talking.

"And stop making fun of us, otherwise I'll put handcuffs on you and I'll pull them! Well, now give me your identification please."

Emma took her papers and showed them to the officers, trying to appease the spirits, and especially, to make a diversion before he asked for Jocelyn's papers which had nothing in common with those of that world.

"Joss, I told you not to repeat this scene with real officers!"

"What are you insinuating, Madam?"

"So you don't recognize him? He's Jocelyn Beaumont, the stuntman… and after the stunt in Paris he has to do this week, he turns some stunt scenes in a visionary with the famous histrion Roland Fabious! And there's a scene similar to this one."

Jocelyn was listening to what she was saying, but he understood nothing. Emma didn't let anyone answer and kept going.

"In fact, Professor Thibault, whom we came to look for, worked with him on the shooting of the visionary 'Elsewhere' with Jon Jospinaus and Mylène Loyal in the lead roles. You're surely familiar with it?"

The officers looked questioningly at each other, and then looked at Jocelyn, stared at him.

"It's true", one of the officers said, "look closely, he appeared on the videophone the day before yesterday!"

"Now that you mention it", his colleague said scrutinizing his face like a painter looking for a flaw on a master canvas, "I saw the ad of the stunt on the videophone that he's going to do in Paris, and it's him we see at the end of the spot, touting the merits of road safety. Now I remember! Imagine that, Jocelyn Beaumont, the intrepid is in our police station!"

Now Emma didn't exist for them anymore and was more vigilant about what Jocelyn might be saying.

"So, Mister Beaumont", repeated the officer, with a friendly pat on the back as an excuse, "what brings you to our beautiful region? You came to see the professor, if I understood correctly?"

Jocelyn was a little embarrassed in regards to Emma, but given the situation, he had no choice but to take things in hand.

"Yes, exactly, that's it! Where is he?"

"Do you know him well?", asked the officer who looked very

serious.

"Very well, we have often worked together on the filming of mo… visionaries."

Emma wasn't saying anything and was observing with a smile from time to time, and without realizing it, she was looking at him with the eyes of love.

"Alright", the officer said, "before giving you the sad news I have to ask if you're family, or give me the contact of one of his relatives."

The couple looked at each other intrigued by what the officer had said while evoking 'the sad news'. Preferring not to react to this by opting for patience, Jocelyn responded to Emma's gaze by staring straight into her eyes.

"Darling, will you give me Benjamin's phone number, please?"

He then turned to the officer and continued.

"No, we're not family, just close friends. Of what sad news are you talking about?"

Emma wrote the number on a piece of paper and gave it to the officer who handed it to one of her colleagues. He stared at Jocelyn, and declared as solemnly as he could.

"We think your friend has lost his mind. This is why we preferred that he discussed with our shrink-officer at first, so that he could give us his opinion."

The two lovebirds, gaped and let a few seconds pass before talking. Still, the idea of an experiment that the professor could possibly have done as part of his research was very much in their minds. The main thing was now to show the officers that he was surely not so disturbed, but perhaps a little eccentric.

Emma wasn't worried about Benjamin; he was used to seeing his father at odds with his entourage. She took over and asked to see the professor. Having been informed of their arrival by

Benjamin, the chief-officer announced the officer in charge of the sector in which he was locked up.

"It's alright chief-officer, they can go!"

Jocelyn was glad the officer hadn't asked for his papers. As for Emma, reassured to be able to express herself instead of her 'new husband', the fear of seeing him do or say a something stupid had faded.

APPRENTICESHIP.

— *"Statistically, with enough time,*
anything could happen."
Elisabeth Vonarburg.

S he gave him a very explicit stealthy look; he immediately understood the message and tried to retreat without totally disappearing.

"Very well, Mister Beaumont, I will accompany you and you will certainly be able to take him home, now that we have talked with his son. Please follow me, it's through here", said the officer, indicating with his hand the direction to follow.

As they walked along the corridor leading to the place where the professor was, the orderly told them in a few words the reasons that had made them think the man no longer had his wits about him.

"Your friend was picked up on the road to Paris, hitchhiking. When we stopped near him, he barely looked at us. He seemed lost. Then, stopping in front of him to offer help, and when we asked him what he was doing there, he became completely incoherent, but I would rather you be the judge of that. Here we are..."

The professor was sitting at a table, and the psychiatrist who had been talking to him was watching him from a neighboring room through a two-way mirror, as if he were a criminal.

"Oh, there you are", he said, seeing the couple, "You wish to see him?"

"Yes, officer", Emma said, "we even wish to take him home, for Mrs. Thibault, his wife, is very worried about his disappearance."

"And it's precisely about that I wanted to ask you some question before letting you see him. Your friend said he moved in inter dimensional space, what can you tell me about that?"

Emma was trying to hide her embarrassment, while Jocelyn was beginning to see hope.

"What answer could I give to that?", she thought.

"We are not aware of his activities", Emma answered, "we only know that he does some research and some experiments from time to time, but I am unable to tell you exactly what he does. On the other hand, I can tell you that he's not always wise with them, much like Hitler when he invented the theory of relativity."

At that moment, Jocelyn felt his eyes desorb, but kept silent.

"Yes, I see", said the psychiatrist-officer, perplexed.

He briefly looked at his colleague and continued.

"If you want to go in, please do, I'm sure he'll be happy to see you."

"Thank you, officer", the couple said, timidly.

They entered the room without really knowing what they were going to say to the old man.

"Hello, professor", Emma said, in a cheerful tone.

"Emma, Jocelyn, you cannot imagine the joy of seeing you both…"

He thought for a moment and continued.

"I thought you had divorced, I must have understood wrongly... So, how are you, kids?", he said, taking each one in his arms and patting their backs. "And you, Jocelyn, weren't you supposed to be in Paris?"

"Yes, professor, we're going there, we stopped to pick you up."

"Professor! How polite you have become... There was a time when you used to call me Allan!"

"Of course", Jocelyn said, "I was teasing you..."

Emma was fearing, more than ever, a new blunder from him. It was necessary to get Allan out as quickly as possible and explain to him the situation she was in, despite herself. As to the professor, surprised by Jocelyn's reaction, he was a little worried and wanted to know more.

"Something worries you my young friend, you don't look so well."

"I confess that lately, I am no longer quite myself", Jocelyn said, looking upset, but inwardly, proud of his response. "I promise to tell you, Allan", he concluded, thanking him with his eyes.

"I'm counting on it, my boy!"

He was looking at him strangely, he was suspecting something.

"Professor", Emma intervened, cut off in her tracks by the latter...

"I'm going to relieve you of that girlish burden and explain to them that my mind has wandered. We will avoid a situation as embarrassing for you, as for me", he said, giving them a reassuring smile.

"And I, who took him for an old fool", Emma thought, now relieved that they would finally be able to consider a solution for her 'new ex-husband'.

Jocelyn was eager to get out of that place, and the psychiatrist

-officer who had listened to their conversation felt 'the scam', he saw that the trio seemed to get along well and decided to question the strange hitchhiker professor again.

"Ouch!", Jocelyn thought, seeing the officer approaching, not seeming like one who was ready to let them go.

"What is it now?", Emma thought, having noticed the same thing.

"I heard what you said, professor Thibault, and I would like to know what you were doing on that road."

"It's very simple my dear fellow, I took the train in Paris thinking I was taking the one for Lyon, but I was wrong, and I boarded the one that took me to you!"

"How come you didn't notice that earlier? They didn't announce it on the intercom?"

The professor put a reassuring hand on the officer's shoulder, who didn't know what to think of this eccentric man with the mysterious look.

"They surely did, but I wasn't paying attention…"

"So be it, but I'm still surprised that the wind didn't convince you to turn back…"

"There wasn't that much!"

"Enough to get a few wind turbines move from their place…"

"You exaggerate, my boy!"

"I'm not your boy!", virulently resumed the exasperated officer.

"Alright, Officer, as you wish!"

"Are you mocking me!?"

"Oh, come on now, I would not dare!"

In that moment, the officer defused the nuclear warhead who threatened to mate with his rising rage, and continued calmly.

"Professor Thibault, you were at FIFTEEN KILOMETERS

from the train station", he went on, pressing on his words.

"It's true, but I was doing a new experiment right then, of which I cannot talk to you about..."

"Why can you not talk about it, would it be doing something illegal?"

"Oh, come now, Officer... You're not thinking straight. Do you believe that at my age I would venture into illegality? I am well placed, a life of a scientist that is a little sassy certainly, but organized, what interest would I have to put myself outside 'the law'!"

He was so convincing in his manner of speaking and in his behavior that the officer finally gave up, and now addressed the two lovers.

"Alright, follow me, I need your signature on a document and then, you'll be free to go."

Emma took charge of the task, while Jocelyn and the professor recalled some memories of their past collaboration. But you can't teach an old dog new tricks... Allan was aware that something wasn't adding up. But he very much preferred to wait for the right moment to state it.

Perplexed, the officer handed one of the signed documents to Emma, and all three went to the exit.

"Still, there's something that's not quite right", the psychiatrist–officer said, while watching them leave, "what do you think, chief-officer?"

"They don't seem dangerous", the latter said, "that crazy old man seems to believe what he's saying, and he's lucky to have people around him like that young couple to take care of him!"

"If you say so..."

They went on about their business while the 'Old Fool' and the 'Young Couple' headed for their car.

Emma suggested that the professor sit in front, but he refused, leaving that place to Jocelyn. They started the car and drove. None of them dared say anything, but Emma finally decided to start the conversation.

"If you're tired, take advantage and get some rest, we'll arrive around eight o'clock tonight."

Impatient, Jocelyn cracked and addressed the old man.

"What are you working on at the moment, Allan?"

"You don't remember anymore! Wilfried Hitler contacted you and me for a new collaboration, such as we did for filmmaker Jack Choupla… That was only three weeks ago, Jocelyn. It's not like you to forget a professional appointment!"

"You say Hitler?"

"Come on, Joss, my little Joss, you don't know of whom I talk about, Adolf Hitler's son, one of the greatest scientists of the world."

"Yes, of course, how could I have forgotten! Reassure me on one point; the 'BRITANIA' existed, didn't it?"

"The BRITANIA, you say? I don't know what you're talking about. Alright, now you can tell me the truth, I am aware that you're not the Jocelyn I know! If what happened to you is what I think it did, it won't be easy to get you back, this is the case, isn't it?"

In that moment, he looked at Emma like asking for her help, but the urge to get out of that situation quickly took precedence over the embarrassment he felt, and he grabbed the hand the professor had handed him.

"There' no Wilfried Hitler, is there?"

"Of course there is, my young friend, but there's no collaboration. I must admit, however, that if you had continued to question what I was saying, I would have hesitated a little longer by laying out other traps such as this one!"

"So, what did you find so different that made guess you so quickly?"

"Your attitude and the way you addressed me. And forgive me, but someone who is out of place, it shows like the nose in the middle of the face! But does that matter?"

"No, professor, you're right. What do you suggest we do?"

"Start by telling me in detail what happened to you, and call me Allan, please!"

"Yes, Allan, thank you for being so direct, for, between us, I don't how I would have started this talk with you."

Even before starting his story, the classic ring' of the phone of old that he had selected among the numerous ones on his mobile phone was heard. Jocelyn looked at his pocket for a moment, somewhat puzzled.

"Excuse me, prof…, Allan, I'm going to answer."

"Please do…"

"It's strange that he can take calls", he thought.

"In all logic, this couldn't happen."

"You again, darling, I hope it will work this time."

"Hello… Hello!"

He heard again the same phenomenon as with the first call, without being able to distinguish anything. He hung up again, desperate to never have news again.

"You seem worried, my young friend, problems?"

"I don't really know much. Apparently, someone's trying to call me, but when I pick up, nothing!"

"It's very surprising that you can receive a call, since the waves aren't the same."

"How come?"

Some seconds passed. Allan was 'gone' in a deep reflection

that made him seem disconnected from this world like a toy whose battery would have reached the end of its load.

"Allan, Allan!"

"Yes, excuse me, I was thinking! I understand that it may come as a surprise, but my entourage did this! Well, do continue your story now."

"Yes… you're certain that…"

"Yes, I'm certain", thought Allan, getting impatient. He urged him on with a wave of his hand to begin his story.

"I was driving on the highway towards Italy…" Jocelyn recounted his mishap while Emma and Allan listened with great attention…

"Until I arrived on this viaduct…"

"What time did you say it happened?"

"It must have been around ten o'clock."

The professor was thinking and seemed to be making calculations in his head.

"One would barely believe it", he said looking at the ceiling of the car. "This won't be easy", he continued.

"What do you mean?"

"I'll explain all this in detail when we get to Paris. But, right now, I need to think; so you can understand in a few simple words, my assistant created a mechanism to move in several dimensions, generating 'gaps' that open, close and move constantly across the globe. And that happening to you last night in the place you described, I conclude they have already made the complete tour of the planet. It remains to find out where all these gaps are and how fast they're moving. But it's not only this, for if my theories are correct, they could just as easily move in the same world. We would then talk about traveling in the same time line, even if it's only for a few minutes."

Allan continued his reflection aloud without regard to his surroundings, as usual.

"Perhaps the experiment of this particle accelerator has left undetectable traces on the surface of the Earth. It must have caused interferences in our magnetic field. But then... Not everything comes from that damn device designed by Garvey. The phenomenon was already latent and all it did was press a switch created during the start of this infernal underground machine. It is perhaps thanks to it that his command worked so well. It would then only resume these existing phenomena by amplifying them. It would interfere directly with the time that passes here, while revealing the snippets of another time."

"That's it, he's gone again!", Jocelyn thought.

He remained silent for a few moments, then went on in his scholarly reflection.

"If we take relativity into account, the phenomenon is not possible. So we must ignore the laws of our physics and see further. So, no causality or logic. It is now possible to intercept other times, other dimensions. There would be places that would have turned into a kind of giant tube where time accelerates until reaching the vibrations of another time, inaccessible until then... It's amazing! We discovered the machine to go back in time... or to pre-empt it! Just as we have our own perception of what surrounds us, this command perceives all that is around our universe by accelerating or braking at will. At the switch of an unfortunate touch, we change at will our glorious past. If the past exists, then the future does as well. It's a balance thing, like the Yin and Yang, white and black, day and night. We can change the future, but not the past, because if the act has not been accomplished, there is nothing to change. That's why we have to go back", he concluded, approving himself with a nod.

"Go back where, Allan?"

"Sorry?"

"Nothing, never mind!"

"We need the past to live the future…"

"He's gone again", Jocelyn thought strongly.

"Many live in the past; so, there's no possible future in this case…"

"Allan?"

"And it was simple, this was the link…"

"Allan, please!"

It was in these moments that he perfectly illustrated the almost caricature image of the old mad scientist.

"I'm annoying you, aren't I? I'm listening, my friend…"

"Would your assistant accept to help us?", said Jocelyn, who seemed to be wondering about his possible return.

"As soon as he gets back from his interdimensional getaway! Indeed, he has also disappeared two days ago, but I do not yet know everything on this subject, because I went to another world for a very short time, then I reappeared where you know."

"How can you be sure he'll come back?"

"He's equipped with his 'generator' and can therefore go where he wants, at the moment of his choice."

"Then, the problem is solved", Jocelyn exclaimed cheerfully, "we only have to wait for him to come back and program my return on his device."

"I'm afraid it's not that simple, my boy, because when I will show you the extent of the problem, you will understand without me even having to explain it to you."

"If you had to quantify my chances of getting out of here, how would you estimate my chances to be?"

"It's almost like hearing the Jocelyn I know, maybe in the end, you're not so different after all! To answer your question, I would have to go back to my calculations."

Jocelyn noticed Allan's sudden change of attitude. He had just switched from casual speech to a formal one from one sentence to another, and even if his fate seemed to be sealed, it comforted him somewhat.

Emma drove and didn't intervene in their conversation. Nevertheless, she paid attention to every word they said; in doing so, she discreetly watched Jocelyn. A myriad of thoughts crossed her mind.

Having slept little in the last two days, Allan felt a sharp fatigue that invaded him little by little.

"Children", he said, "I will think intensely for the next two hours. Forgive me in advance, but I feel the weight of my eyelids take precedence over my vigilance."

That said, the professor took a comfortable position in his seat, with his head back and fell quickly asleep. Jocelyn turned towards Emma and shared some observations.

"I'll remember you with your permissive officers!"

Emma giggled.

"It's normal", she said, "you made fun of them. You addressed him 'Mister Officer' instead of 'Officer', and those who were there and who heard you felt mocked too."

"It's not all that bad, I didn't insult them!"

"Insulted is not the word, I would rather say a provocation."

'Officer' is considered a first name in a way, because they are supposed to be listening to the people. It's like you would call me 'Madam Emma'. That said, for some time now, there has really been a return to the essence; they are indeed listening to us and without being provoked, very respectful of us, as much as of 'the law'."

Bored by what he heard, Allan intervened.

"You're very nice, but I've been dealing with officers for the last two days, wouldn't you want to change the topic of conversation?"

Frustrated, the lovers looked at each other with a smile.

"Of course, professor", Emma said, "we'll talk about something else". As Allan fluttered his eyes, Emma and Jocelyn continued their dialogue, evoking their respective lives. The meeting of the two couples in both worlds was similar, only some details were different. Their entourage was the same except for the two children they had in this world. Only their life was different by the decisions they had made in their world. Everything was similar and everything was radically different. Similarly for cars to name just this example, which, in this world were mostly branded 'Smett', created at the turn of the century, and later resumed by his son known to everyone for his music in our world.

It had been about an hour since they had begun chatting, and Emma was beginning to show signs of fatigue.

"I see you're starting to struggle", Jocelyn said, "do you want me to drive?"

"Yes, I would, I'm not used to drive so many kilometers in one go. Do you know how to drive this car?"

"It doesn't seem too difficult, the fact that there is no shifter, I assume it's normal?"

"That there's no what?"

"Never mind, I got it wrong", he said, wanting to avoid endless explanations.

He took advantage of the time remaining for Emma to drive until she found a place to park, to examine the way she was driving the engine.

"Not complicated this car, I hadn't noticed earlier, it must resemble our automatic shift", he thought, with his eyes fixed on Emma's hands and feet.

"Two pedals, surely the accelerator and the brake, the counter stuck at a hundred and fifty, this thing drives itself!"

"There's a parking", Emma said, slowing, "I'm not going to give you any instructions, a seasoned driver like yourself must know how to drive!"

She, therefore, didn't feel the need to tell him that it was necessary to accelerate progressively when the 'Road' position was engaged, as it was currently the case. There were indeed three driving positions on all cars in this world. The positions 'City', 'Road' and 'Sport'. The difference was in the power level at start-up and on the road. This device allowed to drive up to one hundred and forty kilometers an hour for one minute to double other vehicles, without hindering. Of course, that was marked on the speed recorder, but there were no warnings for the one who didn't abuse it.

So, Jocelyn took the wheel, looked at Emma confidently and fastened his seatbelt, one of the few common points between the cars in his world and this one.

"Here we go", he said, accelerating so violently that Emma found herself thrown back into her seat without being able to move, and the professor, who had fallen asleep in the back seat, felt his head thrown back as if he had caught a right punch straight in the face!

Emma laughed heartily.

"If you accelerate so suddenly, it automatically goes into 'Sport' position!"

"In 'Sport' position by itself? What are your engines running on? Over boosted kerosene?!"

"You should have seen your face!"

She let a few moments pass and then resumed.

"It's crazy how much you resemble each other, and at the same time, you're so different.

Jocelyn preferred to avoid the remark.

"Why not leave the choice to the driver by offering, for example a switch?"

"It's simply faster in case of overtaking other cars."

"Yeah... Why not!"

Just as surprised as his passengers, Jocelyn quickly found the right mix to avoid a new strong sensation worthy of the 'Roller Coasters'.

"Forgive me for this wrong maneuver", he said, trying to avoid laughing out loud.

Allan had his hands around his neck, like an electrician screwing a big light bulb and Emma smiled, kindly making fun of the apprentice driver.

"If we fall asleep now, do you promise not to eject us from our seats?"

"It's a promise, I won't be surprised anymore, you can rest easy!"

Along the way, he saw officers busy checking a driver.

"Here are the cops controlling the 'snitch' of a car, I really have seen everything!" he told himself.

In that moment, he was caught in a quiet panic.

"My license... it's surely not valid if I'm arrested!" Neither him, nor Emma had thought about it. What to do? Wake her up so she could take the wheel again? She had fallen asleep so quickly.

"Anyway, I'm already caught in this world, what more could happen!"

He chose to continue without saying anything. He was looking at the landscape in front of him, the road, the cars, at the signs that weren't blue, but burgundy in this world, but the indications remained about the same as those he was used to.

The distances seemed to be marked in kilometers like 'PARIS 328'. He was reassured to have the professor in his company, as he had the necessary knowledge to make him go back to his dimension, and Emma who slept soundly, always close to him... here, as elsewhere.

It had been an hour and a half since he had been driving. A blue car had been in front of him since he had started. He was driving peacefully, occasionally taking his eyes off the road.

"I can't wait to get there" he thought. His eyes began to flutter because he had had trouble falling asleep and had been able to rest for only two hours. While his attention was drawn to a building with unusual shapes, he examined it for maybe two seconds, and turned his eyes as he saw it in his field of vision. Having passed it, he put his eyes on the road again and didn't realize right away that the blue car was no longer there. He realized it ten seconds later, ten seconds too late... Perplexed, he slowed down; he hadn't noticed any exit or any area. Only a truck was driving far ahead. An unexpected voice came suddenly to disturb the 'Driver Jocelyn'... 'Slow down'...

"You again!" he thought. Having already met him, be listened to the advice without going crazy about it. He was looking at the behavior of the truck's driver who was braking bit by bit.

"What is he doing?"

He saw the latter slow down considerably, while continuing extremely slowly. Prudently, he did the same, trying to see what made him react like that. Getting close, he noticed that the tar shone like a 'mirage effect'. But when he got there, he realized that something abnormal was happening. It wasn't a mirage; he had trouble believing what he was seeing.

"I'm dreaming, it's not possible!" he thought.

Water seemed to come out of the ground and the amount kept rising. He didn't understand what was happening. Water was coming out of nowhere. It wasn't falling from the sky, nor was it overflowing from a ditch, as there were none in that place.

Impossible to image rain without any cloud in the sky and its singular way of falling to the ground. The flow was becoming more abundant, it was growing visibly. Water was spreading everywhere and farther and farther. Surprised by so much water, the vehicles that arrived in the distance began to zigzag, hydroplane, brake suddenly and roll a little in all directions. Water was coming in, as if something was blocking its flow in the 'piping'.

At the same time surprised and curious, some drivers who had just passed stopped two hundred meters away to contemplate the show and film the scene with their mobiles. But the water was spreading quickly and came to the feet of the image fans. Some went back into their cars to flee, others more adventurous, soaked just to film until the end. There was a nascent current in this improvised river that was beginning to make them stagger.

But the events that followed left him speechless and forced him to react urgently. Suddenly, there was a huge storm, much bigger than the already existing stream, only slightly higher than the ground, like a huge open valve with a high flow and a pressure similar to that of the fire hoses the firefighters use, using the power of a thousand. It was surreal. But that was only the beginning! To his amazement, he saw a small boat appear in the same stride a hundred meters away. The latter appeared with a certain momentum as output of a large faucet.

It was there, on the wet asphalt, with a man and a child on board.

Seeing this, he braked suddenly, provoking this time to his two passengers, the opposite effect of his departure on the tips of the wheels.

Having buckled up, Emma was shaken like a plum tree, but managed to remain in her seat, as for Allan, he found himself directly on the ground between the front and the back seat. Awoken with a start, and somewhat annoyed, he climbed the seat to sit down again.

"I prefer your double's driving, at least when doing a stunt with him, he warns ahead!"

"What's wrong?", said Emma, still shocked.

"Am I the only one to see it?", Jocelyn said, getting out of the car.

"How does he do that?", Emma thought.

As for the professor, he immediately understood what had happened. He got out of the car, approached the boat and found a father and his son completely frantic. Jocelyn suspected strongly what they had gone through.

"They must have been terribly shaken", he told himself.

First on the scene, Jocelyn rushed to the boat.

"Nothing broken?", he asked, getting close to them, ready to come to their aide.

The father was as shocked as his son and Jocelyn could only sympathize with their emotions having himself crossed this kind of 'accelerator tube' who had made him visit a black hole where nothingness reigned, to make him land in this world. Emma and Allan got there too.

"What happened, dad, where are we", the young boy asked,

scared, "and what stings?" The two boaters didn't know where to send their hands to scratch themselves.

"I don't know, my son", replied the father who was trying to keep his cool, if only for his boy.

"Don't panic", the professor said, getting to the boat.

The father looked at him strangely, as if he had guessed that it was the only thing left at his disposal.

"Who are you", the child's father resume, "and where are we?"

"If I answered you, you would certainly not believe me", continued Allan, who was beginning to wonder where all this was going to stop! "Get off your float, and come with us, we'll help you."

"Sir", snapped the father, "you still haven't answered my question! Who are you?"

Allan took the situation by the horns, and approached the father.

"You were on the water, right?"

"Yes, and this much anyone could have guessed!"

"Listen to me and trust me", Allan continued calmly. "I know what happened to you and I know how to solve it! Are you ready to listen to me?"

Then he pulled himself together and added, assuming all the responsibility for the events:

"I'm professor Allan Thibault. I teach at the University of Paris, and I work on different projects, at one in particular, right now. Sadly, there were some malfunctions and that's why you ended up on this road!"

"I don't understand a thing of what you're saying", continued the father, snuggling his son against him with his left arm, while continuing to scratch himself everywhere with the other.

Allan looked at Jocelyn to make him understand that he might well need his help. He agreed with a nod, which allowed the professor to embark on his crazy straightforward explanation.

"You're in another world!"

"It's as I thought, you're as crazy as they come! Don't come any closer."

"Listen to me and shut up! Obviously, you were sailing on the water, and now you're here! So, it's certain, something inexplicable happened... Do you want to have a chance to know what it's all about, or do you prefer to wait here in your float?"

Worried and still scared, the man agreed to listen to Allan's explanations.

"It may be that you only made a trip back in time", announced the scientist seriously.

There, Jocelyn frowned, for he had landed in another dimension, why would it not be their case as well?

"A trip back in time, just that", said the child's father, stunned.

"I know, all this might seem crazy to you, but it might be the case."

"Alright, very well", said the father, "you do seem a little crazy, but not very vindictive, and since you say you know what happened to us, I'll listen to you."

The itching was starting to fade...

"Let's not stay here", Jocelyn said, "we'll end up causing an accident."

Emma decided to intervene, thinking to appease the anguish of the boy and his father.

"He's right", she said in a soft voice, "we'd better put this float on the side of the road, and go a little further to talk about it."

"Alright, we'll follow you", the father answered.

In the distance, a car was slowly coming, probably due to the crowd on the road, and the water was still flowing, flooding the roadway through and through.

"What's your name?", Jocelyn asked, approaching the float.

"I'm Hubert and this is my son, Félix."

"Help me put your float in these bushes, please."

While the water still didn't stop flowing, and Allan watching the phenomenon closely, everyone was getting into the cars to get their feet out of the water, which had reached a level of about three centimeters on the tracks that formed at that place a long and light bowl like shape, thus retaining the mini ocean carpet.

Then, the professor noticed another phenomenon... The water stopped flowing. He could hear the distant cry of a woman, as if someone was trapped in the air calling for 'help'. But it didn't last. Two seconds passed, and the voice disappeared.

"Did you see, dad", Félix said, "the water stopped flowing!"

All were amazed by what they had just seen. Allan was still in the same place and was slowly moving his arms in front of him like a fly hunter, walking just as slowly around the 'gap', now closed.

"Are you coming, Allan?", Emma told him, taking her head out of the car.

He seemed thoughtful, but was starting to move towards his friends, reflecting intensely while observing the 'castaways' of the road, who had apparently stopped gesticulating.

"Professor", Emma said, impatient, "let's not stay here!"

He got in as well and Jocelyn started the car slowly this time.

"What are you thinking about, Allan?", Emma asked, turning towards him.

"I admit there are certain details that still escape me, and I have been thinking about it all this time."

"Would you kindly explain to me what you know, or at least what this is all about, and most importantly, how did we get from the lake to this road?"

"Of course, dear Sir, I promised I would. But for starters, tell me what you saw from the moment you were on the water until you ended up here, please."

At the thought of reliving the scene, Hubert was uncomfortable. Allan thought he knew the answer to some details, but he was far from suspecting what Hubert would explain. He told the facts thus:

"We were in the float on the lake, we had just waved to my wife Tiffany, and then, I still don't understand what happened. The landscape became crazy! It started accelerating all of a sudden. We felt like we were in a whirlwind, but in a straight line! Everything happened so quickly, and I even thought I saw something pass below us."

"How come?", Allan asked, taken by surprise, "you mean there was something else, and that it crossed you?"

"Yes, at least that's what it seemed like, when we fell into this 'Rectangular Whirlwind', but it went so fast, it was so surprising, so scary. I confess that our spirits were elsewhere at the time. We were suddenly itchy all over our bodies. Personally, I thought I would explode, although the pain wasn't as big as it was for my son. Do you have an idea about that tingling?"

"I think so, but, again, the answer might amaze you..."

"Do tell us, at the point we are now!"

"The tingling comes from your atoms, if my theory is correct."

"From our atoms?"

"Yes, we're all made of atoms. It's important to know that they are linked together according to the needs of the Earth, in this case and among others, 'us'. We are only a collection of atoms that are eager to graft elsewhere when we die. I'll save you the detailed explanations, but you have obviously started a process of 'atomic decomposition' during your crossing and this explains the tingling."

"Did you say 'atomic decomposition'", Hubert said frightened.

"Yes, I did use 'decomposition'. Know that atoms only consist of vacuum and remain assembled only under certain vibrations. At the atomic scale, we are a poorly-crafted canvas of extreme resistance, paradoxically. That said, if we exert sufficient force at each end, that is if we change the vibrations, it will eventually give way starting at the edges, then they will tear completely if these vibrations last. It's the same thing for us. If the latter change, it is normal for atoms to no longer interpret their presence in any body, human, animal, plant or chemical, and seek to settle elsewhere. I won't give you a course in chemistry, but there are some fundamental 'rules' about atoms as to their attraction to each other. There are too many factors to take into account, but if our environment changes, we also change, one way or the other. In my opinion, there was a lapse of time when your molecular structure was put into question, the time needed for your atoms to find their landmarks, their marks, a bit like a stealthy floating, you understand?"

"I'm afraid to understand it", Hubert approached Allan so his son couldn't hear, we are "'dislocatable', are we not?"

"Under certain vibrations, yes, like I just explained, and further more, your son can understand…"

"Why do you say that?"

"I don't really know, but I'm telling you!"

Allan ventured, frankly, in various assertions, but he had a doubt about his theory. Was reconstitution complete once the gap closed… His eyes suddenly widened. He glanced at Jocelyn.

"Weren't you dislocated?" he thought, *"the vibrations of your world can not in any case correspond to ours... Or they are not so far apart. Yes, that's it, why haven't I thought about it earlier? Each vibration depends on a fact and a specific moment, but the 'structure' stays the same. There is nothing different with us and if it can evolve among us, this molecular dispersion only occurs during crossings. The adaptation time is decided in just a few seconds... If we adapt so easily to new vibrations then our mind is obliged to follow... Hm, something to ponder."*

"Professor! Professor!"

"Yes, I'm sorry, I was thinking."

"You have an explanation for the whirlwind?"

"These whirlwinds are the result of the meeting of these two worlds. Even a simple shift in time generates this kind of phenomenon. The world we are in is different from the one where I started this phase, as many things have happened almost everywhere."

Allan thought again for a few moments.

"Which would involve absolutely going back to the exact spot where they appeared, unless... if the invention of my assistant's mule head was well thought out, then some problems might disappear. So they went through a 'wormhole'. But how could it stay open for so long and especially how did it become so big? Garvey, you found a way to produce an antigravity field. I will never tell you, young man, but you are prodigious. You created 'The eye of the inter-dimensional cyclone'. Anyway, this man and his son do not only have 'their spirit elsewhere'. We have to bring them back to their world."

"Sir, are you alright?"

"Yes, I'm sorry, I think not everything is lost. If what I think is true, you are already saved!"

"That's good news, but what are you saying?"

"I mean that despite what has just happened to you, the situation may not be as dramatic for you as it is for our driver!"

"Sorry?", Jocelyn said, worried.

"I'll explain. My assistant who has been missing for three days now has developed a machine in the form of a small box, which allows 'gaps' to appear in interdimensional space-time; that is to say in other realities, whether or not they are part of who we are, and especially where we are from."

Hubert looked at him strangely.

"I don't understand anything!"

"It's normal", Allan resumed, "it's not easy to explain it in simple words. Alright, I try to keep it simple so that everyone can understand. There are other realities apart from others, other universes if you prefer, and my assistant Garvey, has created a device that causes flaws in our universe in the form of point distortions and consequently, in other realities, as if you were spreading your arms to open a curtain. And that's a little of what happened to you and your child. But you obviously haven't landed anywhere other than in your own dimension, and that, I cannot explain yet."

"You mean to say there are other dimensions?", Hubert said, a little amused.

"There is nothing to laugh about, my young friend, as according to you, what happened?"

"OK, I admit to not understand anything of what happened, but from there to talk about other worlds, or time travel, there's a huge gap!"

"Think again", Jocelyn interrupted, "the same thing happened to me, except that I had to admit that I did not just go back in time."

"Of course, you will conclude by saying that you come from

another world, won't you?"

"Yes, Hubert, I am not of this world."

"You're an alien then!", said Félix, amazed.

"I had forgotten about him", Jocelyn thought.

"If you could avoid telling that kind of joke in front of the kid, you would avoid frightening him", Hubert objected strongly.

At that point, Jocelyn braked almost as brutally as the first time, sidling as best as he could on the side of the road. There he turned back, speaking sharply to the incredulous father.

"Listen well to what I'm going to tell you, you were on the water, and you found yourself on our road, that's already a first reality. Even if you want it or not, something happened that is not trivial, and that is something the professor has been trying to explain to you since just now. But you're not making it easy for him by stubbornly going on as you do, forcing him to look for words so that you understand. And please, don't talk to us about your son, he was with you, so he is concerned as well, kid or not, 'Capich'? So now you're going to shut up and let him speak!"

Determined, he turned around and restarted promptly. In the car there was a climate of wonder and astonishment.

"He's something else, this one" Allan thought looking at Jocelyn, and Emma was of the same opinion. Feeling free to continue his explanation without being interrupted every two sentences, Allan continued.

"Hm... Alright, as I was saying, I'm not absolutely sure that the gaps consistently lead to other dimensions, since there are a few people missing here in our dimension, which were found the next day, for some, two days later, for others at the other end of the world. And this continues to happen, both for appearances and disappearances."

142

"I don't understand", Hubert interrupted, "are you insinuating that it doesn't stop?"

"Not for the moment, in any case. Please turn on the radio, Emma. Don't leave it on too loud, so that I can continue to talk to our new friend, and when you hear pertinent information, tell us and turn the volume up. I bet they will announce other appearances and disappearances."

"Yes, professor, I'm on it", she said, turning on the radio.

"I won't go into detail", Allan continued, "it would be too technical, but what we can observe for the moment, is that all of this happens randomly, and as long as I don't have any more data at my disposal, I prefer to refrain from any explanations that might otherwise prove inaccurate thereafter."

"If you'll allow, Professor, there is a simple solution to try to know if it's a simple journey in time, or if they're in a dimension different than theirs", Jocelyn interrupted.

"And what is that, my young friend?"

"If they're still in their world, they should be able to reassure their family or loved ones with a simple phone call."

"That is so true!", Hubert exclaimed, "with your interdimensional stories, it didn't even cross my mind!"

"He's right, this guy" Allan thought, *"Why didn't I think about it?"*

"Could you please borrow me your phone, Jocely", Hubert said, boiling with impatience, "if you're right, I'll be able to talk to my wife and tell her everything's alright. We went to a dwelling in Italy and I should be able to easily find the number…"

Jocelyn didn't answer, but inside, he was laughing.

"Dweller, you're very lucky", he thought,

"You're still in your world!"

Suddenly, Emma came to disturb the serenity that had just

settled in the car. She handed her phone to Hubert and manipulated the radio.

"Listen!", she said, gently ordering everyone to shut up, and increasing the volume of the radio.

"Ladies and gentlemen, hello", said the voice on the waves, "new inexplicable phenomena have occurred since this morning."

In that moment, everyone in the car kept silent, and had ears only for the words of the reporter on the radio.

"In addition to all these disappearances and appearances in the last two days, yesterday evening, a strange event in the sky was observed. Some evoked comets, but after careful observation, it was concluded that it was not fast enough for comets, and far too much for planes. The authorities have not yet declared anything on this subject."

Hearing that, Hubert felt reassured. He officially heard that they were not the only ones. To believe that one should give more credit to the word of an electronic box than to that of a man. As for Allan, he was now wondering about these strange things observed in the sky.

In his presentation, the journalist spoke of seven new disappearances and as many appearances. But the big novelty of the day was the observation of the event in the sky. In recent days, the news was like a trailer for 'disaster, science, fiction' movies, and each passing day announced a new phenomenon.

* * *

Meanwhile, Enke and Klaus, disappeared two days earlier had ended up in a dimension that was not that of the professor and Emma, let alone that of Jocelyn. For them, the passage had been rather gentle. At first, while Enke was giving some advice to Klaus to appease him in regards to the control he was afraid to miss that morning at school, the landscape as well as the clouds in the sky had accelerated in the same way as for Jocelyn on the viaduct; but it had happened in such a short time that, concentrated in their conversations, they didn't realize it immediately. It was only a few seconds later that Enke had found it strange that the tar they were trampling had turned into earth, and when they looked around, everything had changed. They had been paralyzed with fear and astonishment for a few minutes, while scratching their bodies with virulence…

"Where are we mom, and what's making us scratch like this?"

The boy wasn't particularly scared, but rather intrigued.

"I don't know, darling, stay right next to mom."

"It stings too much mom, do something!"

The mother was gesturing just as much as the child and had to contain herself not to explode nervously. As she was trying to relieve her son, she felt the itching gradually start to fade.

"Do you still feel like scratching as much?", she said, sighing.

"Looks like it's going away, and you?"

"Yes, darling, it's beginning to pass."

She was trying to hide her fear; what had happened?

Why had everything changed from one simple step to another? Enke didn't understand and couldn't believe what she was seeing. Although her reaction of hugging Klaus against her to protect him was that of a protective mother, in addition to the surprise, she felt one of those ill-being announcers of bad omens. The houses, the buildings, the streets, as well as the car and the hubbub of the city had disappeared almost from one second to the next. Furthermore, it was impossible for the sun to begin to set when it had been just 8:15 when they had started.

Around them, there was only nature. High mountains stood upright in front of them, and all around was a multitude of pristine lands and meadows, but no houses, not even a farm, let alone a living soul. Thus, Enke couldn't even give Klaus an approximate answer. She could not articulate much anyhow.

The idea came to her to turn around to check if they could go back again, but the gap had already closed.

"Where are we, mom?", the child asked again.

"I don't know, Klaus", the mother said, worried.

"What do we do, mom?"

Enke stressed easily, and she knew she shouldn't panic so she wouldn't panic her son, but it was too much for her; she lost it for a moment under the constant assault of Klaus's questions.

"I don't know anything!", she retorted curtly, raising her voice.

"It's not my fault we're here", the child answered, crying and letting go of her hand.

Realizing her error, she felt guilty for not having mastered herself more and quickly made up for her mistake. Having gone a few meters away, she joined him and crouched at his height. She looked at him, put a soft, warm hand on his face and reassured him.

"I'm sorry darling, I shouldn't have reacted like that. I admit this scares me, but I'm going to be a courageous mom and I promise not to get annoyed with you again. Will you forgive me?"

Understanding the situation in part, and succumbing to his mother's love on the other hand, Klaus dried his tears and snuggled against her, showing her, at the same time, that they had to stay together in such a moment and that at the height of his ten years, he too would be present to watch over her.

Now sure of herself, Enke decided to take things in hand. She glanced at a three hundred and sixty degree angle, got up and took Klaus by the hand.

"We're not going to stay here doing nothing", she said, staring at the meadows. "We'll walk there and we'll eventually find someone, a house or a farm, are you ready?"

"Yes, mom", said the boy enthusiastically, "let's go!"

So they began to walk with the firm intention of putting an end to that nightmare. In that moment, they didn't know they were being watched. Eyes had watched them since their arrival and followed them step by step.

Klaus continued to ask questions and harassing his mother without realizing it, as he saw that what they were going through wasn't normal.

"Why are we here, mom? Why has Berlin disappeared? Are we being punished? Do you think we'll return home?"

Enke thought she needed to reassure him more.

"Don't be scared Klaus, we'll soon go back."

"But it's not that mom, I'm not afraid, but you're the adult, maybe you didn't tell me everything so I wouldn't panic!"

Enke realized that she wasn't dealing with a brainless young child, and that she should now talk to him like she would a little man. She stopped, lowered herself to his height and spoke to him putting aside the child he was.

"I can't answer your questions right now, but what I can tell you is that I want as much as you do to find Berlin and our habits again."

"Alright, mom, I won't annoy you with my questions anymore."

"I know Klaus, do you want to continue or do you want to stop?"

"No, mom, we can go on."

They resumed their walk, when suddenly a huge shadow flew over them. On the ground, it was as big as a plane flying at low altitude. They immediately raised their eyes to the sky and saw what appeared to be a huge raptor looking like an eagle or a vulture. To tell the truth, it didn't look like anything known in their dimension, but it was gigantic and seemed to follow them from a distance.

"Run", Enke screamed, panicked.

There was a place two hundred meters away, filled with trees tight enough for the monster not to penetrate. The animal was making flights closer to the ground, and seemed to be waiting for the slightest opportunity to grab one of them.

Enke and Klaus beat all records to reach that mini saving forest. The trees got closer and closer, another hundred meters and a true eternity to reach them. The giant bird continued its incessant passage, and this time flew less than a meter above them. At the next passage, for sure, it would open its long claws and take one in stride. More than fifty meters before the shelter, but it was still too long. Enke took Klaus by the hand and ran at full speed; the animal turned around and got ready for a new mudflat, more than thirty yards to go to be safe, but the bird was coming, it was there, very close, like a building with giant wings, its great claws opened, and planted themselves directly into the ground, encircling them within twenty yards of the trees.

Enke took Klaus in her arms, thinking about the worst. The claws would certainly wrap around them, picking up a piece of earth in the process. Enke looked her child in the eyes; impossible to escape from that prison made of giant claws. I love you, my son... I love you, mom...

Both were huddling together, but the claws didn't move,

they didn't close and there, in addition to the huge cry of the animal, resembling an eagle gleam amplified a hundred times, another, much more grave cry came, recalling the hiss of a snake accompanied by a huge roar. Enke and Klaus faced facts, if the bird had wanted to catch them, it would have done so long ago. Suddenly, the claws flew away and violently grabbed a huge, long, large snake, putting it several kilometers away. Enke and Klaus were paralyzed, watching the spectacle.

The snake was at least sixty feet long, and its body was as wide as a tank truck. For it, they had to be what a mouse was to a giant python. Given the violence of the hold, the snake must certainly be dead, as for the bird, once its package deposited, it turned around and went back to the mother and child. It was hard to believe, but that monster had saved their lives, even though they had never felt death so close. Having taken refuge in the trees, they watched the animal approaching, and then land about fifteen meters away from them. It was then they realized its size. Wings folded over its body, it was there, planted in front of them, perched on its two huge legs. It was as tall as a three storey building, and as wide as the kitchen and living room combined. It suddenly made a yelp that looked like a victory cry. Only listening to his instinct, Klaus went out of the trees and went towards it.

"Klaus!", Enke cried, trying to hold him back.

So she decided to follow him. Klaus wasn't scared anymore

The animal leaned a few degrees forward and seemed to fix him in the eyes. Enke couldn't believe hers, but remained cautious about the possible reactions of the raptor.

"Thank you", Klaus said.

The animal replied with a short yelp, less noisy than the first. Maybe it had answered 'you're welcome'?

Then, it flew away, generating huge dust from flapping its wings and went off in the sky.

They didn't know where they were, but apparently, someone or rather something was watching over them.

"Come, Klaus, let's not stay here…"

GROUND ZERO

— *"And remember time and again
that each and every one lives only the present,
that small infinity."*
Marcus Aurelius.

Thomas, Kévin, Kurt and Robert are the four American workers gone missing from 'Ground Zero' to Jocelyn's dimension. The passage for them was as radical as a blow to the buildings around them. They found themselves in a sanitized and futuristic place. From one step to another, they were in a large room painted white and without any decoration. There didn't seem to be anyone, and yet in the distance some noises could be heard...

"What the hell!" Thomas said.

Kévin, who always had an answer for everything, even when he didn't know the answer, wasn't late in formulating one.

"It's nothing guys, don't worry, we did the same kind of experiment in the army and we always came back."

As for Kurt, he often had answers, but only when he was certain not to tell nonsense. He said things as they were, without frills, without manners, sometimes awkwardly. So, he was 'the friend Kurt' whose smile amused everyone due to the arrangement of his teeth that recalled the raw unfinished wood keys of a grand piano.

"I'm like this. You take me as I am and that's it!" He defended himself often.

He had a different opinion about these unusual events, but he preferred to shut up by asking Kévin to deepen his own just in case, for once, he wouldn't tell stupidities.

"What do you mean, what experiments are you talking about?"

"It would take too long to explain, never mind!"

Robert, who was a placid fellow, was quickly exasperated by these capricious childish quarrels.

"Shut it!", he said in his deep, shrill voice.

It was radical, everyone shut up immediately. It's true that his wrestling style, tamed by a woman and two children, didn't invite one to annoy him. Not even Kévin commented in those cases.

"I don't know if we're part of an experiment", he continued, "but something weird happened during this acceleration and now we're here! So, let's concentrate on what we're going to do."

The large room made of white walls and windows didn't appear to have any doors. Only an iron footbridge, overlooking what looked like an artificial garden, seemed to lead into another great hall similar to that one.

"What do you say, guys?", Robert said, fixing the latter with his eyes.

"You… you really think it's OK to leave this place?"

"Do you see any other solution, do you see the building site anywhere?"

"Alright, very well, let's go", Kurt said. "STOP!", he suddenly screamed.

"What now?", said Thomas, who officiated from time to time in curative speleology and was now in action.

"Look, here, on our left! Do you see what I see?"

"Shut up", Robert whispered, "maybe it wants to communicate with us."

On their left stood a man whose head seemed to have been too swollen; he stood still and stared at them intently. The man was dressed in light clothes, as if to be confused with his surroundings.

"What's that?", Thomas said, frightened.

"Someone who seems to be wondering what we're doing here", Kurt said shyly, "in my opinion we are with an 'ET' who apparently has found his home!"

A voice was suddenly heard in their heads.

"Who are you?"

"Did you hear that?", Thomas said looking at his three stooges, "I had a feeling I heard that in my head!"

Robert looked at his three colleagues, stopping on Thomas.

"We all heard that in our heads. Now, let me talk to him."

"Hello, sir, we are construction workers working on Ground Zero in New York, we finished our work day and wanted to go home, but we have come, god alone knows how, here, in your humble abode."

As Robert tried to hide his fear and keep his cool, 'Watermelon-Man' was heard again, in the same way.

'I know how you got here and we can help you get home.'

"Did you hear that?", Kurt said, "we're going to be able to go back. But, actually, where are we?"

"The question is not where, but when!", 'Big Head' answered.

"This kind of 'Mr. poorly imitated doesn't inspire me any confidence", said Kévin, approaching his right hand to the hammer hanging on the waistband of his trousers among a pair of chisels and other tools serving him in his work.

"Kévin, calm down and shut up", said Robert dryly "and leave your hammer alone!"

Kévin hesitated for a moment, shooting 'Mister nice' with his eyes. Suddenly, all of Kevin's tools, as well as those of Robert, Thomas and Kurt, came out violently of their places to fly in the air and land ten meters behind them, to their great surprise.

"Did he do that?", Thomas said, impressed.

The four workers looked at each other without any reaction.

"OK", said Robert, putting both his hands forward in order to make 'ET' understand that they wouldn't do it again, "tell us how to get home!"

Then, he turned towards Kévin.

"Start messing around again and I'll plant your hammer in your brain!"

For once, Kévin had no answer. One could see fear had motivated his act. Robert saw it well and tried to calm the situation by putting a friendly hand on his shoulder.

"We, too, are scared at least as much as you."

"I'm sorry, guys", Kévin said, a little embarrassed.

Thomas, who was often, and despite himself, the scapegoat with Kévin, gave a discreet smile, forgetting for a few moments the situation in which they were.

"You must have missed the flight the day they did this experiment in the army!" he thought.

Robert was used to be the natural spokesperson for his colleagues. He looked again at 'The man who spoke without his mouth' and told him calmly.

"Alright, we're ready, explain it to us."

The voice made itself heard again in the four minds.

"You are on Earth and I am not an alien, but a human, like you. I was born in the year 4502 and we are in 4657."

"In God's name", interrupted Kurt, "he's a hundred and fifty-five!"

"Shut it, Kurt and listen", Robert said, whispering.

So, 'Mister nice' continued with his explanation. His words had the effect of a blow to the workers' head at the end of each sentence. When he had finished, he invited them to follow him to another large white room…

IT IS TIME.

— *"Simplicity is not a goal,*
  we come to it despite ourselves as we come close
  to the real meaning of things."
  Aristotel.

Emma's small white 'Smett' was heading towards Paris. Having been able to talk to his wife, Hubert was presently reassured. As for Tiffany, she had understood nothing of the brief explanation her husband had tried to give her, the most important thing being she was able to talk to both of them, until then, they had been missing. Only resolving the mystery of the car in the water remained.

"What have you decided", Allan asked him; "do you want to go to her?"

Hubert appeared to hesitate for a few moments.

"All in all, I'll wait to get to Paris", he replied, nodding to an only for your ears discussion.

"I'm listening."

"Now that everything is in order, we will accompany you a little way if you don't see any inconveniences, Félix is eager to see the rest of the events unfolding; a little like me, I admit."

Allan looked at him with a huge grin that seemed kind of

dangerous.

"You're making fun of me, aren't you?"

"No, not at all, it's not what you think."

He was about to interrupt, but Hubert insisted.

"Please, listen to what I have to say."

Allan kept silent, but nodded with a slight movement of the head.

"There's something I haven't told you. Félix had a strange behavior which lasted only a few moments, but still managed to capture my attention, despite what happens to you in that kind of infernal whirlwind. He was reassuring me that we would get out of it, then the next moment he was scared to death."

"I don't see anything very mysterious given, the circumstances."

"You didn't hear him then, otherwise you would be asking yourself the same questions as me!"

"I see. Have you asked for an explanation afterwards?"

"No, I'm thinking of telling him about it when all this ends, unless he does it himself."

"That would have been interesting to know. So be it, you'll explain it to me later, for we have things to do now. You want to come with us, but it would be nice if he went back just to exorcise what he saw or heard. Moreover, only his unconscious could remember."

"What are you saying?"

"Nothing happens by chance, my brave Hubert, think about it."

He turned on his heels and acted as if nothing had happened, leaving Hubert to his thoughtful and caring father thoughts.

"As you wish", he concluded.

"You don't want to see your wife?", Emma was surprised.

"Of course I do", Hubert said, "but this is an experience you only get to live once; furthermore, there are direct flights from Paris!"

"I understand…"

Emma was debated by Hubert's behavior.

"He disappears in front of his wife and he only thinks about will happen here!" she thought. She forced herself not to give him a piece of her mind, but in spite of herself she was starting to react like a woman's rights activist.

As for Félix, he was very excited by this supernatural situation.

"Are you alright, my son?" his father said with enthusiasm.

"Oh, yes, dad!", replied the latter with the same enthusiasm.

Emma, Jocelyn and Allan opted for silence, but they were of the same train of thought. The car continued its ride towards Paris. Suddenly, Félix noticed a huge shadow in the sky. It was not without reminding him of still fresh memories in his mind.

"Look", he said, "it's Julius!"

"This huge mass?", his father said again.

"Yes, dad, I'm sure, I would recognize him among all the others", continued the overexcited toddler.

"But, Félix, there are billions of birds on this planet, you know; maybe it looks like him, but it's a hundred times bigger than the one you picked up with your young friend."

The child looked at his father seriously and went on looking.

"It's him, dad!"

Hubert realized that the toddler wasn't joking and decided to observe the raptor in more detail.

"Look at the way it flies, dad, you don't remember his wing?"

"Of course son, I remember, but this one is huge; you think he could have become what we see up there?"

"I'm telling you it's him", the child insisted.

Jocelyn was also trying to observe the animal while driving, and soon, all the occupants of the Smett were watching him closely.

"If it was a flying elephant, I would understand that he remembers", Allan thought, good scientist that he was. *"But a raptor!"*

"You took him in when he was young?", he asked Félix.

"Yes, sir."

"I guess it wasn't bigger than a canary at that time."

"Yes, professor", the young boy resumed, eyes bright with cheerfulness, "and I'm sure he saw me too!"

Hubert tried to reason with him.

"Félix, he's at least three hundred meters from us."

Intrigued, Allan couldn't help but ask him for some more details.

"Show me with your hands how big he was."

Félix spread his hands about ten centimeters.

"Strange" Allan thought, « *what breed of bird can become so huge in such a short time. Unless it's him, and by the way, then animals too keep the same traits no matter what happens in other dimensions... Would there be another me, ten times bigger or maybe much smaller? A possibility to take into consideration, without losing sight of the fact that any animal always adapts to its environment if it wants to survive. What could have provoked this? They must have adequate space to land on, I can't imagine one of these behemoths landing in a city in the middle of the day. Would the Earth have become an immense desert populated by giants? But then, where do people live? Perhaps there are fewer, much fewer in this case? What have we done to ourselves? What destructive controller did we operate? Maybe all of this is the normal biological evolution for both man and animal. But if it becomes big, there is bound to be a moment when air becomes rarefied? This bird is obviously not his, but if his food has grown*

at the same time as him, there is something to worry about. I am curious to know more."

He looked at the child again and questioned him more precisely.

"Do you remember his beak? Was it straight, horned or a little rounded?"

Awakened from his thoughts, Félix answered promptly.

"It was straight! Why do you want to know that, professor?"

"It's to try to determine which species it belongs to."

As the animal flew nearby, it suddenly disappeared before their eyes.

"Did ya see dad, we can't see it anymore!"

Seeing that, Hubert realized that the same thing had happened to them, and his first thought went to Tiffany.

"My God" he told himself, *"she must have really been scared".*

He turned to his son, stroking his hair.

"We'll go find your mom who must be eager to see us again, what do you say?"

He also really wanted to see his mother again. He said nothing, but all the words of instant approval were in his eyes when he looked at him, snuggling in his arms.

"I told her we would be back in three days, but we're going to surprise her by trying to get there tomorrow afternoon."

The child still didn't answer, but approved with a sign of his head. Emma stared at the sky where the raptor had disappeared, and smiled a smile of satisfaction.

"You go up again in my esteem", she thought.

They stopped about two and a half hours later to take a break. Jocelyn, whose eyes were literally coming out of their sockets, went straight to the toilets to cool off his face and try to fight against fatigue.

This pause was welcomed by everyone. Emma stretched her legs, lost in her thoughts, her heart between the two Jocelyn, this unusual situation they were living and its future.

Allan was leaning on the door of the Smett, both hands in his pockets, thinking very intensely too. Was there a way to master all this? Would he ever see his assistant student Garvey again? Was he lost in the space-time continuum? Was he still alive? And it wasn't just that. If the human brain overheated in case of great reflection, his would probably catch fire!

Finally, Hubert and Félix walked towards the side of the mountain that bordered the parking. Hubert was trying to put some order in his mind and assimilate what had happened to them.

Leaving the toilet, Jocelyn stopped a few minutes after taking a few steps and looked at Emma.

"Please", he told himself, *"Don't fall in love with me!"*

His gaze then wandered for a little while, over everything and nothing at once. His attention was suddenly drawn to the other end of the parking lot. The landscape seemed to dance there. He narrowed his eyes to focus better.

"What's that again?" he thought.

He started walking towards the place in question, without taking his eyes off it. The rock of the mountain as well as the trees at that precise place were dancing; what seemed to be a kind of 'snake dance' and the closer he got to it, the more distinct it was. The phenomenon stretched about three or four meters, and seemed to start from the ground to the sky, as if the Earth had been disemboweled within it. Suddenly, a man appeared for a few seconds, then disappeared immediately.

Surprised and amazed by this sight, Jocelyn stopped short for a moment, then ran to the dancers trees screaming.

"Professor, Allan, come quickly!"

Everyone in the car park turned towards him without paying attention to the phenomenon except for a little boy Florent, whose parents were parked nearby and left for two unfortunate seconds their offspring unattended. He too had noticed what was going on and was heading straight in. Jocelyn was running as fast as he could and was still screaming.

"No, don't go! Come back!"

The boy was too fascinated by what he was seeing to hear anything and now his parents, Jocelyn, Allan and Emma were running behind him. The other people in the parking lot didn't understand what was going on; all remained frozen, watching the scene. The child was only a few steps away and was far from realizing what would happen to him.

"Florent!", his parents were screaming.

"Stop!", Jocelyn cried.

The child entered directly into the gap that closed immediately behind him. He disappeared under his parents' horrified eyes. The landscape had gone back to normal. Jocelyn arrived like a bombshell, turned around, felt the air with his hands in case there would be a tiny part of the gap.

"Where is our child?", asked the parents, panicked.

Allan, Emma and Hubert who had told Félix to stay close to the Smet, arrived in their turn, breathless from the two hundred meters they had run.

"Florent!", the mother cried desperately.

She was looking everywhere, vainly seeking a sign, a noise, a cry, but there was only the vertical wall of the mountain.

"Give me my baby back!", she continued, crying.

Her husband was panicked and upset as well. He rushed to the mountain, stirring the air with his arms.

"My son, where are you?", he thought as if he were addressing the mountain, *"Give him back to me!"*

Then he turned to his wife and tried to comfort her by taking her in his arms, but there was nothing to do, she became hysterical, and only wanted her baby. Distraught, he looked at Jocelyn.

"What have you seen? What has happened?"

He didn't know what to answer. What do you think of:

"He disappeared in space-time, or maybe in another world!" he thought. *"I really don't know what to say, old chap."*

But he still tried to provide an explanation while the officers, alerted by the general panic arrived, sirens blazing.

"They were the only ones missing", he said to himself, still searching for acceptable words to describe the situation.

"To be honest, I haven't seen much", he tried to convince him.

Frustrated by this response, the father reacted strongly by taking him by the 'Colback'.

"You're joking! Why were you screaming for him not to go? Where wasn't he supposed to go?"

Taking him out of his arms, Hubert and Allan tried in their turn a vain answer.

"I know what you're feeling", Hubert said, "I lived the same thing the day before yesterday".

"Calm down, sir, it's not his fault", Allan said.

Out of their cars, the officers silenced everyone and separated the two men.

"Here we go", Jocelyn told himself, *"think of something, Allan!"*

He was looking at Allan, Emma and Hubert, who now understood the situation they had been in when they found him in the float with Félix.

"What's happening here?", one of the four officers asked.

"I want my baby", the mother of the missing child kept screaming.

"It's our son, Officer, he disappeared and the man who is there", said the father, pointing to Jocelyn, "has seen everything and now pretends that's not the case."

"Damn it, he wants to send me to prison", thought Jocelyn, who was seriously beginning to worry about the turn of events.

The officer turned, looking at him like a bandit.

"Well, tell us what you saw!"

Seeing him in a pinch, Emma intervened again.

"The child was just here", she began to explain pointing to the place with her finger, while heading there. But the officer stopped her in her march.

"Madam, please, I was talking to the gentleman, if you have seen something, tell it to my colleagues."

She didn't insist. *"I'm sorry, Joss, this time, you're going to have to take care of it yourself"* she thought, looking at him with apologetic eyes.

Against all odds, Jocelyn answered most seriously.

"I might be taken for a crazy person, but I'm going to be honest" he told himself.

"Very well, Si… Officer, I'm going to tell you what I saw."

"Yes, and also explain the reason that made you scream at my son not to go there", the father resumed.

Jocelyn went to the exact spot where the child had been.

"Here", he said, sure of himself, "he was right here, as this young lady began to explain" he pointed at Emma, "then I saw this beam, a bit translucent appear right there…"

At that moment, everyone's eyes grew round.

"No, Jocelyn, what are you doing?" thought Allan sending, him a look that meant:

"It's not a good idea."

"What beam are you talking about?", the father asked.

"Do you want me to tell you what I saw or not?"

Annoyed, he let him continue.

"So, I said there was this light beam, a bit translucent here, the child approached, and when I saw him, the only thing I told myself is that it could be dangerous and that the child shouldn't get any closer; it's at that moment I screamed at him not to go."

"And then", the officer continued.

"Well, then, he disappeared!"

"What do you mean, disappeared?"

"He got close to the beam, then I didn't see him, just like everyone else in this parking lot."

The officer approached the place to inspect it.

"Where did this beam come from?"

"From the sky, Officer, from the sky."

"I see, don't move please, I'll come back."

Perplexed, he made a sign to his colleague who was questioning Emma, inviting him to join him. They stood aside for a moment to talk, then joined the other two who were taking information from Hubert and Allan, as well as from others present in the car park.

Jocelyn got close to Emma.

"This doesn't smell very good at all, what do you think?"

Astonished and trying to smell, Emma didn't immediately understand what he meant.

"I don't smell anything special, why do you say that? Don't you think we have other bigger issues to settle at the moment?"

Jocelyn glanced at the sky as if to ask for help.

"Forget what I said, I'll explain later."

Still not understanding, she didn't insist. The four officers continued to discuss among themselves, and evoked, among other things, the recent disappearances and appearances that had made the news of all the news flashes for two days. Five minutes later, they came back, but this time to talk to the child's parents.

"Have you watched the news lately?", one of the officers asked.

The still-collapsed mother let her husband answer.

"To be honest, no; we left the day before yesterday to our second house in the mountains, and we weren't at all concerned about what was going on. Why the question, Officer?"

"Now I understand better."

He asked one of his colleagues to borrow a newspaper from among the onlookers. He came back almost immediately with the newspaper of the day in hand.

"Here you are, Chief Officer."

He took it and showed the couple the first page directly. Seeing the headlines, the man got alarmed.

"What does this mean? Where have they all gone and who are these people from nowhere?"

"It's been two days and we know absolutely nothing about these phenomena. Apparently, there is be a light beam that triggers we don't know what!"

"And what do you plan on doing to find our child?"

"To start, give us his details, we'll distribute them to all the officers and patrols."

"Do you think it's the aliens?"

The officer was silent for a short moment.

"No, Mam, even though that beam intrigues me. But we won't draw a conclusion until we have more information in our possession. For the moment, I will ask you to follow us to the station so that we can put on file your testimony."

"You're not looking for our son?"

The officer looked at the mountain which was accessible only from a height of about ten meters.

"Unless your child is a high jump champion, I don't see where he could have gone."

Offended by what appeared to her to be nonchalance, the young woman objected fiercely.

"Leaving this place is out of the question! And I can't believe you're not doing more to find him. What if he comes back?"

"I understand your dismay Madam, but in truth, there is a small visionary of a few minutes that we will show you, which I think will help you better understand what is happening. We can't do anything for the moment, but I can assure you we're working on it. Come with us, we only wish to help, believe me; maybe you'll find him sooner than you think."

Confident, her husband complied with this and finally managed to convince his wife.

"Very well, Officer", the husband said, "we'll follow you".

"Very well, we'll leave in ten minutes, the time we need to take the witnesses' contacts."

The young couple turned towards their car, but the man changed his mind and turned around.

"Where are you going?"

"I'll come back shortly. Go sit down, I'll join you in a minute."

Jocelyn saw him come in his direction.

"*Ouch*", he thought.

"Sir, I apologize for earlier", the man told him in a desperately sad voice, "I had no control over myself. Are you sure you saw that beam, because I've been thinking about it since you alluded to it, and I didn't notice anything like that?"

Mistrusting his reaction as an unhappy father, Jocelyn decided to offer help in a certain way.

"That man you see there", he resumed, pointing to Allan, "is a science professor at the university of Paris, and since these phenomena have begun, he is working on the problem and has some ideas to develop. But he prefers to remain silent for the moment, and if you give me your contact, I will communicate them to him and ask him to call you if he finds something. What do you say?"

"All the help we can get is more than welcome. Here is my card."

Jocelyn took the card, reading the content.

"Laurent Cullier. Don't worry, Laurent", he said, putting a friendly hand on his shoulder, "you're not alone".

The way he told him that, gave the orphaned father a lot of heart.

"Thank you, sir; and who are you?"

"Jocelyn Beaumont."

"Strange, I already heard that name somewhere."

"It's normal. Go on now, don't make your wife wait."

Intrigued by these words, Laurent, whose gratitude was in his eyes, returned to his car.

Emma and Jocelyn's turn arrived.

"Emma Beaumont, you live in Aussillon, at what number?"

Emma provided all the information she had been asked. It was then Hubert's turn, whose identity papers corresponded to this world, Allan, and finally Jocelyn.

"Here we go again", he told himself.

"And you", the officer said, "your identification, please."

Only Emma knew the problem. She got ready to intervene again, when suddenly, understanding what was happening, Allan took the lead. He approached Jocelyn and undertook a comedy worthy of the greatest actors, to Emma's big surprise.

"When will pay attention, you dummy", he said, resting his left hand on Jocelyn's forehead, "at your age I would never have forgotten my papers at home, they're way too important!"

"You don't have them with you?", the officer asked.

But Allan didn't give him time to answer and continued his game, pretending to get annoyed.

"But, no, he doesn't have them with him! The gentleman has forgotten them home! The gentleman doesn't care! The gentleman's head is empty; and if you get into an accident, what will you do?"

The officer tried to calm him, but it was in vain.

"Come now, Sir, calm down, it's not that bad."

"Not that bad, you say? But it's the contrary! He deserves you put him in prison so that it serves him as a lesson once and for all!"

In that moment, Jocelyn wanted to put a big pad on his tongue. *That's enough, Allan, he got it!* he thought.

"When I think this big 'Dummy' is forty-five years old!"

Hubert was a little amused to see him so belittled.

"Sir", the officer said, "as I have already stated, it's not that bad."

He continued by addressing Jocelyn and trying to hide a growing smile.

"Just give me your name and your contact, that would suffice."

What number will he give him? Emma thought. But this time, he didn't need any help and got out just fine from the situation.

"My name is Jocelyn Beaumont, I live at number three on the road that goes through Aussillon in the Tarn and as for my phone number, ask my wife, as we changed a little while ago and she was the one who took care of it."

"You really do forget everything! Your uncle is right, you really should pay more attention. One last thing, where are you going?"

"We're going to Paris, and to answer your statement, I will not forget, though in the future", he said a little embarrassed, "I will remember!"

Emma uttered the number and the officer went off to join his colleagues.

"Thank you ladies and gentlemen, we will keep you informed. Will you be available in the next three days?"

"I can't tell you exactly, but it's very likely."

"Alright, if there are any changes, let us know. Our contact details are on the document I gave you. Here sir, this is yours. Have a safe journey."

"Thank you, Officer."

Jocelyn went back to the Smett and buckled up.

"Emma, Hubert, Uncle, are you coming?"

He's not upset, but the way he had said it amused his fellow travelers. Everyone took their places in the car in total silence; little stealthy glances went from all sides. Jocelyn started slowly. A few kilometers down the road, Félix who had briefly seen what had happened, stepped directly into the heart of the matter.

"Are you upset, Boss?"

"Joss, please. No, Félix, I'm not, I'm just trying to find some pride again!"

He then glanced at Allan, and his look said *you didn't hold your punches, if I have to go and see the officers in Paris, I will be the laughing stock of the whole station!*.

"Yes, Boss, you're angry, I can see it", the boy insisted.

Hubert patted his leg slightly to make him understand not to go any further. There, it was too much, Jocelyn exploded and answered dryly by raising his voice.

"JOSS, damn it! JOSS! Capich?"

No one spoke, for fear of putting oil to the fire, but after a while, Allan decided to attack the abscess.

"Come Joss, calm down, you musn't hold it against me, I only got you out of an awkward situation for you and for all of us, actually."

Félix interrupted the conversation, as a question puzzled him.

"Can I ask you a question, Joss?"

"Yes, Félix, what is it?"

"Are you upset with me, tell me?"

"No, Félix, I'm only annoyed, I let myself go and it's me who asks you not to blame me, you agree?"

Enthusiastic, the child responded quickly.

"Yes, Boss!"

Jocelyn quickly realized that he was dealing with a nice 'Little Poison', but he didn't lose his sense of humor for that.

"Hubert", he said calmly, "would you twist your son's neck, I'll return it to you later!"

Félix came back with another question.

"Joss…"

He was starting to tap the wheel with his fingers.

"Yes, Félix."

"What's your surname, 'Damn it' or 'Capich'?"

Meanwhile, everyone laughed, as for Jocelyn, he only giggled.

"You really don't miss anything!"

"Quentin is the same, you know!"

Seeing her awkwardness, Emma swallowed the last words of her sentence, but it was said.

"I didn't mean to say it like that, Joss, I'm sorry."

In his world, he had made a choice, but in this one he was the

Jocelyn who had no children. He felt a void right then. He took comfort, however, in the idea that all of this wasn't his life, it was elsewhere, and he was happy with his Emma.

"It's fine, Emma, don't worry about it."

Allan understood the heart of the matter. So he put an end to that incipient rancor.

"Now I'm sure you won't hold it against me, and I know you won't ask me to feel guilty for wanting to help you. Furthermore, I'll continue to do it when we get to our destination."

"I know, Allan. For the moment, I felt belittled, I confess, but I still owe you one."

"I don't want to know why you're telling me that Joss, but I prefer to use my insight!"

Seeing that this expression wasn't current in this dimension, he didn't even try to explain the meaning.

"Alright Allan, as you wish."

Hubert didn't dare intervene, but curiosity won and he couldn't help questioning him about his world. Now calm, he answered all the questions, even Félix's.

They were only twenty kilometers from the capital. Until then, the highway was virtually identical to what he knew, but he had never seen what was announced on the road signs. The end of the road was only a few kilometers away, and the indicators only showed parking areas with different names from the city neighborhoods. Not really knowing what to do, he first spoke to Emma who couldn't answer him precisely.

"All I know is that we don't go to Paris by car. There is a multitude of car parks on the outskirts of the city where you can park and then take an eel that will take you to the neighborhood of your choice. The underground is very efficient! You don't have it in your world?"

"Of course we do! But we eat them!"

"Idiot! Better ask Allan for where to park. I'm going to wake him up."

Emma shook him gently.

"No need to shake me like a plum girl, I just got a little sleepy and I heard you talk. Follow number '7', that eel will take us directly."

"Alright, Allan, number 7."

Jocelyn was secretly having fun. An eel! Why did not they call it the rattlesnake train!

Arrived at the entrance where other cars were also waiting, Jocelyn was in the mood to joke.

"Look, here's the toad's hall from which all the flies that are going to be swallowed by the eel will take us directly into the cockroach nest. Homo sapiens friends, get ready to land!"

Emma laughed heartily. Allan meanwhile, made a wise remark.

"It is necessary that youth be done and that old age is done!"

"Come on, you should wake up Hubert and Félix, it would give them time to get themselves together."

"You're right, Emma."

He didn't joke often, but when he put his mind to it, he had a special kind of humor. He started gently waking Félix by waving his finger in front of his mouth in a sign to say nothing.

"Since you like laughing, I propose you observe this, it works every time!"

He approached Hubert, who was sleeping peacefully and shouted:

"The ravine, we'll fall!"

Hubert, who was sleeping peacefully awoke with a start, his eyes distraught, clinging with his left hand to the front seat and pinning Félix against him for protection. A few seconds passed before he realized the situation. There were only two cars left in front of them at the entrance gate where there was a guard, surveying the operations. Some had their appointed place, others, like them, were directed to the so-called temporary places of reception, summing up a few places.

Hubert was still in shock, his eyes rounded, his heart pounding and a few drops of sweat due to the stress he had experienced, dripping on his forehead. He looked at the professor with contempt.

"Are you done, did you have fun?"

Everyone in the Smett was laughing with tears in their eyes. It was certainly not a popular joke, especially coming from a science professor like Allan, but these last two days of intense stress had provoked an irresistible desire to relax, whatever the means used. Wiping away tears, Allan apologized to Hubert.

"Forgive me, Hubert! I know it wasn't very nice, but I needed it."

Their turn came.

"Good evening ladies and gentlemen, I don't recognize you, I presume you want a temporary place?"

Allan intervened and answered in Jocelyn's place by presenting his university card.

"Good evening, my friend! We're going to the university neighborhoods. These young people accompany me and will leave in three days."

"Well, then it will cost you twelve crowns for parking, and a round trip eel. You'll follow the letter 'A' and you will park in the place with the number '2382'. The car park is guarded day and night and if you have to stay more, you have the opportunity to pay for additional days in the eel hall at Beaulieu University.

Have a nice stay!"

"Thank you, sir."

The barrier opened, they reached their parking place and then headed for the eel entry hall 'South-Paris'. Apart from Allan, who often used the eels for his Parisian trips when his motor-scooter wasn't working, Jocelyn, Emma, Hubert and his son were discovering them.

The hall dug in the underground was huge; the height of the ceiling could easily have contained an eight-story building. Everything seemed to have been repainted the day before, as it was clean and modern. Soft music was broadcast for a more pleasant wait. No speaker was visible. The sound seemed to come out of every wall. Advertisements were scrolling to targeted places. Impossible to see from where they were projected. The walls seemed almost alive and seemed to manage the atmosphere of the place themselves. Judging by the faces of the people present, there was a much quieter atmosphere than anything they had seen so far, similar to the one he had seen on the highway.

Probably this world had succeeded on this point. Maybe it was just a matter of manners in the minds.

For a city like Paris, it must have been a real feat to achieve such a result. Jocelyn couldn't help but question Allan.

"Has it always been like this?"

"What are you talking about, the color of the walls, the atmosphere?"

Jocelyn smiled in response.

"No, there were a lot of Pique-Pockets at one time. The officers rumbled throughout the hall. But one day, there was a general chill. You don't know it, but mentalities had unified, not very long ago and it reproduced the same thing in the eel sector. It would take some explaining, but…"

"Emma told me a little on the road."

"She told you about this 'road unifier'?"

"A little, yes."

"Well! It's what happened here. All eel travelers unified. They helped each other whenever there was a problem; so much so that when a person was attacked, it was no longer two or three officers that intervened, but a mass of people present at that time. The decision was taken. It worked great with the Command, so you can imagine with purse thieves!"

"That's right, billions of grains of sand can form a mountain."

"You understood, my young friend."

Four men dressed in dark red uniforms crisscrossed the length of the platform, but they didn't seem to be on the lookout for malice. Indeed, one of them headed towards an old man overloaded with suitcases and bags to help him. Jocelyn looked at all that with interest, trying to make comparisons. Emma, Hubert and Félix were stunned by the excesses of the place. Observing their behavior and their amazement, Allan welcomed them to Paris. Curious, Jocelyn questioned him.

"There is no ring road around Paris? You know what a ring road is, don't you?"

"Come, my young friend, you're talking to an active scientist. I'm not completely out of it!"

"That's not what I wanted to say Allan, but some of the terms you use are different from ours to designate similar situations."

"True, you do well with words! To answer your question, there is one who has six kilometers over all."

"Only six?"

"Not all the decision makers were in agreement with the project and it was abandoned two years after the beginning of the works, which caused a real controversy. So today, only taxis, ambulances, fire trucks and small trucks are allowed to circulate in the capital. There are only thirty access points, all the others have been closed."

Jocelyn couldn't believe his ears. Impossible to imagine in his dimension. Suddenly, a light and noisy slip was heard, an eel appeared like a mini TGV, all white.

"Here it comes!", Félix said, excited to take one for the first time in his life.

It stopped, the doors opened and everyone boarded, as well as the old man accompanied by the man in red.

Jocelyn was still making comparisons and smiled on seeing the scene.

"How can our mentalities be so different with our brains a priori identical!" , he thought.

In the same way as his friends, he discovered the inside of the vehicle, where burgundy and center seats, with metal bases fixed from floor to ceiling and arranged every two meters were placed on each side of the walls and on the whole length. A sound signal indicated the closing of the doors and the departure followed. People who had just arrived and embarked in the last moment settled next to them.

"Good evening!"

"Good evening!", they replied.

Félix remarked the little girl who was apparently the same age as him and looked at her with the eyes of apprentice lovers. The blonde girl walked towards him with an electronic game in her hands. To Jocelyn's great surprise, her parents didn't stop her from getting up. Clumsy, Félix didn't know if he too should get up or sit, keep his legs folded on the seat, or extend them to appear more 'relaxed'.

Arrived at his seat, she smiled at him and made contact.

"Hi!"

Félix opted for an attitude of lover jaded by life.

"Hi, what's your name?"

"Céline, and you?"

"I'm Félix!"

"You live in Paris?"

"No, in the south of France and before arriving here, we were in Italy."

In that moment, his father, as well as his new friends looked at him out of the corner of their eye with concern.

"Wow, in Italy! You travel a lot; you came with the zinc?"

"No, with a float!"

Céline laughed, but this response worried the girl's parents, who in turn began the conversation with the group, which was forced to return to 'vigilance mode'.

"He's your son?", they asked, addressing Emma and Jocelyn.

Hubert answered promptly.

"No, he's my little boy."

"And the lady is your wife?", they continued, pointing to Emma.

"That's right, I'm sorry, I tend to appropriate him, that's how much I'm proud of him! And while we're doing the introductions, this is my cousin Jocelyn and my uncle Allan, science professor at the Beaulieu University."

By saying that, they were trying to reassure them. But suddenly, between two phrases, they could clearly hear young Félix's voice continuing to explain to Céline the way they had arrived there.

"And then, everything accelerated and we ended up on the road with the float. We traveled in time!"

178

A deathly silence is the exact term to describe the minute that followed when everyone watched each other with fried whiting eyes. Jocelyn made an attempt to save the situation.

"My nephew has an overflowing imagination!"

"Come Céline!", her parents told her.

They got up and advanced to the door to get off at the first eel stop, near Allan's house.

The girl didn't want to break the contact, but orders were orders! Better not upset a closed brain. When they got off, she turned her head towards Félix, and in her eyes was: *"You seemed nice"*. She gave him a discreet hand gesture and looked back at him: *"Pity"*. Hubert looked at his son with compassion and sought to comfort him.

"Don't worry, my son, if it's meant to be, you'll see each other again sooner or later. And in the end, you don't even know her."

He wasn't really sad, as they had just gotten to know each other, he only regretted that parents could interfere in these stories that are not theirs.

"You're upset with her, aren't you?", Hubert resumed, talking about the girl's mother.

He looked at his father, sad.

"Yes, a little, it's not fair."

"She simply must have been scared for her daughter; in a way, she wanted to protect her and that doesn't make her a bad mother. Come, give me a smile, I don't like to see you sad."

He gave him the requested smile and was flattened against his father.

"Come here, son!"

Jocelyn was looking at the scene, his eyes empty and added a little dipper.

"A little stuck at the edges this woman, don't you think?"

179

Emma, who was watching the couple and the little girl advance in the hall, saw something alarming and alerted her friends.

"Look! They're talking to a security guard…"

The latter turned to look at them.

"They're looking this way!", Emma said, a little worried.

Suddenly, the men in red hurried in their direction. Jocelyn couldn't help but comment.

"This can't be, what did she say to them?"

"At home, we go crazy when getting into a car and here, just get off a fucking eel", he thought.

The doors were still open and in the hall they were getting closer and closer.

"Will they never close?" Allan told himself.

While they were only a few meters away, the signal sounded and the doors were activated: 'Clack'.

"Saved by the bell", Jocelyn continued to think.

The men arrived at the eel, clapping their hands on the glass behind which they were sitting. Worried, Jocelyn asked Allan.

"What should we expect at the next stop?"

"In my opinion, they will have warned their colleagues in the next hall."

"Do they have the same authority as the officers do?"

"No, but they can warn them, in accordance with each case."

"In short, our situation looks bad; who has an idea?"

Seeing that no one reacted, he added.

"Today, it would come in handy!"

Knowing him through the Jocelyn of this world, Emma knew how to get around to calm him. She used her charm by putting her hand on his and looking at him tenderly.

"We managed so far, we'll be fine from now on too."

"So, he resembles me that much?"

"In this particular case, I would say 'You' resemble him!"

He looked at her the same way he would at his Emma. Actually, this made him uncomfortable. Allan saw something was happening, but it was not his business. Félix regretted his words and began to feel guilty.

"All of this is my fault, I'm sorry!"

As an interim grand-uncle he was, Allan reassured him immediately.

"You don't have to worry about it, little one! After all, you only told the truth. Obviously, if you hadn't done it, we wouldn't have had this problem, but having behaved this way, you unintentionally chose honesty, you didn't control yourself. Whatever the consequences, you acted very well and I advise you not to change. You're honest; stay the same, even if in certain situations, you have to deal with the world you live in, the most important thing is to never forget who you are."

Those simple words, sounding corny, didn't seem to fall on deaf's ears, given the boy's attention.

"I'll call the day I'll be in the mood to sell him", Hubert joked, "you would make a great interim father!"

"Grand uncle would suffice, my young friend! I have always been more understanding of other people's children than my own. Maybe it's due to the fact that I'm much more demanding with them and that I have never been able to take enough distance to take them as they are."

"And I, who took you for an old fool! I realize my mistake now, you're a good man, Allan."

"This is it, we're getting to the next station!", Emma said apprehensively.

"Yes", Jocelyn confirmed; "and I think we have a welcoming

committee!"

They looked at each other as if to say 'the goodbye of the condemned'. Allan assumed the role of the old sage with the 'good words of the just'.

"Comfort yourselves by saying we did nothing but help people who needed it."

During this time, Jocelyn got overheated in reflection.

"We won't let ourselves be taken without doing anything", he thought *"there's surely a solution"*.

This thought didn't even have time to go around the edges of his brain that the solution presented itself, under the bewildered eyes of five other travelers present in the train.

It began with the vision of a landscape enclosed in what appeared to be a breach, a bit as if what we could see from the rest of the inside of the train was damaged in that place. Only Allan, Jocelyn, Emma, Hubert and Félix could see what was in that breach; the other five passengers only saw the appearance of a person from nowhere.

"Garvey", Allan exclaimed, "finally, here you are!"

While the five spectators sank in their seats as if wanting to pass through them, Garvey, box in hand, invited Allan and his friends to follow him.

"Come", he told them, "we don't have much time ahead of us!"

Allan was subjugated and especially very angry with his pupil.

"But how did you know?"

"No time to explain, let's get out of here!"

The eel was already skirting the platform of the hall, they had only a few seconds left before total stop.

"Come on", Garvey insisted, "it's now or never!"

They all glanced at each other and headed for the still open gap, one after the other, then it closed behind them just after Emma's passage, who hesitated a few moments before launching. As for the five witnesses of the scene, they now seemed to be an integral part of their seats. The red security guards who, too, had seen them disappear, couldn't believe their eyes. When the eel stopped and opened its doors, only the five seats and their new occupants remained.

They tried to interrogate them, but none of them could get a word out, as they were frightened and feared to be considered crazy. Five new disappearances were therefore to be deplored, but this time there were witnesses who could swear that someone had knowingly provoked them.

CALL TO ORDER.

— *"What we now refuse,*
no eternity can bring back."
Heraclitus.

T he crossing made, all were virally itching all over their bodies for a few seconds.

"What's happening to me?", Emma gestured in all directions, as did Allan, who seemed to have gone on a flea hunt.

"This is precisely what I explained to our friend Hubert earlier."

"Yes, I did think about it when I asked the question, but it's hellish, I feel like I'm in a chopper!"

"It's going to pass soon", said Jocelyn, who was also finishing his dance at the same time with Garvey, Hubert and Félix.

"Are we at the university, Garvey?"

"Yes, professor."

"What day is it?"

"Still today, same time, same year, same day."

"Well, I'll take care of you soon, young unconscious mule head."

Garvey had an evasive look, frustrated by Allan's reaction,

who knew the young man's reactions very well.

"I get him out of a bad situation and this is the thank you I get!" He thought.

"You may have saved us, but all of this happened because of your accursed invention and especially, your disobedience! You think I don't know you, young man?"

Surprised, Garvey didn't insist. Allan worried about Emma, for whom this experience was a first.

"Everything alright, young lady, not too shaken?"

She wasn't especially shocked, but only surprised by the effect the trip in space-time had.

"Everything happened so fast, I felt like I was traveling at three thousand kilometers an hour and at the end, I saw the moment when we were going to hit hard the parking lot where we are, not to mention the tingling."

"Personally, to me it made the same impression when we arrived on the road", Hubert noticed, "and you Félix?"

"Yes, the same and when we arrived I put my arms in front of my face to protect myself."

"And how did you take this new experience?", Allan resumed.

"It was great, keenly the third!"

This remark amused them and relaxed Allan a bit, but without weakening the anger he felt towards Garvey.

"And you Jocelyn, was there something different for you?"

"A small one, but not too much! This time, I was prepared."

"It's true that it removes the element of surprise, especially for you who did it with your truck the first time… Perfect, since we're all OK, I propose to sleep a little, as we're all very tired. There are some free rooms on campus. We'll go to the guardhouse to ask for the double of the keys."

He suddenly noticed Jocelyn and Emma's bags that he had

ELSEWHERE

not paid attention to until then. He observed them for a while. An attitude that became almost normal in the eyes of the group.

"Here we go, we're there again!" Jocelyn smiled ironically.

"Are they heavy?", Allan asked, looking at him.

Surprised, Jocelyn glanced stealthily at his bag, which he held with one hand over his shoulder.

"Yes… Uhm, no, why the question?"

"For a reason far too technical to start an explanation."

"Oh, OK!"

"Can I?", Allan asked, holding out his hand.

"Of course, here you go", Jocelyn answered and gave him the bag.

"No professor, you're on the wrong track", thought Garvey, who could see where he was coming from.

Allan grabbed the bag with energy from the information given by the 'Nice Driver', but the latter was used to heavy loads, unlike Allan, who, surprised by the weight, put the bag on the ground without letting it go. Everyone smiled and smirked at the scientist who was glaring at Jocelyn.

"I'll teach you the definition of the word 'heavy' when we'll have time!", Allan said, a little vexed.

"Sorry, I…"

"It's okay, don't worry about it, I saw what I wanted to see."

He ended the mood by his somewhat childish behavior, as well as the tone with which he concluded by addressing his pupil.

"As for you Garvey, you'll get off the hook tonight, but we're going to have a talk tomorrow. I'm going to call Auguste to inform him of our arrival." He composed the '213'.

"Security station, Auguste speaking. Identify yourself, please, you're calling from the science room and Professor Thibault is

186

absent."

"Not at all, Auguste, I came back with a few friends and I would like to have the keys to the two available rooms, please, as there are six of us, with Garvey!"

Allan had been missing for two days and Christian, who had seen the scene, was at home for a while to recover from his emotions. Auguste was therefore intrigued and very surprised to talk to him, especially at such a time, especially since Garvey was also missing, but no one here knew anything about it.

"Professor Thibault! Where have you been? And why call at this hour? It's not in your habit to do so."

"I'll explain later, Auguste, just tell me if we can have the rooms, please."

"Of course, professor, come down with your friends, I'll get the keys meanwhile."

They went down to join the guard post where Auguste was waiting for them outside, in front of the door. Arrived a few meters away, Allan greeted him from a distance, raising his arm.

"Good evening my brave Auguste, how are you?"

"Very well, professor. Good evening ladies and gentlemen, good evening Garvey."

They answered in kind.

"Say professor, from where did you get in, I didn't see you pass?"

"We came through the back, as it was shorter from where we were coming from."

"Very well, professor, I won't insist. Must I announce you came back?"

"Why are you asking me this, Auguste?"

"The back door has been condemned for over a month, professor!"

There was at that moment a furtive look of stealthy and anxious glances, like those that might have been burglars caught in the act. Allan was very upset by this situation, which was really bad. This made a real case of conscience for him about lying to Auguste, as he appreciated him a lot and had great esteem for him. On the other hand if he did, he could still catch up later by trying to explain the situation to him without passing for a mental patient. It was difficult for him to imagine the scene: *"I'm sorry to have lied to you the other day, the people who accompanied me, some had actually traveled in time and others changed dimension".* It was just not thinkable.

"One must know how to lie sometimes, for a good cause", he told himself. He, who made it a point of honor to respect the people he met and who always had an answer to everything, was caught off guard. He was clueless, trapped, and didn't know what to say.

"Don't worry! Of all the teachers who teach here, you're the one I appreciate the most. If you ask me not to say anything, it will be so and if you need something, call me."

"I'll owe you a hundred times, my dear Auguste, and I prefer that you keep it all under wraps. For the time being, anyway. Thank you, Auguste."

"Here! The keys. It's the pavilion that's right here, a hundred meters away. Good night, everyone."

A few seconds passed, then he added.

"Don't get up too late tomorrow if you don't want to be seen!"

On the way to the pavilion with his friends, Allan turned around and thanked him with a wave of his hand. Auguste returned to his post to prepare for his first round.

RECIPROCAL VIGILANCE.

— *"What we are looking for is here
if only our spirit's peace
doesn't leave us."*
Alphonse Allais.

Allan opened the door and Félix glimpsed a white silhouette in the distance.

"Dad, dad", he said, shaking his arm and pointing his finger to the other side of the campus, "look!"

Astonished by this sudden precipitation from Félix, everyone looked in the direction indicated, but to the boy's surprise, it had disappeared.

"What did you see?", his father asked, looking in turn.

"There was someone all in white there!"

Jocelyn was also looking in the same direction. He had caught a glimpse of it, but he preferred to keep quiet, because the little he had seen made him hesitate between fatigue or hallucination, which was nevertheless shared with Félix. Were they being spied? If that was the case, for what reason?

That wasn't the first time Félix had seen it; but he had the strange sensation that this white silhouette had looked at him more insistently this time. However, it didn't frighten him as

189

much; for sure, he was still curious, but he felt inexplicably confident in its presence, as if it had been a close friend. That night, he would be in the grip of resolutely realistic dreams in the vision, as in the apprehension of the contents with an extraordinary touch at certain moments.

The small blonde head was about to live the first moments of his future life without even knowing it.

Hearing this, Garvey scanned the place and the surroundings again.

"Why are they here?" he thought *"maybe I'm mistaken, they wouldn't do that".* He had what he commonly called a 'Theoridea', a mix of theory based on an idea. He was fully aware of what he had seen elsewhere. He knew that the few answers he had were a tiny part of millions of other possibilities.

One certainty: everything awakened in him the mad scientist so often crushed and stopped dead, and yet so present in his lonely attitude. He literally enjoyed the excitement in front of all these phenomena. No question of restraining oneself for decency and respect for the experience of the elders. He intended to store as much information as possible before a term was put to this crazy adventure in one way or another.

Seeing him react like that, Allan wondered in his turn, but didn't show him.

"Come on Garvey, are you coming or are you planning to stand guard at the door?"

"Eh, yes, I'm coming!", he said awkwardly.

Grouped in the main room, Allan didn't waste time.

"There are three rooms with two beds each, I imagine you will sleep with your son?"

Hubert nodded.

"Emma, you're going with Jocelyn, right?"

"Yes, Allan", she promptly answered.

"Perfect", Allan resumed; "are you coming Garvey?"

He reluctantly complied, not daring to make known his desire to sleep on the living room sofa. Allan was pleased with this state of affairs, as he intended to steal the 'breach box' from him. But knowing his professor, he took some precautions. Pretending to arrange things, he took a plastic bag folded it into a ball, put it in his pocket, as well as the magic box, making sure that nobody would notice and went without saying anything in the direction of the toilet.

When he got there, he locked the door, took the bag and box out of his pocket, sat down on the toilet and prepared it discreetly, but quickly so as not to attract attention in case anyone came in to relieve themselves, with a mind to the box in the water tank, convinced that no one would think to go there.

His little business finished, he flushed the toilet, while waiting for a possible problem. Apart from a slight sound of crumpled plastic that was heard, but was lost in the sound of the mechanism when operated, everything was fine.

Satisfied, he went back to the room where the professor was already sleeping like a log. He glanced at his bag to check that nothing had changed, but Allan had apparently and against all odds, had managed to abstain.

"At times, I really don't get him" Garvey thought,

"I would have looked in his place!"

He lay down on his bed and relaxed. He thought about what he had discovered, the people he had met in those two days.

"If only you knew, professor" he said in a low voice.

Tiredness soon took over his thoughts and his eyes closed without him even noticing. Only a few minutes passed before Morpheus also welcomed him until the early morning.

191

Hubert and Félix were lying on their respective beds, and exchanged a few words before falling asleep.

"Why didn't you believe me earlier?", Félix asked shyly.

"Because there was no one, although I turned right away."

"But I saw him!"

"Then, it disappeared…"

"Had it been Benoit, you would have believed him!"

Hubert noticed his mistake and caught up immediately.

"No more than you, Félix. Don't think I make differences between you and your brother, but it turns out that he was older than you and when he issued an opinion on a subject, the age difference would be noticed, he understood some things that you still couldn't, given your young age. That's why you must have had this impression of favoritism. But there was none, his opinion was sometimes more sensible than yours, that's all. Remember that the only difference between you two was your age and nothing more. Mom and I love you very much as much as your deceased brother. Have I reassured you, son?"

Félix felt again his importance to his father and that was enough for him.

"Yes, dad, I miss him often, you know."

"You speak to one of the two people who gave him life, son. We also miss him, and terribly sometimes. But fortunately, we have you!"

Then, he got out of bed and approached his son, staring at him.

"Félix, your mother and I love you so much that words are not enough to express it. In the future, you'll hear us often talk about Benoit, probably because we won't be able to berate him for stupid things he won't do anymore, but you'll never have to see any difference with you because you are just as important to us. Do you understand?"

"Yes, dad."

There, he put his arms around his father's neck before adding, "I also love you guys very much!"

"Will you be able to go to sleep now, my son?"

"Yes, I'll be fine."

"This small tear on your face", Hubert noticed, "is it for your brother?"

He couldn't answer promptly and just nodded in answer.

"Don't worry, son", said Hubert, cajoling him, "we'll get through this together, I love you, my son."

Félix literally lurched and cried in his father's arms. Also close to tears, Hubert concluded the conversation.

"We would better get some sleep, because we are both tired and I don't know what tomorrow will be like. And don't worry about your white silhouette, I believe you."

He gave one last hug to his boy and went to settle in his bed. Like Garvey and Allan, they fell asleep just as quickly. Only Emma and Jocelyn were still resisting sleep.

"How will tomorrow be, in your opinion?"

"I really don't know, Emma, I think Hubert and Félix will take the train or plane to return near their lake. Garvey is obviously going to get scolded, after which he will look with Allan for answers regarding my return, or I least, I hope so."

"Plane?"

"Sorry; I wanted to say the zinc…"

"Jocelyn…"

"Yes…"

"I think I want you to stay", Emma said shyly. She suddenly heard the specific ringing of Joss's mobile phone. He took it out of his pocket and answered by reflex. It then happened the same as with the previous calls. He looked at the screen, it was Emma… his Emma.

"One would say divine intervention is possible between two different worlds", he said, almost sorry; "should we take this intrusion as a sign? Do you believe in one or more Gods here?"

"Yes, we have our beliefs."

"You, like me, didn't intend to play cards, true?"

"Well…"

"It's too timely to be random. Powerful thoughts and strong emotions must not have dimensional and temporal limits. I think we should pull ourselves together and go to bed directly and wish each other good night."

Emma was both admiring and disappointed. He showed such sentimental righteousness, which came from the manners and certainties in which they had each evolved in their world. At the same time, it kept them from being happy in this world. She saw it as an injustice, a malfunction in this universal situation.

"We wouldn't hurt anyone", she said, sad.

Jocelyn would have let himself go too, but he knew he could no longer take looking the Emma of his world in the eyes. Even if thinking twice, he wouldn't have been fundamentally unfaithful since only one world separated the two women, which were one and the same person, with a different evolution. Maybe it was an exam, a test.

"It's the other me you love, not me and I don't intend to give up your double, she doesn't deserve it, and … I love her."

Emma felt this love coming into her for this man who was exactly the same as the one she had married a few years earlier. She found in him, however, a small difference, so tiny that she couldn't yet define it.

"We would better go to sleep, Emma."

He saw one of those awkward situations on his horizon appear, for him as well as for her, and he didn't want to go there, not tonight.

"Good night, Joss."

"Good night to you too."

Sometime later, while everyone was sleeping in the pavilion, the man in white appeared in the main room. His intentions were, in all evidence, peaceful. He only took a short walk in each of the bedrooms watching them sleep, then disappeared in the same way he had come.

At the same time, Emma heard Allan grumble after Garvey about the light while Jocelyn started snoring.

"You couldn't have gone earlier?"

She realized he was talking about the toilet. *"It's now or never"*, she told herself. She got up quietly and headed for the room on tiptoe. Hearing noise again, Allan lit his bedside lamp.

"What now?", he said dryly.

"Ups, I mistook the room, sorry."

"That's OK. It's only the second time, after all!"

"No! Why do you say that?"

"You mistook it not five minutes ago."

"No, that's not true. You're mistaken."

"Where is she?" she thought.

"I could have sworn the contrary. It's nothing much, have a good night."

"You too, thank you", she said, shutting the door after her.

At that moment, an illumination came. He should never have

let it out of his hands. Seeing this, Garvey felt the need to return to the toilet. It was enough for Emma to understand.

Ouch! It was still there. But looking a little closer, he noticed a difference in the data he had entered. It couldn't be Emma, at least not now.

TEMPORAL ACCOMMODATIONS.

— "It's not in knowledge that happines
lies, but in the acquisition of knowledge."
Anatole France.

Auguste was making the last round for the night; likewise, he thought it would be useful to wake his surprise guests in passing, making sure they didn't forget themselves, and also to avoid problems with the management for having welcomed, in addition to Allan and Garvey people from outside the University without informing anyone.

He walked to the front door and knocked three times. Only Allan heard him. He got up quickly, his eyes still half closed, and opened the door a notch.

"Oh, it's you! Hello Auguste, what time is it?"

"It's 5:50, professor! It's the last time you'll see me today. You'd better get up and leave the rooms, because Christian's replacement will be here soon and he doesn't know you."

"How can I ever thank you for the great service you have rendered us? As soon as all of this ends, I'll explain everything, you deserve to know."

"Don't worry about it, leave the rooms as soon as possible.

For the moment, it's what I care about the most."

"Very well, my friend, we'll get on the move and thanks again, Auguste."

He went back to his station, watching the pavilion out of the corner of the eye. Half an hour passed and no one had come out. He decided to go back, taking care this time to take his universal key. Arrived at the door he knocked again, but without any answer. He tried a second time with the same result.

"If they had come out, I would have seen them" he thought.

So he decided to open the door and discovered an empty pavilion as if nobody had stayed there. He was helpless; questions were flowing in his head.

"Where are they? And yet, I watched the pavilion all this time!"

"Professor", he screamed, "hello!"

Intrigued, he looked in all the rooms so his conscience would be at peace.

"Hello", he continued, "anyone?"

Only silence answered him. He had to face facts, they had gone.

"Strange", he told himself, knowing it took about five minutes of leisurely walking to reach the main building or the exit. Furthermore, admitting that he hadn't seen them, Allan would never have passed his station without greeting him one last time. Expressing his incomprehension with a sigh, he came out, locked and returned to his post. On his way back, he glanced curiously at the window of Allan's room and noticed the light on.

"Damn that Allan!" he thought.

He still took his phone to check and dialed the room number. While Allan was lecturing Garvey about all these events, the phone rang out with all its sounds.

"I'm not done with you, young man, I'm going to answer that and I'll be back."

"No!", Garvey objected vigorously.

Certain it was Auguste calling, he didn't give him time to finish his sentence and promptly answered.

"Yes Auguste, it's only us, don't worry."

"I was sure of it, professor, but I had to check."

"I understand Auguste, you're only doing your job, and the University is in good hands with you, my friend."

"Thanks for the compliment. How much time are you staying this time?"

"How come, I don't understand, Auguste. What do you mean?"

"Just that your room was lit every other night and when I came after phoning in vain, there was no soul alive and even less light. Please tell me it was you!"

Understanding that it was Garvey, Allan took responsibility.

"Yes Auguste, and I apologize, but let me explain."

"No", he interrupted him, "I don't want to know anything! Avoid me only problems with you know whom, I don't ask more of you."

"As you wish. Just so you know, we won't be staying long and we'll leave as we arrived... discreetly."

"If you delay too much, you risk being seen."

"No, don't worry, no one will see us."

Auguste put his hand on his head before answering and sighing again, like a father would do with his son who causes all kinds of problems.

"Very well, professor. Good luck in what you do and in the future, warn me when you jump here."

"You're an angel, my friend, thank you again and see you soon."

"And, of course, I haven't seen you. Goodbye, professor."

But Auguste couldn't help but watch the windows of the room. Jocelyn, Emma and Hubert had stood in the back of the room to let Allan and Garvey have their talk. Watching them out of the corner of their eye, they evoked certain differences between their two worlds and Félix was fascinated by their conversation. Allan turned towards Garvey and resumed.

"I don't yet know what punishment I will inflict on you, but I'll make sure that in the future you don't do the opposite of what I tell you. For the moment, we must repair all the harm done, even if it doesn't bring back the poor Chinese man who fell on the wagon."

To that, Garvey lowered his eyes. He had heard about it in the news and was feeling a lot of guilt.

"Please, professor, I feel bad enough about it as it is."

"I know Garvey, but as the one in charge of you, I have to answer for you, so I'm just as responsible as you are. But, right now, the most important thing is to find a solution for all of this. We'll get back to this conversation once this is over. For starters, show me the box, please."

He took it in his hands, looked at it on all sides and was astonished at its simplicity.

"There are only two buttons! One for the date and the year, the other for the place and time. How could you reduce all the settings to two miserable buttons?"

Garvey didn't dare show how proud he was. He watched Allan's expression, apparently fascinated by the object.

"And this small LCD screen allows you to view the programming! It's amazing! And I guess that's where you put the 'Neutrinos' in question… You're a mule head… And you are prodigious."

Despite what he had said just before 'mule head', he became

again for the space of a few moments, the young Allan Thibault thirsty for crazy discoveries. Garvey noticed, but didn't say anything.

"How does it work, show me Garvey."

He took the box again, entered some data by pressing the first button, then pressed the second.

"There's something you need to know professor, everything is relative!"

"If this is really the case, I'll give you the opportunity to explain, but for now, show me."

Garvey complied.

"Is there anyone who isn't from here in this room?", he asked solemnly.

"There's Jocelyn… Hubert and Félix only move through time", Allan said seriously.

"They are from here?"

"Exactly."

"Did they tell you what happened to them?"

Allan told him their story in a few words. With this information, Garvey addressed Hubert.

"Do you remember what time it was when you disappeared with Félix?"

Taken aback by the question, Hubert interrupted his conversation with Jocelyn and Emma, then tried to answer with precision.

"It was about eleven o'clock, maybe a little less."

"That's when you were on the water? Had you been sailing for a long time?"

"For about an hour."

While questioning him, Garvey was pressing the buttons on his device.

"Does Félix know how to swim?"

"Why are you asking?"

"Because it's better that you reappear in the water rather than on the shore where you were."

"You mean to say we don't need to take the train anymore?"

"Exactly Hubert, are you ready?"

Hubert and Félix looked at each other. They were both happy and scared.

"Of course, Garvey, but we're going to fall in the water, if I understood correctly; and there will also be that tingling?"

"Yes, Hubert, you got it right!"

Hubert got down to his son's height for a moment.

"Are you OK with this, Félix, doesn't it scare you?"

"You're going to be there."

Hubert smiled and got up.

"It's OK, what must we do?"

"I'll open a breach here and you'll have a little less than ten seconds to enter. It will be like in the eel."

"Will we arrive in the water or on the water?"

"That, I cannot say. I think you'll be above."

Allan made big eyes and raised a problem.

"Tell me, Garvey, if they to arrive in the water and the breach doesn't close immediately, don't you think that we risk flooding this room and incidentally all those around us and on the ground floor?"

"How could I not have thought of this detail?"

"This detail", Allan exclaimed; "Garvey you're a genius, doubled with a mule head and a linnet head! From now on, I'm going to take things in hand. First of all, we will print on paper the notes we might need, which are stored in the calculator. So, we will not have to come back here and worry poor Auguste.

Now Garvey, I'm going to ask you to enter my home address in your device, because my wife must be worried and I want to reassure her first and foremost. As for you two", he continued, addressing Hubert and Félix, "we will go to a field in the suburbs. Is that OK with you?"

"Of course, professor. It will be an honor to meet Mrs. Thibault."

At that moment, Allan preferred not to answer, but thought nonetheless.

"That's it, if you're as excited after our passage, I'm the Beatles."

Allan often made puns and sometimes invented them. In his world, the Beatles had never been created, but there was a mystery there to be solved. With Garvey, they had often asked themselves this question during their research experiments.

"Are we capable of seeing elsewhere?"

Hubert wondered at the reaction of the old mad scientist and grew pensive for a moment.

Allan, in turn, perceived the astonishment hanging in Hubert's eyes and answered him in a tone of assured jest..

"Don't worry, she's only grumpy, but so delicate when she wants!"

Hubert and Félix showed a clear smile while looking at each other. Both had to see the same face in their intensely expressive gazes: that of a smiling Tiffany, but immediately replaced by the same image as a complementary backdrop, all the stress and anxiety she must have been feeling at that very moment.

"Don't worry, son", Hubert continued, showing his smile again, "we'll see her soon."

"I know, dad, and I'm not worried, you already talked to me about this!"

"Tell me, young Garvey", Allan said coming in front of him

and putting his right hand on his shoulder, "your device doesn't allow the arrival point to be at a different location from the initial departure point?"

"I don't really know, professor, I haven't tried it yet."

"Normally, all relativity issues should not occur since you haven't taken them into consideration."

"Yes, but it's not about that. The passage caused by this command is not what I expected."

"What's the problem, the 'Negative Matrix?'"

"You know…"

"I was making experiments well before you, so I'm listening!"

"Alright professor, there is actually this negative energy all around us inside the vortex. This keeps it open long enough for our passage and gives it a comfortable, but growing size because it's the only way to keep it open. The problem lies precisely with this movement. The bigger it gets, the less accurate it is."

"I see, I admit not having an answer at the moment, but we will think about the solution when we go back to the University."

"But you were saying…"

"Yes, Garvey, but let's not risk it. It's not about sending them back to be skinned in their world!"

"They're not risking anything at this level, professor."

"Maybe in the same world as is the case with Hubert and Félix, but for another world. The disturbance is more and more unstable at each opening. So, I suggest you check some calculations before sending our friend Jocelyn back to his world. Will you agree?"

"Of course, professor, you're absolutely right. We shouldn't send the image and sound separately!"

Allan turned abruptly, looking at him sternly.

"I'm sorry, professor", Garvey said like a penitent boy.

"Alright, as for you, Jocelyn, we'll go to the place where your cart is and we'll see how to send you home."

Jocelyn nodded his agreement and Emma was surprised that she was dreading that moment. Could she take it? Was she not going to crack at the last minute trying to hold him back? So many questions going round in her head. She loved him again, with a different love, of course, but she loved him.

Allan turned to Garvey.

"So, my young friend, are you ready?"

"Yes, professor, I'm waiting for the coordinates."

"You don't remember where I live?"

"Professor, I only came once to help you carry documents two years ago and I didn't stay because I was in a hurry! All I remember is the neighborhood."

"Well, your device does the 'Latitude-Longitude' conversion, doesn't it?"

"Yes, professor, that's right."

"Alright, then enter this: Boulevard Saint-Clair n°. 5, in Paris, of course. Perhaps it would be better to arrive in the garden at the back of the house, otherwise my wife might have a heart attack! Can you do that?"

"Now, yes."

"What do you mean by that?"

"I'll tell you about it professor, you'll be fascinated, I'm sure! But we don't have much time ahead of us."

"For once, you're right, let's do that."

Surprised by the steadiness of his student, Allan smiled and continued.

"You see Garvey, when you want, you think!"

Garvey saw that it was a clumsy maneuver to assert his status as a wise old man. He entered all the information in his box

205

and was ready for the transfer.

"I'm ready", he said, seriously. Seeing them look at each other, he added:

"It will have the same effect as the passage from the eel to here! Can we go?"

Allan had trouble admitting it, but he admired his teaching assistant. He made a quick tour of the different expressions on all present faces and said solemnly, majestically raising his right hand like a tenor...

"Come on, young man, create a miracle!"

Garvey executed and created a new breach. Another vague landscape could be distinguished inside. It surprised Jocelyn who had already noticed it during the previous trip, but he had preferred to keep quiet, so as not to disturb Garvey, nor his scientific tutor.

"For how long will it stay open?"Allan asked.

"I can open and close it at will", Garvey answered, modestly.

"Really?"

Allan looked at him with an ounce of pride in his eyes, as if to say:

"It's me who formed him!"

Auguste, who was still watching the room, regularly glancing at it, suddenly saw the light go out and another whiter light appear, trembling, disappearing fifteen seconds after his appearance. He tried to understand for a few moments, then went back to his flask of whiskey, because serious as he was in his work, he was also a former alcoholic and didn't hesitate to take a sip when the need felt itself known. He didn't get drunk, but it was a happy medium he had set for himself, that was his way of being reasonable.

"Don't do anything stupid, professor Thibault", he thought.

The room had fallen back into darkness and no longer showed any signs of life. Jean-Claude, Christian's replacement, arrived.

"Hello, Auguste."

"Hello, Jean-Claude, how are you today?"

"Excellent, thank you. And you, any problems last night?"

Auguste smiled reassuringly.

"No, nothing to signal, I could have fallen asleep! Here are the first arrivals, I leave you to your sad fate, dear colleague. Have a good day, see you tomorrow."

"Thank you, to you also Auguste, or rather good night."

"That won't be too difficult, to go to sleep. I'm going; see you tonight."

Auguste took some things, then went on foot, with a bag on his shoulder. He didn't realize it, but there was a man hidden in the park near the university who was watching him without following him.

TIME CONNECTIONS.

— *"Having a body is the great threat to the spirit."*
Marcel Proust.

Allan was one of the lucky inhabitants of his neighborhood, because he had a 'usable' space with small shrubs, and a variety of different flowers that Damiana, his wife, took pleasure in cultivating and arranging. The walls encircling the place were adorned with climbing plants and this little piece of paradise of half a hectare where one could easily hide from indirect glances, was the ideal place to 'appear'.

The first to arrive was Jocelyn, then came Emma's turn, who arrived directly in his arms. Shortly afterwards came Hubert and Félix, followed by Allan and Garvey to close the ride and immediately activated his box to close the breach. Emma was still in Jocelyn's arms and seemed to feel great pleasure in being there. Noticing, Allan wanted to tease them.

"You never miss a chance, you two!"

Caught in the act like two toddlers who had just caused a disaster, they separated immediately, probably guilty of being good together and braving there the worst of taboos.

Allan laughed heartily, regardless of how early it was.

"You're two teenagers!"

The two lovebirds looked at each other furtively, not even daring to speak.

"What do we do now, professor?", Félix asked.

"Now, I'll go wake my wife and try to find the right words to explain the story of the past three days. So sit on these benches, I won't be long."

Suddenly, a desperado-like female voice came to interrupt them.

"Don't bat an eyelash or I'll be happy to ventilate your spirit!"

Armed with a hunting rifle, Damiana didn't immediately recognize her husband's back, who was finishing his sentence and was about to head inwards. Impressed by the lady's determination, no one except Allan had the guts to answer.

"I forgot to tell you about her character! Especially when you disturb her sleep!"

He slowly turned around with his hands raised, in a burst of humor.

"I beg you sweetness", that was the pet name he had given her, "when I told you I wanted to spend the rest of my life with you, I was serious!"

"Allan!", she exclaimed, her eyes rounding.

Listening only to her heart, she threw the rifle to the ground and ran to him to kiss him and show him all the distress she had felt in the past forty-eight hours. But in the heat of the moment, when the rifle hit the slabs that formed a path that then went to different parts of the small city forest, the shot went off surprising everyone, as well as a few neighbors around, making them jump in their beds. Some even went to their windows to try to see something.

"Sweetness, pay attention, it's not a toy and you could have hurt someone doing what you did!"

At the same time surprised, frightened and confused of her thoughtless gesture, she couldn't find the words to express her dismay, because the rifle she had was actually a trick to dissuade potential visitors. Weapons were repugnant to her and she was afraid of them, especially when one pressed the trigger. Had she known it was loaded, she would never have taken it in hand.

Everyone had been surprised, with the exception of Félix, who was smiling, seeing the poor lady caught in her own trap.

"She's flipped, Mamie Nova", Jocelyn thought.

"One must not oppose this nice, gentle lady" , Hubert said.

"I'm going to help you, you need it" thought Garvey, adopting a transcendent attitude for a few seconds.

Emma felt caring.

"She must have been really scared to react so violently! What would I do if something happened to Jocelyn?"

She looked at him briefly, then changed her mind.

"For a nice old science teacher supposed to have a peaceful life, I go through time breaches and my wife shots everything that moves", Allan thought in his mind.

After being surprising and almost dramatic, this situation looked a little funny. Overwhelmed by emotion, she managed to apologize and gradually recovered her wits by machine-gunning questions.

"Where have you been? What happened to you? Are you alright? Who are these people? Where did you go? Why are you here so early?"

Allan didn't even have time to answer that the next question came.

"Let's go in", he said, "it will be easier to talk inside."

Looking at her surprise guests, she wanted to rectify the

situation.

"Pardon this welcome, but we had an intruder some time back. Please do come in, I'll prepare breakfast."

Then she approached the boy like a loving grandmother.

"I didn't scare you too much with my clumsiness, did I?"

Having been rather amused by the situation, Félix laughed heartily.

"No, madam, it was great!"

The little man definitely relaxed the atmosphere with his reaction.

"He's cute. Is he yours?", she asked, looking at Hubert.

"Yes", he answered. "and we're very proud!"

"It's strange, your face seems familiar. Haven't we already met in the past?"

Hubert didn't have time to answer, Damiana continued in the same stride.

"Yes, that's it! I saw you on the videophone last night and you… disappeared!"

"Sweetness", Allan interrupted, "we'll tell you all about it, I'm coming with you to the kitchen to prepare the coffee."

Before leaving, she looked at Jocelyn and Emma.

"I'm happy to see you two again, but I thought you were divorced and I understood that you could only come this afternoon. Well, it doesn't matter, now you're here and you can tell me all about what you did in the last five years."

Emma and Jocelyn looked at each other, a little worried.

"What will we be able to say."

The old couple headed towards the kitchen, while the five guests waited patiently and comfortably on the upholstered fabric chairs in the living room. While waiting, they looked all over the big room. There was beautiful furniture of a rustic style, but indefinable. The decor was basic and discreet. The few frames affixed to the walls, as well as the photographs of the couple and their children, could be counted on the fingers of one hand. Still, Allan's three diplomas, which proudly stood on a splendid dresser in the back of the room and were beautifully framed in wood and gold, were exceptions to the rest of the room.

As for Garvey, he was scrutinizing the garden, admirably arranged in his eyes. Something stunned him; he could not put his finger on it, but it emanated from those little shrubs, flowers and other plants, an indescribable serenity. Much more than admiration, he felt an uncontrollable fascination. Like guardians, the trees seemed to watch over the house. Jocelyn noticed Garvey's interest in the green space.

"Wonderful, isn't it?"

But Garvey seemed literally absorbed and obviously didn't hear anything he was being told. Jocelyn, who in these cases didn't get upset or even resentful, answered himself.

"Yes, I'm absolutely right, this garden is beautiful, a treat for the eyes!"

Hubert, Emma and Félix smiled of this good-natured simplicity. Also amused by what he had heard, Garvey got out of his silence.

"I'm sorry Jocelyn, my mind was elsewhere."

"Don't worry about it, Garvey, in these times, having your mind elsewhere is normal! For my part, I'm better than you are right now. Not only do I have my mind elsewhere, my body also followed! Had I only had this problem, I admit that knowing that 'I' had to come this afternoon makes me ask myself three thousand questions a minute. I think it's all starting to scare me."

"Don't worry, Joss, we'll come up with something."

"It's not that I'm worried about, it's to see myself in the flesh in the body of another person. I wonder what my reaction will be!"

At those words, Emma had a twinkle in her eyes.

"What are you thinking about?", Jocelyn continued.

"I'm wondering the same thing you are!"

Félix looked at his father.

"I don't understand anything, dad, what are they saying?"

"I doubt you would be able to understand, son, but apparently, there are many other ways to travel, as we did in the float. Destinations may vary and bring us to places where we could meet people like us."

"Like twins?"

"Yes, like twins."

"And us, will we see us?"

"No, for we are still in the same place."

"But we're not, we're not on the lake anymore."

"The place I'm referring to is 'Our world', we are still in our world."

Seeing that Hubert was having a hard time, Jocelyn came to the rescue.

"Remember what I was telling you yesterday in the car."

"You told me your name was neither 'Damn', nor 'Capish', nor 'Boss'."

Emma smiled.

"Yes, but before that."

"That you were an alien."

"Exactly, Félix."

"You were saying you come from another world."

"Another dimension, more exactly. Same world, another

dimension, you understand?"

"Then you are an alien!"

"No, Félix, an alien is outside the Earth, and therefore, nothing of a human, this is not my case. As for you, you only changed places in the same dimension."

"I didn't understand anything!"

Garvey was amused by the situation and Jocelyn noticed.

"Say Garvey, after all, you're the scientist here; why don't you give it a try?"

Garvey looked at Félix for a few moments, then got up and went into the garden.

"It's really higher spirits, that", "Jocelyn said in a tone of exasperation, "you ask them something and they go away!"

Félix seemed thoughtful and calm, much more than usual. He looked Jocelyn in the eyes and said in a serene voice.

"You'll go back to your world, Jocelyn, but you won't find your life again!"

At that moment, everyone was silent and was watching the boy with concern.

"What did you say?", Jocelyn asked, surprised by his words.

"You understood very well and you're going to like it!"

His manner of talking had changed. It was that of a grown-up adult, in the body of a child, with his little boyish voice. It almost sent shivers down the spine to see such assurance emanate from that little human.

Hubert immediately directed his attention towards Garvey...
"What did you do to my son?"

He was watching Garvey standing with his hands behind his back in the garden. He seemed to meditate or chat with the clouds. Hubert refrained from getting up from his chair to ask an explanation of the young mad scientist who was becoming more and more strange.

"What's happening here?"

Allan came back with a small basket filled with pastries.

"What's Garvey doing in the garden?"

To his great surprise, it was Félix who answered, and it was in the same tone he had used with Jocelyn.

"He's meditating, professor, he's meditating."

Allan cast a suspicious glance at Hubert, who turned his head toward the garden, pointing to Garvey as the one person responsible for the metamorphosis.

Damiana arrived with a tray of coffee, sugar, cups and a jug of water. She put everything on the table, inviting everyone to serve. She took a seat herself, and noticed Garvey who still hadn't moved from his place. She wanted to call out to him, and when she opened her mouth to call, everyone could hear.

"I'm coming!"

Astonished at this readiness at the limit of clairvoyance, everyone kept silent.

Damiana now received her guests with dignity, without a rifle; she made a brief conversation with everyone, throwing a furtive eye at the strange Garvey from time to time. She turned to her husband and told him of her impressions.

"This is the young boy with whom you came two years ago, isnt' he?"

"Yes, it's him. You have a good memory, especially as he hasn't stayed for more than five minutes."

"It's true, but he has a head one doesn't forget. But today I find him strange, what is he doing there, all alone?"

"I don't know sweetness, but it has lasted long enough and I'll go see what he's up to."

Allan went out and when he turned his back, Garvey seemed

to sense his arrival and turned in his direction even before he had time to put a foot on the gravel part of the door step, likely to announce his progress by the sound of his footsteps. Surprised, Allan stopped short, looking at him strangely.

"I'm coming, professor", he said simply, smiling. Allan remained speechless, stunned with astonishment.

"You're starting to scare me, my young friend", he thought . By the time he reached Garvey, the latter stopped him in his tracks for good.

"Don't be afraid professor, I'll explain everything in due time!"

The two men returned to the living room and settled down again. As he sat down, Garvey exchanged a knowing glance with Félix. Seeing the exchange, and eager to break this atmosphere of suspicion, Damiana asked for an explanation on their presence.

"Allan told me something extravagant earlier in the kitchen."

She looked at Hubert.

"And you, what planet do you come from?"

Assisted by Garvey, Allan spent the next hour explaining their mishaps, like Félix who had understood in record time the root of the problem. Garvey, on his part, didn't even try to do with Damiana what he had done with Félix. Not that she wouldn't understand, but there was now between him and Félix a unique connection.

Damiana was stunned by what she had just learned. If someone other than Allan had told her such a story, she would never have believed it. Still, she only knew their adventures, but just like her husband, Emma, Jocelyn and Hubert, she didn't know everything, the 'big part' still remained to come.

ACCELERATED LEARNING.

— *"What an hour brings,*
a century cannot give."
Horace Nelson.

She scanned all the faces present and stopped on Emma's.
"You, I know; we have already met with Jocelyn, well,
I meant to say... You understand, don't you?"
"Yes, Madam Thibault."
Then came Jocelyn's turn.
"Wasn't it you I was expecting this afternoon?"
"No, ma'am, it's the first time we see each other."
And finally, Hubert and Félix.
"And you two? You arrived here with your float from Italy?"
"Yes, ma'am", Félix answered, still very serious.
Hubert looked at him for a brief second, then looked at
Damiana again.
"It's like he said, ma'am!"
"And you've all come here with the help of this little device
that Garvey made?"
Allan noticed that she was not in her normal state, and spoke.
"Garvey will give you a demonstration my angel, so you'll see.
Garvey, please!"

He watched for a moment the stunned lady and operated his box announcing what he was going to do.

"I'll disappear and reappear before your eyes, it will only take a few seconds. Are you ready?"

"I don't just want to see it, I want to do it with you!"

Allan strongly objected.

"No, sweetness, don't do it!"

"And why not? Do you think I will let such a phenomenon take place before my eyes without taking a closer look at it? I want to do it; whether you agree or not!"

"Her character remains well beyond her awakening!" Jocelyn thought.

"Do it gently", Allan ordered.

"Don't worry, I know what to do."

He set his box on the year 4657 and scheduled an arrival forty-eight hours before their departure. So that for everyone, their absence lasted only three seconds, but the reality was quite different. When they reappeared, Damiana was no longer the same. She stared at Félix and smiled a smile that the boy simply returned to her on the same wavelength. Seeing the change, Allan panicked, approached her and took her in his arms.

"My angel, are you ok?"

She smiled the same way and kissed him greedily in front of everyone.

"Damiana, what's wrong? What happened?"

Circling his neck with her arms, she simply replied.

"It's wonderful, Allan, we must continue!"

He didn't understand anything, just like the others.

"What must we continue?"

"Our evolution, Allan, our evolution."

"What? What evolution?"

"I told you, Allan, ours! We live in a virtual world Allan, we veil our faces, but the day we'll open our eyes, everything will change."

He looked at Garvey anxiously, then resigned himself, exhausted.

"If you say so, my angel!"

He moved away from his wife to go and collect himself alone in the garden and in passing, he heard the voice of young Félix.

"She's right, professor."

He paused for a moment, studying him, then resumed his desperate walk, lost in thought, wondering if he was losing his beloved. He walked nonchalantly, sadly, bearing on his shoulders the weight of all the misery of his world.

"What's happening here?" he told himself. *"Are these the first fruits of madness?"*

Damiana joined him.

"No, my darling, they are the first fruits of the evolution of man!"

Almost scared by his wife, he responded with a surge of courage.

"You're saying…"

She interrupted him and continued in his place.

"Yes, it's what I'm doing and we can all do it."

Allan didn't understand anything; she looked at her like never before. In his eyes there was mistrust, fear.

"I admit all of this scares me a little. Will you tell me where you went?"

"You'll be the first person to whom I'll tell, but not right now, we have to take care of Hubert and Félix."

"I'm the scientist of the group and it's you who tells me what to do! Well, go ahead, I'll tell them goodbye."

Garvey and Damiana advanced towards them to announce. Seeing that, Jocelyn and Emma got close.

"Well then", Jocelyn said, "everything comes to those who wait. It was nice to travel with you, especially with you, rascal!"

He took a beautiful pendant from his neck that he had offered himself in a key moment of his life and knelt in front of the child.

"Here Félix, it's for you", Jocelyn put it around his neck.

Surprised, Félix was silent for a few moments.

"What is it?"

"A souvenir from another world, little one; my world!"

"Why?"

"Crooked atom, quite simply..."

The child carefully scrutinized every detail of the pendant and returned to the organized lethargy. Joss waited a moment before continuing.

"Do you like it?"

Impassive, the child continued to study the object with great attention.

"You've never seen one like it, right?"

"That's it!", Félix said suddenly, like a research scientist who had put his finger on the solution to an enigma!

Hubert got worried.

"What is it, son?"

Félix stared at his father with some intensity.

"That's what I want, dad."

"You want to make medallions?"

"Dad..."

"I know, my son, I understood, I'm afraid."

The expression on the child's face was different, more confident. Like an adult, he had made a decision, the one who was going to change his future. Félix had surely changed in his behavior, but he still didn't have his words with him and answered in a tongue-in-cheek way.

"I also appreciate 'Boss Capich'!"

It had the advantage of relaxing the atmosphere and Hubert messed the little man's hair with a certain pride.

"Happy to have known you, we could probably follow the progress of your actions on the videophone! Be careful. And while I think about it, here is our contact information, this is my business card."

"Your business card? You don't waste chances, do you! But I don't know if my phone will want to go through time."

"To be honest, right now, we kind of lost it a little", he joked. And as for the doors, only the ones we do not explore remain closed."

Jocelyn smiled, assessed the card and began to read aloud.

"Hubert Doran, travel agency manager 'Paradise'. Of course you are!   So, you want to make me travel in the fourth dimension!"

"That's an idea to explore. But I think you already travel enough with your job. I just won't be opposed to the idea of being in touch, I like you. Anyway, even in temporal or interdimensional travel, we can meet interesting people!"

Jocelyn was stopped by the boy who was watching him intently. He seemed to want to say something, but didn't. Feeling the weight of this insistent gaze weighing on him, he did the same for a second or two. They exchanged a smile, then he resumed his conversation with Hubert.

"I'm convinced", Jocelyn said.

He looked at the card again, put it in his back pocket and continued.

"Hubert Doran". He looked up and stared at him, "we'll think about you, Mr. Doran, give us a call after you reunite with your wife."

Hubert gave him a friendly hug.

"I sure will 'Joss Damn'!"

"I can see Félix really is your son!"

Then came Emma's turn, which was entitled to the same favor. In doing so, he slipped a message into her ear.

"Don't make the same mistake with him."

She looked at him smiling.

"Thank you, Hubert."

Then she got down to Félix's level and kissed him on the cheek.

"Good bye, little man, maybe we'll see each other again?"

"No Emma, that won't happen!"

Surprised, she looked at him questioningly. Allan and Damiana were also entitled to goodbyes in their own right.

"What an adventure, professor!"

"Quite so! Take care of yourself, my friend. What will you say about the float?"

"Don't worry about it, professor, I'll think of something!"

"Good bye, big little man", Allan told Félix, "and never disappoint yourself!"

He looked at him with great intensity and held out his hand.

"Well, look at that, just like a grown up!"

'Big little man' remained unperturbed. Allan held out his hand as well. The roles were reversed. He felt like a clumsy boy with him since his 'Mental Metamorphosis'. Everything he said always fell flat; he thought more than he normally would have done before speaking, like a student who wanted to give the right answer to his schoolmaster, and it was starting to frustrate him a little. While they were shaking hands, Allan thought:

"If I don't ask him now, I'll never know the motive and especially the how of this radical change."

Like Emma, he got down to his level, not to give him a kiss, but to satisfy his curiosity by speaking softly to him, not to be heard by anyone, knowing that he would be understood, he went straight to the goal.

"Tell me, Félix…"

He got closer to Allan ear.

"It's pointless, professor, you already know, but you don't know that you know!"

"And I presume it will come to me without asking?"

Félix didn't answer and only smiled. Allan let it go in the end.

"Have a safe journey, little one."

While his son was talking to Allan, Hubert greeted Damiana who had told her good news about Félix. Presently, Hubert was reassured and proud of his son. She went towards 'Einstein Junior', showing a wide smile. She also stood at the same level as him and took him in her arms.

"Thank you, Félix, with all of my heart."

Having become an adept of speechless language, he again, for an answer, simply smiled.

"I hope we'll see each other again soon", she continued.

"Yes, Madam Thibault, do hope!"

"You're cute. Now go and find your mother who is worried."

Félix joined his father who was waiting for him with Garvey.

"Are you ready?", he said pressing the keys of his box.

"Yes, Garvey", Hubert answered, looking at the "little prodigy" with the loving eyes of the father he was.

"OK", continued the young scientist, "I'll accompany you in case I make a mistake."

Hubert and Félix waved to everyone once again, then a breach within which one could distinguish the 'Timeless Disorder' opened. All three were engulfed in it, then disappeared completely. The breach closed in the same way a few seconds later. Everyone was watching the happening, somewhat fascinated by this magic. Returning to his wife's changed behavior, Allan thought:

"Maybe it's not such a bad thing after all?"

Similarly, Emma, on the other hand, was rather satisfied.

"That's what sent me my new Jocelyn!" No one saw her, but her eyes were shining.

Jocelyn was also thinking.

"And to think that the situation in which find I myself I owe to that thing! But I have to admit that it's worth a thousand times the internet when it comes to connecting people!"

As for Damiana, it was much more solemn.

"Without that, I would never have known what I now know."

They were all four planted there, having concretely appreciated the phenomenon at its fair value as privileged spectators, lost in their thoughts and feeling to a greater or lesser degree, a feeling of lacking something. These two days that had been a little crazy, lived alongside this dad with his little boy, arrived on the road riding in a boat, had marked them and they were already regretting not remembering after all the gaps would close again.

As was his habit, Allan had entered a new phase of long reflection and suddenly understood something essential: the surrounding waves had been disturbed by all these breaches that didn't just let human bodies or water or vehicles pass.

"Yes, that's it" he thought *"everything is just waves. They took advantage of openings to mix with those already present in each world.*

Little Félix, as well as Damiana and the others, were unknowingly in constant contact with their respective double, who must have also had unusual feelings. That was why he wasn't truly himself. No matter what, everything should be in order for them when everything would be over. The strangest thing is that Hubert and I didn't experience these interferences. Maybe our doubles are dead. Garvey must have discovered it, I'm sure."

Meanwhile, Hubert, Félix and Garvey had arrived at their destination, or rather, 'Elsewhere'.

THE BENEFITS OF THE UNIVERSE.

—*"Write the joyful song of healing,
the precious song of deliverance. This
is how you'll remember your future."*
Winston Churchill.

The landscape had nothing in common with that of the 'Lake St. Cross' in Italy. Hubert and Félix had noticed, but maybe they had landed not far from the lake in a place they hadn't seen. Seeing them looking for a landmark, Garvey told them.

"Don't look for something familiar, we're not in Italy."

Félix stared at Garvey and immediately made big eyes as he glanced at his father. Noticing it, Hubert questioned him with his eyes.

"Look", resumed Garvey "and most of all, don't intervene, because you could trigger a series of disasters. Just tell yourselves there is a good reason for our coming here."

At that moment a big luxury sedan-like vehicle came, driven by his eldest son, dead in this world in a terrible car accident a few years ago. His father, as his younger brother were shocked by this vision. It was eight o'clock in the morning and Hubert could see his disappeared son in the flesh getting off the vehicle and going to work. The emotion took over and Hubert, as well as like Félix couldn't contain a tear that escaped from a well-anchored sorrow deep inside.

"Why show us this?", Hubert said, shaken.

"Because it's going to help you", Garvey said; "I know that for you the urge to go hug him must be great, but you will have to override your feelings this time."

"You think it gives me some comfort to see him there, like that, as alive as he will never be again?"

"But, of course!"

"How can you say such a thing?"

"Because in this world, you and your wife died, and your two children were taken by a foster family. Furthermore, you will know from now on that somewhere he still lives, with the responsibility of his younger brother Félix certainly, but he lives!"

"We died, you say?"

"For him, yes; in this world, you are dead. But imagine for a second what he would experience, just like the young Félix of this dimension, if he knew that you too are alive somewhere?"

This simple remark made him think so much that he began an 'Express Psychotherapy' in his head. After all, he was there, right under their eyes and well alive. For sure, he had to get used to the idea of not seeing him again, but luck offered him the ultimate opportunity to find that he was not quite dead. And even if that feeling of lack still persisted, they had had the opportunity to see him again. Could we say life wasn't just? No, on the contrary, it was just a question of balance.

Félix apparently had more ease in dealing with the shock. But this meeting, or better said, this vision, was going to change their point of view entirely. Hubert couldn't take his eyes off his other son.

"Live your life, my son", he thought *"Now I'll know that, somewhere, you're happy."*

A tear was rolling down his cheek, but it wasn't a tear of distress, but rather of hope. Félix was equally moved, but these voyages, as well as the knowledge he had gained, helped him to take the necessary distance so as not to sink into deep sorrow, for now, he dreaded things differently. Hubert looked at Félix and spoke from the heart.

"You're right, son, we're very lucky. An opportunity like this won't happen again soon."

In that moment, Félix became thoughtful…

He then turned to Garvey to express his gratitude.

"Thank you from the bottom of my heart, Garvey! Your device doesn't only cause disasters, it also saves lives."

"I knew you would be convinced and that finally you would come out happy! Shall we go?"

"Wait another minute, please, let me enjoy these magical moments. You don't know what the death of a child causes for parents."

"That's true, but Jocelyn will never have this chance in his world."

"He cannot?"

"No matter, the thing is he will never know the birth of a child. That said, nothing is written; everything can still change from one moment to another, without warning. All depends on what we decide to do…"

"I understand; and how do you know about Jocelyn, did he tell you?"

"Let's just say I found out in my own way."

"I see, you saw him while he was with us!"

"In our time, Hubert, he is here with us and has adapted to our vibrations, but there, they are different. He has become his own double, in a way. You understand?"

"I admit that this... But I will think about it."

"You won't be able to. Or rather, yes; in your unconscious... Well, we have to go now. Come, come!"

Hubert couldn't. It was impossible to bring himself to stop looking at his son.

"Hubert, let's go! You don't have your oldest anymore, but your youngest is waiting."

"I only ask for ten more seconds, ten more miserable seconds, Garvey, please."

"Alright, OK, but not longer, because I gave you this opportunity to help with your mourning, not for a relapse. And that's exactly what will happen if you stay too long, you're going to want to get him back, which is normal somewhat, but unhealthy for everyone."

"You're right, but still, there's something that escapes me. How do you know of his existence since I haven't told anyone?"

Garvey stared at him for a second; but preferring not to embark on an interminable explanation, he opted for a satisfactory answer.

"You said it yourself just now Hubert", he replied, putting his breach box maker forward, "this device doesn't only cause disaster, it also does good deeds. There are many things that escape us in this world, as well as in others! But there are some where there are people who are very... how to say it... different, people who react in the opposite way to us. That is to say, to whom nothing escapes, on the contrary, they are the ones who escape their world!"

Thinking he hadn't finished his explanation, Hubert was

waiting for the rest. Then, seeing he hadn't said anything, was surprised.

"You're done?"

"Yes, Hubert, I'm done."

"Don't hold it against me, but I didn't understand anything and I imagine I'm going to have to be OK with that?"

"You got it, Hubert!"

"Well, in that case, I won't insist and if we have to go, so be it."

Then he put a friendly hand on his shoulder before continuing.

"You have reached your goal by leading us here and I will be forever grateful."

In that moment, Garvey had an amused thought...

"Since I tell you, you won't remember anything!"

"It's a shame my wife, Tiffany, couldn't enjoy this opportunity, but I'm sure that now I'll find the words to comfort her. Thank you again Garvey, and continue to disobey your professor!"

"Don't mention it Hubert, it would have been a shame if I hadn't done it, since I created the possibility! I will accompany you now?"

Hubert looked one last time at the building where his beloved child was working in, taking Félix's hand.

"Goodbye, my son, we'll always love you."

"I'm opening the breach; come!", Garvey said.

Everyone went inside and ended up at the 'Lake St. Cross' in Italy. Hubert and Félix looked at the landscape and said,

"It worked! We're back!"

"You musn't speak too loud here", Garvey said.

"Why?"

"Because we came back ten minutes before you disappeared and you are currently on the lake where you are going to sink shortly. You'll have to dive again and join your wife."

"You hear that, son?", he said, impressed. "Your mother will only worry for a few minutes. We'll leave here and we'll only have a hundred meters to swim. It's phenomenal! But you haven't told anyone", he remarked.

"Exactly, you have a sense of observation, Hubert"

"May I ask why you kept it silent from everyone, but not to us?"

"Yes, of course."

He let some seconds go by without saying anything.

"Garvey!"

"Yes, Hubert?"

"Well, I asked you a question!"

"I know…"

"You don't want to answer?"

"I did!"

"Come on, Garvey, what are you playing at?"

"I'm not playing, Hubert, you asked me if you could know why and I said yes!"

"I understood, it's really funny and I'm hilarious! Now tell me why, please!"

"Why "?

"Garvey, please, stop being a clown!"

"I was asking why you want to know."

"Alright, never mind, let it be!"

"Anyway, you would have forgotten it in ten minutes".

"I just wanted to know the reason for this difference."

"There isn't one!"

"I don't understand."

"You came back home, just like the driver you crossed."

"Sorry?"

"Yes, don't you remember? This means that by returning to your dimension, the same goes for this driver. It's what I call 'The balancing effect.'"

"If we hadn't crossed him, he would still be in the same point, then?"

"That's right."

"But we didn't cross him in this voyage, did we?"

"It's normal, we're a little advanced on time. He will find himself on the road where he was driving before 'falling into the water' and he will not realize or remember anything, since all this will never have happened..."

Hubert looked at Félix from time to time to see his reactions, who didn't seem particularly surprised by what the fearless scientist explained. Then, he looked at Garvey again to ask for a clarification.

"Tell me Garvey, this sudden change in Félix..."

He interrupted his momentum and reassured him.

"He received much information at once and this explains, in part, his behavior; but all that will soon fade, he'll become the little boy you've always known, for in the ten minutes to come, he won't remember anything, just like you, Hubert! You will only remember having been overthrown."

At that moment, Hubert showed some disappointment.

"And what you showed us in the other dimension?"

"The same! And it's normal, since when that breach will close, it will mean that you have never lived that adventure. But if this can reassure you, the human brain stores everything that it has seen and heard and you will never really lose it."

Resigned and sorry to hear such news, Hubert asked one last question.

"What is the other explanation about my son's behavior?"

Garvey looked at him solemnly.

"Your son is an 'Indigo'."

Having misunderstood, Hubert felt touched in his heart, as well as in his pride. He then had a strong reaction by strafing his eyes like a soldier in battle.

"I'm sorry; my son a fool?"

Amused, Garvey went for a rectification.

"Hubert, I..."

Exasperated by what he had interpreted, he didn't even give him a chance to explain himself.

"Shut up! Telling me such a thing about 'MY SON' after what you showed us, takes the cake! I know he sometimes happens to be on his own planet, but then, to treat him as a fool looking me in the eye!"

In his pleading of a protective father, he consoled his son with a look and saw, to his great surprise that he was smiling.

"Son", he fiercely continued, "you don't have to smile when someone disrespects you this way!"

"Listen to him, dad, really listen."

Stopped in his tracks and somewhat disconcerted, Hubert calmed down and let Garvey continue.

"Very well, obviously, something escapes me, keep going!"

"Read my lips, if necessary! I didn't say 'FOOL', but 'IN-DIGO'[3]."

"What's that? A new way of qualifying people who don't fit into the mold?"

"No Hubert, the Beings 'Indigo' don't know what they are. They realize it with time, growing up without being able to put a qualifier such as this one, but feeling different from those that

---

[3] Word play in French – "nigaud" / "indigo"

surround them. Furthermore, they really are different. Félix has always gone in his own rhythm, hasn't he?"

The boy remained impassive, took out his cell phone and began to press the keys. Hubert eyed his son for a few moments. He was concentrated on what he was doing.

"We talk about him, and what does he do, he types a message!" Hubert told himself, disoriented by the child's behavior. *"What is he writing? Joss C... Why is he writing that on his phone?"*

Hubert suddenly understood the approach of the little prodigy who had become apprentice genius.

"He wants to remember! You're really smart, my son!"

Garvey saw Hubert watching his son with compassion and was still waiting for his answer.

"Hubert? Are you still with me?"

"Yes, I'm sorry. What were you saying?"

"I was telling you about the rhythm."

"Yes, it's true he's out of it often, as you can now see, but..."

"Curious about everything, and yet impassive?"

"Yes, that's right. Since he was very little."

"You've often been told that he has a psychological problem. Whereas in comparison it's not him, but those who tell him that have one. They don't understand and they probably never will. Félix has some mental gates that open more easily than average. He is able to understand everything a quarter turn, much faster than anyone."

"So, Indigo Beings are geniuses who ignore others, if I understand what you're saying?"

"I would rather say people normally formed in a world of 'spiritual loafers'. The indigos don't allow their minds to be polluted with the failures of life. They may be turbulent at the beginning of their existence, the time it takes to adapt, but often become men or women dreadfully strong and wise."

"When you say strong, you mean physically?"

"Not quite, Hubert. But in this world, someone who is able to walk in the minds of the people he meets throughout his life is elusive; I will say even indestructible."

"I see, my boy is an alien altogether!"

At that moment, Garvey smiled evocatively.

"We could almost define him like that, Hubert."

"But 'Indigo' is a color!"

"Right, Hubert."

"What do you mean, right? Hey, what are you doing?"

"He won't leave me like this, right?" he told himself seeing Garvey leave.

"Garvey! Garvey!"

"Dad, let him; the breach could close."

Either way, he wouldn't have said anymore; he turned around and headed for the breach, waving goodbye. Surprised, Hubert tried, in vain, to know more.

"Wait! Don't go! I didn't understand what you said."

"Goodybe Hubert, goodbye Félix may all three of you have a nice life!"

Garvey continued to advance towards the breach, went in and disappeared with it. Hubert was still trying to understand, a little worried.

"An indigo! What's that?"

The breach closed, the memories of the past few days were slowly fading away, one by one.

"Let's get into the water before we forget what we're doing here", Hubert said, taking Félix by the hand.

"To say that if we meet him again we won't even remember him, it's extraordinary, but whether he likes it or not, we have indeed experienced this story!"

"What are you talking about, dad?", said Félix, who no longer remembered their misadventure.

"Well, I'm talking about... about..."

He hesitated a few moments and then recovered.

"I don't remember what I wanted to say, son, not even what I was saying. Strange! Come, let's go back to your mother, maybe it will come to us while swimming."

Suddenly, cries of panic sprang from the water and from Tiffany.

"Look, dad, the float came back!"

"I'll say, it's true! We must be really under shock not to remember!", Hubert thought.

"Come Félix, let's go reassure your mother..."

METAMORPHOSIS.

— *"Must we really marry the situation?*
Yes, but with all due seriousness."
Simone Weil.

In the Parisian house, everyone had resettled around the living room table and re-served while continuing to talk about parallel worlds and other breaches. For them, it was only a few minutes ago that Garvey, Hubert and Félix had gone. While they were still stirring their cup of coffee for some and chocolate for others, a gap opened in the garden, delivering the young physicist alone.

He could have reappeared instantly, but he had chosen to do this to avoid unnecessary questions. Everyone stopped to observe the phenomenon which, even if it became familiar, still remained an extraordinary sight to behold.

"Ah! Here you are already!", Allan said.

In a hurry to fix an error, Garvey was ready to leave.

"Yes", he answered; "and I'm now going to take care of the most urgent cases. As for you Jocelyn, you'll go back last since you know where you are and what happened to you. This is not the case for other people who have been victims of my invention."

"I understand", Jocelyn answered, "do what you have to do, I'm no longer an hour away, anyway."

With these words, Emma looked at him sadly.

"I have to do something", she thought. Then, she stared at one of the surviving cookies next to her bowl of chocolate.

"So come sit with us for five minutes, my young friend, and have a cup of good German coffee that my wife prepared. Your rescues may well wait three minutes, don't you think?"

Jocelyn stayed silent, surprised: "The good German coffee?"

Garvey had a similar reaction: *"My young friend... the premises for an apology?"*

"Alright, professor, you win, I'm going to taste the savior coffee your wife made."

He took a chair and sat down with his mates. Emma was staring at him and literally boiling with impatience to share with him a decision she had just taken. But impossible to tell him in front of everyone, she had to wait for an occasion, she had to 'corner' him alone. But above all, was it wise to talk about it?

Damiana noticed the distress that pierced the young woman's eyes. She tried to use some of her new skills to help her. She tried to cross her gaze and it didn't take long in happening.

As Allan was about to speak again, she literally jumped into her chair and shouted in an almost disillusioned way.

"Emma, we have to talk as quickly as possible!"

All eyes were immediately on her, and those of Garvey, who immediately understood the problem. Allan and Jocelyn were looking at each other without understanding anything.

"What now?" they thought.

Emma felt embarrassed and didn't know what to do to avoid a confrontation. Having drunk only a sip of the 'good German coffee' and anxious not to embarrass anyone, Garvey got up from his chair.

"Emma, Damiana, follow me into the garden, please!"

Allan tried in vain to understand and started to get up at the same time as the two women. Of all the strange behaviors that he had witnessed in recent days, Jocelyn, meanwhile, began to no want headaches and adopted a pacifist behavior, preferring to wait and see.

Garvey stopped the professor's enthusiasm, making him understand with his hand placed in front of him like an 'officer' stopping a car, not to insist and to sit down.

"No professor, only your wife and Emma! I will tell you all in due time, I promise you."

"But, Garvey, what's happening? I remind you that you are my assistant, I don't dare say my student anymore!"

"Please, professor, don't complicate things, they are complicated enough as it is", said the young man, going outside where the two women were already waiting, seeming in a serious and grave discussion.

Allan was again sidelined and this exasperated him more and more. So he found himself in his home, sitting on a chair in his living room, not able to do anything, except observe and act almost obediently.

Amused by the situation and the fallen expression on the scientist's face, Jocelyn couldn't control the beginning of a smile that Allan noticed.

"This makes you smile?", he said dryly.

Jocelyn hesitated a moment before answering.

"Don't be upset Allan, but yes, it makes me laugh!"

Allan stared at him, trying to stay cold and serious, but couldn't contain an amused expression as he smirked. Meanwhile, the summit was rampant in the garden; we could see among others Emma, who was decomposing from second to second and Damiana who spoke with a certain virulence.

"Do you realize what you want to do, my child? Are you not thinking? Have you thought about the consequences? Have you talked to Jocelyn?"

Garvey calmed the tone of the conversation and offered a solution.

"Calm down Damiana, it's not a big deal as long as everyone agrees. We'll just go and you'll say what you have to say, do you agree Emma?"

Surprised and happy with the proposition, Emma didn't wait to be told twice and quickly accepted. Damiana was surprised by the taken decision, according to her on 'fast-forward.

"I suppose you know what you're doing, young boy!"

Garvey stared at her without saying anything. From that moment, it was, in the eyes of Allan and Jocelyn, who watched the scene attentively, a conversation without words, as well as the disappearance and immediate reappearance of Emma and Garvey. A bit like a ray of sunshine blurring their bodies for a moment. When all three returned to the living room, 'Medor and Brutus' who had not moved an inch, followed them like two watchdogs waiting for an order. Jocelyn looked at Emma and even ended up scrutinizing her face. Something was wrong with her attitude, something had changed. What had they talked about outside? Why did Emma seemed to be shocked after looking happy just two minutes before? Garvey didn't even sit down, he took his cup of coffee, still warm and swallowed the rest in a gulp.

Almost like a little boy eager to be accompanied to the carnival rides, Allan spoke timidly.

"So what's the schedule now?"

Feeling, in spite of appearances a deep respect for Allan, Garvey opted for a solemn response.

"Professor, you have 'taught me almost everything' and I have always admired you; you and your bad temper."

At that moment, Allan had a reaction that he curbed immediately.

"That is why you will accompany me in the operations to will follow, because as I told you, I will explain everything and show you everything. You have well deserved it! If you don't mind, we'll start by making the disappeared appear again and make the appearances disappear!"

Pleasantly surprised, Allan decided to let himself go and close his eyes to the 'dirty character' evoked by the young man who had passed from the state of student to that of master in the space of two unhappy days.

"Very well, Garvey, I'm with you."

"Not so bad, this little one!" he told himself.

At that moment, Damiana approached him and kissed him on the cheek.

"You'll see, this kid really has more than one trick in his bag, have a nice trip, my beloved."

"Finally, you found a little humanity! And I, who thought you lost!"

"You have never lost me Allan, I'm just in the process of getting acquainted with myself! Go quickly, we'll resume this conversation later if you wish."

Garvey was ready, all he had to do was press a key.

"Are you ready, professor?"

"Yes, my young friend, let's go!"

Garvey activated his command and the two men disappeared

into the garden. Jocelyn saw Damiana talk to Emma like a protective mother.

"Don't worry, my child, nothing has yet been decided."

He saw Emma behaving with care and he began to wonder about these incessant changes. He let Damiana finish and then wanted to have a clear heart. Before going to work a little in her garden, she finished with this sentence:

"Will you be alright?"

Emma didn't answer and only nodded. Jocelyn looked at them in silence, thinking,

"What is happening to you, my beautiful?"

He had the impression that she had forbidden herself not to look at him. Why this sudden distance? Not caring for it, he decided to join her. Emma was vainly trying to hide her apprehension that emanated from her thousand fold. Reaching her, he put a hand at the top of her back to comfort her.

"Everything alright?"

"Yes", she said in a trembling and fragile voice.

"In these kind of cases, when I see the Emma of my world in this state, I take her in my arms and I hold her very tight against me. But I…"

She didn't even give him time to finish his sentence and snuggled up against him, grabbing him like a rescuer who would have saved her from drowning. A little embarrassed, Jocelyn tried to take some distance, but the hug was so strong he could barely breathe.

"Emma, you're squeezing too tight!"

He didn't see her, but a tear ran down the face of the tearful young woman.

"Emma", he said, "I'm suffocating!"

A smile appeared then on her face and she let go.

"What's wrong? I have found you very strange since earlier. Is it because I'm leaving?"

"Yes Joss, I think that's it."

"But we talked about it, you know very well I can't stay here."

"I know Joss, just leave me time to get used to it."

"That's exactly what we don't have: and I already have an Emma who loves me in my world, you know this, and you, a Jocelyn who loves you."

She looked at him strangely, with expressive enough eyes, through which everything she felt came out as clearly as if she had expressed it verbally. Conscious of his mistake, Jocelyn recovered.

"Forgive me, I had forgotten, but even if you're divorced, he loved you and maybe loves you still; now if he's as awkward as me to say what he has to say, you'll never know!"

"I don't know what to think, Joss."

"Furthermore, I could never stay here knowing that another me lives under the same sky; it might cause an imbalance somewhere. I probably express myself badly, but you understand what I mean, don't you?"

"Yes, I understand very well."

She paused and then continued.

"Would you be willing to give up your world if the Jocelyn from here went there?"

"Now, you're scaring me, Emma. Are you serious?"

"Just answer me!"

"No Emma, it's not my world, my life is elsewhere and I love the Emma I met. Why are we still talking about this? I thought we had covered it."

"Don't be upset with me Joss, I'm a little lost at the moment."

"You're certainly in love, but not with me; the man you love is him and not me."

Emma seemed to really lose her footing. Was it Joss number one she loved or Joss number two? In her eyes, number two had behaviors that she criticized the absence of in number one. From her earliest childhood, she had always been told that everything could be done when you knew what you wanted and by putting in the necessary motivation. But can we change a person against their will? Wouldn't it be wise to take what you've always wanted and is right there at your fingertips? There was really enough to bang your head against the walls.

Noting her distress, Jocelyn worried.

"Everything alright? You know that's not possible."

"I know Joss, I know", she answered, sadly.

Jocelyn tried a maneuver to lighten the atmosphere.

"There's something else I'm thinking about."

"What?"

At that moment, he would have taken her in his arms, maybe even kissed her to show her compassion, even love, but he refused, because his departure was too imminent, and a certain wisdom seized him.

No, it was decided; he didn't want to complicate matters further between them. He put a hand on her face, almost tenderly. She approved the gesture of his hand on her forearm, which disconcerted Jocelyn. Until then, only Emma to whom he remained faithful had reacted in that way.

"It's crazy how much you resemble each other right now…"

OTHER TIMES, OTHER CUSTOMS.

— *"Man may want to stop his imperfection,*
still, a human being remains
evolving at his own pace."
MM.

G arvey and Allan were now in Pékin, China.

"What are we doing here?", Allan asked.

"We're going to remove the dead from the news of the last two days!"

"What happened?"

"In this factory, nothing; a man named Ching Changsung Boudsang will have finished his day's work in less than five minutes. He'll take his bicycle to go home, like he does every day, but a breach will open in front of him and he will have no choice but to hit a cart head on upon his arrival. But we'll make sure that never happens."

"Yes, now that you mention it, I did hear talk about it. But then, it's sensational! You can also control time with this device?"

"Yes, professor, we can."

"But tell me, it's not the same as the one you showed me at the university, or am I wrong?"

"No, professor, you're not wrong, it is different and has many

245

more functions than the first model."

"You created it at the university, didn't you?"

"Only in part, I'll introduce you to the people who helped me."

"Where are they?"

"Elsewhere! Watch the exit of the factory please, they won't be much longer."

Deep down, Allan was in heaven, he now lived what he had always dreamed of.

"What are you going to do, Garvey?"

"I am simply going to reverse the process."

"I can imagine pretty much what you're going to do, but I'm forced to admit that I've been a little out of it for a few days."

"Don't worry, professor, I propose we put everything in order first and then, you'll know everything." And… seeing Allan was a little embarrassment, Garvey reassured him.

"Yes…"

"The only difference between us is our generation. I dared put into practice what you have always been forbidden to do."

Allan looked at him a little biased.

"Anyway, no one will be able to take away your franchise, my young friend!"

Garvey smiled and resumed his surveillance. Suddenly, a bell sounded throughout the factory.

"Attention", Garvey said, ready to activate his box, "they're coming out and we musn't miss them."

On the large parking lot in front of the factory where the two scientists were camped like two tourists contemplating the difference of the arrangement of the stars with the sky which usually shelters them, tall bushes could be found in the back, inside which hid a man who seemed to be watching them. Sensing his presence, Garvey turned around and distinguished him in the distance.

"They really don't trust me", he thought.

"Here they are, coming out, come professor, we have to be in the place where the breach opened."

They disappeared discreetly to go on the boulevard where Ching Changsung had tragically disappeared.

"It's him, I musn't miss it, for it will be impossible for me to go look for him in our dimension!"

"Why?"

"Because the unfortunate man arrives directly on the grille of a cart and I have to close it as soon as it opens. He'll wonder what it is, but I have no choice, it's the only way to save his life."

Although slightly overwhelmed by the events, Allan understood very well what was going on. Ching Changsung arrived at the exact moment the breach opened and Garvey made the first move, so that the nocturnal cyclist saw something in front of him that he could never explain because it only lasted a hundredth of a second. But, he will be present to tell his children and grandchildren.

"Good for me", Garvey thought; *"It wasn't obvious."*

"Well, it's done", Allan exclaimed, "where are we going now?"

"We're going to join 'Enke and Klaus', who have made a formidable discovery."

"What's it about?"

"Another evolution."

"And how is it different?"

"You'll see, it's a surprise."

Garvey caused a new breach; they found themselves in the world where birds seemed to protect the human race. Looking around him, Allan was astonished.

"But it's a desert here! Are we in prehistory?"

"No professor, there is no date here, but if there was one, we would be in twenty-four thousand three hundred and thirty-seven!"

"Strange, I don't see any sign of civilization."

Suddenly, Allan realized that this world was not unknown to the young assistant.

"Tell me Garvey, you have already been here, haven't you?"

"Yes, professor, nothing escapes you!"

"In this case, why not do the necessary the first time around?"

"I was too fascinated and little Klaus wanted to stay a little longer when I went to get them. Right now, it's still possible to get them back."

Allan remained speechless; he went from astonishment to astonishment.

"I hardly dare ask the question, what is so fascinating?"

Garvey waited a few moments before answering. He looked at the sky and smiled.

"That!", he replied, nodding at the clouds.

Allan looked in turn and saw a shape in the distance that never stopped getting bigger. Alan was intrigued, impossible to take his eyes off of it.

"I could swear that zinc is alive!"

Garvey had a wide smile, while Allan, frightened, began to understand what he was seeing.

"It can't be! It's not what I think it is?" He thought.

'The thing' began a descent in their direction; Allan, panicked.

"Run, Garvey, run!", he shouted, starting to run.

Running and looking straight ahead, Allan kept talking.

"Did you see that?"

Getting no answer, he looked at his side, stopped, then turned. He noticed he was alone and that Garvey seemed to be wisely waiting for the arrival of the 'feather plane'. The yelping of the animal became more and more powerful and worrying for Allan.

"What are you doing, Garvey? Come!"

Not seeing him move, he first thought that the young man was petrified by fear.

"Poor Garvey, I can't live him there!"

"I'm coming, my friend", he said, tracing back his steps.

'The screaming plane' was about to touchdown, but too bad if he had to help relieve the bird of some feathers, because deep down, he highly esteemed this gifted student, whom he secretly admired for his talent and insight.

He didn't have time to go more than ten meters that the bird landed just a few steps from Garvey, generating such a cloud of dust that it was impossible to see more than two meters away.

"Garvey, is everything alright?", Allan continued by groping his way.

"Reassure yourself, professor, we have nothing to fear."

The dust gradually faded and Allan began to distinguish the enormity of the beast and to his surprise, he saw the intrepid young man sit on one of the animal's two legs. He was stunned by this surrealist scene.

"What's happening here?" he told himself. *"That bird is as big as my house!"*

"Do you know what you're doing, my boy?"

"Yes professor, come with me, we musn't stay here too much, for here, if these giant raptors are our friends, there are other less welcoming creatures that roam."

"Alright, I'm coming."

Allan couldn't help but contemplate from top to bottom and up and down the exceptional size of the flying giant.

"I can say that right now, you managed to totally surprise me, my friend!" he thought as he walked in the direction of the paw where there seemed to be arranged a kind of nacelle stowed with rudimentary ropes.

"All that doesn't tell me anything worthwhile."

At the foot of the flying building, he inspected the installation.

"You are certain of the solidity?", he asked, a little worried.

"No professor, but the others trust it and that's enough for me! Furthermore, they use it every day."

Perplexed, Allan hesitated to embark.

"Yes, maybe, but still."

Suddenly, Garvey's tone hardened.

"In God's name", he said, his eyes tousled, "come professor, climb quickly!"

"What's happening to you, Garvey, a little respect, please!"

The giant, who had spotted the same moving bump under the sand, grabbed Allan without hurting him and flew away immediately. Allan understood nothing of the action. Both were now in the air, Garvey comfortably seated and Allan curled up on himself in the clutches of the black giant.

"What's happening?" he thought, *"We're flying!"*

He could see the landscape going by between the claws. For him, the situation was unlikely. This poor professor of science, with a good life, found himself in the clutches of a kind of eagle fed GMOs, more than a hundred meters from the ground, flying at high speed, going to meet people he knew nothing about and all in another dimension!

The journey only lasted a few minutes. In the distance, one could distinguish small wooden buildings perched on a huge rock approaching. They seemed to be inhabited by a handful of people who seemed to be watching for the arrival of the airbus with squeaky reactors.

Garvey let himself be peacefully carried, while Allan wondered what other misadventures he should expect. The landing wasn't relatively difficult for Garvey, but poor Allan found himself dropped from scratch to the ground to finish rolled-off with no choice but to make a new indigestion of dust.

"You should have gone up with me, professor!", Garvey teased.

The first thing that jumped to Allan's attention was the size of those present. Men and women measured three and a half meters and the children arrived up to almost two meters.

The tall man approached the eagle from about ten yards. The latter lowered his hairy head of a golden brown color, apparently already old and stared at the man in the eyes a few seconds, then flew to his huge nest perched on a reef a little further. Seeing that, Allan thought to understand what had happened, but was surprised.

"Did they do what I think they did?"

"Yes professor, obviously, these two just communicated with each other. But it's nothing professor, you're not at the end of your surprises!"

While they were talking, Allan was fascinated by all those tall people who seemed to have been kicked in the backs since their earliest years, so impressive was their size.

The inhabitants of the place seemed to embody beauty in all its splendor. One of them approached what was for them 'little beings' by gibbering something quite incomprehensible to them. Only Garvey made the reply to Allan's amazement, who was still dusting himself off.

"What did you say between yourselves?"

"They welcomed us and I thanked them."

"I'm not surprised any more with you! I imagine the fact you understand this language is due to the recent acquisition of your potential?"

"No, professor, allow me to tell you that you are wrong! I only acquired the key and I used it."

"Hm, I see."

The tall man continued his greeting and spoke to Garvey again. Allan looked at him without saying a word.

"He's inviting us to follow him, professor, come."

Along the way, they passed by what appeared to be a fifteen meter long barbecue. In the embers, a huge sausage seemed to simmer. Allan couldn't help but look at that huge length. Suddenly, something intrigued him.

"Well, this sausage is weird, it looks... ."

At that moment, he was terrified.

"It's a head! My God, it's a worm, a giant worm! Did you see that, Garvey?"

"Yes professor, when I came to this world and they're going to eat it!"

"They're going to eat this horror? Unless they have evolved with their size, there is only one esophagus and two large vessels to eat!"

"As you say professor, they have had to evolve over time, because here, as you can see, they may be eating it, but if one of them has the misfortune to walk in places without trees, they are the ones being eaten!"

"Earthworms that eat meat?"

"They have apparently become carnivorous!"

"Unbelievable! I would never have believed it had I not seen it with my own eyes."

"Everything changes professor, just look at the size of these men, as well as their faces..."

"This as well, had I not seen it…"

Garvey watched Allan behave like a child marveling at the discovery of the world.

"You can deny it yourself, dear professor", Garvey thought, *"but you are like me; we are very similar".*

The three men were heading towards a large wooden hut in which there was a large crystal 'pebble' in the middle of the room. Amazed by its beauty, Allan couldn't help but admire it aloud.

"This stone is beautiful, is it not, my young friend?"

"Yes, professor, it's magnificent!"

The man told them with his hands to sit on one of the wooden chairs installed all around.

"Do you know what we're going to do?"

"No professor, but let's follow his directions and we'll see."

The three of them sat down and the giant presented both his hands, the palms directed forward, towards the crystal. Allan and Garvey were a little impatient to see the unfolding of events. 'Goliath' closed his eyes and concentrated as if he were going to pray. Some moments passed, the crystal was tinted with several opaque colors one after the other. And suddenly, images started to appear. They were 3D images. Allan and Garvey became the privileged witnesses of human history since its appearance on Earth.

All times and important facts were in some way recorded there. The two 'little beings' were like in front of a good film at the cinema. Thus, they could see bits of every era up to ours, but also, all those that will mark our future until twenty-four thousand five hundred and twelve precisely. They also found that man had reached his egocentric and more simply selfish climax some seventeen thousand years after our era and that gradually became aware of this, he radically changed his way of life by advancing, adopting and living in perfect harmony with what appears to us to be pure madness today, but still very real in that time; nature in all that it can offer to help us evolve, starting with animals, such as birds become real behemoths.

Seen from the outside, a conclusion imposed by itself... Return to the 'Prehistory of the future'. But therein lay a great difference. Man was now able to concretely share things in vital need, because there comes a time when by force of too much comfort and assistance, man is no longer a man, but a kind of human robot living only to be 'comfortable', without taking into account his own evolution. So, by focusing only on futility, like a child who has been spoiled rotten from a young age and who becomes aware as an adult that the most important thing is not there.

Seeing them so much absorbed by the film, their host spoke.

"As for the animals, they are like us, they adapt to what surrounds them. And the fact that for example, raptors have become true 'warm-blooded Boeings' is not due to chance. The men, as well as a multitude of animals, grew partly because of the climate, but not only. There is a persistent phenomenon of which we are not aware of and which is, nevertheless, part of what we are. Some call it 'Psychoactive Evolution'. We could just as easily call it 'Suggestive adaptation'. At all times, man has shaped his image according to his feelings, be it fear, the need to protect himself, or to prepare for an event announced or secretly guessed. Our destiny is not written, we create it day by day, basically with the decisions we make throughout our life."

"Well, he talks like us, the animal!", Allan thought.

In the in '3D' film, there were also present scenes for the

least disconcerting, that the great man continued to comment upon…

"Men of the future visit their ancestors for, among other things, see what they were and observe their evolution since the times when man thought he knew who he was and why he was there, sending intelligence and surveillance missions in the form of 'human spies'. Whether in our time, in the past or in our future, man will always make a kind of inventory of humanity by helping him from time to time to grow and evolve in the right direction. We had no trouble melting into the mass since all this amounted to studying ourselves without knowing it a few times. It's so much easier; at first, we think it's science fiction, but later, we end up believing it.'

"I'm sorry to interrupt, I don't understand! Who is 'our'?"

"I'll answer you shortly! I have not been clear, I admit, but still, we are what you will become! Just like your children. I noticed you were staring at my son just now. Surely because he doesn't look like me and that's exactly right because he's not mine!"

"He's not your son?"

"Today yes, but he hasn't come from me. You are still appropriating your children while ours are part of a clan. They alone have a whole group of parents whose recognition they have. There is no longer this phenomenon of exclusivity and belonging. They find themselves all the less disturbed because whatever happens, they always have the recognition of someone. Cohesion was created between our children and the group. There is no longer this feeling of rejection and they experience a serenity deep in their souls all their lives."

Looking closer, it could be seen, felt. All the children observed by the 'visitors' at that time didn't seem to be disturbed by anything. A simplicity of life reigned that they had never seen until then. Was it the key to well-being? Certainly, judging by the 'old toddlers' with all their parents. This called into question all their certainties. And maybe, who knew, they might engrave this information somewhere in one of the many drawers not often opened in their minds?

Even though Garvey had rather suddenly acquired some knowledge, he was just as stunned as Allan at the sight of this very informative show. Presently, many things could logically be explained in the many researches carried out in their dimension, as well as for the many paranormal questions frequently raised.

When the movie ended, the two friends who were shocked by this new knowledge remained a few moments in awe before the crystal, which had become a decorative object again.

"Did you see that?", Allan said. "We change planets and we realize that our destiny is the same."

"It's logical in some way, don't you think, professor?"

"Certainly, but what is the purpose of all this?"

"Always the same existential question. Why do we exist?"

"Yes, my young friend, why? Whether on this Earth or a bigger one, our future remains sealed."

"That is to say that we ask ourselves the same questions here and elsewhere."

"How to continue living normally knowing all this?", Allan observed.

"I don't think you'll remember", Garvey assured.

"Because there will be no relation between the two worlds, correct?"

"That's correct, professor, can I make a comment?"

"Of course."

"You only miss the audacity of my generation."

Allan gave a wry smile and added:

"Don't exaggerate, Garvey!"

"I'll be careful, professor."

Goliath suddenly interrupted the conversation.

"How are you feeling, gentleman?"

Perplexed, Allan reacted on the spot.

"Why not welcome us in this language since you understand it?"

"I wanted to see where you are exactly."

"I don't understand."

"We started talking differently when we became aware of what we are. And when we realized that we could communicate other than with speech, our language gradually evolved into a much simpler form. We don't talk with words anymore; we express our emotions and desires! The time in which you live is made up of a communication through words and writing, but it will evolve. The writing will be simplified, it will no longer be great literature, but phonetics. Then, the era of drawings will come."

"Drawings?"

"Yes, phonetics is born from electronic communication tools. But when they ceased to exist, they gave way to drawings. It was done in less than seven generations. It must be said that there was only one step between these two means of communication. In the beginning, it was a clever mix of both. We put a drawing from time to time, then systematically in each 'written' exchange to brighten up the phonetics."

"Sorry, but this is our generation, not yours, is it?"

"I had forgotten! Yes, that is correct. Then, we found it more fun to make each other guess what we wanted to say with drawings in the form of charades, for example. To end, we have come to try to guess ourselves without words or drawings and we have all, little by little, learned to read our thoughts, even from a distance."

"Everyone took to it without saying anything, so easily?"

"Of course not! It started with clans communicating this way only between them, then it gradually spread to the whole world."

Garvey and Allan literally drank the giant's words, but they still had a lot to do, even though they had discovered that time was no longer a major problem.

"Sorry to interrupt", Garvey said, "we won't remember anything anyway, will you accompany us to Enke and Klaus, because it is for them we are here."

"I know", the 'green giant' said serenely, "still in a hurry, aren't you?"

"There's nothing to teach you", Garvey replied proudly.

The man smiled and made a sign for them to follow. All three went towards a 'Big-Small' house. Allan couldn't help but observe everything around him again with the same look of disgust at the sight of the strange sausage.

"I agree with you, professor", Garvey said, amused.

The green giant noticed their behavior, stole the information and then decided to distract himself.

"You want some?"

Allan made as if he hadn't heard anything, but Garvey manifested his desire to abstain.

"Don't tell me our food doesn't attract your attention since you were already watching it."

"God, keep him from insisting", Allan thought, who was ill beforehand.

As the winged buildings came and went over the small perched village like sentinels on the lookout, Allan and Garvey cast a second, and therefore deeper look at the big people, who all seemed to measure their degree of knowledge. The green giant saw they were trying to make as if he hadn't made the invitation; he reiterated his proposal.

"Come on, don't be embarrassed, follow me, we will have a tasting. No, Allan I haven't forgotten about you!"

"You should have, I wouldn't have held it against you!"

"Well, are you researchers or not? You should be curious about everything you see!"

The disciple and his master looked at each other nonchalantly.

For sure, they would never have the opportunity to be offered such a dish, but for the time being, they were ready to do away with it. Their steps were becoming more and more hesitant as they approached the merguez. What they saw in the dishes caused them the sudden and yet cruelly real desire to search within them for a hidden talent of screenwriter to pretend at any cost, to pass the test.

"You at least have the possibility of not remembering, professor", Garvey said, trying to give himself courage.

"My young friend, in these cases, it's not the memories that count, but the experience."

The sausage was not ready yet. It was cooking at small fire along its entire length and only a circumference of about ten centimeters thick was edible. Seeing them approach, one of the giant women prepared three dishes filled with what they considered to be the best: the still-raw top of the gray-black bratwurst.

"Oh, my God!" Allan thought.

"We have to find something!", Garvey told himself.

The tall lady handed them a good plate. It looked like a sticky, gooey blank of whitish color.

"This part is not eaten, it is gobbled!", green giant junior clarified.

"Look!", he continued, showing them how.

"You don't have to think Garvey, go with honesty!"

Then, everything happened quickly. The two scientists, on the point of vomiting, couldn't speak for the next three minutes, to the greatest amusement of their host. To the question: "Did you like it?", they could only answer with a nod of reassurance. *"Yes, we liked it so much that words fail us!"*

The small household was only a few strides away now. Great asparagus beckoned them to follow him. He opened the four-meter-high entrance door and invited them to enter. There, they found the boy and his mother in conversation with one of the children of the clan. The child spoke to them like a teacher talking about his poor life experience.

Allan didn't know that life expectancy had changed along with height. The young giant was three hundred and twenty-six years old, twenty-four years before adulthood.

"Forgive the interruption", said Allan timidly from the height of his one meter sixty three, "we came looking for Enke and her son Klaus."

Despite his age, the young man seemed to be only twenty years old. He looked at him coldly and put poor Allan in his place.

"Who are you to dare interrupt me when I am in conversation with my guests!"

Surprised by that reaction, Allan reacted the same, determined not to be disrespected by who was, in his eyes, an insolent young man. Amused, green giant and Garvey let things flow.

"A little respect for your elders, young man, haven't they taught you this?"

The young giant, as well as Klaus and his mother, laughed heartly. Allan turned towards Garvey. Offended is the right word to describe what he felt.

"Ah, evolution is beautiful! Personally, I don't see anything changed with our time apart from the size!"

"You forgot the age, professor", Garvey said, trying to calm him.

"What age are you talking about? That of this disrespectful young person?"

"Yes, professor. Here, they age much less quickly than in our world and this young man is, alone, five times older than you and I."

"What do you mean?"

"He's over three hundred years old, professor!"

"You say over three hundred years old?"

Allan couldn't believe what he was hearing.

"Yes, professor, this young man can afford to ask for silence when he addresses people like us!"

Unaware of what to do, Allan fell silent, letting the 'Young old man' continue his story before Enke and Klaus who were, literally, absorbing each of his words.

"Today, we don't visit each other anymore", quietly pursued the three-hundred-year-old boy, "because we were still suspicious of ourselves a few centuries ago, but since we know why we are here, we no longer feel the need to do it". Enke and Klaus were fascinated. Although he spoke to him in German, 'Big Guy' understood easily, since he had learned it at the community school. They all learned the different languages of our time during history."

"When you say visits, what are you referring to?"

"We moved in inter-dimensional spaceships that could exceed

the speed of light, which allowed us to travel faster than time, well beyond all the rules of your science."

Allan and Garvey began to understand little by little where he was coming from. They listened with great attention.

"And what did you do then?", continued Enke, who was also beginning to ask herself philosophical questions.

"At the beginning of civilizations, we came to visit you. We gave you plans and writings. We thought it would help you evolve in the right direction. But in that period of our evolution, we didn't know we were working for ourselves. Those plans provided you with the knowledge to build great mortuary monuments within which your prophets and gods were supposed to rest for you to have a sense of acquiring wisdom. They also explained how to live in your environment, use what you have at hand, like iron hidden on the rock that comes from space."

"You're talking about meteorites, aren't you?"

"Exactly! Before our arrival, the men you were back then weren't even aware of fire. It is from then on that you began to realize the possibilities of your planet. But, you have also started a long war of territories which is also still relevant, even if it has cooled lately."

"Perhaps more civilized."

"If we can talk about a civilized war, then yes. It is also due to our visits that you have been able to develop more and more deadly weapons. One day, one of your scholars recovered debris from fallen ships on Earth. You must know our vessels have organic properties and in the case of a crash, these elements are recyclable. After a good number of tests, he realized the possibilities of this matter. To sum it up, at first he intended to make an elixir of youth and ultimately he created gunpowder!"

"It's not really the same use."

"Indeed and despite this misplaced pride that stifles you, it is fear that guides your steps."

"Fear of what?"

"Of everything, beginning with yourselves! As for the writings, it was simply the code of your Bible that is part of the teaching of wisdom and knowledge. All this was going on about two thousand five hundred years before your Jesus Christ. We later learned that among other things written in this teaching that we, ourselves had inherited from our ancestors, a phrase to which we had not specially paid attention that said:

"A prophet will come, will engender a new race of men who will be taken as gods."

"It only took us a few generations to understand it was about us. Our descendants did as much a few millennia later. But that time, we came to see the results."

"Excuse me, but will we do the same thing in thousands of years to men who will be in our stage of evolution then?"

"I cannot precisely answer, because all evolutions are different by the multiple decisions that it is possible to imagine in every situation and at every moment."

"We never go back to the same point. Our instincts, our moods, the circumstances."

Everyone looked at Allan who had obviously forgotten himself again. He noticed it only moments later and was embarrassed.

"Excuse me, you said you came back?"

"Yes, we were watching you, studying you and sometimes, we borrowed you. But we didn't exactly have the same look as today. Our evolution had been so fast in such a short time that our head had almost doubled in volume. It was only about eight thousand years ago that we stabilized and continued to grow evenly. Thus, we understood that you and us were one and the same race. We are your future!"

Garvey wasn't surprised, he had discovered it recently, but he wanted to know more.

"Allow me to interrupt", he said cordially, "something escapes me. Did your last visit go back a long way?"

"Why this question? You may be wondering how we do it?"

"Exactly, I see your houses without any technology, your way of living, your habits, and apart from your giant eagles, I don't see any ships or vehicles for travel."

"I understand your surprise; but don't be fooled by appearances, they are misleading. We have mastered technology for millennia and we have not banned everything. It is not only harmful, it also has its virtues. We have access to a huge shed built inside a mountain a few kilometers from here where we can move in the eras of our choice. This is for us a way out in case of; and we are a whole team to watch over it. But although everything is regularly maintained and in excellent working order, we have not used it for centuries."

"As you say, you never know. And it's also practical."

Green giant was looking at him with a small smile, without saying anything.

"This changes everything" Garvey thought, *"So it was they who came three thousand years ago. It is they who transmitted their knowledge to the ignorant savages that we must have been in their eyes".*

"Is there something else?", the gentle colossus said to Garvey, who seemed to want additional answers.

"Yes, two more questions, if it's alright with you. What kind of event would you reuse this facility for except a cataclysm?"

"Today, nothing, as we are at a stage in our evolution where we do not want to change anything of the past. But we prefer to have an escape route anyway if our decision changes, because even if we have decided not to live in fear anymore, we grant ourselves the right to want to save our species."

"It's logical, you have already changed the past!"

The big man showed a little discomfort that he erased immediately, then resumed:

"We made this mistake a few times for the sole purpose of giving evolution a boost, but as with everything, some errors are sometimes good to make us understand and especially to know how to concretely look at the consequences of our acts."

"It's a human reaction!"

"Of course, we haven't lost it. There was a second question, I think?"

"Yes, thank you. This one is going to be more down-to-earth. What kind of world have you visited?"

"I'll give you the short version, if you don't mind. We have seen a world where the Earth is not the one we know. It is there we understood that some evolutions caused the destruction of the planet for another, a little larger and just as hospitable. But it was necessary to eradicate monster species that were far too dangerous for humans arriving, and thus survive and evolve in complete peacefulness. For these earthbound people, the operation lasted eight hundred years for things to return to normal after the nuclear bombs sown almost everywhere."

"The big-bang" Garvey thought ironically. *"But then, what are we chasing after? All these theories, all these formulas, all this time and all that for this! Are we as bad as that? After all, man is able to destroy the planet a hundred times then... As long as men try to kill each other, there can only be one left! Who said this already?"*

Allan watched young Garvey begin to unconsciously mimic the behavior of his master to think. Equally enthralled and amazed, the other guests were also deep in thought. Young Klaus was definitely hooked. As for Enke, she couldn't believe what she was hearing.

"But then you're…" Garvey said, in complete reflexion.

"The beings you consider exterior to your world. But as I was saying, now that we know the reason for our presence on Earth, we are no longer doing any research and your turn will come in a few thousand years."

"Extraordinary!" said the eyes of Klaus and his mother.

"And why are we here?" Allan and Garvey thought at the same time. To their great surprise, the young giant turned and answered simply:

"To live, gentleman!"

"Us too!" the two scientists continued in silence.

"No, gentlemen, you're wrong! Try to take a step back from your respective lives."

Those who were in the eyes of the giants only two mentally retarded stayed mute for a few moments. Still, Garvey tried to save face.

"I think I understand what you're saying!"

"And what do you understand?", green asparagus resumed.

"Just that we have other interests."

"Yes, you can put it like that."

"I'm sorry to go back to it", Allan said, "but we came to take back your guests!"

Amused by what he was hearing, 'Father giant' made a pertinent remark.

"Now I understand why it took us so long to evolve!"

Feeling the need to justify himself, Allan replied serenely.

"I see very well where you want to get at, dear friend, but we must live with our times or else we will be unable to find a place in the world in which we were born."

"A very interesting remark, small human!', junior green giant teased.

His father stared at him without saying anything. He must have been sending a thought, maybe even a reprimand, judging by the looks they were exchanging. Garvey tried to intercept the contents of the silent conversation, but couldn't. Sending a last message to his son, he glanced briefly at Garvey.

"You won't succeed, we're blocking you!"

Surprised, Garvey raised his eyebrows and was in awe at the ease with which they mastered this ability. Enke and Klaus were also amused by the situation, they would have almost stayed in this world had they not had their lives organized and full of projects in the world of stress. They got up and went to their saviors.

"Wait a minute", said Allan, the avid scientist of knowledge, "I still have a question or two to ask."

Their two hosts looked at him and both started to answer before he even had time to say anything. Surprised, but not amazed, Allan listened attentively to the two giants.

"Yes, Allan", Junior said, "what you saw in the crystal are embryos we placed in different worlds, including yours. In your time, you still don't know it, but when they will finally convince you of who they are, not by saying it, but by their behavior, you will have a reaction of rejection for a long time. But you will gradually compare yourselves to them and eventually accept them as such. This will happen soon; about one hundred and fifty years and you will give them the qualifier 'Indigo Children'. These will be regularly and systematically taken for study, like some other 'non-indigo' for comparison, because at the point of evolution that we acquired more than five thousand years ago, we didn't understand this difference between you and us. It wasn't so much for what we had developed, but rather for our appearance. Our heads had grown in the space of two millennia. We had become pale caricatures of ourselves. Later, we discovered the reason. Having found a way to exploit our dormant resources, we focused primarily on that. The more we tamed them, the more we wanted to discover more. We have largely left out our physical aspect in favor of the cradle of our brain. It was not until much later that we found our balance, as we told you two minutes ago."

"Two minutes!" Allan thought, *"at least twenty passed!"*

Everything he thought was read by the two human pylons and it was the father who spoke this time.

"That's right, Allan, time passes a little less quickly for us than it does for you."

The man smiled and continued.

"I see you're still asking yourself a lot of questions and I'm going to answer one of them. You, your wife, as well as Garvey, all three are Indigo children who have evolved in the world from which you come from, and you were all three regularly taken at regular intervals without you even suspecting anything. You have no memory of it, only a few absences at certain moments in your life."

Continuing to read the questions, he came with another answer.

"We manipulate your vision. To remember, you would need to wake up your unconscious, because we cannot intervene at this point or we would lose ourselves."

"Yes Garvey, your unconscious protects you."

"Of course Allan, there are thousands, even millions, we do not know exactly. We evolved differently. It is written in our history books that we no longer exist in some worlds, in others, evolution has been delayed by the technology used on men for different reasons; elsewhere, it is technology itself that has survived by creating its own evolution on the human base and eradicating all lives on the planet. And I'm not talking about the evolution of the planet that has been constantly reshaping itself again and again by causing natural disasters, balancing the human quota. In this one, the animals evolved with us, thus allowing us to be in total symbiosis with them."

He heard Garvey, who in turn wondered about a few things.

"Yes Garvey, you are entirely right, there is no such thing as chance. What you learn now, as well as Allan, Enke and Klaus, will forever be engraved in a corner of your mind and you will all use it one way or another, sooner or later without being aware of it."

"The answer is yes, Allan. The two people you came to recover are like you. They will also contribute to fundamental changes."

"Obviously Allan, I understand very well. When we became aware of our achievement, we decided to make a final journey back to you only a few thousand years ago. We put in writing what was in our eyes the main rules of life, as well as some of our knowledge, and we gave them to you so that you could evolve more quickly. That amused us, because we were then about twenty centimeters tall, the size we have today, and you simply took us for gods, because we were coming from the sky at the speed of lightning. But unfortunately, you have misinterpreted most of the advice we gave you, apart from a few exceptions that you quickly assimilated; greed prevailed on almost every level. You are only barely beginning the process that will bring you peace."

"What peace?"

"The one that will not force you to be wary of each other. As long as there are armies, there will always be something to defend. No one is forced to follow a dictator in his madness, but we always come back to the same problem: you need a guide, whether it's good or bad. But no one will move for a long time in your world of egotism and cowardly pestilence."

Allan didn't give him time to read anything and responded promptly.

"We're not all like that, you know!"

"No, I didn't say that, but people like you, are in your world what small islands are to the ocean!"

Then, he looked at Garvey and concluded.

"You will go home with knowledge that will not serve you; not consciously, in any case. But I see that you will meet other people, who can also teach you and who knows, to share with you some of their experience."

"You're talking about…"

"Yes Garvey, what we used to be. In their world, they also do 'Placements' and 'Visits'."

The two giants turned to Enke and her son.

"Maybe we'll see each other again, in your thoughts. Did you like your stay with us?"

Klaus looked at them smiling.

"Sehr gut!" ("Very much!") he answered spontaneously.

"Danke schön" ("Thank you very much!"), Enke added.

Giant senior sent a thought to the winged mastodon, a call without words. A question still tapped Allan, but he dared not ask. Intercepting his thought, Junior answered.

"So we are frightening", he joked; "we keep our own count of

270

days gone by, my father is eight hundred and forty-three years old!"

"Eight hundred and forty…"

"Three years, Allan. If you evolve in the same way, you'll get there too."

These few words left him dreamy. He glanced at Garvey and headed out. It was then that the 'beefy moss' eagle arrived, redoing Allan's 'make-up' the dusty way.

"Garvey", he screamed, "is there no way to go from here?"

"Of course there is professor, it's enough to enter the coordinates of this place and we'll be done!"

"Hm… We don't need your services anymore, bird of misery, you can go back to where you come from."

He turned to 'senior green giant' who was very amused by the scene.

"You knew it, didn't you?"

The man laughed out loud.

"Goodbye, Allan, take care of yourself."

Allan sighed as if to express a flush.

"I will do so! Garvey, Enke, Klaus, are you coming?"

They greeted their host one last time and joined grumpy. When they were ready to go, Garvey turned to junior, who answered him immediately in the same way …

Then Junior resumed,

"If you wish not to, you won't lose it. Just work on it and, especially, maintain it."

Garvey greeted them with his hand: *"Thank you"* and Allan did the same. He activated the command and opened the gap. Suddenly, he realized with horror that he was wrong in his settings and summoned everyone to stop.

"Don't go in! I forgot a small detail. I have to correct an error."

"What is it, my young friend?", Allan asked.

"If we had crossed this gap, we would have found ourselves in France twelve meters from the ground!"

"Yes, indeed, it is wiser to start again", grumpy joked.

While the open gap was about to close, the eagle resumed its flight on the orders of his master and, unintentionally, rushed inside. Having seen it disappear before their eyes, the panic began to take over the small community immediately after the surprise effect. 'Green Giant Father' approached the group, running.

"Look for him and bring him back to me", he said dryly, "don't make me do it myself. We're counting on you!"

Sorry for what had happened, Garvey reassured him.

"Yes, you can count on us, we'll bring him back. What do you tell him when you call him?"

"I don't tell him anything. I send him an emotion."

"Very well, I understand."

"This won't be easy", he continued, thinking. He turned towards Enke and Klaus, determined to repair his mistake.

"Prepare yourselves, we're going! You'll relive the same thing that brought you here. Are you ready?"

Klaus and his mother nodded without need for a translation.

"Professor?"

"We're waiting for you, my friend!"

After double checking his programming, he activated the magic box and created a new breach.

"No error, right?", Allan asked before going in.

"None, professor, rest assured."

Allan went into the breach, followed by Klaus, his mother and Garvey, who, with a guilty look reassured one last time the nice giants. The breach closed only five seconds later. A silence of death reigned in the small community of big people. Worried, junior and his father looked at each other, exchanging thoughts in their emotional dialect.

"Let's hope he'll keep his word", continued junior, who had intercepted Garvey's last thought.

"Yes, son, let's hope so. Maybe it went back from where it came from. Remember the little bird he was when we took him in."

"Yes, but it was dear to me."

"To me too, son, to me too."

"Did you see the reaction he had with them? He wasn't afraid!"

"I have observed his behavior more closely with you for all these years. He always felt good in your company."

"With the children we are?"

"Yes, son."

He didn't want to hurt him, but he knew he would never see him again, just as he was convinced that memories and feelings are transmitted from generation to generation, even among raptors.

SON OF GOD...

— "Utopia is simply what
hasn't been tried before."
Benjamin Franklin.

To definitively stop all these 'crazy breaches' that continued to open up everywhere, causing new disappearances and appearances, Garvey had the heavy task of go back to each of them to put things in their place. Having improved the system of his box during a visit to a parallel world, the latter emitted a beep with each new unforeseen phenomenon. Allan, like the others, didn't pay attention until Garvey reacted to the last beep when they arrived in Germany. After asking for an explanation, Allan felt a certain discouragement.

"Well, we're not out of the woods yet!", he exclaimed.

Garvey had scheduled their arrival barely a second after Enke and Klaus's disappearance, who suddenly immediately disappeared and reappeared under the bewildered eyes of the old man sitting nearby on a bench and who will, thus, never report the disappearance. But rather an apparition followed by a disappearance two minutes later. That of Allan and Garvey. For him, the result was the same; if he talked about it, he would be considered someone 'disturbed in the head'.

After thanking and greeting the two scientists, Klaus and his mother continued their initial journey with a second behind, forgetting as they went about their misadventure, which got stored in their subconscious.

Allan and Garvey continued to run after the breaches for a long time, bringing people back to their homes, not without difficulty for some, considering the surreal side of the problem. They arrived in a spaceship where Florent was, the young boy who had disappeared at the foot of the small mountain near the rest area where his parents had stopped, as well as two other children. Everything seemed to go well for them, but Allan wasn't quite reassured. The place was even whiter than can be defined by the name of the color and portholes could be distinguished, through which only black and tiny suns appeared.

"Where are we?", said Allan worried, and yet intrigued by the place.

"We are in the spaceship where there are only friends!"

"Don't tell me you have already been here?"

"As you wish, professor."

"Garvey, you're taking some liberties that you would never have taken before!"

"There's nothing mean here professor, you're just not comfortable in this place, I just turned your attention away from that feeling. To answer you, yes, I've been here before and they've helped me improve the box so that I can fine-tune exactly the place, the day and the hour where I'm going, and a signal for each new breach."

"Yes, you told me. What are we doing now?"

"We're waiting for our hosts. But I have to warn you of a detail before they arrive."

"What is it, my young friend?"

"They don't look at all like us."

"Eh! Don't worry about me, I'll control my emotions and between you and me, I have seen some in my life!" Allan assured with great wisdom.

Some minutes passed and no one came.

"You're sure we have to wait here?"

"Yes, professor; and we couldn't go anywhere anyway since all the exits are protected by a magnetic field."

"Then how could we arrive?"

"Only the exits in the ship are secured. They protect the entire ship only when absolutely necessary."

"I see', Allan said, contemplating the big white hall.

In doing so, funny impressions came to disturb his mind. He isolated himself for a few moments in the recesses of his brain.

"I know this place" he thought, *"how is this possible,* we're aboard a spaceship supposed to house aliens".

Garvey remarked Allan's mind retreat.

"All is well, professor?"

But he was too far gone to hear anything. The more he looked at the white hall, the more this impression of déjà vu was accentuated. Was the old sage losing his reason? He was eccentric enough to behave like that, but from there to feel like home in a spaceship that was light-years away…

Turning his back to Garvey, a hand posed itself on Allan's shoulder who, thinking that it was his young assistant now his equal and even more, turned towards the owner of the hand.

"I told you, you don't need to reassure me, but it's nice of…"

When he discovered the face of the being in front of which he found himself practically 'nose to nose' with, he emitted a short, but powerful cry of fear and surprise.

"I tried to warn you, professor! I admit I was as surprised myself the first time!"

This vision reminded him of some bad nightmares from his childhood. For two seconds he behaved like a seven-year-old waking up after a restless night. The being was tall and had a head disproportionate to his body. The latter seemed frail, fragile like a man who might have taken a relatively heavy blow to the skull to make his brain swell and his eyes dilate by dyeing them black. The whole covered with a kind of blouse, letting his little arms and his skinny calves appear. Allan came to his senses by acquiescing in the situation.

"Who are you?"

"A human being five thousand years after your era and my name is Isos!"

"So this is what we'll become."

"Not necessarily, at least not everywhere."

"Yes, I know, we'll make decisions in some worlds that will lead us to a whole different result."

"That's right, but between us, you're on the right track."

"You mean we're going to know a healthy evolution?"

"We could say that, since your children are not too disturbed by what they have seen so far today."

"The children from our world, right?"

"Yes, that's what this is about", 'big eyes' sent to Allan through thoughts.

"You too, I presume you greeted my assistant in the same way when you surprised me?"

"We can't hide anything from you, 'Great Indigo'!"

"Now I'm taking up the ranks!"

"Come, let's find the three children we borrowed from you."

They headed for an airlock not far away, to enter another

room, a little smaller, where there were other 'big heads', children and adults, in the company of the toddlers they had come to get. Unlike many preconceived ideas about people like them, the welcome was pleasant, even warm. They were very far from the fear or suspicion that one could probably have imagined in such circumstances. What was obvious was that they seemed to have been waiting for their visit. It was simply surreal.

"Ugly, but obviously very nice", Allan thought. Garvey intercepted his thought and took care to prevent it.

"Pay attention to what you think, professor. Around here, it's better to empty your head!"

Isos came back to them after having askes them to wait a moment while he went to talk with his peers.

"He is right, Great Indigo, we read all your thoughts and for your information, in our eyes it is you who are ugly!"

He invited them to sit on two of the fifteen seats arranged in an arc.

"Take a seat, we'll quickly finish."

Isos sat next to them, looking at the three little beings they were studying simply by talking and doing measurement exercises with them. All three had been scared when they had arrived, but that was in the past.

"You don't look surprised!", Isos said to Allan.

"You don't read my thoughts anymore?'

"Even if I allowed myself to do it on your arrival, we don't do it constantly, haven't for a long time."

"You used to do it before?"

"That's right. This goes back more than four thousand years, when we had recently discovered a multitude of abilities in us with which we played at first, then gradually learned to live with."

"Allow me a question, my good fellow. What is the point of borrowing these children?"

"There are only children. We study the evolution of all beings that we place in different worlds to better understand our own evolution, no matter their age."

"You mean to say these children are yours?"

"Yes and no. Their souls were implanted in the belly of different women in different worlds. They therefore have the appearance of those around them."

"The souls, you say?", Allan wondered.

"Yes, some are caring, others less."

"What are you saying? The souls you place may be bad?"

"That can happen, no one is perfect. Some took advantage of the situation. Most didn't know their origins, but had in them powers they discovered throughout their lives. There were also mistakes made in the placements. And even today. The entourage of a child can be decisive in its future. Of course, when we realized it, we tried to fix it, but we realized that it was better to let it continue, because it takes all kinds of happenings to make a world, like you would say, and this allows differences to come in being. It's also a good way to observe and study various reactions."

"You say 'powers'; what are they?"

"To summarize, all those who compel people to act against their will like the power of advanced persuasion, mental manipulation, etc."

"Advanced persuasion?"

"Yes, or the ability to get into people's heads without their even realizing it."

"It's fascinating! Still, something eludes me. What happens to souls that aren't reincarnated?"

"They wander while waiting to find a host. They are waiting their time."

"What is the difference between yours and ours?"

"They are all alike. It is later they stand out. Some do not have the patience to wait and will be reborn in another universe. They move and can sometimes make long trips."

"I would have never imagined it!"

"But yes, Allan, since it's already inside you."

Suddenly, he had an awareness that left him speechless.

"So my deep self is an alien!" he told himself.

Isos intercepted the conclusion without saying anything, only a little look out of the corner of the eye to study his reaction. Garvey listened and watched without saying a word either. Isos resumed the conversation and changed the subject.

"Allow me to clarify one of the thoughts I intercepted despite myself just now."

"Which one?"

"You think we hurt the people we take. On this subject, you must know there have been evolutions almost similar to ours, or very close to. Some have greatly benefited from their advantage over beings such as those around you and others also continue…"

"What do you mean?"

"Look at these children, they are hardly evolved compared to us, but their base is healthy. They are your future and we bring them here to make sure they move in the right direction. It's true that everything needs to evolve, both bad and good, because it makes it possible to see concretely where mistakes have been made. That said, as long as we won't have all our answers, we strive to guide the worlds that we think need it the most. Thus, we immerse some of our old souls in newborns to try to bring something positive regarding wisdom in those worlds where everything goes wrong. Still, some of you having acquired the same knowledge as ours have only sought to abuse this situation; and that's still the case today in some worlds, including yours."

"These children would be the key to our spiritual success?"

"Exactly Allan, just like your Garvey, or Jocelyn, or should I say 'the Jocelyn Beaumont' of each world."

"All the Jocelyn?"

"Just like all the Allan Thibaud or Emma Dumont or Damiana Duquesse with their maiden name, the Hubert and the Félix Doran, etc. You are precisely one hundred people per world to be selected because it is easier for us to identify you afterwards."

"But don't the others do as you do?"

"Unfortunately yes and we cannot control anything. We opted for this solution, but they proceed with transmitter implants for their identification, because this is unfortunately not the only reason why we are studying you."

"You're starting to scare me, which is the other reason?"

"There is an important factor in the law of space, because it evolves in the same way as the inhabitants of different worlds. It is only creation and destruction. All is only an eternal beginning and no one can change it. The big space consists of a multitude of small universes. Sooner or later, they are irretrievably self-destructing and we know that it will happen to us, just like with you. Obviously, on our time scale, we can afford to search in peace for another universe where to live."

"You mean we will have to leave our planet one day soon?"

"That's right, but to achieve this, you will have to develop the necessary technology as we are now doing, because each dimension has its own vibration; and unless you create a huge 'wormhole' that will remain open long enough for the entire population to leave, which is not physically feasible, it is the only solution. I see the term vibration poses a problem?"

"We can't hide anything from you! I think to understand what you're saying, but I'm not sure."

"These vibrations come from the power and speed of magnetic fields that are different in each dimension. For example, what you call the 'beyond' is a dimension that is certainly different from yours, but it would take a small acceleration of your field to perceive it and rub shoulders with your dead."

"Some people do, however..."

"Each being is endowed with an energy of its own. When an individual certifies to communicate with the dead, it is actually his soul that does it and it is true that in some cases, the mind intercepts certain things and can therefore do it consciously, but it cannot do it for too long, because it will run out of energy quickly and risk stagnating between two dimensions. Each world, each being releases its own energy. When we manage to distinguish another dimension, whatever it is, without moving from ours, it is a little in the form of a hologram that it appears to us, except in the case where we can access it obviously as you have been doing since yesterday."

"If I understand correctly, we all have our own energy bubble and we are ruled by a huge bubble."

"It's very simply said, but it's actually the principle. This is how we visit worlds without being seen. But we cannot always limit ourselves to that. In addition to the different evolutions that are given to us to see, we examine various places and their inhabitants, to see if compatibility is possible."

"Then, you haven't told me everything earlier! These Indigo

beings that you place in all these worlds are somehow witnesses or telltales, are they not?"

"Yes Allan, we choose the same people in each world of many universes and we insert our souls at birth. It is the potentially more advanced beings such as you, who will gradually advance the evolution of your respective worlds and you will also explore the same way as us for your race to survive. They all advance their world in their own way; they are not only there to live a life, but they are not aware of it. If we look in our memories that go far beyond all the lives that we can have, we would find that every world so different is a step ahead of the previous one, because we are always reborn within the same evolution, but at different times obviously."

At the end of the sentence, Allan could be seen raising his hand like a schoolboy.

"Yes", said Isos, smiling from his toothless mouth.

"You're talking about the different lives we have here, aren't you?"

"Of course, in your era, we talk about previous lives without really knowing what we are talking about and most often exclusively under hypnosis. You simply don't know that these memories come from other dimension around you."

"If I understand well", Allan continued, "we haven't lived these lives, we live them elsewhere."

"Exactly! You are insightful for a man of your era!"

"Thank you for the compliment!"

"You will also know voyages to later worlds, much like you do now, but it will become a mere formality. Some worlds have self-destructed like the images I send you, you see?"

"Impressive!", Allan exclaimed.

"In his soul, man went to the end of his nuclear madness.

Nothing and no one survived. Still, life will come back the next day, an umpteenth restart."

"And there have been several", Garvey asked.

"Of course! Many other races of men and humanoids evolved. Besides, we have just visited one before yours."

"Could we see the images?"

"It's possible, but I won't do anything about it, because it's not your evolution and if you don't have any image in the conscious state, they'll be there anyway."

"Yes, I know", Allan said, not really knowing why.

"It's a bit like a battle over our heads, if I understand correctly. Everyone will visit one day or another!" Garvey added.

"In a way, yes. And I think we ourselves need to be researched by other more advanced civilizations than us."

Allan raised his head to the sky or rather to the stars and had a moment's hesitation.

"Hm... Don't ask me why, but I think you're wrong."

"Alright, I won't ask why. Are you sure?"

"I don't really know, I can't remember, but I think that one day soon, we will not want to prospect anymore and we'll end up settling down."

"Nothing is due to chance, whatever happens; I will even go so far as to say that it is a universal law!"

"Something escapes me", Garvey said, his mind fluttering. "You tell us about the worlds and universes you visit. You say we have to ignore certain things, so why let people see you because, since you have the possibility to make yourselves invisible?"

"We have to let ourselves be seen by your satellites in orbit just so that you realize that there is something else, that you are not alone. Furthermore, it's sometimes a real show for us when we watch you. Your getaway to your satellite, which you call

'Moon', greatly amused us. Isturias you see in the back of this room couldn't stop laughing seeing you evolve in space with this big tree trunk smoothed technology as evolved as my to do list! We even followed you for a short time."

"All in all, you're having a good time watching us!"

"We would be wrong to deprive ourselves. After all, we are just human beings, more advanced than you! This allows us to put ourselves before our mistakes and to rectify the eventual backfire. And if we wouldn't visit you to give you some of our knowledge, we might not be what we are today."

"You would have become later on", Allan punctuated.

"That goes without saying! All worlds evolve. Maybe we are tired of traveling. Perhaps we are impatient to settle. It's true we pretend to give you knowledge, but the mold from which we are made of is identical to yours. We all as we are, were little humanoids whose size didn't exceed ten centimeters."

These words provoked general astonishment in the small inter-dimensional group.

"Really", Garvey asked, "ten centimeters?"

"Yes we were a little different, but we were men. It's normal you don't know it, because for you it goes back to forty two million years and you don't know anything about your evolution."

"Ah! I'm sorry", Allan virulently objected, "we have learned much more than you think!"

He enumerated some fossilized finds, as well as old writings found here and there, emphasizing some points that seemed important to him. Isos laughed with his beautiful smile with teeth as an option and continued.

"It's as I was saying, you don't know anything!"

"May I?", Garvey said, seriously.

"Of course, I'm listening."

"You're more evolved than us, you can go to all existing worlds. Why not go directly to a world that resembles yours? A world in which you would find your peers?"

"Because it doesn't work that way. We would only stagnate in our evolution. We have to follow it, not continue those of others. You understand?"

"Yes, but how did the first ones do it in this case?"

"Besides our evolution, in all the worlds of space, you must not confuse beginning and evolution. One is precisely the continuation of the other. Worlds were born from the beginning of our appearance, and it is only from that moment that the multiplication started according to the lived experience and our decisions."

"Yes, but where did these little men come from at the beginning?"

"Any life whatsoever is microscopic at the beginning of its existence, then it evolves and adapts little by little to its environment. It begins with an organic development, then the birth of a spirit created by the needs and desires of the 'said organism'. Both then evolve in osmosis over time and the perpetual change of their environment, which shapes us in a certain way. Some organisms choose, if we can say so, to become a man. Others go to other spheres more or less basic or more or less animal."

"You mean we choose who we will later become?"

"Yes and no. It's a choice that is done slowly, step by step. Some stopped in the course of evolution and have become, to name just one example, the monkeys you know. Although they too have evolved in their own way. Others continued to become lynxes, mosquitoes or snakes. It's mainly their environment that made them become what they are, just like you."

"Yes, but man resonates much more than animals, who have undoubtedly, made the easiest choice…"

"What you say is not false. Easiness has been for them what in your world the remote is for the TV, but taking a closer look, each of these species excels in their specialty."

"It may be so", Allan continued, "but I still believe we will one day reach saturation and we will sooner or later want to stop and rest. Maybe we'll get to the end of our abilities."

"Why do you think such a thing? Even if, I admit, it has some value to it."

"Because when we'll know who we are and, especially, why we are, we may not feel the need to survive anymore, but only to accept the time we have to live and to give way to other beings, to other evolutions. This may be the law of the great spaces."

Garvey and 'Oval Pumpkin Face' looked at him strangely. They were both voiceless and impressed. As for Allan, he didn't even know why he had said that, but he had a deep conviction.

"How could he remember? He should have forgotten what he has seen."

As long as he was connected to his box and all time gaps were not closed, Garvey was the only person who could consciously remember all the comings and goings in different worlds. This connection was made possible thanks to the organic micro system that had been added to, in the eyes of Isos, his simplistic device. Moreover, that could have been dangerous, even fatal for the young assistant to not remember. Isos wanted to get the information in his own way, but his attempt was unsuccessful because Allan was blocking any unsolicited intrusions. To the amazement of Isos and Garvey, he was already beginning to develop certain faculties. Garvey wanted his heart to be at peace.

"Say, professor…"

"Yes, my young friend", Allan said, smiling.

"Would you like to come with me to recover the eagle from earlier?"

"What eagle are you talking about, my dear fellow? No, wait, don't answer, my mind is a little confused and I don't understand what's happening to me, but even if I have no memory of that eagle, what you tell me doesn't surprise me."

"I think something's going on inside you, professor. If you feel anything unusual, you will tell me, won't you?"

"Of course Garvey, given the circumstances, you would be the first to know."

Garvey felt that something strange was hovering in the air. Suddenly, Allan addressed Isos, as he would have done with a friend and the latter who had not let anything show until then, seemed to be worried.

"You don't intend to settle on our planet, do you?"

Isos seemed to break down a little more with each word coming from Allan, under Garvey's interrogative eyes.

"What makes you say that, Allan?"

"I wouldn't be telling you that if I didn't know it."

He was looking at Isos with intensity.

"I wasn't supposed to discover it, was I?"

Then, Garvey was, in turn, completely stunned. Some, looking like Isos, heard Allan's words and turned to the three men, leaving aside their occupations for a few moments. Allan seemed shaken and continued to expose his discovery.

"Is that why you helped him?", he continued, pointing to his pupil with a nod of his head..

Now everyone had their eyes on them.

"There's a little of that Allan", Isos said with emotion, "but it's not the only reason."

No longer able to contain himself, Garvey cracked.

"What's going on here?"

No one paid attention to him. Allan was heading towards the colleagues of Isos and arrived in front of one of the men, or rather one of the women. He stood in front of her for a few moments, then put his hands on her face. Garvey was beginning to understand and couldn't believe his eyes. Allan was acting like a child. His hands were shaping the face of the alien who seemed moved as well. Then he took her calmly and tenderly in his arms, placing her head against his chest. Surprised, and yet happy she put her two thin arms around Allan.

The scene was surreal. These two beings with diametrically opposite appearances had obviously hooked atoms and, who knew, the same DNA and therefore the parental consanguinity, which had often worked for Allan's good health. It was true he had never gotten sick. Moreover, it had become a game in his childhood, if we can say so.

In his time, a man, a real man, should not be weak. Allan had often used that advantage. His adoptive parents regularly had white hair with this hypertensive child whose brain had worked from the start at two thousand miles per hour without any respite. The poor boy had often been bridled, but he had caught up since. Allan was serene, soothed. All remained like that for three long minutes. A total silence reigned. Isos turned towards Garvey.

"This was never supposed to happen. You understood it, we placed him in that world. Allan is our child!"

Garvey raised his eyebrows. What news!

"I think I had understood it. I was expecting all eventualities by creating this toy, but that!"

"Normally, he won't remember upon leaving."

"He shouldn't, it's true, but with everything I've seen, I wonder."

During their embrace, a question crossed Allan's mind. Intercepting his thoughts, Keisha peeled off her sacrificed child and explained to him.

"You don't remember us, because before injecting you into the belly of your adopted mother, we made sure that your genes mutate and be like theirs. Then, nature followed its course. And sending you in that world, we counted on you to contribute to an evolution similar to ours, so that our race could survive the future chaos of our world. Unfortunately, you won't see the result, for your life expectancy has now become inferior to that which you should have had; normally, anyway... We will not be able to consider settling there for centuries, or even millennia. It all depends on your evolution. But nothing is certain, for we have traveled beyond your space-time; and what we have seen doesn't encourage us to persist in this path. That said, everything can still change according to decisions taken in the 'key moments' of your history."

"Is it according to the decisions we will take, that our planet will continue to be or not?"

"Yes, that's exactly right. As well as with your personal evolution, all decisions you can take, will make the difference."

"If only I had the knowledge I should have had if I had stayed here, many questions would not arise again."

"Yes, my son, but if you had, you couldn't live in the world you have been born in. You have to advance at the same time with your peers."

Allan felt in that moment an outburst of revolt as to his fate.

"Why choose me?"

Keisha gave a shrill cry that only vocal cords like hers could emit.

"You turn the knife in the wound my son, as you're not the only one to have been sent elsewhere. Some of your brothers and sisters have been appointed to help the evolution of the different worlds you were born in. Do you think I watched you go away from us cheerfully?"

Allan remained speechless.

"That's not the case", Keisha continued, "I was heartbroken every time we sent one of you to those backlogged places. You will never be able to imagine what the definitive separation with one of your own children can be like, whatever the cause; even to save an entire race. So, all I can tell you my son is… Show them… Be their guide. Make me proud!"

The questions jostled at the portico of Allan's brain.

"Have you ever tried sending us into an era closer to ours, if only to find people with a similar evolution?"

"One time only. Their world was at the same level as ours and since all this was happening in real time compared to us, we preferred to repatriate him with his family, because that didn't lead us to anything. To tell you everything, he was the first to leave and it was all the easier because there was nothing to do in terms of integration, as everything was the same as our world. But when we realized this failure, we realized that all worlds, whatever they are, have a life span that is more or less identical. Today, we think we only have one window of time to evolve in all these worlds; it's up to us of we want it or not. That's why there are many worlds that go in the right direction and others that run towards disaster. It's like wanting to catch a bird in the middle of a flight and never reach it in the end. We have surely not done all of this for nothing, it was necessary for us to be able to see it, but it's been a long time, too long have we looked for a land to welcome our race; and we wonder sometimes why we do all this. We start to doubt what it is we chase. And if evolution was like this?"

"You mean you doubt the reason for which you sacrificed me?"

"I'm sorry my son, but for now, yes, because it will be necessary for your world to start again. It's an endless story and it's a real problem of conscience for us."

"Maybe you'll open yourselves to something else."

"Yes, certainly, but to what?"

"We'll look for ecological solutions to save our planet, we'll only delay for a moment our sad end, won't we?"

She smiled and squeezed him against her again.

"I very well recognize that in you, my son."

Garvey caught his attention by waving his hand. *"We still have things to do!"* But Allan wasn't paying attention, he was too busy finding his own.

"You won't remember", 'Mother ET' said, "but you will now be appeased. Your life is with them and I will have to cry after you a second time. Go my son, give us hope, confirm our choice and be happy."

Allan knew he would have no memory of it and wanted to savor this unique moment to the fullest. He would never have such an opportunity again. On the other hand, there will be a sort of unconscious equilibrium that will take place instead of this lack, which he didn't even suspect existed, such as a subliminal order injected into his head. Without knowing it, Allan was going to leave more solid, stronger maybe even more human.

EVOLUTIONS.

— "We can kill time or ourselves;
strictly speaking, it is the same."
Elsa Triolet.

Bollène, the next morning.

While Béatrice had come out late in the evening to ensure the well-being of her guest, she had spent a restless night and had had very little sleep. The soreness of her wounds pulled her skin and caused her a slight limp. She thought of only one thing, to see her strange guest. But it was better not to arouse suspicions. She prepared coffee for the whole family. Her parents, who were always the first to wake up, were surprised to see their daughter getting busy in the kitchen.

"Good morning, darling", her mother gave her a kiss on the cheek, you didn't suffer too much from your wounds last night?"

After her father placed a kiss on her forehead, she sat down on a chair, which had the effect of accentuating the pains she felt, at times feeling like she felt them all over her body. She knew that her parents had to be away for a good part of the day. Only one problem remained to solve, 'Annie', who was struggling to get up on the first ring of her alarm clock.

"We'll leave towards nine o'clock", Gabrielle said and we'll be back around four o'clock this afternoon. I have prepared 'basquaise' chicken for lunch, the one you like."

"Thanks, mom."

"And you'll cleanse those wounds, they're not pretty to see."

"Yes, don't worry."

Suddenly, a voice was heard in her head.

"Hello Trice, I'll take care of your wounds, if you wish."

"You can do something?", the girl said aloud.

She suddenly realized her clumsiness and her parents looked at her strangely.

"What do you want us to do?", Roger asked, interrupted by the strange behavior of his daughter since the day before.

"I have to think of something", she thought. It didn't take much time, as her imagination was very active.

"I would like you to get something for me if you have time, because I will have a little trouble getting around today."

"What do you need?"

"A red fluorescent marker."

"The one you have doesn't work anymore? I thought I saw you had a practically new one in your hand just a fortnight ago."

"I use it a lot at the moment."

"Alright, we'll get you one."

"She's strange, she's hiding something" Roger thought, looking at Gabrielle who wasn't paying attention.

"Good comeback", the flying voice resumed, "what's a fluorescent marker?"

Béatrice let out a barely audible grin, similar to that of the day before, but a little less obvious. While Gabrielle was busy preparing Annie's breakfast, Roger noticed.

"Are you sure everything's alright, my girl?"

That was the way he called his two daughters.

"Your daddy seems to quickly understand and know you well", the voice continued.

"Shut it!", Béatrice couldn't contain herself to say it aloud again.

Roger saw red and put the indelicate girl in her place.

"My daughter, that you have a problem and do not wish to speak to us about it, only regards you, but I will not tolerate you speak to me in this tone!"

His serious tenor voice woke up little Annie who came down more out of curiosity than out of concern. For once, she was not being shouted at!

Gabrielle was looking at her daughter with concern. At the moment, she released the bread she was preparing for Annie, asking as many questions as Roger.

"Talk to us Béatrice, tell us what's wrong. These reactions are not like you."

The girl was upset. What to say?

"If you hear me think, I need advice, now!"

"It's the right time", the voice answered.

"Couldn't we joke later?"

"Tell them you're discovering mediumistic gifts and that you're hearing voices!"

"They're going to think I'm crazy!"

"Absolutely, but if you add that you don't control anything and it scares you, you have a chance to challenge them. Also tell them that they will have a minor incident this afternoon."

"What?", she said aloud again.

Annie had just entered the room and was surprised by the atmosphere that prevailed there. At the moment, she thought her sister was addressing her.

"I didn't say anything, Béa!"

She looked at her parents looking at her big sister as if she came from another planet.

"Tell them", the voice insisted.

"Alright, OK, I didn't want to talk about it, but I do, indeed, have a problem."

Having calmed down, Roger asked for more details, while Gabrielle sat around the table to listen to her daughter explain her sudden change.

"You won't believe me and it's a little sensitive to talk about."

Roger put a reassuring hand on the shoulder of the unlucky girl.

"Tell us, my girl, it will surely do you good to talk about it."

"I'm hearing voices and I think I can see the future!"

Her parents looked at each other, telling each other with their eyes: *"What did we miss?"*

Annie smiled and wondered how she could take advantage of this new situation. A question passed through Roger. He wanted to have peace of mind.

"Are you taking drugs, my daughter?"

In those cases, 'my girl' went into the background. Distraught, Béatrice could only see that she should never have embarked on such an adventure, but she still tried to cope.

"Alright, you asked for it! You will have a slight incident this afternoon, and NO, I don't take drugs!"

"You never mentioned it to us", Gabrielle remarked, "why didn't you tell us sooner?"

Béatrice didn't know what to say anymore to get out of that conversation.

"I'll never get out of it" she told herself, *"I have to find something to end this charade."*

"I was afraid of your reaction."

"But you know very well that we're not narrow-minded", Roger said "and it seems to me that we have often shown understanding with you girls."

"Tell them their judgment is much too important to you, so that you take the risk of making a bad one", the voice advised.

She repeated everything to the letter, by adding:

"Could we talk about it later, when you come back, for example?"

Worried as the mother she was, Gabrielle preferred to reassure her.

"Of course darling, but don't be afraid to talk to us. This is not what we showed you, OK my daughter?"

"Yes, mom, thank you."

"A last detail, my girl", added Roger, who seemed preoccupied, "what color is the car we'll have the incident with this afternoon?"

"Dark blue", the voice said.

"Thank you!"

She passed the message to her father, then got up from the table to go isolate herself in the living room. In the kitchen stupor reigned. Annie felt two oppressive looks upon her.

"Ouch!" she thought.

"You were aware of your sister's vision gift?", Roger asked.

"No dad, this is the first time I hear about it."

Gabrielle interrupted the conversation, but was no less worried.

"Roger", she scolded, trying to deflect attention from Béatrice, "we'll talk to her when we come back if you want, but we have to be in Orange at half-past nine. We'd better finish our breakfast and get ready if we don't want to be late."

Roger knew very well where she was coming from saying this and although nothing pressed, reasonably speaking, he nodded and resumed painting his bread.

Meanwhile, 'Irma' who was sitting on the sofa staring at the outside landscape, was silently conversing with her friend.

"How did you get on that road?"

"There is certainly someone in your world playing with the corridors of time."

"Someone from my world? The corridors of time? I know I can be naïve sometimes, but there, even if you master the extra-sensory communication, it's too much!"

"I'm not looking to scare you or lie to you; but did you just realize that you do it very easily too?"

She kept silent in that moment.

"That's right, you're right, I didn't pay attention. That's it, I can't believe it, I have the gift of telecommunication!"

"Why do you say 'the gift'? It's just another capacity you've developed."

"But I had never done it before."

"If you didn't have anyone around you to practice with, that's normal."

"It's logical! Maybe that's why I could talk so casually with you, I didn't realize it either, I didn't even see it coming."

"You're funny Trice, you amuse me greatly. This must be due to the fact that we are on the same wavelength."

"Maybe! For communication, anyway. Can I ask you a delicate question?"

"Of course, Trice!"

"Béa, why do you have such a big head?"

He laughed frankly.

"We're like that."

"You're still saying you're not from our world?"

"I knew I was changing dimensions when the landscape I was in suddenly started to accelerate. It went so fast that I didn't have time to react and I can clearly see that I'm elsewhere. Everything is different, starting with you."

"Very well, admitting you're not from here. You often have fun at this little game?"

"Never! Only a few men of science venture from time to time as part of temporal space experiments. So we know the existence of the phenomenon, but it's not a mass attraction. You're thinking I'm an alien, right?"

"Yes, and…"

"I don't resemble at all to the image you have of us."

"Correct again, and…"

"It's normal, we're human beings like you, but we changed with time. In what year are you?"

"In 2016."

"We're in 3717. We have a little more than 1700 in advance of your evolution!"

"Human beings like us?"

"What else would you like us to be?"

"I don't really know, but different from us, in any case."

"What is your basis when you say that?"

"Your appearance, your powers."

"Of what powers are you talking about?"

"You know very well, all these things we do together and you seem to find normal."

"But this is part of man, dear Trice and if we can have this type of communication, other men and women in your world can, unless you're an alien yourself!"

"You're kidding, right?"

"Yes and no. To be honest, that's what you are on this Earth as well as us, actually. It's what you'll discover by researching your origins. We weren't born with the earth, we are imported from different universes."

"A giant hand dropped a man and a woman on a beautiful morning in May!"

"We could compare your giant hand to the assault of space on the planets and the man and the woman to microorganisms with an adaptation without limits."

"You know more than us on this subject?"

"To really know it, you would have to go, but the weather conditions of that time do not allow it. The air is unbreathable; Earth is very hostile. We tried to send a 'roboman' some time ago. The implants he had received allowed him to evolve in places inaccessible to us. But we never heard from him afterwards."

"What is a roboman?"

"Simply a man with a multitude of implants making him more technological than human. Have you ever heard of nanotechnology?"

"From time to time, in some scientific programs on a cultural channel."

"In my world, there are two distinct races: 'Us' and the 'Plugged'. This is one of the nicknames we give them and we try to separate from them because we are afraid of what this situation is going to cause. Some robomen started giving birth to babies with nano integrated circuits. I can't quite believe it myself, but now it's part of their anatomy and now more than ever we don't want to mix with them at any price, because it is out of the question to take the risk of being born 'preimplanted'."

"I would be scared too!"

"They swear by it, unlike us, who think that what we are doesn't stem from our abilities, but from the choices we make. I may have a bigger head than you, but the rest of my body is the same as yours outside your belly."

"What do you mean by that?"

"No one is deformed where I come from, unlike your father, for example."

"If he heard you, he would knock you one immediately!"

"That's nice, a what?"

"A wallop!"

"I don't know what it is, but it surely leaves a good feeling."

Béatrice smiled. She was beginning to fall in love with friendship.

"So, let's hope he doesn't develop good feelings towards you! Anyway, you'll probably never meet."

"It's been a day that I'm here and I find you very strange at times!"

"Maybe, but for me, it's you who are strange, because even if you seem sincere, I don't meet every day someone who certifies coming from another world with a watermelon as a head, who speaks without moving his lips and has three hairs on the pebble at Homer Simpson!"

"I never counted them, but I think I have more than what you say."

"It was just a manner of speaking, we tend to exaggerate everything!"

"I understand."

"Everyone has so much hair on the skull where you come from?"

"Yes and no!"

"That's a clear answer!"

"My peers have none or very few."

"Even the women?"

"Especially the women!"

"I can hardly imagine what they should look like!"

"To very beautiful women."

"I'm sorry, I meant no disrespect."

"I know, I'm not upset. Still, there are other people in our world who still have as much hair as you do."

"The robomen?"

"Yes; we respect that community, but we don't live together. Their choice is their own, we don't immerse ourselves in their lives and vice versa. So there are two different governments, two police forces and we are two worlds in one. Our coexistence has been serene for four centuries, but the beginnings have been difficult and our ancestors have almost lived an ideological war. To come back to my appearance, it is similar to yours, we only use more of our brain. But if there's something I know, is that we were once like you."

"Really?"

"Yes, we discovered a multitude of psychic abilities that had slumbered in us forever. We had not really exploited anything until 2020, in any case nothing but our 'technological intelligence'. But that year marked the beginning of a new era. Some continued to believe in technology and others to their own psychic and intellectual abilities of which I am a part of, and we quickly split into two distinct groups: men and robmen, also called 'hairy'."

"Now I understand better; tell me more about these robomen?"

"Like I already said, we called them that, for they were born human, but they don't have much human traits besides the base

302

and the physical appearance; and they can transplant micro circuits in their bodies to outdo themselves, however they don't live as long as we do. We think that man is like a repository, a software store that he never uses."

"So, thankfully not all of them use it, because if we take into account that it has only 'bugged out' since its appearance, it will be better to secure access to software with a password written in concrete!"

"You use concrete in your computers?"

Béatrice burst out laughing.

"No, forget what I said and continue your explanation."

"I just understood, but your qualifiers are sometimes different from ours."

"What do you say in these cases?"

"We talk about the crystal."

"Only that! Note, this doesn't surprise me."

"You know its virtues?"

"Vaguely, I equate it with purity."

"Well, this is precisely our workhorse. We started a long work on ourselves by learning to 'click on the right programs'. Man underestimates himself all his life by putting himself his own barriers, whatever the reason. The human body is nevertheless able to bear much more than we thought, starting with life. Our wounds, like yours, close and heal. Our body cares for itself and this is part of our active programs. But we can only be and react according to what surrounds us. The subtlety is simply to find our balance."

"'OUR' balance?"

"It depends on the personality and desires of each individual."

"This is not obvious, but you are perfectly clear and concise."

"Why do you say that, Trice?"

"Because it's so simple to hear."

"I see, but it's been centuries since the process began. I grew up in this context and I would have a hard time feeling how you do, but I must admit that I was very good at history!"

"In history, one would think to hear about prehistory!"

"It's very old for us. To be honest, you represent the beginning of what we call 'the beginning of the peak of the end'."

"Yes, to sum it up, we are only mentally retarded in your eyes!"

"No, is this how you consider your ancestors, which incidentally, are the same as yours, but from even more distant times?"

"No, you're right, apart the exceptions, we admire them."

Homer smiled discreetly, alone in his cabin, guided by wisdom.

"Very good, you got me, but don't add up!"

"Since we have started talking, it's the first time I've heard an expression we also use. We nail ourselves in our world, surely remnants of our prehistory..."

"That's it, make fun, at the first opportunity, you're entitled!"

"To what?"

"Back at you."

"We also use that one!"

"I don't care", Trice said dryly, "about the way you joke! And the robomen, can they travel as you do?"

"Not to my knowledge. That's due to their state."

"How so?"

"We haven't looked into these experiences much, but I know by having read about it that the settings are different for us and for robomen. That said, we think they have already tried it without making it obvious."

"So a man and a roboman can't travel together?"

"Certainly not, because one of them would disintegrate. This is partly why we plan to travel in different universes in search of a new home to separate ourselves from them once and for all. But this takes time, a lot of time, because we have only known inter-dimensional trips concretely for barely 200 years, and even if our scientists have been testing for more than a century, it is not yet developed, so not in the public domain. With a little luck, maybe I'll see the beginning."

"What are the other reasons?"

"We know, among other things, that our planet is heading towards destruction, no matter what we do to save it."

"Then, you're closer than we are", Béatrice said "for we began to talk about it here too. It's not for the day after tomorrow as a happening, but we're convinced we're going to live it too. All the research we systematically do goes in this direction."

"I'm not surprised, because even if we don't yet travel, the researchers who put it into practice make public reports. But they are censored and filtered by the authorities. To summarize, only the one who wants to understand, will. By the way, since I'm here, how are yours?"

"Our authorities?"

"Yes."

"Why the question?"

"Because there is a pivotal period in our history and I am curious by nature."

"It's starting to be the anarchy of justice."

"I understand what you're saying. By noting that they can afford almost anything, high-level positions attract all neurotics in your world! All governments are the same. In some ways, they don't have a choice. Normally, constitutions are designed by and for man, but he will never be more than the result of his own evolution as such."

"Well, say, one has to hang on and out with you!"

"Where?"

"I wanted to say one has to follow you."

"I agree, but where?"

"Just let it go!" Béatrice said nonchalantly, exasperated.

"I hold nothing in my hands."

"It's not true, you're doing it on purpose!"

"Yes."

"Because... Sorry?"

"I said YES!"

"Perfect, now you're mocking me!"

"Excuse me, I found it funny. I won't upset you anymore. Continue your presentation, please. We were evoking the fools of power. That's how you say it, right?"

"We don't say, but we truly think it. That said, it's not a first. Today, it becomes difficult to elect someone in our democracy, because we don't know if they are there for ideals or for their career, not to mention the retribution. Recently, a president has multiplied by ten his salary on the pretext that he didn't get enough compared to his ministers, whereas it would have been so simple to lower theirs. This way, they would have been equal by respecting the difference of status. But when you see that, it's hard to think they're not there for the money. But they are apparently still trusted because there are still many members. In a way, I find it rather sad. Where will it lead us?"

"I think I can answer that question, Trice, because our history relates similar facts and the result is not very joyful."

"Something escapes me in what you explain"

"I'm listening, Trice."

"Béa... You seem to say that there are several different evolutions, are we in agreement?"

"Yes, Béa, that's what researchers in this field are telling us."

"So why would there be multiple worlds if they all evolve the same way? And add 'Trice', please!"

"Yes Béa and Trice. There are several worlds, we are certain. But there are also a multitude of details that differ. Recently, one of our scholars came back with more instructive affirmations. Basically, all these evolutions were not alike that much. The first say that the same characters are found in all universes, but in different ways. To put it simply, the decisions that one person can make in one universe will not be the same in another and all in the same period. But we're discovering that this phenomenon is not unique. There is also the time factor."

"How come? And my name is BEATRICE!"

"Space is made up of holes through which time is questioned. That is to say that when traveling in other dimensions, we travel or rather we are called to travel also in time."

"There are about fifteen billion people currently and…"

"How much did you say?"

"Fifteen billion. I know that in your day you are about eight billion and you are about to change poles. This will obviously have unfortunate consequences, but you will survive in spite of a natural selection, because nature is not made to obey us. It always takes back its rights. If the planet is overloaded, it will make it so it will be lighter. We're like fleas on a dog, except that the Earth shakes in its own way. It balances itself, somehow."

"How do you know?"

"I know my classics."

"I see", 'Trice' grumbled; "and you still manage to find space on Earth?"

"Of course, there are many more than you imagine and at the risk of surprising you, there are still a lot of exploitable places."

"That represents so many possibilities of different worlds…"

"Exactly since each one of us can have a multitude of different reactions to each situation, which can in turn change those of others. It may be that robomen don't exist elsewhere. We make and shape our world every second that passes and in every new birth there is a new dimension."

"I don't dare imagine living and evolving in this spirit, it must be great! But say, for someone supposed not to know, you have a lot to say!"

"As I was telling you, I keep myself informed."

"But these dimensions which you speak of, don't exist in the beginning?"

"Obviously yes, but they are waiting their turn, somehow."

"You mean they are waiting for births to exist?"

"No", Homer said, laughing, "they don't wait for a signal and aren't stopped until the activation of a giant switch! I say there are many dimensions for each of us in which we can very well go and come back many times, and we discover them throughout our life. Moreover, it can happen that some mix together."

"Hey, excuse me for a minute here. When you say 'We discover them throughout our life…'"

"Yes, sorry. We don't discover them, we go through them without knowing it."

"Without knowing! But you were saying…"

"It's a bit complicated to explain to an ignorant. I'll give you an explanation you can understand!"

Béatrice didn't react, but she thought no less. She was, literally, boiling.

"The universe is like an enormous pendulum, each element of which it is composed has a precise function and is always activated in due time, simply because it is necessary. It is our freedom to take into account or not. This can sometimes cause occasional irregularities, like seeing one of your cars come out of nowhere, when there was nobody in the beginning."

"Yes, it's true, it happened to me a few times."

"It is then an interdimensional shock that never lasts more than a few seconds."

"Something intrigues me. If all dimensions collide, we should have already seen other civilizations more advanced than ours!"

"No Trice, my presence here was knowingly provoked, if we can address it so. But otherwise, only similar dimensions attract and intermingle regularly. One of my dimensions may be that of my neighbor. But there are so many factors that come into play, that it is difficult and I cannot even see anything in advance."

Homer let a few seconds pass, then continue with an unexpected remark.

"You have on your face the expression of a person who doesn't understand my words. You have to tell me if that's the case!"

"You can see that?", Béatrice asked, surprised.

"Yes."

"Stop me if I'm wrong. We discover our dimensions at every moment of our lives, without even realizing it, do we not?"

"You can put it that way; in so doing, we become acquainted with ourselves. But I don't know if it's a good method."

"Why?"

"Because some things are better off not knowing. Because if, as they say, memories fade, our eyes also have a memory and as you know, waves and vibrations never stop."

"I don't understand."

"We are thousands if not millions of people, and when there is one who sees something, it is as if the information is engraved simultaneously in the brain of each of them. It's what we call 'déjà vu.'"

"If the same people appear in each world and they get married and have the same children, then everything comes together!"

"Yes, Trice, that is correct."

"In this case, what good are all these worlds?"

"Each of them is a part of ourselves. They all have a reason for being because nothing happens by chance. We have the robomen because we haven't been virulent enough. I'm convinced that there are other worlds similar to ours where they don't exist. Worlds where we have evolved in differently."

"These passages to other dimensions always lead to worlds that resemble us?"

"You probably refer to the low vibration dimensions where we are only wandering spirits without a carnal form?"

"Yes, that's it. Spirits or ghosts, I don't know how you call them in your world."

"We use the same terms. Language evolves, but thoughts stay the same. To answer your question, I don't know enough, so I can't be precise, but if I understand correctly, it's just a simple adjustment."

"Then, it's possible?"

"I even think they started with that, as these dimensions are the closest and the most accessible and when they saw it worked, they looked at other dimensions as well. We designate them as parallel dimensions, because they resemble ours on almost every point. Only the evolutions are different. However, we are certain that information is being transmitted between each other."

"What do you mean?"

"Each person automatically informs their double when they learn something important to them. This would take long to explain. To resume, we think we all inform ourselves as much as we can about how we are so as not to lose ourselves in the different personalities we are capable of having."

"It's crazy, I'm telepathically talking about something you only see in sci-fi movies with someone from elsewhere!" Béatrice thought.

"I heard that!"

"I forgot again!"

"Just a small clarification. I don't come from elsewhere, I arrived from elsewhere, it's not the same thing; even if the result is the same. I didn't want to be here. I only hope I can find a way to get home."

"For that, it would be necessary to find someone who is interested in this field and personally, I don't know anyone in this area."

"Don't worry Trice and Béa, I see you're falling asleep, so I'll do the same by putting a screen in front of me in case one of your family members comes here."

"I'm sleeping? Why do I feel like I'm floating in the air? But… what's happening? I see myself. I can see myself from the top of the room! Should I be scared?"

"If 'Screen-Spirits' and outside the body experience scare you, then yes; otherwise it's part of the process of telepathy, or rather of one of the processes, I should say. You chose the easiest way. Thus, our two spirits met, for I was forced to do the same."

"Okay, but before I fall asleep, how did I do it?"

"You already did it without knowing. That is to say, you continue to react to what surrounds you, to what is the most important, but your mind is elsewhere. And it's something that you apparently do often, because you do it with great ease."

"And what do you mean by screen?"

"It's a 'thought form' I use to give the illusion I'm not there."

"You become invisible?"

"In a way, but I would rather say I blend in the scenery, or that I make the person who approaches me blind when she looks towards where I am."

"A bit like putting a big picture of the empty room in front of you?"

"Exactly, you got it! You better watch yourself and don't lose sight of yourself ... 'It's Béatrice'. Because it's a blow to not be able to come back if you're not paying attention. Sleep well, Béatrice and see you soon."

"See you soon... One last thing... It's amazingly huge to have met you!"

"We're not as big as that."

"Never mind, see you later."

"Yes, 'Trice-Béatrice-Béa'. You're really strange, it's hard to understand you without analysis."

That 'one-to-one' conversation lasted only ten minutes. While Annie was finishing breakfast, Roger and Gaby went to get ready. They stopped a few moments in the living room to observe their daughter who would now be the subject of special attention.

"We'll have to be very open-minded with her", Roger said.

"We already are, it's not in that direction we'll have to put in an effort, but rather to the consequences and changed in our lives this new situation will bring", Gabrielle answered.

"You're surely right. Let's get ready."

Annie hurried to swallow her last sandwich to go see her sister. She was both excited and worried. She, who being the youngest, compared to her elder sister, now she should probably share her 'untouchable' status and put her little life into question. A certain jealousy, almost a rancor was beginning to settle in her young spirit. No one, not one person would take away the privilege of being able to do stupid things with peace of mind, but above all, out of the question of losing the spotlight. What to do? A certainty was growing.

'Miss little plague at times' was on the right track for her nickname to make sense. She went back to her room to think of a solution. She lay on her bed, took a comic in her hands pretending to read it and imagined a multitude of stratagems to discredit her sister.

"Having a 'gift' in turn? No, that had to be proven; say she's taking drugs. She's much too serious, no one will believe that; spread a rumor that she bonded with the local 'Billy the Kid'? Why not? That would be a start... I'll keep that in mind."

She was suddenly hit by an illumination that made a smile of satisfaction appear.

"To begin with, there's nothing better than to bring the parents back with their feet on Earth..."

She closed her book, threw it on her bed after getting up hurriedly, checked her sister was still sleeping and waited patiently for their parents to go away. She turned on the television, sat on one of the chairs in the living room and saw some cartoons, taking care to adjust the volume so as not to wake up 'Trice', throwing a look at the eyes of the latter from time to time.

"When mom and dad will see that, they'll think I'm an awesome little sister to respect her sleep."

Satisfied with the success of her plan, she comforted herself in a victory, to her advanced eyes. Finally ready, Roger and Gabrielle were about to leave and made some recommendations to the girl.

"Be good and listen to your sister. If she doesn't wake up by the end of your shows, shake her up a bit and don't quarrel!"

For the first time, it was her, young Annie, receiving the instructions; she had to watch over her older sister.

"Yes, dad, of course mom, no problem."

The time to board their car and the two sisters were soon alone in the big house. She watched her parents leave, waving her hand and implementing her plan without further ado.

She returned to her room to change and went quietly in the garden shed to take her bike. 'Homer Simpson' had recently been out and about from his four wooden walls. She got on her gear, went out into the middle aisle and took a last look at the house before leaving. She started pedaling so fast that she could hear the wind bumping into her bike, causing a light and steady breeze.

At the first corner, she hesitated a moment, changed her mind, then continued to pedal even more rapidly. On the road, she saw Madam Lambert, a close neighbor to whom she didn't fail to make big signs to greet her, but especially to show whoever wanted to see that she wasn't accompanied.

Arrived at the second corner, she decided, took her courage in both hands and continued straight, closing her eyes. She felt in her mad rush that she had left the road, but she wasn't falling, nor did she hit any obstacles. It lasted for about five seconds, then surprised by that state of facts, she opened her eyes. For a second, she couldn't believe what was happening. She was flying!

"Not possible!" she told herself, *"I continue to advance without touching the ground; I'm flying!"* she screamed inside, *"I know how to fly!"*. She could see the grass, the bushes and all that was the forest running at full speed under her wheels and the most fabulous, was that her bike seemed to be guided and avoided

the trees like a skier doing a slalom. She was more amazed than scared. In a moment of lucidity, she asked herself a question.

"How am I doing this?"

Still guided by a force invisible to her eyes, the bike slowed down more and more, until it stopped in the middle of the trees, in the undergrowth. She had traveled more than two kilometers and was now among the chestnut trees, her feet and the wheels of her bike anchored in the weeds and other nettles that flourished in that exact place. She looked all around her and went to the obvious. She would have to backtrack, without being able to use her bike, on that very inhospitable carpet for her little thirty-two feet, covered with simple tennis shoes in fine linen, strung over socks not much higher than her 'low ankles'.

She was not pleased with this state of affairs, but she had plenty of time to think and reflect on the situation in which she was in, in the hour and a half it took her to rejoin the road, fighting against the green nature with every step she took.

When she finally reached the tar, she looked at her legs, which made her suffer from all the scratches and scrapes caused by the wooded walk. She got back on her bike without resting even for a minute and returned home. This time, she didn't bother to make any sign to anyone. Madam Lambert was again present during the passage of the one that had become a real human rocket, as she quickly pedaled.

Back in the garden at the bottom of her house, she didn't even bother to put 'Ariane' in the shed. She threw the whole thing on the floor, hurried inside, rushed into the kitchen where her sister was preparing lunch, and setting the table, encircled her with her arms as if it was the last time she could do it and offered her apologies in good form. Surprised, and most of all worried,

Béatrice stopper her younger sister's momentum.

"Where have you been? Do you have any idea of the time I wondered what had happened to you? It's been more than two hours!"

But Annie wouldn't release her grip.

"Forgive me, Béa", she said without letting go.

It wasn't in the girl's habits to lose herself in apologies. Béatrice often showed patience and bravery towards the little pest, but there was something unusual about her behavior. She seemed to be really sincere. It was different from all the excuses she had made so far. Béatrice got out of the hug and asked her this simple question, without any anger.

"What happened?"

The girl had tears at the edge of her eyes.

"I feel guilty Béa, I feel really guilty."

"If it's for the worries I had, not to mention the reaction that mom and dad would have had if anything had happened to you, it's forgotten, I don't hold it against you, but there's something you're not telling me."

Annie didn't have to find the courage to explain everything, the words came out of her mouth simply and without detours. She recounted her misadventure, the reasons she had acted that way, not to mention the inexplicable aspect of the 'Forest Sequence' and completed her story about the awareness of her feelings towards her sister, as well as a complete wondering about what her act had done to her.

"So this is why I couldn't talk to you", she thought.

"Yes, that's why", 'shaved head' answered, "your little sister isn't a bad person, she just got a little lost!"

"I know, thank you for what you did."

"It's nothing, Trice."

Annie realized her sister's sudden absence.

"Béa?"

"Do you think I can tell her?"

"Yes Trice, she is able to understand and her presence will be useful."

"Well, I'll come with her in this case, the time to prepare her for what she will see and hear."

"Talk to you later, Trice."

"Béa... Trice please, talk to you later."

Getting no answer, Annie asked again.

"Béa, can you hear me?"

At that moment, she 'hung up' and finally answered her little sister.

"Yes, Annie, I'm sorry."

"You didn't react when I told you about the bike in the forest, you didn't seem surprised when I was sure you would think I'm crazy."

"It's normal, little sister, when you'll see what I'm going to show you, you will understand my reaction and many other things."

"What are you talking about?"

"Isn't she too young to get involved in such a story", Béatrice thought. On the other hand, her help would be welcome, because it would be far too complicated to hide this from everyone. She took Annie by the hand, brought her to the other room and invited her to sit on one of the chairs around the dining room table.

"Wait for me here little sister, let's discuss all this while eating."

The preparation didn't take long, she didn't need more than five minutes to bring plates, cutlery, drinks and hot dishes. She took a seat as well, served and started to tell the story.

When she had finished, Annie couldn't believe her ears, but she was, however, excited to discover 'ET'. She hastened to finish her meal, boiling impatiently. Béatrice was observing her and smiled.

"We're going to go Annie, five more minutes."

She finished in turn and went to the kitchen to prepare coffee.

"Is he really scary?", questioned little repentant pest.

"I was really surprised", Béa said, coming back with her cup of coffee. "The way you're going to see him is not at all like the one I was introduced to him. It's his head that surprises the most. It's just a little bigger, that's all."

"Could I ask him about my future?"

"No Annie, he's very nice, but most of all, he's lost here, I would even say stranded!"

She pouted, but settled with the answer anyway.

"Have you finished your coffee?"

"No!"

There, she swallowed the last sip and calmly put the cup on the saucer. Annie saw the teasing, she was on the verge of implosion.

"Have you finished?", she said, annoyed.

"Yes."

In a cartoon, smoke would probably have come out of her head.

"We're going!"

"You're in a hurry?"

"BEA!", said Annie, in a tone of rising decibels.

"Yes, little sister", Béatrice continued, joking.

"WE ARE GOING!", she growled.

Béatrice stopped the torture and headed for the front door. Annie expected a new setback and didn't get up quickly. Seeing this, Béatrice turned towards her sister.

"Then, what are you doing? I'm waiting!"

She didn't let herself be told twice, jumped up and hurried to the exit.

"Come on, I have sufficiently teased you."

Annie didn't say anything, but looked at her sister like a weasel waiting for his hour of deliverance. At three meters from the shed, Béatrice stopped.

"You remember what I told you sister, he surprises the first time."

"It's alright Béa, you told me, explained it in detail."

They were now in front of the door of the 'extraterrestrial temporary guest house'. Béatrice looked at her sister. She didn't show it, but she was worried about her reaction. She seemed enthusiastic, for sure; but if by chance she got scared and ran away, she would alert the whole neighborhood.

"We'll see", she told herself.

"Then, what are we waiting for?", Annie was growing impatient.

"Are you ready?"

"Come on!"

"I can go out or you can open the door, if you wish", Homer proposed.

"I heard a voice", Annie exclaimed; "he has a nice voice, heard it in my head!"

"Don't worry Trice, everything will be fine."

She opened the door and a shadow caused by the sun penetrating the 'was ist das'[4], appeared on the floor.

"He's so big!", Annie wondered with her big little girl eyes.

---

[4] 'was ist das' – 'what is this' in German (translator's note)

The shadow suddenly disappeared, leaving inside as only image the tools and other machines of gardening and DIY.

"Where is he?", Annie asked, all excited.

Béatrice wanted to immediately put an end to the joke.

"Homer!", she said seriously, aloud.

Some seconds passed without an answer.

"Homer!", she repeated dryly, like a mother exasperated by the nonsense of her child.

The same shadow suddenly grew from the back to the front creating the expected surprise effect and a hand came to rest on Annie's left shoulder, which surprised, turned at once, discovering Homer's face. She uttered a short cry and succumbed to fascination in the next moment. His body was dressed in white, loose clothing hiding all the contours of his body, yet not able to hide its large size and oversized head.

"He's strange, but he doesn't seem mean", noticed Annie, behaving like a tourist visiting a zoo.

"Be careful", Homer said in a joyful voice, "I bite and I also devour", he added, growling.

"That's it, we had our joke, could you be serious again, please", Béa said, trying to distract Annie's attention.

"You want us to help you or not?"

"No reason to get annoyed Trice, look at your little sister, she's ready."

"Béatrice, damn it, it's not that complicated! Ready for what?" She said, adopting the behavior of the protective big sister.

"To assume what she is. She's always going to be the little pest you know, but she will now favor the feelings she feels toward the people she loves."

"It's profound, what you say."

"Profound? How do you measure words here?"

"Let it go", retorted Béatrice who had no desire to embark on an endless explanation.

"I have nothing in my hands and if that were the case, I wouldn't let it go, it might break! You're really strange in your world, even foolish at times."

Annie was smiling, she was starting to find him amusing.

"I wanted to say that we have other ca… that we have other more important issues to deal with."

"You want to talk about my leaving your world, no doubt?"

"Yes, I have no plans at the moment, but I'm counting on you to help us."

In saying that, she realized there was no conviction in her words. She had the exact opposite and this thought frightened her somewhat. Homer adopted a resigned air, without exacerbating it, but it was stronger than him. What emanated from his person at that moment was not very pleasant. Feeling like a slap, Annie couldn't contain herself.

"You're going to stay here, right?"

Although aware of an impending disaster, but also anxious to keep the morale of the troops intact, Béatrice was offended.

"Annie!", she said militarily.

Homer looked into her eyes and shared his impression.

"I don't think I'll go back Béatrice, your little sister saw right."

"How can you give up so easily!" she was indignant.

"In the same way that I know your parents will hit their car, I won't be able to go back."

"For how long have you known?"

"Just for a short while, since I woke up this morning."

"But then, everything you told me about your world?"

"Beautiful memories Béatrice, only beautiful memories."

"Then we just surrender ourselves without doing anything!"

"It would do good to try something, just in case, if only to not have this feeling of regret, but anyway, I saw the result. Two men will come here to help me, but the attempts will be in vain."

"And how can you remain impassive by saying that?"

"I am not! But what else to do?"

"And who are these two men?"

"They're from a world different from yours, but they look like you, they are only five years ahead in time from your dimension. By the way, I use this word, but it is inappropriate. It would be more accurate to speak of a universe, because to each of them, a very precise world corresponds. I'm not a connoisseur, but that I know!"

"By your scientist explorers?"

"That is correct, Béatrice."

"At this point in time, you can call me Béa if you want."

"I know what I want, but you, do you really know it?"

"How do you see all these things?", Annie asked, a little curious.

"It's written in time."

"How so?"

"We all have a soul and if we wish, we let it frolic wherever it sees fit, which is an opportunity for it to bring us all kinds of information more or less interesting."

"So that's having the gift of clairvoyance?"

"Yes, we could call it that, but it's not a gif in my world."

"Then what is it?"

"It's normal!", he said, smiling.

"And you, Béa?"

"It was him, little sister, he communicated the information because I had to get out of the situation I was in this morning with dad and mom."

"So you cheated!"

322

"Yes, little sister, I was forced to! And if you say anything about it, I'll strangle you!"

"She's serious, your sister!"

"So, what do we do now?", Annie asked.

Béatrice looked at Homer sadly. She knew very well that there was no doubting his word. Until then, the situation was strange, exciting maybe, but it had become desperate. How to return someone from another world to his home? With whom to talk to?

"Don't worry, Béatrice", Homer said, "where I come from, we believe in our destiny and if mine is to stay stuck here, then so be it!"

Béatrice was clueless. She wanted so much to tell him he was wrong, that his visions might not be 100 percent reliable.

"Those two men you were talking about, when are they coming?"

Suddenly, Annie's attention was drawn to a glow from the back of the garden. Homer watched the show out of the corner of his eye and seeing that, Béatrice finally turned around. Annie moved closer to her sister, putting both her hands on her arm.

"What is… what is it?"

"It's a time gap", Homer said.

In that moment, Béatrice made the connection with the appearance of Homer on the small road at the back of the house and questioned him.

"Is this how you got here?"

"Yes, or at least, I think so."

"Then, it's done! You only have to go inside and you'll go home."

"I don't think it's that simple. Let's see what happens."

More than eight seconds passed before Garvey and Allan

made their appearance. They came 'in bulk', unlike their other escapades. This arrival was much more eventful than the others. The time spent inside the passage had lengthened and their landing had been more chaotic. A ping pong ball would surely have bounced back by throwing them on the ground. A little shocked, the two men got up and found their footing.

"My God, Garvey", Allan said, upset, "what happened?"

Garvey was lying on the ground; he started to get up, then asked himself. The gap had closed too quickly. *"Something's wrong"*, he told himself.

"I don't really know what, professor. Unless..."

"Unless what, Garvey?"

"Something's not right. It's quite strange."

"Are you going to unravel the mystery or should I first answer a trick question?"

"Look Allan", Garvey said, showing him the small screen of his box, "among the openings that we have to check, there is someone from another world here."

"A stranger to this world?"

"Yes."

"So, we've got this. I don't understand your surprise!"

"He apparently comes from the year 3717!"

"From so far away! How is it possible?"

"Anyway, it's what's shown here. I don't understand how this could have happened by itself."

"Surely the same as the others."

"I don't think so, professor."

"And why not, young man?"

"Simply because I visited all the others, but not this one."

The two men looked at each other, worried.

"I think we're thinking about the same thing, my friend. The law of the universes.'"

"Yes, professor, this device has its limitations."

"We would be too presumptuous to think that this tiny box could indefinitely defy the grand universe. Here's a lesson to remember!"

"As you say, professor, and we must hurry if we don't want to get stuck somewhere around here."

"Look, Garvey… No, behind you."

"Where are they coming from?"

"For them, I think it's us who came out of nowhere."

"It's strange, professor, nothing works in this voyage, I can't even say who we must help. Let's go meet them. This is also strange, they don't seem surprised to see us!"

They were no more than thirty meters from the trio and could now distinguish their faces.

"Mystery solved, my friend, we know who we came to get!"

"Are you sure, professor", Garvey joked. "He seems to be between two evolutions?"

"Garvey, with each stroll, I need some time to remember what we're doing, unlike you and I have no memory of the worlds we visited. So I have no term of comparison. That said, I can't explain why I'm not surprised to see him."

"I know, professor, and I don't think I'm going to remind you. Furthermore, I don't think I'll remember when all this will be over."

"Hello", the two men said, taking the last steps to arrive.

"Hello", answered Homer and his two savior apprentices.

Garvey remained thoughtful in front of Béatrice.

"I could swear I already saw you somewhere. Could I ask what you do for a living?"

"Garvey, come on, we're not here for that!", Allan admonished.

"That's ok", Béatrice said, "a bit dated as approach, but I'm used to it!"

"It's not at all what you think, I was just saying..."

"Garvey, please!", interrupted Allan by making him understand with a nod of the head to put a big block on the tongue.

"That doesn't bother me", Béatrice insisted.

"Forget my question", Garvey continued, realizing that he would probably spend more time in useless explanations than building an Eiffel Tower in every world; "my colleague is right, we don't have time."

"His colleague" Allan thought, *"he's quite arrogant!"*

"Alright, colleague; and if we took care of what we came here for, what do you say?"

"Yes, professor."

Garvey addressed directly the person in question.

"It's the 29th of October, 3717, is it not?"

"Indeed, but your command is malfunctioning, right?"

Surprised, Garvey looked at Allan, then answered Homer.

"That's right! But how do you know?"

"It is of no matter. You should leave while you still can."

"You really know things! But the answer is no, not before trying everything and we'll start right now."

He entered the coordinates in his magic device, but nothing worked.

"I was expecting this", he thought *"But he can't stay here and we don't have much time! How to go about it?"*

Homer intercepted his thoughts and hastened to reassure him.

"Don't worry, Garvey, take care of other people who need you and who are waiting for you."

"How does he know my name?"

"How do you know? I see, I understand... But I refuse to

abandon you!"

"You don't have a choice, young man, you have to leave before everything rushes down on you."

A loud, muffled sound was suddenly heard. It seemed to come from the sky, more precisely from the stars. In that moment, everyone looked up and watched a huge, indefinite shape high enough, just above them. Béatrice couldn't believe her eyes. Annie wasn't even scared.

"Look!", she said pointing her finger at the sky.

Allan was equally astonished and Garvey had the expression of someone who understood what was going on.

"Well, very timely! Mom and dad come to the son's rescue" he thought, looking at Allan from the corner of his eye.

Allan noticed and gave in to curiosity.

"Is there something I should know?"

"No, professor, reassure yourself."

He didn't believe a word, but he knew that his young friend now knew very well what he was doing.

Homer didn't understand what was happening, he was terrified, much more than Béatrice, unlike Annie who was fascinated by the show. All had their eyes fixed on the gigantic vessel, which more or less, measured at least one kilometer in circumference, like a floating city. It was so low that the whole city and maybe even a good part of the area could see it. It wasn't moving. Only the multitude of white, blue and green lights glittered under the hull. The authorities soon deployed a fleet in case something happened, as well as some experienced pilots in the air ready to shoot. All this took no more than ten minutes to set up.

"What are they doing?", Annie asked.

"They're here for me", Homer answered.

"You saw it?"

"Earlier."

"But what are they waiting for, like that?, Béatrice thought aloud.

"They're only setting a few time parameters to bring our friend home", Allan was sure of himself and surprised the next second to have answered thus.

Amazed by what he had just heard, Garvey looked at him with a frown, but let nothing be noticed.

"It's not possible!" he told himself *"He can't remember... not here."*

"What do you know?", Béatrice continued.

"I... I just know, that's all!"

Homer asked him the question in his own way, in a nominative and discreet way so that he was the only one to hear it.

"That's where you come from, right?"

Allan turned to Homer, looking at him with satisfaction and approval. Garvey had vaguely observed the scene with an evasive, but focused look.

"Well then, I don't understand anything anymore!" he thought, *"What are they doing, did they plan a family weekend?"*

Sensing something coming, Homer looked at Béatrice and Annie smiling.

"Thank you for your help", he said aloud.

"We didn't do anything", the big sister answered, "it's rather you who helped us!"

"You supported me when you could have reacted quite differently."

"We have only known each other since yesterday and you changed our lives forever. I will never look at the sky the same way again."

"Me neither, 'Trice.'"

"Please, between us, call me Béa…"

"You're not as strange as I thought."

Béatrice let a small tear fall, filled with emotion. Annie wasn't as moved as her sister and she couldn't help but do what she had recently decided to do. She motioned for Homer to bend down and gave him a kiss on the cheek. Surprised, he did the same, saying out loud what she had in mind.

"Well, it's done, little girl, you kissed an alien!"

"Wow!! It's exactly as I thought!"

The eyes of wisdom looked at her intently for a few moments.

"You're still young, small one. Your age forgave your acts. But you grew with the lesson you received today. Know that your actions may not always be the best. Those who pretend to be perfect lie."

"Why? You think that's possible?"

"Who can boast about it besides those who seek precisely to show it? Certainly not those who have the potential. Learn that those who want to appear so hide their true nature. If perfect beings existed, they would not show it, especially in a world like yours! Continue to make mistakes, to go wrong, it's the best way to achieve perfection."

Allan and Garvey didn't miss a word. They were attentively listening to the 'Voice of the future'.

"Why were you surprised by my kiss, don't you do that at home?"

"There's not much contact. It disappeared little by little with time. We give more importance to who we are and what we think. We are much more cerebral; we have other interests, if you prefer. Everything in our existence that lasts longer than yours, is changed from the past that will one day be your present. Our taste in food evolved. We eat less meat, we sleep a lot less and are practically no longer sick. Our lifestyle is very balanced. There, young lady, did I answer your question?"

Annie nodded.

"How do they have children if there's no contact? Not by thought transmission, surely!" Allan thought. Homer looked at him, smiling.

"Exactly like you Allan, but what is for you an enjoyment is for us only the means of procreation and our women carry the child five to six months on average and three to four months for the premature."

"Hm, thank you sir!", Allan said, a little embarrassed.

Then he turned towards Béatrice.

"Do you want to kiss an alien as well?"

"Homer, that could be badly interpreted around here!"

"Very well. Do you want to do the same thing as your sister?"

She smiled in turn and answered.

"After all, it's not every day that we have a three degree encounter... If you want!"

Béatrice did the same, or rather wanted to do the same, but Homer suddenly disappeared before her eyes, apparently removed by some kind of light beam straight out of the center of the ship.

She gave a little cry of surprise. It only took one second and Homer didn't have time to greet the two men who had come from elsewhere to help him. Entering the beam, Homer could distinguish in the background a tiny part of the landscape of his world. The goods shipped, the beam disappeared; then it was the ship's turn, rumbling like a giant hornet for a few moments, starting to slowly gain altitude and went at the speed of lightning.

From the black dot it quickly became, everyone saw it

disappear from the landscape at once, as if a door had opened in the sky to close suddenly behind its passage. The authorities, still on alert, didn't understand the goal of the maneuver. Who were they? Why did they come to leave less than a quarter of an hour later? Would they come back? These were the questions; in other words, it was a general panic.

"Well, home he goes!", Garvey said.

"Let's hope so!", Béatrice said, looking at the stars. "There are sometimes brief meetings that mark us for life. Some make us discover the feelings that make happy, an alter ego, others what is worse in human behavior, but whatever the nature, they change our life forever."

When Gabrielle and Roger would return in the afternoon, their car would have indeed suffered a shock. Béatrice will even take a picture of the impact and make it a symbolic memory. Her parents will talk to her about this revealing gift. She will simply say that this is not the time for her and that when the time comes to develop it, she will look into the matter.

Annie will never doubt the interest of her close entourage, as well as the extra-familial relationships she will have the opportunity to develop later. In other words, she will have confidence in herself and in life. And above all, the two sisters now knew that somewhere, far from there, elsewhere, other civilizations existed.

Garvey and Allan were no exception to the show and although they had reason not to be so amazed, they had watched with the same fascination.

"We should go now, professor."

"Yes, my young friend, time passes."

Before pressing on his command, Garvey made one last remark to Béatrice.

"If by chance you feel like singing, don't hesitate, you have a splendid voice where we come from. And you", he continued, talking to the 'little one', "you are the no less famous sister of our great voice singer. You don't sing, but you've been able to put repetitive journalists in their place during a live interview with your big sister. You've been able to show off your steel character in front of millions of eyes and we love you both!"

Perplexed, Béatrice asked this simple question.

"How do you want her to put anyone in their place at her age?"

"I'm sorry, I had forgotten, you're twelve years older in our world ..."

He paused, then added a detail.

"Both of you, of course!"

"Time shifted?", Béatrice was surprised.

"It is a contentious issue, but I will be tempted to tell you there is no time."

"There is no time? How is it possible, we can measure it, so it exists!"

"It's not as simple as that, but you'll have to find the answer to that question yourself, for we have to leave now. Goodbye, or rather farewell and a beautiful life to you both."

"Goodbye, Miss", Allan went further.

Garvey pressed the small keys and the little green light came on. A new gap opened before their eyes.

"It's time, professor, we can go."

The two sisters watched the phenomenon with as much interest as they had the first time.

"It will be difficult to tell this to our friends, what do you think, sister?"

PERMUTATION?

Back home, Allan and Garvey arrived in the garden.

"Look! Our two time travelers", Jocelyn looked at Emma, who didn't seem to be herself, somewhat distant and relatively agitated.

"What is it, why are you waddling like that?"

"It's this jumper that's itchy."

"Seeing you, it really looks like you're coming back from an interdimensional walk!"

"I already saw this jumper", Jocelyn told himself.

"You didn't have this jumper yesterday?"

"No, I took it as a spare luggage, why?"

"Nothing, just curious."

"She's hiding something."

Emma felt Jocelyn's skepticism. She tried to divert his attention.

"Look", Emma handed him a precious stone, which she had bought some time back, thinking of him.

"You're giving it to me?"

"Yes, take it."

"You know I'm not really a 'jewelry' guy.

"Yes, but this one has value because I offer it to you and maybe it will make you think of me when you go back."

"In that case, yes, or at least I hope so!"

Something was bothering the young woman. She tried not to let anything sweat, but it showed; a blind man would have seen it.

"Is everything alright, Emma?", he continued, getting close to her.

She looked at him like she had never done it since his arrival.

"What is it, Emma? You're looking at me like that because I'm going to leave?"

He suddenly noticed a detail and looked at it twice.

"What have you done to your hair since just now? Looks like it lengthened!", he said, wanting himself funny, and yet intrigued.

Seeing that she didn't react, he didn't insist, smiled at him and pressed her against him.

"You and I know it's not my place here. I'm sure my double can be reasonable by looking at what has always escaped him for so many years. It's up to you to allow him and not to seem to want to bite him as soon as he gets near you. If I am able to love you in my dimension, he must be able to do the same in his."

He was silent for a few moments, then continued using psychology.

"Give me a chance to come near you, to come to you in this world. Help me show you what I feel for you. After all, we're all the same characters with different destinies and lives. And if all goes well, we'll forget this adventure when everything is over."

Still stuck to each other, he ran his hand through Emma's back, as if to wipe off a rebel stain.

"We must not seek to correct our mistakes with people other than those with whom we committed them with."

Jocelyn was starting to be on a streak of beautiful philosophical phrases that wanted to be comforting. He was disarmed in this situation, which seemed to have no solution.

"What to do?" he thought *"What to say? I can't stay here because she doesn't want me to go? Don't let me go like this, please. I don't need this."*

It was as if her heart had stopped beating. She wasn't saying anything, she was only looking at him sadly.

"No need to go back to that, right? We already talked about it."

He suddenly saw a tear flow on the sweet face of young Emma; she seemed to be broken.

"Emma, please, don't do this to me. It's her I love, not you, you know this!"

She got up suddenly and went away, alone in the garden. Seeing this, Allan was surprised and wanted to comfort her.

"Come now, my child", Allan stepped forward as a protective father, "what's happening?"

She was now really crying, unable to utter a word. Jocelyn watched the scene while stopping any momentum of love.

"Talk to me, young woman, make me your confident, I authorize it."

She folded back on herself and continued to pour the sad liquid of her thoughts by succeeding to utter these few words.

"I can't, professor, I can't…"

"You can't what?"

She was in the uncomfortable stage of being inconsolable.

"Leave me", she said, moving away towards the back of the garden, "it will pass!"

"Something escapes me", Allan thought.

He looked at Jocelyn, who was still inside the house, making him understand that he couldn't do anything. Garvey followed the scene without saying anything, but began to ask himself some questions.

"Why such a brutal change?"

An idea touched his mind, but he didn't think it was possible. Jocelyn really didn't know what to do anymore. What would happen if he stayed here? Did he want to stay in this world? And Emma... his Emma? He was desperately trying to turn the problem around, but the outcome was still the same, he had to go back... he wanted to go back!

To see her collapsed like that broke his heart. He noticed, however, a difference in her behavior, then changed his mind, thinking that they were both identical, but...

While Allan was a little helpless in the situation, Garvey hesitated to use his new faculty of persuasion, then he saw Jocelyn go to her and preferred to let him do it. Damiana watched the scene from the living room and also felt that something had changed. Arrived two meters from the unfortunate woman, Jocelyn took a plunge.

"Emma..."

He didn't have time to say more, she threw herself in his arms, excusing herself between two sobs.

"But what's wrong? I thought we had clarified all that. If you give yourself the chance, you can recover it by making one or two concessions; and you also have two wonderful kids who..."

Hearing that, she literally collapsed, interrupting him.

"Come on, Emma, I don't have a place in this world, and even if the children wouldn't notice, I would never be able to lie to them."

"Don't be mad with me, Jossy, I'm sorry."

He frowned, disengaged from Emma, stretched out his arms, stared into her eyes and made her say the words again.

"What did you call me?"

Confused, she tried to make it right.

"Jossy, I used to call him that from time to time and it escaped me."

"There's only her who calls me that and since I have been here, you haven't called me that!"

"I'm not myself today, pay no attention to what I say."

"Why do I have the strange feeling you're hiding something and what's happening here will change the rest of my life?"

Daring to approach the couple, Garvey suggested hurrying before all gaps closed, causing irreparable damage.

"I'm coming, Garvey! Could you answer two questions before?"

"If I know the answers."

"You did not separate from your device for a second, did you?"

"No, I don't think so, why?"

Emma looked at him, concealing her panic.

"That way, it's only a question and you keep the memory of your world for long when you're in another, that is to say, like me?"

"You're worried about losing your memories? Because in this case, reassure yourself, as long as the gap through which you arrived is still active, even closed again it can open again as long as I have not put an end to it and in this case, you keep your memories."

"I see", Jocelyn concluded, preoccupied.

Before leaving, he turned towards Emma to ask her a last question, making sure no one else except her heard it.

"You didn't do it?"

"What are you talking about?"

"Kitten", he replied, thus giving her a reactionary trap, for it was with this cute little nickname that he sometimes addressed himself to 'his' Emma.

Emma pulled herself together and showed of presence of mind this time.

"You also call her like that?"

"You want to tell me he calls you that too?"

These few words reassured him, he doubted no more or very little.

"Yes, it happened to him sometimes, in privileged moments."

"I admit I was wondering if…"

She put her hand on his mouth, looking at him lovingly.

"No, Joss, don't say anything anymore. If Garvey authorizes me, I will accompany you to be there for your departure."

The look they exchanged at that moment was intense, emotionally charged. Allan also interrupted the love birds.

"We have to go Jocelyn, say your goodbyes!"

"Can I accompany you?", asked Emma calmly, seeming less upset.

"I don't see any inconvenience", Garvey said.

She returned to the living room to pick up her vest. Damiana hadn't said anything, but she was seeing clearly now. When Emma got to where she was, she spoke to her in a monotone voice and so simple and natural that it destabilized the young woman.

"You're certain it's what you want?"

"Yes", Emma was surprised, "I'm only going to watch him leave and I'll be back with your husband and Garvey."

"Don't pretend not to understand, it's you, isn't it?"

"Please, don't say anything!" , she answered with her eyes.

"I will be here if you'll need help, young girl. Furthermore, Jocelyn will be here this afternoon, 'your Jocelyn' from now on."

Emma smiled and thanked her the same way, without saying a word.

"You have nothing to thank me for! Come, go now!"

She joined the three men and Garvey got his box out of his pocket.

"We must first go to Aussillon for you to recover your cart and then in the Vosges where you appeared; am I right?"

"Yes Garvey, that's it", confirmed Jocelyn, who was both sad to go, leaving these friendly people, as well as this Emma with whom he had spent nice moments with, but also happy to find his life and 'his Emma'.

He went to say goodbye to Damiana and then returned to the group.

"Are you ready?", Garvey asked.

"Wait a minute", Allan said, looking at his wife.

"Do you want to accompany us, my angel?"

"No, leave without me, I would rather stay here."

"Alright, let's go then!"

Garvey opened a new loophole and everyone went in. Having missed nothing, Damiana thought:

"I don't think I'll ever get used to it!"

"Wait", Jocelyn said, "I have to take my bag!"

"Go ahead, we'll wait!"

METEMPSYCHOSIS.

— *"Living, we always
learn something"*
MM.

G arvey had entered the coordinates of arrival in
the woods, not far from the neighborhood where
Jocelyn's truck was parked. They all arrived safely
and headed towards the house of Jocelyn and Emma of this
world. It didn't even take ten minutes before Emma recognized
the color of the truck.

"It's there!", she said cheerfully.

However, knowing she would never see this truck again
saddened her. Walking in the direction of the vehicle, Garvey
briefed Jocelyn on the upcoming events.

"We'll go on a road with little traffic so that you can disappear
in peace. There, you'll go to the Vosges where we'll meet, and
it's from that place you'll continue your journey in your world."

"Say I still have more than half of the week to go", Jocelyn thought.

Arrived in front of the truck, he seized the keys, opened the
door, climbed and started the engine.

"It's a strange vehicle you have there", Alan remarked; "I never
saw anything like it!"

"Well, that's true", Garvey confirmed, "the carts from this world are quite different!"

"Don't you want to take advantage to take some things home?", Jocelyn asked Emma.

"We only have little time", Garvey objected, "and you weren't supposed to come here with us!"

"Very well, come up in the cabin, in that case. We'll go on a little road three kilometers from here; there is never anyone over there."

Sitting on the berth at the back of the cabin, the two scientists surveyed the inside. It was the first time in their lives they were in a truck, especially one from another world.

As for Emma, she had a big chip on her shoulder, but wasn't showing it. In the passenger seat, she watched Jocelyn drive out of the corner of her eye. It was the last thing, the last movements, the last tics, the last moments she would spend with the man she loved. She wanted to remember, even if at the end of this adventure, she knew, the memories would fade irretrievably. Though; who would be able to say it? Can't they fall into one of the many 'information files' that our brain would be able to store, somewhere in a place where only the unconscious can access?

It was with this meager hope that she reveled in a heavy silence. Jocelyn glanced discreetly from time to time, smiling. Smiles that expressed, in turn, compassion, sadness and desolation. He suddenly broke the mortuary silence that reigned as master, to announce their arrival on the small deserted road.

"Here we are! Deserted road, two minutes stop, everyone down!"

He left the contact and looked mechanically at the various gauges on the dashboard. He realized that the level of gas oil was only half, instead of three-quarters, as it should have been.

"*Damn it!*" he told himself "*I hadn't thought of that! How will I explain it to him?*"

'*Hello Gérard, I'm missing three hundred liters of diesel because I was forced to fork into another dimension!*"

"*If I tell him that, he'll immediately tell me to shut up, stop taking drugs and he wouldn't be wrong. I would do the same in his place!*"

Emma was looking at him with great tenderness. She was smiling. She wanted to let go of her impulses that were becoming more and more oppressive.

"What is it telling you?"

"Huh, what?" Jocelyn said, seeming to be coming out of a semi-comatose state.

"The dashboard, what does it tell you? You seemed to be in full transcendental communication with it!"

Jocelyn smiled in turn.

"Yes, we were having a great conversation. It told me that I had used about three hundred liters of diesel to get off the Vosges and he was sorry for me when I go back and explain this to my boss on Friday!"

"Why do you worry, the flow goes well between you two?"

"Yes, but this isn't nothing. You can steal one hundred liters at a time two hundred, but three hundred is a big amount. My thief shouldn't be in a car! But by the way, how can you know about our good communication... I don't think I told you?"

Emma blamed herself for not paying attention and immediately found the right answer.

"Yes, you told me about it when we walked past the store near the house. You told me it was the place where you worked..."

"If you say so, I don't remember."

"Well, I'm going, see you!", she said, worried by her mistake.

She hurried to get down, but Jocelyn took her hand and pulled her towards him, inviting Allan and Garvey to get out first. The two scholars looked at each other with a smile and executed themselves.

"Please close the door behind you!", he ordered, gently

Emma was feeling good. She would have wanted the moment to last forever. Without saying a word, they looked in each other's eyes with one of those looks that say very much in a few seconds. In that moment, neither of them controlled anything. They approached without looking away and kissed tenderly for more than two minutes. Allan and Garvey were patiently waiting outside.

"They're taking their time", Garvey exclaimed, "he must be treating her!"

"Patience, young man, you wouldn't like to be interrupted when your turn comes!"

"Why are you telling me this? You think I don't know what this is?"

Allan looked at him seriously, put a hand on his shoulder and replied bluntly.

"Yes, my young friend, that's what I think!"

A little embarrassed, the young man didn't answer, but Allan added a little ladle in order to reassure him.

"Me neither Garvery, at your age, I didn't know what it was".

Fortunately it was only them on the road, because he was now really uncomfortable. Seeing that, Allan didn't add anything and preferred to let time pass. While the two lovebirds were still stuck, Allan decided to relieve himself.

"I'll be back shortly", he said, "I have never pissed this far!"

This simple remark had the advantage of relaxing the atmosphere, which had become somewhat more cumbersome since

343

the reminder of their experience as a man. The young couple was now verbally saying goodbye.

"With a little imagination, we could say we're going to find each other, elsewhere, in another world", Jocelyn joked.

"Who knows?"

"I think it's time, I'm going to Emma, 'mine'. I didn't buy it, but..."

In her grief, she succeeded in displaying a smile.

"It's so like you! It's really your style!"

"You want to say his?"

"Yes, I want to say his... and..."

Suddenly the radio turned on at full volume. Even if the was used to it, he jumped systematically. Emma jumped too. At the stroke of surprise, she threw herself into his arms again.

"You should fix that!"

"If this is what it takes to make you happy! By the way, just now when we were kissing, I was with her..."

Those words filled her with happiness.

"I know, Joss. You should not delay, our mad scientists are making a new rut on the road with their paces!"

"Anyway, another stop is planned for the Vosges, do you remember? I would tell you to stay with me until then, but you never know what can happen."

"See you soon... there."

Emma finally got off the truck to the delight of the 'round walkers'.

"Ah, finally", Allan said, "we were preparing to pass the night here! You can say goodbye once you arrive in the Vosges. Giddy-up!"

Then, he turned towards Garvey to ask a last detail.

"You know the traffic on this road where he will land?"

Embarrassed, Garvey ran to see Jocelyn.

"I was sure", Allan said, "he didn't think about it! Stupid!", he sighed.

After talking to Jocelyn for a minute, he came back in a hurry and pressed the breach making key.

"Then, young man without a brain, what's the situation?"

"It's alright, professor, he didn't meet anyone other than a little old man in his old car when he arrived and from what they talked, it's always like that."

"OK, if you say so, after all, it's you who have the situation in hand."

"Is there a specific pace that he is supposed to achieve?", Emma worried.

"Absolutely not, my child, but he must still drive! Be careful, he's coming."

Jocelyn remembered the vibrations, what he had experienced during his first visit at the wheel of his truck and he feared his arrival in the gap that was approaching at fifty kilometers an hour. Maybe with a reduced speed, the disturbances would be smaller, he said to himself. He didn't let go of the eye hole. Attention old man, it's now! He was gripping his steering wheel as if to keep it fixed on its axis. Three, two, one... The craft entered the rift under the eyes of Emma and her friends who had to do the same, just behind.

"That's it", Garvey said, "it's up to us now!"

They ran inside, then it closed a few seconds later. They arrived in the correct place. It was the road on which Jocelyn had come into this world. Stopping right after landing, he went to meet the three followers.

"Not too chaotic this crossing?", Allan asked Jocelyn.

"Much less so than the first one! Say Garvey, a question came to my mind after you came to talk to me about the other road."

"When I arrived for the first time, I was coming from a highway. It might have been early evening, but there were still people driving around."

"It's a risk to take", Garvey answered, "because even if I make a reconnaissance crossing, nothing says that there won't be someone on your arrival. I'm sorry, Joss!"

"That's not very reassuring!"

"I can't tell you anything better. You must go back to the exact place and time of your disappearance, even though... maybe not..."

Allan was again lost in his thoughts.

"Garvey you have already managed this feat, it seems to me, no?"

Wanting to reassure, he intervened.

"This won't reassure you, but you're on the point of taking a calculated risk, just like your double, whom I know very well. You could be him!"

"You're right, Allan."

"You see!"

"That doesn't reassure me at all!"

"Do you remember the traffic that was there when it happened?", Garvey asked.

"I think I was alone at that moment, but I have a doubt, I was quite tired."

"Normally, you should end up in the same conditions as when you left. But there is always a slight shift, because everything is in perpetual motion and even setting the device on the precise second where you have gone, you will not arrive exactly where you want. So there's a risk and I can do nothing about it."

A distant engine noise suddenly caught their attention. Jocelyn smiled.

"Papi Mousot!"

"Let's hurry", Garvey said, "someone's coming!"

"I know who it is", Jocelyn assured, "leave it to me!"

Hearing that, Allan interrupted sharply, cutting off the momentum with his arm.

"You're talking about the old man?"

"Yes, it can only be him."

"Think for a moment, we are on the day and time you met him, so he doesn't know you!"

"You're right Allan, I didn't think of that."

"You should leave now."

"Prepare your device", Jocelyn said in a decided voice.

He approached Emma for a moment, put his right hand on the cheek, stroking her face with his thumb.

"Safe trip Jossy", she said with intensity "and don't worry, you're not sick."

He smiled at her with all the tenderness that a man in love can have, then bid farewell to the 'brains'.

"Goodbye Allan", he said, shaking his hand. "I'll try not to forget you, but I guarantee nothing! The same for you Garvey, take care and thank you for everything, all three of you. I would be tempted to say it was a memorable adventure, but…"

"Come on, go now, the vehicle is getting closer!"

He climbed in his truck, restarted it and began his advance. He waved one last time, throwing a last look at Emma. She felt a great void, more than a few seconds and she would never see him again. She knew he had to leave, but she wanted him to stay.

In that precise moment, she would have suffered less if her heart had been torn out. She watched him leave, dying inside. She was restraining herself from cracking, but she couldn't contain a tear that was slowly running down her cheek.

"Goodbye my Jossy, have a good week and be careful."

Garvey was preparing the opening of the breach, while Jocelyn continued to take up speed. He too was unhappy, but at the same time happy to go home. The straight line offered by the road at this point was nearly five kilometers. He was now at his maximum speed, ninety kilometers an hour. The entry wasn't far. He was reviewing everything he had lived in this world until Emma's last words she had told him ten minutes before: *"They're making a new rut with their paces", "Have a safe trip, Jossy", "Don't worry, you're not sick".*

His thoughts jostled each other. Besides, he had to, because he would remember nothing after the next quarter of an hour. The breach was about to open and he was apprehensive. The first time, when he arrived, the surprise effect didn't give him time to look at the action in detail. But this time, it was different, he was waiting for it. He absolutely wanted to see the process from A to Z, even though he wouldn't remember, but he would have seen it at least once in his life, even though it was from elsewhere!

He watched the panorama, seeking at all costs to capture the first second of the timeless opening. The landscape was escaping faster and faster on each side of the vehicle again for the occasion an ICO (Identified Crossing Object). Suddenly, the great boom, similar to the one he had heard on his first voyage. Everything before him began to float, to wave as if he was under water. Despite the situation, he was almost amazed at the appearance of the flaw that Garvey called 'set up'.

What an extraordinary and striking sight for Jocelyn's eyes on the birth of the phenomenon. He tried to see the outlines, but the magnitude of the phenomenon was such that it would have taken at least five kilometers. He could already hear the growing and incessant buzz that followed the 'set up'. It was as if a huge, well-tuned engine was idling to power this huge machine like the purr of a UFO immobilized there.

Difficult to define the distance to the entrance to the infernal gallery, but the crossing seemed imminent. Now, everything around him was being questioned: the trees and the landscape seemed to disappear and reappear with every second that passed. He could now distinguish the whirlwind where everything seemed 'Demolecularized', named 'Gateway'. That landscape towards another world that was emerging in the distance, supposed to bring him home, looked more like a decorated black hole than the solution to his problem. He thought again and again about these few days spent here, as well as Emma's reactions and words. Something wasn't right.

He was only a few meters from the opening and understood what had happened. He was horrified and couldn't understand the choice she had made. Impossible to stop now, he had to continue. "Emma NO" he was screaming; "Why?". He was disoriented, lost. As he stepped into the gap, Papi Mousot stepped out of the bend at the wheel of his old car and witnessed, to his utter amazement, the iron giant's disappearance. He stopped short. He couldn't believe what he had just seen. He was looking straight ahead, beatific, in shock.

"It's not true! Yet I stopped drinking alcohol six months ago, darn it!"

Then he saw three people talking on the road, in the distance. "What's that about!"

At that moment, Garvey opened a new breach to return to Paris with Allan and Emma. They were walking in the direction of the old man. He couldn't see the back of the gap, as only the entrance was visible. For him, the show ended with three people walking on the road for a few moments, then disappeared at once.

"Darn it, what's happening to me, I swear never to drink a drop of alcohol!"

Jocelyn had arrived safely in a calm traffic. By chance, there was no one in front or behind when he appeared. His mind wandered with sadness and despair. Why had she left him? He couldn't remember how many hours he had left to drive. It wasn't far from nine o'clock and his day was likely to be about to end. So he decided to stop to get the record out of the snitch and check. It had been about five minutes since the fault had closed and his memory was starting to get confused. He was still grieving, but he didn't know why. Two kilometers separated him from a highway area and memories of the other world gradually faded away. He was now thinking of Emma and was languishing the end of the week to find her. Lucky, he found a parking space just released and parked there.

When he removed the record where all the information such as the city of departure and arrival, the speed at which he was driving, the number of hours he was driving and the stops, he didn't understand anything. It appeared to have run for two days during which the truck had not rolled. He looked at the date and time indicated on the device ... Wednesday, May 7th, 2016.

"What do you know!" he thought, *"What's this mess! I fell asleep, it's not possible otherwise!"*

He also noticed the level of diesel on the gauge of the tank gauge. It had practically halved. Plus, he had the strange feeling of having been through a 'black hole'. He didn't even remember getting there. On the other hand, he remembered the disappearances and appearances at the beginning of the day. In any case, those of Monday…

While a lot of questions jostled at the door of his mind, his phone rang; but he was too busy thinking about finding a rational explanation for all of that to answer.

"But then, I also disappeared! Why can't I remember anything? Maybe I was taken by aliens and they just erased my memory! No, even better, my two hemispheres don't resonate anymore."

He had the idea to go down to check if one of his two tanks wasn't pierced. He conscientiously inspected the slightest stain on the ground, then looked around the tanks without noticing anything.

"It's still strange" he thought *"Unless it was pumped. If that's the case, they didn't leave me dry!"*

He went up to his cabin, decided to no longer beat himself up; well, almost! He noticed suddenly the absence of his locket in the reflection of the windshield.

"Well, hell! What did I do with it?"

He never got it off, so to speak, and couldn't remember when he had detached it. He rummaged through his cabin for a few minutes, then finally settled on the fact that he had probably left it at home. He grabbed his phone and called Emma, who immediately picked up.

"Hello, good evening sweetie."

"It's not too early, I was worried!"

"Why? I often call you at this hour!"

"Eh… yes, it's true! I'm sorry."

"Are you sure everything's alright?"

"Yes Joss, wonderful."

"You're a little strange today. Maybe I woke you up?"

"Yes, that's it, but it's better now."

"Yeah, if I didn't know you, I would say you're hiding something… But let's leave it. I called for two reasons. I'm looking for my medallion everywhere and I was wondering if it's not in the room. Would you go check?"

Emma knew perfectly well where it was, but what to answer? She pretended to go look for it and then resumed.

"I can't find it, Joss! What's the second reason?"

"I wanted you to tell me what day it is."

"And you tell me I'm strange!"

"Oh! I'm fine, but say, just tell me what day it is!"

"It's Monday, my love, and you left this morning. Why?"

"I'll call you in a quarter of an hour, I'll explain."

He finally put this quirk on the account of a malfunction of the device. After having put everything in order, he prepared his cabin for the night, cleared his berth of the few documents that dragged there, pulled the side curtains and called Emma again to tell her, among other thing, of his dismay.

On her side, Emma was settling gently into this new life. This Jocelyn certainly didn't have his double's notoriety, but he was much more attentive, more involved in his relationship and he led a simple life away from the spotlight. She savored in advance what was waiting for her. The decision to let her double take the maternal control of her children hadn't been easy, but she knew, however, that a mother similar in every way would take care of them with the same love, the same desire to make them happy and make them good men.

Also, she could give one or two children to the new 'Jossy' with only a few years behind. For 'Joss the stuntman', the Emma he was going to find, was the same, so to say, but without the liabilities of their separated couple and the reactions she would have had in seeing him, they would be guided only by the love she felt for him and not by the discord and all those tense situations that there had been with his double. There was, therefore, a good chance that she would succeed in reconquering him. But she now had a bonus, a gift from the gods: two beautiful children she would raise as if they had come out of her womb, which could have happened elsewhere in the place she would spend the rest of her life. This crazy adventure, an incredible and fantastic start had finally filled a gap in four people whose lives would be forever different.

Taking a closer look, everyone gained something from it. Béatrice and Annie would never be the same again. Their lives would be calmer and better. Young Félix wasn't aware, but he had changed. Sure, he no longer behaved like a sleepy schizophrenic, but this experience had unlocked something in him; a door had opened. Hubert didn't feel anything special, but his behavior changed, he no longer reacted to his old ghosts, he was just what a man can be, if he didn't rely on the traumas he had experienced to live. Someone at peace with himself.

FAMILY BRIEFING.

— *"Arrived at a certain stage*
of questioning, we can
only find answers."
MM.

Allan, Garvey and Emma were just arriving in the garden. The man in white was also there, but invisible. He was watching their every move.

"Everything went well?", Damiana asked.

"Yes, Madam Thibault perfectly fine", Garvey answered.

"And you, Emma, are you alright?"

"Thank you", she answered, lost in her thoughts, barely looking at her...

"Did I make the right choice? What if I was wrong! If I was only blinded by the children? I will never see Jossy again. I can still ask Garvey to take me back. He'll be right to be angry when he finds out. My God, what to do, what to do?"

Seeing her so bothered, Damiana approached her and gave her a friendly hug.

"Don't be so sad, you're giving me the blues! Think of your children."

Those words made her smile, but she felt a huge void again.

354

She couldn't remember how Jocelyn had gone, but she knew it. She was tied with Allan on this point. The difference was in her memory of the other dimension, the one where she had lived so far. Her memories there, as well as her double's, couldn't fade, because they couldn't exchange their memory, but they had briefed each other on the consequences of inter-dimensional journeys.

The Emma of this world had told her that she might be confused when she arrived in this dimension, but that she should never forget the reason that had led her there.

The situation was becoming fantastic, but in this reality, Damiana had appreciated her double in a short time. The difference between the two was in their reactions due to their respective education.

The Emma of this world who was currently in the dimension of police and boats, had had a happy and full of consideration childhood, unlike the new widow, who had been shelved since her early childhood. So that her relationship with her brother and sisters had nothing to do with what she was going to discover here. Her father still lived, her sister Mira really loved her just as her brother and her other sister; and the atmosphere could be described as something pleasant, friendly, simple and fraternal. Her parents had never made any differences between the children. The Emma, who was now part of her native world, was going to discover a completely dislocated family, victim of all the unspoken that only increased their anger, their hatred and their stupidity.

In this world, her brother and her sisters had been raised as adored children, as opposed to her double. This had largely contributed to the fabrication of adults with often selfish behavior, insane and without any values. People whose biggest concern was how they looked through the material and the goods. Their greatest skill was to have the 'False-Worship', to say that they were innocent before the fait accompli. Rather die than assume their responsibility. It was normal, sad, but normal; because thus had been their education.

Denying a loved one was the easiest in the world, commonplace, just like stabbing in the back at arm's length. One of their specialties was to get involved with each other in their personal problems so that they could eventually blame themselves and thus have an ideal offender at their fingertips!

It was a permanent public exhibition of teeth and real parts of reciprocal and frenzied sodomy. But to give up thus, couldn't it happen that the shoulder blades wouldn't remember the movement to lift them in surrender?

Some members of the family no longer spoke to each other without knowing why. The reasons that were the initial cause probably had to be noted on a notebook so as not to forget them. There was also poor Axel who had been raised by his mother and who had joined the army for fifteen years. He hadn't escaped the rule either. The first reason had been a good one to get angry with his mother at the age of twenty-four and since, he was running after a surrogate family, trying to make himself accepted by everyone as a child or a man of the family, and thus have bits and pieces of little happiness that he had never had before.

This conjunction made them different from what they were in this world. Here, nobody was trying to make a claim in one way or another and to be accepted at any cost; because all had evolved in a healthy atmosphere that hadn't turned them into sentimental competitors.

They both knew it when they exchanged places. One didn't

have children, didn't get along with her family and was to live the contrary with a man, true, a bit more selfish and egocentric, but still 'made of the same mold'; and the other who had never known how to attract the attention of the man she loved and who had only her children and her family to comfort her, was going to be able to build a new home this time with a man who would take her existence into account.

They had each a share of sacrifice, but they would live what they had never dared to hope until then. Garvey's invention had, in the end, more benefits than he had imagined.

Allan had joined his wife to talk about this whole story and Emma went to isolate herself for a moment in the garden.

"You're not bothering us, young woman, you can stay", Allan said, gently.

She didn't have the heart to answer and went out in silence.

"Let her be Allan, the small one is unhappy, she's breaking my heart. Leave her time to get used to all this."

"Alright my angel, but things have become what they should be and she will have to get used to it anyway."

Damiana would never betray the secret. Maybe she would tell him one day, but later, much later.

"You're right 'Panou'", she said, "everything goes back to normal."

Panou was a little name she gave him from time to time and that meant nothing in particular. It was just cute.

"How are you feeling?", Allan continued.

"Fine. Why?"

"I'm asking about earlier, the strange behavior you had."

"I wouldn't really know how to explain it, but I feel like I'm losing it little by little."

"How come you were able to do that and not me? I confess

that it intrigues me a little."

"I told you, I couldn't give you an exact explanation, but on the other hand, I can talk to you about this clarity in my mind. Now I know what we feel when we die!"

"When we die? How do you know?"

"I know it, that's all, and I've seen a lot of things too…!"

"Could I know?"

"What happened with your device is very close to the reality we are in here, we don't see it."

Allan frowned, it meant : *"Continue!"*.

"It's nice to see you don't know everything, from time to time", she joked, "it makes you human!"

"Yes, my love, I am only human!"

"Maybe we'll talk about it one day…"

"What do you mean?"

"Souls, spirits and entities mix all around us."

"You mean there are ghosts around us?"

"Yes, Allan, it's a whole. Death is to wandering spirits what life is to our future beings."

"Wait a minute! You're telling me that men of the future visit us and they are in the same state of mind as our dead?"

"Yes, and I'm going to tell you even more! They communicate with each other."

"And you could see all this?"

"Yes, my darling, I saw them. I see your brain of Cartesian scientist prevents you from listening to me openly!"

"No, it's not that! But recently, it's a lot of information in one fell swoop. But the strangest in all of this is that I have the feeling, I would even say the conviction, that I have always known it."

Damiana looked at him smiling.

358

"What is it, my angel?", Allan asked, smiling back.

"Nothing, I just love you!"

"Me too", he continued, taking her in his arms.

Damiana looked at poor Emma who seemed to be in full conversation with the skies.

"Let's comfort this little girl, she needs it."

"I don't understand her reaction, she knew he had to leave!"

"Don't look into it, it will pass."

"Maybe I should ask Garvey to open a breach so she could go straight home with her car?"

"Maybe…"

Garvey sat on a chair in front of the living room table and continued to brainstorm for the eagle.

"So, my young friend, what are you thinking about?", Allan asked.

"I'm thinking about the giant eagle."

"The what?"

"Ah, yes, that's right! Never mind, it's nothing serious."

"Do you think you could accompany Emma to her place?"

"You mean with this?", Garvey said, showing his box. "Yes, it could be done, why?"

"We don't think she's in a state to drive, it would be better if she only had a few kilometers."

"I see."

"You were talking about a giant eagle earlier…"

"Yes, I think I found a solution, I'll take care of it as soon as I finish with Emma."

"It's you who understands, Garvey! I don't understand a thing, but obviously, you have the situation in hand."

Emma feared the meeting with the children who were now hers. The panic increased as time went on. Damiana went to her, waving her hand so as not to be followed by the men.

"Are you overcoming the situation, young woman?"

"I don't really know, but I'm here now."

"You still have the opportunity to give up and go back home. You're wondering if it was the right decision to make, aren't you?"

"Yes, I'm also wondering if I'm not going to pay the price."

"In what way?"

"I have always thought that we must overcome the trials of life and not get around them. This is an unexpected opportunity for me to have what I have always wanted, but I am not convinced of the merits of what we have done."

"If I understood correctly, you adore Jocelyn and you're wondering if you deserve to be a mother?"

Emma felt embarrassed and didn't know what to say.

"Your double had a word with me before her second departure and after returning for a few hours to Aussillon."

"Indeed, I am in doubt and I miss Jocelyn terribly."

"It's not easy, is it?"

"You're clairvoyant!"

"You see you still have a sense of humor, not everything is lost! Why did you come here?"

"For the children…"

"And Jocelyn, the one of this world, of course?"

"Yes, but I don't know him…"

"That will happen shortly", Damiana said, looking at her watch. "What did your double say about the children?"

"She will never abandon them, since I'm here."

"Do you have the feeling that you deserve them?"

"I don't understand!"

"Do you think you have suffered enough not having children?"

360

"I think I could say I had made peace with it. But Joss had a big contribution to it."

"For sure, but you ended up accepting it, right?"

"I had to."

"Your double had also ended up accepting this situation with Jocelyn, even if she still loved him. Do not you see some justice?"

"Maybe, but…"

"The same as your parents…"

"What are you trying to say?"

"You're in permanent conflict. If they hadn't been what they are, your relationship with them as well as your brothers and sisters would be better, wouldn't they?"

"How do you know?"

"Do I really have to answer?"

Emma simply moved her head from side to side without saying anything.

"Normally, you would have had to know another version of your parents in your next life, but you managed to accept them as they are with their qualities and flaws. Very few people can say as much. Most people live in perfect harmony with their obsessive neurosis. To put it simply, you advanced a little on time. Your double already has these bases and even if she's gone, she will always keep them in her heart because she was educated in this way. But with you, it's different, you were forced to create them after realizing that the shell you had forged was not the answer to everything. You made the choice to see your problems, understand them, accept them and finally, settle them permanently. Generally, it takes a lifetime and even more. But you made it. You have the right now to think of yourself, to look in other directions. It's what we call being free. I understand the situation is delicate for you. You have the feeling of abandoning

Jocelyn, but at the same time, you know that you'll find him in another version, just as your double 'gives you' her children, but she will always be there through you."

"It's to go mad!"

· "It can happen when you take charge, it's not always easy to make the right decisions! Don't react out of fear anymore. Don't let it take over your decisions. A golden opportunity presents itself to you today. Don't be distracted, decide!

"And if you're wrong, what if we're wrong?"

"And if you both managed to turn the page in your respective lives? If you were able to permanently classify your life events among the classified files?"

"I didn't think of it, wouldn't it be by chance?"

"Could you imagine it?"

"It would mean to say my suffering is over?"

"What do you think?"

"And Joss, I love him!"

"Nothing stops you from loving him. The one is this world is different, but they have an identical basis. Loving him, you will continue to love the one you have always known. Maybe he'll even make you forget him!"

"Who says I'll manage to pick up the pieces?"

"I know that he has softened for some time, he has made himself responsible and he has confessed to me that he really wants to pick up the pieces, as you say!"

"I'm so scared…"

"You don't have to be. Try to appreciate the new life offered to you. You deserve it, Emma. A challenge isn't canceled until we understand it, but for you, it's different. You alone can win his heart back, because you don't have all these feelings your double had towards him. You never argued with him. He'll concretely see there is no rancor on your side, which will probably incite him to do the same!"

"And what if he wants a third child?"

"You won't be able to!"

"But he'll be disappointed!"

"But you will love each other and you'll know the happiness of raising two."

Emma crumpled in tears in her arms trying to articulate a last question, barely audible.

"And what if I won't be a Good Mother?"

"And what if you stopped, young woman!"

Tears flowed down Damiana's right shoulder. Emma only managed to whisper two words.

"Thank you."

"You can count on me no matter what. You'll also have the support and love of your family once there. You see, you're not alone."

"My double won't have this chance", Emma continued, wiping her tears.

"Yes she won't, but she won't have your exasperated reactions that could well destabilize her."

The young woman looked at her questioningly.

"I knew that as well", Damiana said.

"I'll try."

"Only try?"

"I'm going to do it", she added, adding a smile to her words.

"What are you going to do?"

"Madam Thibault!"

"Say it!"

"I'm going to live!"

"One more time, but with conviction now."

"I AM GOING TO LIIIIVE", she yelled, under the somewhat astonished gazes of Allan and Garvey!

The doorbell was suddenly heard. The two women looked at each other with an almost complicit and eloquent look.

"Finally someone who will normally enter this house today!", Damiana joked, going to the front door.

Allan joined Garvey hurriedly.

"You should leave now to take care of your raptor, it will avoid unnecessary explanations."

"I'm going, professor."

He opened a breach and disappeared. During this time, Damiana welcomed Jocelyn, took his jacket and invited him into the living room. Emma was a little nervous. Would she manage to see him as Jocelyn or simply as a double? She was very impatient to know which. She heard their two voices coming closer in the hallway. She didn't look directly at the entrance of the arched room, but watched from the corner of her eye. When they arrived, Jocelyn recognized Emma's back and stopped talking for a moment.

"You didn't tell me!", he said, pleasantly surprised.

"It's a surprise, young man."

"It worked, you made it!"

Emma finally discovered him. This one had long hair, he was much more dynamic, sporty and showed an arrogant repentance, but ubiquitous. Nothing seemed to impress him. In spite of this difference of presence with his double, he emanated from his person a certain wisdom which he had acquired over the years. He should have been accompanied, but he had decided at the last minute without really knowing why, to come alone.

Emma felt like reliving her encounter with her double in a

different way. She had felt the same excitement as today. If she let herself go, she would feel guilty for experiencing that, but now she wanted to know, she wanted to know him. In addition, he was his spitting portrait. She was looking straight at him now as he approached, impassive and confident. Emma had a hard time admitting what she was thinking when she had just been crying the departure of the first.

"You have such an expression on your face, you look like I just rose from the dead! Notice, it's true that I definitely buried what I was. I understood a lot of things these last years."

"I ask for no explanation."

He was surprised to hear that answer because he was expecting precisely the opposite.

"I see. Emma, you surprise me. You also changed. But still, I want to say all I have to say."

"Doing stunts was my whole life…"

"Doing?"

"Please…"

She teased him with a look and let him continue.

"Like I was saying, I became aware of a lot of things. Stunts always took precedence over everything. I put it before you, the children, our friends. Till now, I'm not telling you anything you don't already know. But I realized that I needed more to assert myself than I needed the thrills. In everyone's eyes, I have a hectic life, I'm a superman, the one who plays with death, the one who isn't afraid of anything. I am respected for my prowess, for what I am believed to be. But every time I'm about to risk my life, I'm scared. Even if they you calculate everything to the millimeter to minimize the risks, I can't help but think of you. And I don't want to risk losing you anymore. I love you, Emma."

A tear ran slowly down her face. Jocelyn tenderly put his hand on the cheek to wipe it.

"I also love you, Jocelyn Martin", she smiled.

Allan and Damiana were looking at the scene with affection.

"I'll have to make a note for myself on a piece of paper to not forget to punish Garvey", Allan said.

"Why do you want to punish him?"

"It's what I told him at the beginning of this adventure."

"And you have no intention of doing it anymore, if I understand correctly?"

Allan didn't answer and sketched a smile that was all the explanation needed. While he was rebuilding the foundations of his relationship, Jocelyn, satisfied with his speech, he turned to Allan to greet him.

"I'm sorry, Allan, with all this emotion, I had forgotten about you!"

"Nothing major, my young friend, you talked to the most important person, you did what you had to do."

He looked at Emma again, showing his happiness.

"Yes, I had to do it."

"Take a seat near Emma, will you have another coffee?"

Realizing his clumsiness, he recovered in the wake without giving anyone time to react.

"In addition to the one I gave you during our last meeting!"

All were amused for different reasons...

DANCING BACK.

— *"Doctrines pass;*
the anecdotes remain."
Emil Michel Cioran

J ocelyn the Driver woke up the next morning at seven thirty. He had not fallen asleep before two o'clock in the night. Admittedly, he had found a malfunction of his device, but something was bothering him and it was impossible to put his finger on it. The next two days passed quickly.

On Friday morning, he was not very far from Aussillon. An hour and a half separated him. He was driving on the highway and was about to get out of Béziers where he had to take a national road to complete his journey. He could already see himself coming to his place and find his beloved. After the toll, he made a dozen kilometers and noticed in the distance a crowd whose predominant color was blue.

"Damn it!" he thought as he hurried to empty his ashtray through the window. He suddenly saw an element come off and stand in the middle of the road, his arm extended to the left.

"It hasn't happened in a while!"

He wasn't worried; he respected road legislation as much

as possible, because his work was not a regular line, and he sometimes exceeded his driving time by a minute or two. That said, the policemen to whom he had been dealing until then had always been clement at the sight of the overall respect of the twenty-eight days of records to be presented. On reaching the recess where the device was installed, he lowered the volume of the radio, while a young policeman accompanied by a fellow biker approached at a decided step. He lowered his window, prepared the documents for control, then lowered the one on the passenger side to ventilate the cabin.

"Hello Sir", said one of the two policemen while doing the military salute, "I stopped you for a routine check and my colleague who has been following you on a motorcycle has two words to tell you."

"Of course, Mister Officer, here you are!", Jocelyn continued, holding out his papers.

"Please turn off the engine and get out the vehicle, please", curtly replied the young lawman.

"Yes, Mister Officer, I'll let it run a minute for the turbo and then I'll join you."

"I didn't see you with your tricycle behind me, damn it! The ashtray!" Jocelyn thought. *"As long as he didn't see me doing it! »* The biker called him in turn just after spitting a cigarette butt.

"When my colleague is done, I'll take care of you!"

He took off his helmet; a huge ash cloud stagnated for a few moments all around his face, then slowly fell back. Jocelyn wanted to laugh. *"No, not now!"* he thought. *"If I tell that story, no one will want to believe me! Unless he punishes me for untimely flaming!"*

A car suddenly passed at high speed on the road.

"You're lucky, Sir", the 'flamed' officer said, putting his 'ashtray' back on his head, "I have my eye on you and we'll talk about this some other time!"

He rushed to catch the apprentice pilot, while Jocelyn was preparing for the control. In doing so, he glanced briefly at the people in the parking lot. He couldn't help but make a difference with the past, when law enforcement wasn't required to turn roadside checks into a profitable venture.

"I will certainly be entitled to something with the ashtray!" he continued thinking.

He scrutinized the attitude of the men in blue. It's even more than certain, I won't be leaving without a souvenir.

Proudly dressed in his blue uniform 'the young one' seemed determined to enforce the law... to the letter.

There were two other drivers who seemed to have all the miseries of 'the world' on their shoulders. The unfortunate ones had their quota of points reduced off their license, as well as their bank account. Jocelyn stopped his engine, then went down to join the controllers. He was in one of those days where anything could happen to him, while staying Zen.

After having thoroughly checked the authenticity of the administrative documents of the truck, such as the registration card, insurance, transport license and other documents, the policeman began the control of the records. While Jocelyn arrived in front of them to answer any questions they might have, the young controller inspected minute by minute for too much driving time, or too little for the breaks called 'cuts' in the jargon road.

Joss stood in front of them and patiently waited for the verdict. Suddenly, the volume of his radio went up again on a modern, rhythmic music, whose title was 'Four to the floor' of the

'Starsailor' group. It was so surprising that the policeman who was drawing up the report dropped his pen from the sheet of his half-filled notebook. Not so surprised, nor confused, Jocelyn briefly explained the problem he had with his car radio while heading towards his truck to cut the contact. The music was really noisy, but also catchy. At the door, he approached his hand to the opening handle, froze for a moment, then changed his mind. He was in one of those moments when the mountains were reduced to dunes, or to be surprised while having an intestinal relief in public toilets at the fragile entrance door, was no problem.

Of a quiet, calm nature and preferring discretion to arrogance, he was however like everyone else, subject to delusional and slightly crazy thoughts that crossed his mind from time to time. Some even made him smile, even frankly laugh all alone, just by imagining the scene.

Of course, he never practically put them into practice, but there are days when everything seems naturally possible without our necessarily being aware of it; days when the forbidden ones anchored in our minds pause and allow us not to think about the consequences of our actions. A way just like any another to purge the circuit often overloaded with stress.

There was a feeling of freedom in this period of 'grumbling daddy'. Jocelyn was completely elsewhere. He was at that moment as Zen as a Tibetan monk. Sure, he animated the car park alone and seemed to have started on the wrong foot with the authorities, but nothing could reach him and days like this were far too rare to prevent him from just 'being'.

All eyes were on the truck with the anarchist radio. Two seconds later, the volume still set on 'MAX', all were surprised to see him reappear, advancing with knees bent, the bust back, all accompanied by a rhythmic movement back and forth, his arms folded in half and grazing his hips with each pass. The expression of his face was impassive.

The young policeman was screaming as he tried to beat the decibels of the speakers. It also made him look like a grumpy screamer.

"Turn down the volume of your radio and come here immediately, that's an order!"

Jocelyn barely heard him and anyway, at that moment, he had nothing to do with him. He continued against all odds. Grumpy screamer headed for the truck to lower the volume himself before the eyes of his sergeant, who was reminded to order on the spot.

"Meunier! What are you doing?"

He explained with a movement of his fist making him understand what he was going to do.

"Should I remind you of the law, Constable Meunier!", replied the sergeant, advancing towards him with a decided step. "You are not allowed to enter his cabin without his permission."

Seeing that, 'Meunier grumpy screamer' went to the van to take an alcohol test and began to follow Jocelyn in his crazy parade trying to introduce the test into the mouth. Jocelyn couldn't stop laughing. He finally took the balloon in hand and did the test while continuing to dance with Meunier following his every step. The test done, he handed it to grumpy again, continuing his parade.

The latter observed the object with disgust. One of the two motorists who saw themselves with a ticket, looked at the second with a smile, which was returned with enthusiasm. Approaching, he nudged him, encouraging him to follow him in the parade.

"You're not thinking, he's in for a lot...!"

He didn't let him finish his sentence. The desire to brave the prohibition added to the particular atmosphere prevailing on the area and took over reason.

"After all, dancing is not outside the law."

Grumpy didn't know where to turn. Seeing a negative result, the young man summoned him to follow him and stop his antics right then and there. Still serious, he responded negatively with a nod while continuing to beat the rhythm with his left foot, then returned to his mad parade, this time making a mixture of Pharaonic dance and Indian, the Comanche way, dancing around a fire with a hatchet. The two drivers and another one who was also being controlled, left the policemen without saying anything and joined Jocelyn in rhythm by standing behind him, reproducing the same steps and the same gestures.

The vigilante who took care of Jocelyn had now put in mind not to let him escape. Those in charge of the two other drivers didn't know whether or not to put an end to this charade. One of them asked the chief in charge what to do, who was secretly hilarious, but he tried not to let it show. After all, he wasn't hurting anyone by waddling like that, he thought. Furthermore, he would have seen this at least once before retiring. It would have been a shame to miss such a show. He was watching his guys work and applying fines because that was the thing to do.

Seeing the one who controlled Jocelyn's records, check every minute of all the facts of the past monthly period, he felt the same disgust he had experienced entering this period of mandatory profitability. While Jocelyn and his acolytes were doing the show and thus causing slowdowns of astonishment on the road, the young vigilante came to show him some records on which he had noted offenses.

"Look, chief! Here he drove four hours thirty-two. On this one, he made a break of sixteen minutes, so the fifteenth is not complete. On this one, he worked more than fifteen hours, the amplitude isn't good! Here he cut ten hours fifty-five instead of eleven."

Before he showed him the next one, he wanted to see all the records. He found that despite his international work, he made great efforts to comply with the legislation.

"I'm going to get the main note."

"Stay here!"

"How come? He made mistakes and we must punish him for that, that's why we're here!"

"Yes, but we must make the difference between people like him and those who don't respect anything, otherwise what we do will no longer make sense."

"But 'Chiefy'!", he insisted.

"Enough! Listen well, Meunier. When I started this job, I was looking for the culprit. Today, I'm looking for the fault because the culprit, I already know him! I don't even dare go home in uniform, and even less put it in the back of my car as I did before. You see something cheerful about it all?"

Vivid regrets accompanied his words. The nostalgia of the beautiful era was palpable just in the tone of his voice. Grumpy could almost feel it in the same way as his elder did.

"No, chief", he calmly replied.

"The orders we receive, to which we obey with our eyes closed, make us robots of the state without soul, nor conscience. Many despise us today, many are afraid when they see us and I didn't commit for that… did you?"

"Personally, it's to contribute to road safety and perhaps even improve it, who knows!"

"I'm going to tell you something, Meunier. When I was a young policeman like you, the only times we stopped the drivers was either for a big speeding, for a hunt and the truckers called us the angels of the road, rather flattering, isn't it?"

"Well…"

But in that case, nothing and no one could stop that man, somewhere in another world, or in any case, in the eyes of his young subordinate.

"Do you really think we're still those angels, officer Meunier?"

At that moment without realizing it, his face was closer than ten centimeters from Meunier's and he was looking at him with a certain compassion, the sense of wanting to accomplish something was indeed rebuilding and new foundations in progress. No need to run after the culprit, he was already known and had only a few kilometers to go to be punished.

"Sadly, I don't think so chief, but when we look at the numbers, we realize that they are three times as numerous as before and that this is largely the reason why we cracked."

"I know, I know", he galvanized sadly, aware that the infernal machine in which they had almost all enlisted was too good to stop on its way; and it will probably be necessary to wait for it to stop itself after having made the maximum of its productivity.

Then his mind went astray for a moment in glorious thoughts.

"I feel sorry for you, little one; if one day the country goes to war, the enemy will be fined for each bullet coming out of the rifle!"

"I don't know where all this will lead us", he continued, "but as I was saying, I know I didn't choose this job to get here. So, I order you to look at who you are dealing with and to hell with those stupid orders that are turning us into hateful wrecks! Did you get the message?"

"Yes, chief!"

"And stop calling me chief, you say 'yes, sergeant'!"

The other two officers were clueless. What to do? Run behind them and force them back. They arrived in their turn in front of the van.

"What do we do, sergeant?"

"What do you want to do? Draw up a report for abusive dancing? Let's wait for the end of the music and enjoy the show. We would have seen it at least once in our careers!"

Other drivers passing by, who were slowing down systematically could see two trucks, a car, a van and four officers planted there, watching three people dance in rhythm with perfect synchronization. The scene seemed straight out of the shooting of a musical.

Not far from there a walker wearing a white jogging suit also watched the show. That didn't even make him smile. He was just there to watch, like a surveillance camera. No one seemed to see him, as if he were invisible.

On the jovial parking lot, the song was coming to an end. The three dancers were again at the Comanche dance, this time seeming to honor a God by prostrating and standing up every two meters. On the last note of the song, the host took over, announcing the upcoming horoscope and listed the various checkpoints of the day. Hearing that, after having saluted themselves like great artists after a performance, the three unruly drivers laughed heartily and went back to see their policeman.

They were casual, relaxed and a fine wouldn't change anything. On their side, the officers had, without paying too much attention to it, loosened the bridle. Those surrealist few minutes had awakened the man in the uniform. Not the one who tries to interpret the slightest word or the behavior that can lead to the small format paper benefactor of the turnover, no… They simply didn't want to verbalize, except for the youngest, who didn't belong to the generation of protectors of the territory.

Like two sports teams before playing a game, the seven were now face to face. No misplaced look, no provocation or anger, just seven people whose conversation seemed to be outlawed by clothing, professional status and circumstance. After a few seconds, the sergeant broke the silence.

"Will you lower the volume of your car radio please, it will prevent us from yelling to communicate!"

"Of course", Jocelyn said, executing.

He then spoke to the officers who were in charge of the first driver and the motorist.

"Alright, what have we to say about this gentleman!", he said, pointing to the trucker.

"He has two driving times that are two minutes long for one and four for the other."

"What can you say about the other records?"

"All in all, they're good, even if he doesn't often roll at eighty an hour on the national."

"Then listen to me well", he said proudly to his men, "starting today, we're going to make a real difference between those who make efforts and those who do not! We will therefore return his documents to the gentleman and wish him safe roads."

The driver was almost leaping on the spot, he couldn't believe his ears. He took his papers, his records, saluted and thanked everyone in due form, then went to meet Jocelyn who was coming back from his cabin.

"When you're in the mood for a new dance, my friend, let me know!", he said, happily.

"Were they lenient?"

"Yes, they were! They even received new orders! Go, you'll see. Anyway, it was nice as far as controls go! Well, I have to go, I'm already late. You're great… And I should say!"

Jocelyn smiled, shaking his hand. Meanwhile, the officers finished with the motorist, passing him the four kilometers an hour over the speed limit that the radar had showed. He also retrieved his papers and left.

"I see we're mistaken about you! I mean about the truckers", said the man to Jocelyn who had just arrived and who was waiting his turn, a little further.

"Safe roads, Sir! Again thank you, gentlemen", he concluded, addressing the officers.

He got in his car, looked at Jocelyn one last time, smiling and continued on his way.

"It's come to us now!", said the sergeant, who was more inclined to laugh than anything else. "You do the conga every time you get checked?"

Still serene, he answered calmly.

"No, Officer, it was absolutely nothing premeditated. It was just a sudden and crazy urge that went through my head as I was about to get into the cabin to lower the volume."

"Hm… What can you tell us about this week's record of Tuesday?"

"Absolutely nothing, Officer. I didn't even understand what had happened. But what I can tell you, I make efforts to respect everything, even if I lose considerable time."

"You know it's the kind of fault we can't let go?"

"Yes, I know, but it's the only explanation I can give you. Do your job, Officer, it won't be fair, but I'll understand."

"Please make a note of excuse to the gentleman", the sergeant ordered to the young agent after a brief moment of silence.

"But…"

Weary of his attitude of wanting to amend at all costs, he approached him close enough to pin a piece of paper between their noses and calmly told him by gradually increasing the tone of his voice.

"Discuss again a direct order and I will stick you to the broom and mop for the next six months, have I made myself clear?"

Intimidated and embarrassed at having been publicly reprimanded, he ran for the notebook and filled in the green slip that would allow Jocelyn to prove that he had been checked and not to be disturbed for some time with the records. He waited patiently for the officers to finish and still couldn't believe what was happening to him.

"Once I finish here and leave, I'm going to buy a lottery ticket" he thought, *"I won't waste all my luck at work!"*

"You opened my eyes", the sergeant said, "or I should rather say 'reopened' them. That's why I decided to be lenient today. We should never have agreed to become what we are and I even forgot what I committed for more than twenty-five years ago. By doing that, I take the risk of being transferred to the dark places, but never mind, I'm tired of this organized racket and I'll make sure it's known."

Jocelyn wasn't sure if he had to go in the same direction. In the meantime, the ticket of hope arrived.

"Here, sergeant, you can sign."

He signed his signature at the bottom of the paper: Srg. A. Thibault and handed it to Jocelyn.

"Here you are, my fellow, and safe roads!"

Taking the document, he cast a quick glance and was stopped at the signature. He stared at him politely and couldn't refrain from sharing his astonishment.

"We have already met, haven't we?"

"I don't remember, but it's possible. Maybe we have already met in another life!", the sergeant joked, in a serious tone.

The look he had at that moment seemed familiar to Jocelyn. *"Surely one of those feelings of déjà vu"*, he thought.

"Thank you, Officer", he said, still looking for an answer in the eyes of Sergeant 'A. Thibault'.

He walked to his truck while the four men in uniform watched him leave. He climbed up, got in the driver's seat, set off and saw the young agent getting ready to direct traffic in order for him to leave the parking lot in complete peace.

"Thank you, Allan" Jocelyn thought, looking at him one last time. Then he changed his mind. *"Why did I think that, I don't know him from Adam!"*

Looking the vehicle leave, 'Allan' had a small grin at the corner of his mouth.

"What do we do, sergeant?", asked one of the other officers.

"Our job, my friend, just our job. And don't worry about the consequences of the decisions I made. They commit only me and I will assume them alone."

"No, sergeant", proudly resumed the policeman, looking at his colleagues, "we could have refused to obey, but we accepted your orders."

Allan put a friendly hand on his shoulder without saying anything.

IMPLICATIONS.

— *"It is by well-doing*
that well-being is created."
F. de La Rochefoucauld.

Jocelyn was moving slowly on the national at eighty kilometers per hour. He now pushed the button '+' of his car radio to ride in music and eventually find a documentary, with a little luck. He only had one haste: finish his work day and go back home. He felt a certain pride about his attitude during the control. He thought back to the sergeant, who for some reason he didn't know, was familiar to him in his attitude and his look. It bothered him so much that he thought about it until his first delivery, that placed him back on Earth.

It was a huge agricultural machine to be delivered to a dealer. He arrived in the yard of the latter, parked so as not to disturb anyone, then went to the store to learn about the course of his unloading.

"You can stay where you are, you're not interfering, it's perfect! So open the side of your truck, I'll send someone to give you the goods."

"For the papers, I…"

"Yes, they'll be here after my employee informs me about the state of the machine", said the man behind the counter, kindly.

"Thank you", Jocelyn concluded, heading for his trailer to prepare for unloading.

He opened the tarp, removed the boards that consolidated the structure, dislodged, then seeing no one arrive, went back to settle in front of the wheel, which once properly adjusted, transformed into an 'office' to keep the paperwork up to date. A pen in hand, he was preparing to fill in a document on the 'Atlas Office', himself behind on the wheel, when he saw at the bottom of the car park a young boy accompanied by his father, get out of the car. Jocelyn scrutinized their faces insistently.

"You, I know you. I don't know from where, but we have already met", he thought.

At that moment, the child stared at him for a few seconds and waved. Seeing this, Joss returned the courtesy.

"You also know me. How come we recognize each other since we never saw each other before!"

On the way, the child mimed words as if to deliver him a message. Jocelyn didn't let him out of his sight.

"Who are you, little one? From where do we know each other?"

The child's father wasn't unknown to him either. He patted his pen on the paper, searching in vain for an answer to his question. He who had an excellent memory of faces, was unable to put a name on these two there. He hesitated a moment to question them, then not knowing how to approach them, gave up and went back to his office work..

No more than five minutes passed, when he saw an old tractor with forks at the back, awkwardly driven by a young man obviously new to the world of work, wearing a false air of Gaston Lagaffe, the human version. Joss got out immediately, somewhat alarmed by the speed with which Gaston moved with the lock of hair that he regularly removed from his field of vision with a lateral head movement. Jocelyn was amused watching him. Gaston seemed like a caricature on the verge of reality.

"At this pace, he won't even notice the truck!" He thought when he couldn't contain a smile.

The young man passed him, moving in front of him, whistling and greeting him with a discreet gesture of his left hand. He then positioned himself in front of the machine, which had a large sheet of blue painted on it to mask a large part of the mechanism. A good dozen maneuvers later, it was finally over. Jocelyn wasn't saying anything, but he kept a close eye on all the facts and gestures of the young phenomenon, which apparently had difficulty shifting gears when he found them!

"He's going to end my week with a catastrophe!", Jocelyn told himself, his level of anxiety increasing with every decision Gaston made.

Suddenly, everything went very fast. Wishing to align one last time to be well centered, he made a mistake in speed, started the reverse and in panic, crushed the accelerator that the tractor interpreted at its fair value. In the heat of the moment, what Jocelyn saw in that moment, exceeded all he had imagined going wrong. While the forks supposed to be inserted under the machine remained at more than two meters high up, he saw the machine make a jump back encrusting thus the two forks in the blue plate, all in less time than it takes to say it. He was simply flabbergasted. He couldn't believe his eyes.

"This can't be! I'm dreaming! He planted the tractor in the machine!"

Gaston descended quietly from his infernal machine, went directly to his car in which he embarked and left without asking for his change.

"He's OK, isn't he! He plants the forks in the machine and he takes off!"

The din caused by the maneuver alerted everyone in the shop. But we must recognize that in a case like this one, so improbable and almost surrealistic, a certain reaction time is necessary. Distraught, the manager went out in a hurry. The tractor quickly became the main attraction in the next half-hour. Jocelyn explained in a few words what he had seen and felt. Besides himself, the manager was obliged to find a temporary solution for the delivery documents on which Jocelyn was quick to write a double to define the responsibility of each one. Gaston had just had his first lesson. The day was coming to an end, it was half past four, when the companies began to lower the weekly curtain.

He arrived at his depot, where Gérard was waiting for him to unload a little merchandise of which the city of destination was the same as that brought back by his colleague Fanfan. He stopped the engine and went down.

"Hi, Fanfan!"

"Hi Mr. Cosmetic!"

This nickname had been attributed to him after an altercation with customs officers.

"Come on! It's you who still sticks to it?"

Access to this client was deemed to be a real problem at the beginning of the week.

"Don't tell me about it! We can dream better for a Monday!"

"I feel sorry for you. No, it's not true, I'm kidding!"

A white and distant silhouette suddenly caught his attention.

"You OK, Joss?", Fanfan asked, seeing him distracted.

"You see the man in white there, on the other side of the

crossroad?"

"Yes, why?"

"You don't find him strange?"

"He's not moving and he's looking over here. So, what?"

"It doesn't seem weird to you that he's staying there without saying anything or moving?"

"So, what... We don't see people like him every day!"

"Maybe, but he's acting strangely, don't you think?"

"It's true he's looking a lot here. And he's so white!"

"Another follower of Mr. immaculate!"

Jocelyn couldn't see his face, but that silhouette wasn't unknown to him.

"Where have I seen you before?"

"Alright", he resumed, "it's not all, but we have to justify our ten thousand euros a month!"

He put on his gloves and then went to the opening of his trailer. The man in white stayed there about fifteen minutes, then disappeared suddenly, unbeknownst to the vigilance of Jocelyn and Fanfan. Joss wasn't saying anything, but was asking himself a lot of questions. He tried to act as if nothing had happened, but he couldn't help but take a look from time to time, while working. The job done, he went home to find his beloved after discussing the organization of the following Monday with his boss and loaded his things in his car.

Gérard had noticed a change in his behavior, but didn't mention it and watched him from the corner of his eye. He started the short six-kilometer drive that separated him from his nest, as he took pleasure in addressing it, but didn't immediately join the national, located fifty meters out on the left. He opted this time to turn right at the exit of the depot to take the same route that he had taken with Emma in the other dimension.

For what reason? That he could never have said, but a multitude of déjà vu and lived moments invaded him. He felt deeply well, serene. In the other weeks, he was certainly not unhappy to go home, but it had become over time, a kind of ritual that could be summed up as 'Metro Job Sleep', which didn't take away the joy of finding Emma, but he knew he was going to this village, in his eyes wounded by the bad atmosphere of his in-laws. Simply for him today was a new day, better still, a new era in which future problems would systematically have a solution. He didn't think he could be so well…

From then on, the worries related to the in-laws and in particular to his sister-in-law would be completely indifferent to him. They would go to the second, third or fourth plan, because after all, what can be done with someone who has chosen to just be. Happily, Emma was there to raise the level, but he didn't know that she was going to change the rest of his life. He didn't know that some solutions could only be found elsewhere.

For her part, Emma to whom 'Jossy' had phoned to warn her of his arrival had time to discover her New World. She had gone to see her mother where there were already some family members, evoking old memories, as well as her sister Mira accompanied by her faithful nephew Axel, who followed her everywhere. Arriving, she had forgotten the situation and approached her sister to give her a kiss. Only when she saw her react did she remembered.

"Oups! I'm sorry, Mira, I had totally forgotten. Why aren't we talking to each other again?"

Mira was disconcerted by this behavior she didn't expect. The only answer she could articulate was shy, clumsy and barely audible.

"Well, you know!"

This situation she had created turned against her, she was so uncomfortable compared to Emma, who, without highlighting it found the scene perfectly ridiculous and displayed an obvious relaxation.

"Oh, yes! It's true, Max died because of me. I'll write it somewhere so I won't forget!"

Emma hadn't sought out to put her sister in that position, who was literally beginning to decompose under the weight of the looks that weighed on her. Without meaning to, Emma had just brought to light a crappy situation that had prompted the questioning of the whole family about the true character of her sister.

Sometimes there are moments when you feel so good about yourself that nothing or no one could tarnish this condition no matter what, no matter what one might say and no matter what one does. Emma emanated such honesty, such a joy of life, a well-being, that she was indestructible. She didn't need to go into details so that everyone understood the situation. She wasn't in the mood for anything else. But she was strong in one thing: the sisterly love she felt towards her sister.

If her double had decided to erase her sister's existence, she thought that poor Mira had nothing to do with it, that she had only lived through what had been shown to her that it was possible to live and that one day, perhaps, she would find reason. While waiting, she behaved as she had always done, like what she had always known, just simply being her. And this already destabilized a lot this new team of neurotics who was now her family. In addition to some other discoveries she had made in her new dimension, there was only one thing she wanted: to find Jossy again, the very one who had made her want to face all that and give up what made up her life … there.

Impatient, she watched for his arrival. After a while, she saw a car enter the small driveway leading to the house. A big smile appeared on her face.

"Here you are, finally!" she thought.

She headed for the front door, opened it and camped in front, literally stamping. She was expecting to make some small mistakes, but that didn't matter much. Her double had told her everything she needed to know and she had gone through the entire house, including the photo albums. Until then, she had never felt the need to wait for her husband outside, at the door of the house. She felt at that moment nostalgia, almost sadness. She had just remembered a sentence her father had told her, that she would never see again in this world.

"Never fall in love with a body, my girl."

"You're right, daddy" she thought, *"Goodbye daddy, I'm going to miss you."*

Amazed to see Emma wait for him like this, Jossy stopped halfway, got down calmly from the car and walked slowly towards her, adopting a cowboy approach, hands placed along the body, elbows half folded, simulating a possible readiness to draw out a colt.

Seeing this man who, every day had the responsibility of a '40 tons' in his hands have fun like a twenty-year-old, she knew right away that she had made the right choice. She had never had this type of reaction from the one she had married, because he took himself far too seriously and she had always secretly hoped to see him change on this point.

Having the same small grain of madness as her cowboy, she began to advance in the same way. They walked, looking straight in the eyes trying to keep their seriousness by holding back their smiles that only wanted to explode into slavery. They stopped at a meter from each other. Hundreds of messages were being exchanged by their loving eyes. Jocelyn waved his fingers over his virtual colts. He let himself completely go in his delirium.

"One doesn't provoke 'Jossy The Kid' in a duel. What are your last wishes before dying?"

"I would like to see you dance the 'Comanchero' and afterwards, you can do whatever you will with me!"

Surprised by the request, he interrupted the scene for a moment...

"Did you follow me today?"

"Why the question?"

"Nothing, I'll tell you later."

"Two times in the same day, it must be a sign!" he told himself. He thought back to his early morning police check and smiled.

"Bear rolling in the snow", 'Jossy The Kid' resumed, "will dance for you, white woman!"

He did the same dance, accentuating the Comanche side. Emma could no longer restrain herself and laughed heartily. Thirty seconds passed, Jocelyn stopped, managing to keep his seriousness against everything.

"Bear rolling in the snow has danced. He can now do whatever he wills with you!"

"You... You're sure you don't want to talk about it again!"

He approached Emma's face with a normal, serious voice.

"Never, kitten!"

Then he kissed her tenderly, giving free rein to all the messages sent from his eyes to become loving acts. Glued to each other, they spent the next five minutes exchanging their love messages.

"I'll continue to show my feelings for you, my darling, but I feel dirty and I need a good shower. Afterwards, I'll look into your case, I promise. Go inside, I'll get the car and come as well."

Their looks were much more talkative and eloquent than words. He wiped his cheek with his left hand while sketching a smile like John Wayne waving for the last time to the poor lady he had rescued by fleeing the attackers before going back on his horse for new adventures.

Emma was really happy as she hadn't been in a long time. She was now looking at life serenely, from another angle. She was convinced that of all the choices she had been given to make, this one was the best. As for Jocelyn, he could probably have written a novel about what he was feeling at that moment. Something had changed. He too knew he had made the right choice the day he had asked for her hand in marriage, and he discovered that he probably had been asleep for a few years to miss his wife's character, for whom he would give everything. He was just simply rediscovering her. It was now a sure thing. It is quite possible to fall in love with the woman we love.

Although incredible, this adventure had finally allowed beings to meet, to know each other better, to bring out feelings that would certainly have remained buried in the files of ignorance. Maybe that was the magic of well thought out technology. A magic that had brought together a man and a woman who would probably have gone astray in the meanders of a conception of a wrong and obsolete life.

"Wait a minute cowboy!", Emma said, catching up to him.

"'Bear rolling in the snow' obeys! He wouldn't risk saying no to 'little golden diamond'."

"Thank you, bear, but you don't need to conquer me, it's

already done!"

She encouraged him with a last kiss for the road, then returned home to start preparing dinner. Jocelyn arrived quietly and parked in reverse, as usual, not to do the maneuver when he would use the car again. After turning off the engine, he went down, picked up his travel bag, his briefcase and his papers, then went straight to the living room to put everything on the table. In so doing, he fumbled mechanically the pockets of his trousers to prepare them for the passage to the washing machine. In the left back pocket was a business card that he removed carefully, so as not to bend it. He turned it in the right direction, then began reading the content.

"Mr. Hubert Doran, manager of the travel agency 'Paradise.'"

He stood for a moment puzzled, searching in vain for who it could be, then put it in the 'catch-all' dish placed on the dresser in the entrance. He then prepared for the weekend shower which was for him a kind of ritual ending his work week and corresponding to the 'M' moment of the beginning of his weekend. He still thought about the business card without making a fixation on it.

"Kitten!", he raised his voice, to be heard in the house

Emma had gone upstairs to finish a sewing job she had started in the afternoon. She was dying to be at his side, but she tried to act on the advice of her double and forced herself not to be too cumbersome, as if a certain routine had set in.

"Yes", she replied, ready to jump while obliging herself to sit in front of her machine.

"Hubert Doran…"

Her ears rose on hearing that name and she immediately stopped working.

"Hubert Doran? Who is he?", she asked, faking knowing him.

Her mind suddenly panicked.

"Why is he talking about Hubert?"

"I don't know, but we already had to meet him since I had his contact information in the pocket of my pants."

She immediately remembered the scene.

"I had forgotten about it!"

"No, it doesn't ring a bell. Why should I remember?", she lied.

"No, not especially, but I find it just strange not to remember the one who gave me that card."

"Don't worry, if it's important, you'll surely remember!"

"You're surely right."

He paid no more attention and headed for the bathroom. Well, it was done. Emma had successfully succeeded her insertion into this world. As for Jocelyn, he didn't know it, but he would go from surprise to surprise.

15 YEARS LATER.

— *"Big profound events never come*
to those who didn't do anything
to attract them. »
Cabaret Voltaire

The two 'Emma-Joss' couples are happy in their own dimensions. One remarried and two children were adopted by their mother, so to speak, and the other gave birth to two beautiful, unexpected children. The stuntman stopped his risky job in favor of a new, quieter job and now devotes more time to his family.

The driver turned father is thrilled and filled with 'kitten' happiness, who has never regretted her decision.

We are the 17th of August, 2030. 'Trucker Joss' brought his little family to the shore of a lake to spend the day. Both of their children are teenagers and have problems related to their age. But there is still a good atmosphere. They received a responsible education and manage to be wise, even if a few times… Today retired, he knew how to acquire slowly, but beneficial a certain wisdom. Long jealous for his insolent luck on whose account his entourage had prematurely retired because of an irreversible error in his record, as well as the rather plump money he had won at the national lottery ten years ago when he had almost never played. He didn't see things the same way. At the sight of this certainty about which everyone around him seemed to have agreed, he had often thought about it and ended up elaborating his own theory.

Luck is not sent by parcel post. We don't receive it with a divine hand and even less in the form of a built-in trophy when we are ten years old. No, it is something much more subtle in our behavior, something imperceptible for the one who seeks it and so much more eloquent with our interlocutors, but that makes all the difference. It is provoked and can sometimes develop as soon as we see the vein has formed. A kind of thought that is always present, resolutely optimistic and which is refined over the years, thus allowing us to hope no matter what happens. After all, why think that everything is possible when we can afford, to say that it will never happen! The simplest is probably to believe in the same way as in a God. This provides a disconcerting facility to think that one can have. This is certainly what is called 'giving a boost to one's destiny'.

He believed in the existence of a divine balance of which only man is able to activate the movement of. In his eyes, if he had won that money, it's just because he had done the right thing for that, because he was convinced everything happens to those who know how to wait; everything is deserved and always ends up coming to the one who doesn't lose sight of the 'cliché' he made at the beginning of his life. It's our thoughts that make us what we are. The problems of life are about the same for everyone and are mostly related to the society in which we live. However, there is always a solution, so if you can avoid a little stress, it's always the right path to take.

This exacerbated wisdom had still allowed him to pay the

balance of his last mortgage, to buy a second home in a nice little corner of the mountain located three hundred kilometers from their house where he went with Emma and their two sons every winter, to save enough to be comfortably paid in addition to his retirement until the end of his life, as well as to create an attractive nest egg for his children when they were adults, but not before the age of thirty, because he believes that we are not responsible enough before this course and it's not bad to eat a little rabid cow to understand some crucial things about life in this society.

Their car was parked close to the place they had chosen at the edge of the beautiful pond. It was their chosen place when they came here. It didn't bother them to arrive early in the morning to be sure to find the spot free.

"Quentin, Gaël, help us unload the car, you will play after!", said Jocelyn in a tone of passive authority.

Quentin, the protester by excellence vainly tried a timid rebellion.

"But dad…", he said, exasperated.

"Right now!", Jocelyn insisted gently, but still with some natural firmness.

Having no choice but to comply, the two brothers did it all willy-nilly. As she began to set up camp, Emma was looking for bread for the midday meal, but couldn't see it anywhere in what she had prepared.

"Could one of you go check in the trunk to see if the bread is there?", she asked the boys.

"I'll go Mom!", said Gael, returning to the errand.

At the back of the car, he opened the trunk, but saw nothing but the toolbox and the light bulb box.

"No, Mom, there's nothing", he said.

Jocelyn reassured her immediately.

"Don't worry my angel, if you forgot it, I'll quickly go get it with the car."

"Thank you, Jossy", she said with tenderness.

Sometimes she thought about her two other sons she left there when she saw the two children she had given birth to here. She would have liked to have given them different names, but this part of the story was done in the same way as in its original dimension. She couldn't help but find similarities between the four children about their character, their way of being and their evolution. She thought about it with nostalgia and although she was happy in this life, she often wondered if what she had done in the name of love was moral. Had her double matched what she had done in regards to education? What had they become? She had trusted her when she had first laid eyes on her; she had been certain she would be a similar mother, but there were some details she had thought of later.

Their character was certainly the same, but it was not the case with their character, created by their respective experiences. In those moments of blues and questions, her secret was heavy to bear, so heavy... Besides this new life she had here and the negative thoughts that haunted her, there were a few comical and strange situations at once that happened a few times with her children who were seven years younger than their elders in the other dimension, but they had the same character traits and it was as if she was raising her first children a second time. Sometimes she guessed some things in advance, which at times made her pass for a sort of extralucid clairvoyant. She knew in her heart that she should not make these differences, but it was stronger than her. They were so alike.

She suddenly saw Jocelyn come back empty-handed.

"What did you do with our children? I don't see them anymore", Emma said, beginning to think about a moment of rest, lying on a towel she had laid on the ground.

"I got a good price for Gael, as for Quentin, I'll look for him."

"Let's keep at least one of them, he might come in handy."

"You're right, kitten, I will use him as a receiver during our arguments!"

Emma guffawed.

"You're talking about it as if it's a daily occurrence!"

"I won't use him often."

"You would better go look for bread, while waiting. It will save you from talking nonsense!"

Jocelyn prostrated himself like a servant in front of his master.

"Alright, madam, six pack, twelve pack?"

"Go on!", she said, smiling.

"See you later, my angel", Jocelyn staid, going towards the car.

"Hurry, darling", she retorted as she plunged back into her 'uninterrupted rest'.

On the way, he glanced at his children bathing in the lake.

"Don't go too far, avoid making mother's first white hair today!"

They were so immersed in what they were doing that even if they had heard him, they didn't answer. He insisted again, with more authority.

"Quentin, Gaël!"

"Yes, 'Da, we got it."

"To think I contributed to who they are today" , he thought.

He climbed into the car, set off and left for the nearby village. He had to take a dirt road for about thirty meters before arriving on the tar. His 'Dedeuch' could take on any road as long as it was almost flat, but he handled it and rolled carefully so as not to damage it. So he had time to look at the landscape and something caught his attention in the distance, on the tarmac.

A small ball of gray hair seemed to be moving on the lower side of the path. As he got closer, he could see a kitten who had apparently been hit. He paused to take a better look and realized that the poor beast was groggy, but kept alive by the nerves, making it tremble with its whole body. He didn't have the heart to abandon it to its sad fate. He picked it up carefully and went looking for a veterinarian. After making a few phone calls, he arrived at a clinic, took the kitten in the same way he had delicately put it in the passenger seat, and entered as panicked as if it belonged to him.

"Hello, sir", said the vet, "so it's you the kitten savior!", she joked. "Put it here, I'll take care of it right away."

"Do you think it will make it?"

"I can't say very much at the moment. Are you thinking about adopting it?"

Jocelyn didn't know what to answer.

"Hm, I don't know, I haven't thought about it. I just wanted to save it."

"You don't have children?"

"Does this mean it's going to live?"

"I think so", said the vet smiling, "it's not as bad as it looks."

"I'll have to look into it first. Personally, I don't see any problem."

"Here's my card, call me next week. If no one comes to claim it, it's yours!"

"Okay, let's do that, I'll call you!"

Meanwhile, on the other side of the lake, sheltered from the scrub, sat a man, all dressed in white. He was looking in their direction. Despite all the walkers who passed close to him, no one seemed to notice his presence.

Suddenly, he got up and disappeared altogether. He held a photograph in his hands. Emma, who was still lying with her eyes closed, felt a furtive, but intense, current of air on her face, and immediately after, something fell on her chest, or rather, was deposited at the speed of light. That made her open her eyes immediately and she first looked at the package that had been dropped.

"A photo!", she told herself.

She looked around, but no one was there apart from her two sons having fun in the water. She took the photo to take a better look.

"This is a strange photo", she thought, *"one would give them almost twenty years!"*

Then, she searched each detail. Jocelyn, the children, herself and the landscape. She suddenly realized that it wasn't about them, at least not here.

"My babies!", she sobbed.

At that moment, an invisible hand was crushing her guts. She was alone in the world. She couldn't restrain the tears that escaped from their prison to finally give way to a smile.

On this family photo were her double, Joss the intrepid and her first two sons. That little world was happy, their smiles didn't seem to have been the subject of an express order. The image breathed life and happiness. It was one of those 'KODAK' moments that we immortalize to see in an album or a frame later on and remember that moment of joy spent with family.

Her double, Emma, had the same look as she on a similar picture. It was disturbing, almost frightening. Jocelyn's eyes said a lot about how he felt. So seeing him in that photograph reminded her of emotions and the memory of some good times spent with him. Already twenty years... she told herself; twenty long years to remake the world. He would not have needed much more to regret. Of an optimistic nature, she pulled herself together looking at her two current sons. The emotion passed, she scanned the surroundings with the eyes of a detective.

"Who are you? We already know each other, don't we?"

She was unknowingly waiting for an answer, knowing that she was unlikely to have one. And still, against all odds, she saw on the back some words that seemed to have been thrown there, with an ink, at least capricious. It appeared and disappeared according to the brightness.

"Hello, Emma! How is 'Boss Capish'?"

That remark rekindled distant memories, and yet so present. All the adventure she had known was quickly passing through her mind, as well as her whole life from before. More than a symbol, that simple family picture alone represented the confirmation of her choice and the result that emanated beyond all hope. It was a real success. That heavy decision she had made at a turning point in her life, involving all the people she loved and who, in addition to her present happiness, regularly disturbed her well-being, definitely turned into hope and indescribable happiness. She was convinced that she had done well, but something had been missing, insurance, proof, or better, a simple photograph.

"Why wait so long?" she thought.

"We must take responsibility for all our decisions. It's life that takes care of us, to reward us."

"Yes, it's true, it's the t... I see that you reconnected with your sensory abilities", Emma said discreetly, smiling. "Félix... You left, I suppose. It's good, what you did. I won't admit to it, but it was sometimes difficult. Now, I feel liberated from a weight thanks to you little man, who already knew at the time. I imagine you'll do the same with the 'mother of my children'. She must need it too. Do you still hear me or am I talking to myself?"

"I'm a grown man now. Goodybe, Emma."

"You told me we would never see each other again. Goodbye, big little man."

Returning home in the evening, Quentin will notice the disappearance of a photo in one of the frames decorating the large unclosed shelf of the living room and will tell his mother.

"You took the photo, mom?"

Surprised, she will checked and realize that the missing photograph was the one where they are all grouped together, similar to the one she will put in her bag.

"She will surely be happy to see that", she thought.

"No, Quentin", she will reply, "I won't change it, after all."

She will take the picture out of her bag and place it in place of the old.

"It's not the same!", her son wondered.

"I'm used to see it, but take a better look."

Sitting on her towel, she turned her eyes towards another horizon.

POSITIVE INTERFERENCE.

— *"They always say time changes things, but*
actually, time just passes
and you have to change them yourself."
Andy Warhol.

"*T*hank you, Félix", she thought, with great emotion. *"I must pay tribute to you all, your finding changed my life and that of my children. If she could also change the place that makes me a sister in this world!"*

She looked at the photograph again.

"You finally made it Joss, you became responsible! " He could be seen in the background encircling his little family with Emma in the center. She looked at it for a few minutes more.

"I know now I didn't abandon you. I will always love you, my darling."

She suddenly heard the noise, still distant and specific of their 2CH cabriolet four places that Jocelyn had fully restored, and which he was very proud of since it stood out from all the others who only offered two seats. She carefully put the picture in her bag, in which Jocelyn didn't like to look into, turned the written word into a little ball of paper that she hurried to throw in the water, and then laid down again.

A kilometer and a half and some 'Drrrll' later, Joss parked his antiquity, came down armed with two pieces of bread and arrived near Emma whose eyes were closed. Respectful, he approached with delicacy, as not to wake her up. He put the bread over the bag that contained the food, then silently turned back towards the water. Some seconds passed, then…

"Joss…"

He turned, feeling guilty for being noisy despite himself, without knowing when.

"My angel?"

"I'm not sleeping!"

"I thought you were."

"You took some time. Did you have a problem with the car?"

"No, I just saved a life!"

"Saved a life?"

"Yes, a dying little kitten on the side of the road, when I left."

"And what did you do; mouth to mouth?"

"She's pretty tough that one, she'll get through it!"

"Will it live, at least?"

"Yes, it has chances."

"And… ?"

"And what?"

"No idea crossed your mind?"

"You're talking about an adoption or something of the kind? No, not at all. I just have to call next week."

"Of course, it's only for updates!"

"Of course, my angel!"

"That poor little cat hit by a car will be the subject of all your attention because it is simply cute, and nothing else!"

"No!"

"No, what?"

Jocelyn was amused and sighed just for show.

"No, I have no intention of abandoning it, and you?"

"Me, I love your way of presenting things to me, you go straight to the point."

"So?"

"So, it seems to me to be cute like all cats are. What if we took it in!"

"I hadn't thought of it! It's an excellent idea!"

"Luckily I'm here!"

"It's true, would you like to have a cat?"

"You know I love animals. Yes, let's take it in, it will make the children happy, like all children!", she added, staring at him.

He smiled, came back and got closer to his beloved. She opened her eyes but she still carried on her face traces of the emotions she had just had. Knowing her well, he noticed.

"Did you cry? Is there something wrong, kitten?"

"Would we still be together if I hadn't been able to give you children?"

He frowned, thinking: *"She recreated the world!".*

"Alright, next time, I won't forget the bread, I promise!"

"I'm serious, Jossy."

"We talked and talked about it."

"Jossy…"

"I don't know, my darling. I already told you: of course we would, but I couldn't promise to stick to the decision I had taken. I may have realized one day that I was wrong and I am neither more nor less than myself. But feelings can sometimes change everything. I challenge anyone to make such a decision early in life. It might have happened that one day I might have woken up and wanted to be a father. It's the kind of promise I could never have made. Why are you asking me this?"

"Because I often thought about it. If I hadn't healed, Quentin and Gael wouldn't exist and you wouldn't be a dad."

"What do you want me to say to that?"

"I know, you were always honest and you never made promises you couldn't keep. Don't be upset with me, my heart, these are questions I have always thought of."

He lay down beside her and caressed her with a hand on her face.

"We will never know what would have happened, but I love you and I would have chosen you, children or not. Even if sometimes, I happened to ask myself if I will not regret this decision in my old days. But in hindsight, I concluded that my reaction was human and I wasn't betraying you."

"I know that, it was never in question!"

She looked at him tenderly, with a loving smile.

"As usual, you managed to calm me."

"I don't do it on purpose, darling! What if we went to join the children?"

He put his hand in the inside pocket of his jacket to take out a camera. Seeing that, Emma, who had just been shaken by a photo, wanted to know.

"What do you plan on doing with that?"

"A family photo in this little corner of paradise."

"Who will take it if you want all of us to be in it?"

"I'll put it on timer and put the camera on something stable."

They didn't know it yet. This photograph will be like the one Emma had received.

SHARED HAPPINESS.

— « *It is not always easy to take
the right decision, especially when it is
guided by feelings.* »
MM.

At the same time, in the other dimension, in the garage of the house. Emma is busy preparing canned jars of fifty centiliters. She does it regularly. Today, it is twenty liters of tomato sauce slowly simmered in a large pot that she especially bought several years ago. The jars filled, she only had to close them by inserting the famous rubber for sealing.

She loved this life that had become hers. She had quickly adapted. The children, who visited them often, hadn't realize anything. Admittedly, there had been some slight differences in their mother's behavior, but not enough to challenge her identity. The same as her double, she thought of Jossy sometimes. She imagined him becoming a father thanks to that experience. She hadn't told him before she left, but she had long felt guilty about not being able to give him children. The decision, taken fifteen years earlier, had been very painful. She still loved him, but he would probably be happier with a woman who could make him a father, not to mention her new motherhood. She always concluded that she had made the right choice and that nothing was due to chance.

Her 'New Joss' had stopped risking his life for good. His new schedule, similar to those of a civil servant, made him return every afternoon at 5:15, apart from two or three exceptions during the year.

It was close to 6 pm. She wanted to finish closing all the jars before he came home. Realizing that she would be short of lids, she went upstairs to take a new package, stored in the kitchen buffet. It didn't take her more than two minutes. Back in the garage, she opened the package, put a seal on the lid of each pot then put it on a nearby shelf. She then continued to intersperse them until the penultimate, when she stopped the movement of her hand. A note, folded in half with a picture inside, like the one her double had discovered was placed just behind the last one.

The statement was virtually similar to that one. These were the children she never would have had in this dimension. This excerpt of family happiness she held in her hands made her tremble with emotion. Those two children who had often come to visit her in her dreams were just there, under her eyes, printed on that image, almost physically present.

In the snapshot, they were looking at the lens. Their eyes were so expressive that she felt for a moment that they were looking at her. Félix knew very well that in so doing, he would finally free them from the burden created by this situation. She would never know how the photo had gotten there. She only had a vague idea.

Apart from a handful of experienced scientists and some advanced civilizations, only the two of them knew that there was only one step to... elsewhere.

EPILOGUE

* The two agents would never see the abandoned car. Further-more, Michel became an agent for other reasons, he won't go on patrol with Lucien, but with Mathias, who never disappeared. The two formed a good team. The two childhood friends have a bond that their colleagues jealous of. Lucien is wanted by the police for minor offenses.

* Among the students who saw Allan jump into the void, some were enthusiastic and others panicked, like the poor Christian, the guard. These are currently undergoing therapy, although Allan attempted to reverse their dramatic vision by bringing them together to explain that it had been a hologram experiment. We don't know it, but he will refuse to backtrack with the 'magic box'.

* The brave Auguste will begin a short period of questioning, because these events had caused some mess in and around the University and a mountain of problems was and would continue to be raised for some time between officials, including Security. For Auguste, it was going to result in a punctual and somewhat calculated return of a short alcoholic period. Certainly, he knew his penchant and his dependence if he let himself go, but it was necessary to choose between two cases of delicate conscience: do his job by saying concretely what he had seen, or support the most bizarre and crazy of all the teachers, who remained, however the only one to greet him every morning, without

407

exception. He readily admits his weaknesses and although he often behaves wisely, the misbehavior he has doesn't make him forget his priorities. But it would be unfair not to talk about the duration that will only extend over a day. It will be for him a good example of relevance, hiding the truth about what had happened there, he will later confess to his wife.

* The unfortunate Christian will change his arrogance to a low profile for not having accepted his visions and started a reconstructive psychological cure for a while. He who had seen things, had obviously not been prepared for such events.

* The two electricians, Pascal and Henri, will try to share their experience with their relatives, but will soon be forced to admit that it had only been a joke, a bet between them to observe their reactions. So they'll keep the secret their whole lives. Anyway, until time caught up with their adventure in the form of a news flash in 2062, announcing that a tear in time had been made possible after various experiments conducted not far from Paris by a professor of science, a certain Garvey, assisted by a certain Félix. That's the day that Pascal's wife will make the connection. A chance that Henri will never have, having left to a better world a few years ago. Pascal will now be able to leave in peace knowing that his best friend Henri will somehow intercept the good news.

* The young Florent disappeared in the mountains on the highway area under the eyes of his mother, will be found five months later in the North of France. His parents had always believed in his return. They will be rewarded for their patience, their love and the possibility to believe in miracles. They will recover him just as he had been when he had disappeared.

* Félix will continue to grow in the shadow of his possibilities and will meet the one who will become his wife, who is named

Céline. The very one in front of which he had played the jaded man of life in the Paris metro, or rather in one of the many 'eels'. Both will say they have found their soul mate, the complement that they lacked to fully flourish. For him, the drag will have been easy.

"We already know each other, don't we?"

This simple remark, 'remastered' long and hard, had been served in all situations by the biggest hitters on these ladies, but took all its meaning in this almost banal meeting.

* As for the four American workers at Ground Zero, they had no memory of their voyage, but their behavior had inexplicably changed. For sure, they didn't become better than before. Their flaws and qualities were still present, but their minds opened to new horizons, like Kevin for example, whose systematic knowledge began to give way to sensible and measured words. Did interdimensional walks produce magic? Probably not. But they had forced them to appeal to other senses, still in their beginning.

* Ching Chang Chung Boudsang whose experience was initially lethal, will see nothing changed in his life except a sudden fear. He now had a terrible fear of trucks.

* And finally, 'the great eagle' won't be found right away, despite Garvey's efforts. He will not have kept his promise to Green Giant, which will not hold it against him, even if in his world eagles are to the man what our dogs represent to us.

* * *

In all dimensions, an 'UFO' phenomenon will be observed in the next two days. Some will pay attention, others won't.

The other characters who found themselves, in spite of their will in this story, will never remember anything. Some will only have occasional impressions of déjà vu, like everyone else.

Some scientists will argue that time is only a measuring tool, which every civilization uses in its own way. For this, they will basically rely on the fact that in our world, we all have as much as we are our own perception of time. It will be affirmed, some twenty years later, that time doesn't exist and what must happen happens, irrevocably, despite our different destinies.

For sure, Garvey's initial intervention had changed the course of certain existences, among others the birth of Quentin and Gaël, but it hadn't changed the equilibrium of the universe, because nothing happens by chance. They would be born elsewhere, anyway. It was one of the first lessons that Félix and Garvey had received in the beginning. The latter had become his instructor. He had often told him about a particular escapade he had made during his first tests. He kept under wraps that he sometimes had, some more or less precise memories. In so doing, he was checking two or three theories he was working on, including one, in particular. Would he remember all that adventure?

The sequence of events had reinforced this conviction already well anchored in his scientist's brain. But there was something else going back up to more than ten thousand years before year zero. When he realized the potential of his invention when he was only Alan's apprentice, he had the curiosity to go back to the source of our civilization. What he saw that day would radically change the rest of his research career. He realized that each evolved dimension didn't like what they had become. Everyone was trying to change the evolution of others based on their own mistakes. That was reminiscent of the typical human behavior, so nothing extraordinary.

410

Thus, he realized that man was growing in size, but also mentally. The only thing he didn't see was his own neurosis. Whatever the size and apparent state of mind, it had grown in the same way. All sought to correct their own mistakes in others and they did the same with themselves. To sum it up, a snake seeking to bite its tail was probably smarter since it would at least run after something visible.

Félix was this way. But he had a considerable advantage over Garvey. He had already lived this experience, well organized in one of the drawers of his soul. When he finally had the opportunity to put it into practice himself, he wanted to make the 'Journey of Knowledge', as he called it. That day, he programmed a first date on the device that had undergone some modifications since its invention. It was no longer a question of taking into account relativity or any other physical law; it was no longer a problem... Already!

After a few brief adjustments, he left a few millennia later, in twenty-three thousand nine hundred. A time when man had reached saturation and was taking stock of his short passage in different universes. These were much larger and much more evolved. They were about to put an end to their civilization because the result was inconclusive. The planet had drunk the 'polluting cup' six times and with each club hit, the damage had been so great that they had had to live under the earth for more than three centuries.

Such was the sad story of those men who had become tired of that programmed proximity, which had been established over the centuries and millennia, of errors of judgment and of mental decadence, relentless and encouraged by the context. Félix arrived in a specific place, whose details had been provided by Garvey. This place was out of sight as in all the other times he had begun to visit, including the one where he had seen himself as a child on the campus of the Paris University. He could see everything from where he was. The giants were busy preparing a trip... in a flying saucer. The travelers seemed to have dressed for a costume ball compared to those preparing the flight. Their language was different from what he knew. In their hands were held plans seeming to contain far off calculations and pyramid measurements. The hour was at the 'Conference Meeting, serious, as if the future of humanity was at stake.

This departure, which they were preparing with great care, seemed to be one way and it probably upset the people there. Félix didn't miss a beat of the show. After only a few minutes, the five travelers lined up and disappeared in a flash to leave room for a thin opaque smoke that dissipated quickly. Félix was neither surprised, nor astonished. He immediately pursued them, entering the new coordinates Garvey had communicated.

We are now in ten thousand BC. He arrived in an equally discreet place. The ship was already there and its occupants were walking towards a group of Egyptian men. But this visit was almost entirely a scouting mission, as one of them remained on the spot while the other four were heading, less than twenty minutes later, to the ship to return to the stars. Seeing that, Félix returned to where Garvey was to ask for an explanation. There was in fact a third date, two thousand and eight hundred B.C., where he hastened to go. There, he saw the same giants come back with the same saucer, the same clothes and in their hands the famous plans they had brought some seven thousand years ago.

Félix will discover later that one of them will be proclaimed 'God alive', with a historical now name. They will call him Osiris. The plans will be put into action. Universal essential information will be provided to man, grouped in the 'Chamber of Knowledge', located under the Great Pyramid of Giza. But the place isn't unique. There are knowledge capsules around the world. They have been placed in places as diverse as Peru, Mexico or China. In all these cultures, we find the same designation of these men who are not men, but 'Travelers of the stars'. Man doesn't want to see it, but it all started in that time. Every culture imagines to be the one and only to hold the true story of humanity, but they don't know that, in truth, we watch over ourselves. We visit ourselves and guide our choices and our evolution. One of these days, we'll be evolved enough to travel; we'll try to correct our mistakes and we'll visit people who will seem primitive. We'll know that we are acting for ourselves and for our future. So, we'll take stock of our progress knowing full well that the people we'll visit will one day be in our place, while we'll only worry about one thing: our well-being.

This is how we function. We'll always need to burn ourselves to realize that fire destroys us. If we assume that every decision we make creates a new dimension and that we evolve in a different way in each of them, it is then possible to imagine that one day soon, we will not need to be wary of the worst enemy that man can have: itself.

Somewhere, on hertzian waves.

"We interrupt our programs for a special news flash. It has now been more than forty-eight hours since the disturbances ceased. So there is no more fear to have when leaving your home. You won't disappear! Authorities nevertheless recommend caution for the next fortnight in case... Indeed, in addition to the phenomena that stopped, two hunters, Claude and Stéphane have truly lived an extraordinary experience this morning. As life slowly resumes, the two men decide to go hunting and leave at dawn. They aren't beginners anymore and are the type which know what they are doing, but they will probably remember well beyond their lives this extraordinary hunting party. I quote: "A huge eagle, as big as an airliner", Claude confided, still shocked. We were obviously curious and we went there. Our reported, Fabien Plissard, was simply speechless seeing the animal at a hundred and fifty meters away, because the area is secured by the 'NP' (National Protection), first came to help the two unfortunate rifles of these two heads of families, whose projectiles didn't even tickle the giant raptor. Stéphane admits we had the feeling of not being in danger.

"It did'not seem to charge at us when we saw it, but we were scared and we panicked", they will later confide to Fabien Plissard. Still, witnesses claim to have found unusual and rather surprising behavior for an animal of this category and of such magnitude. The first specialists present didn't believe their eyes. They have just watched the images of one of the many passerby who filmed the scene, despite the speed of filming. We can see the giant seriously wounded by the combined ground and air assault, being strafed by the 'NP'. Losing a lot of blood, the latter hovers for miles like a dead weight profile, then suddenly regains consciousness; this is where everyone agrees to recognize the strange aspect of the last phase of the fall. In that moment, it spots houses on the bottom and tries its best to deflect its trajectory by small wing movements. It looks down again and drops without resistance, thus avoiding a certain catastrophe. Did eagles become protectors of man? We doubt it, because even tamed, the balance remains fragile. But this one obviously makes the difference with its 'little congeners', so to speak. It is certain that seeing the bird, one is entitled to think that its size has not traveled alone on the paths of evolution. We just heard that it was sighted in the Sahara Desert, before arriving here. According to the nomads, it wasn't flying at random. It seemed both lost and in search of something, but not food, otherwise it would have taken it. These are the affirmations of this traveler, apparently fascinated by what he saw. Other specialists arrive en masse and prepare to join their colleagues who came first. Still, an essential question remains: how could we have ignored the presence of such a large specimen since the beginning of our existence? Are there others? No one has a sure answer at the moment, but research will start and we will not fail to keep you informed.

Supernatural phenomena rolling, disappearances, apparitions, an eagle more than thirty meters high. Is our world going crazy or is it beginning to unravel its mysteries? If you yourself witness a situation, call the blue number: 0900 600 300. Have a good day on 'Smile Radio' and stay with us!"

PERSONAL MESSAGE.

In tribute to Daniel, whose joy of living is proportional to his natural goodness made the roadhouse 'Les chasseurs'[5], at Berre l'Étang, where I unfortunately no longer have the opportunity to stop, a stop of choice and quality. Today, you have gone to another dimension or perhaps in the "Larzac" and we can only imitate you. Enjoy it, Daniel. I am convinced that the merry man you were with us must be the same where you are. See you soon, Dan.

J-Yves

---

[5] 'The hunters'